". . . As the day wore on,
and the premonition of disaster increased,
the movement to the compound had become
more and more a wild, abandoned flight—
women hastening through the streets,
babies in their arms,
children clutched by the hand. . . .
At every pounding on the gate,
the terror increased;
it approached frenzy.
To Lyle they looked as father
and protector,
possibly to some extent before,
but now implicitly.
In his hands they placed their fate. . . .

". . . He began to sing
the Armenian words of the hymn:
'I love him, oh, how I love him,
And how the Lord Jesus loves me . . .'
A few quavering voices took up the words,
others joined in,
and music began to well forth
as a balm to suffering,
as a long wall reared against despair. . . ."

D1547866

ARARAT

Elgin Groseclose

David C. Cook Publishing Co.

ELGIN, ILLINOIS—WESTON, ONTARIO
LA HABRA, CALIFORNIA

AUTHOR'S NOTE

The English words in which are rendered the verses
of Hafiz which Miriam Verian recites in part 1,
chapter 4, and which Sirani Verian recites in part 4, chapter 1,
are from the translation of Sir William Jones.

ARARAT

© 1939, 1967, 1974, 1977 Elgin Groseclose

Published by David C. Cook Publishing Co., Elgin, Illinois
Printed in the United States of America
Library of Congress Catalog Number: 77-78493
ISBN: 0-89191-078-6

*For my friends
–both present and departed–
engaged in the rescue
of the persecuted peoples
of the Middle East
following World War I*

CONTENTS

PREFACE

For this third edition of *Ararat,* presented thirty-eight years after its first appearance, the editors have suggested that the circumstances of its writing might be of interest.

In 1921, following youth and college in my native Oklahoma, I had gone to Tabriz, Persia (now Iran), expecting to be occupied in the quiet work of teacher in a mission school. I brought with me little realization of the turmoil, suffering, and distress which that area of the world was enduring. Destitute Armenian and Nestorian Christians—refugees from the Turkish massacres undertaken to exterminate the minority races—crowded the city. The responsibility of caring for them had fallen upon the missionaries, and I eventually joined in this task in a minor capacity.

Later, sent to the Soviet Caucasus with the Reverend Christy Wilson, a former football star turned missionary, to obtain supplies, I saw the tragedy of uprooted humanity on a vaster scale—peoples in flight, lands devastated, society disorganized, pillage and anarchy prevalent. And I saw rising above this modern deluge of blood and carnage the great mountain Ararat as reminder of the day God saw the wickedness of men and repented that He had made man on the earth.

To come, as I had, from the then freshest settlements of the New World, a region enjoying peace, plenty, and prosperity, and to be set down in such a region, blasted by human hatred and war, visited with desolation and despair, was to face baffling questions as to the purposes of God, the mystery of His grace, the wisdom of His will. More urgent than a search for the physical evidences of the ark that had rested here after the Flood was the search for the face of God through the mists of perplexity.

One cannot resolve these questions rationally in the turmoil of circumstances; the happenings are too overwhelming for logic to grasp.

There was the promise of God to Noah that although "the imagination of man's heart is evil from his youth," yet He would not again curse the ground anymore for man's sake. There were also the words of Paul, penetrating the heart of the matter: "Where sin did abound, there did grace much more abound."

For in the midst of desolation and despair was also the ministration of hope, the presence of good will. The agency for this ministration was the Near East Relief, an outgrowth of a committee for Armenian relief formed in 1916 through the efforts of Ambassador to Turkey Henry Morgenthau and Dr. James L. Barton of the American Board of Commissioners for Foreign Missions. This had become an immense enterprise of American philanthropy, engaging a corps of relief workers, scores of institutions, all supported by millions of dollars of voluntary contributions—a private enterprise of benevolence still without parallel.

While the characters and incidents of my story are entirely fictional, the work reflects, to the extent that fiction can, the magnitude of this American relief effort—over a million persons fed and nourished, one hundred thirty-two thousand orphans cared for, with thirty thousand of them in one great "City of Orphans," housed in abandoned army barracks at Alexandropol (now Leninakhan). The book also mirrors certain persons who exhibited the range of human capacity for love and hate. Among these was Dr. William Shedd, who in Urmiah received some fifteen thousand refugees in his mission compound, holding off attacks upon them until the ravages of typhus forced him to lead them out through a gauntlet of marauding Kurds—a tragic exodus in which half the number perished, including Dr. Shedd. There was also a prison mate during a period of incarceration by the Soviet secret police—a man of dauntless courage who did much to sustain my spirits, and whom I described in an *Atlantic Monthly* account of that experience. There was the chief of police, a man named Moghilevsky, who (according to a cable dispatch of March 29, 1925, to the American press announcing his death in an airplane accident) caused the execution of some thirty thousand opponents to the regime. Not the least were two evangelists of my youth who drew me to contemplate the Cross—one a powerful preacher, filling a great tent with his Elijah voice; the other a returned missionary, a sweet singer and composer of songs. They all are, in a sense, reflected in the unfolding of *Ararat*.

ARARAT

Part 1

THE ARMENIANS

1. Shepherd and Flock

On the twenty-eighth day of November, in the year 1895, the dark angels of tragedy, roaming the Eastern world, alighted upon the town of Dilijan, Turkey. The town of Dilijan lay in one of the eastern *sanjaks* of Anatolia, not far from the Russian border, in a secluded valley, remote from the outside world, and little touched by the currents of large affairs. The shadow had already fallen upon other parts of the Empire, and the cold winds of death and destruction had been set in motion; but the mountains that lay between Dilijan and the westerly portions of Anatolia had until now screened it and its inhabitants from the blasts.

The predominant community of Dilijan was the Armenian; it numbered some eight thousand souls. There were a slightly smaller number of Turks, and a sprinkling of Kurds, Syrians, Jews and other races. Dilijan was not, therefore, a large place. It might have been destroyed, or it might have continued to exist, and the difference in the then vastness of the Ottoman Empire would have been small indeed.

In times past, Dilijan had been of somewhat more importance. In an earlier historical period it had been a populous Armenian city. The evidences of its former size and importance were to be found in the way it sprawled over thrice or more the area that its inhabitants required,

with great areas of waste land and rubble scattered between
clusters of houses. Still other evidences were to be found in
the marble slabs with indecipherable inscriptions which
might be observed among the foundation stones of most of
the better structures of the town, and in certain mounds of
brick and rubble, half buried in dust and ashes and shards,
that to an archaeologist were eloquent testimony of an illus-
trious past.

Tradition has it that St. Gregory the Illuminator, who was
the Apostle to the Armenians, was born in the neighborhood
of Dilijan. King Tiridates, in the third century, has made
Dilijan into a fortified place which withstood assault after
assault of the Romans. Later, as a Bagratid fortress, it
withstood the Byzantines until finally they took it by
strategy. Apparently, also, it had been a considerable trad-
ing center, though its relative importance in this respect
may be doubted, for it does not appear to have lain on any of
the great trade routes of ancient times.

The Armenian inhabitants of Dilijan in 1895 were but a
remnant of what had once been a powerful and virile population that dominated all this area of Anatolia. The gradual
depopulation of this Christian community—a process
which from many causes had been going on for many
generations—had not been offset by an increase in the Turkish population: the general impression accordingly was one,
if not precisely of senility and decay, of somnolence, a
peaceful, untroubled slumbrousness such as the aged experience before they quietly disappear into the abyss of
death. It was a somnolence, however, that had been disturbed in recent years by certain dreamings and stirrings
aroused by the fresh breezes of a new hope and a new fear
borne from the West.

The Armenian population of Dilijan was not a close-knit
community, as is found in other cities of mixed population.
There was an Armenian quarter, but it was scattered, rather
than compact, and interspersed among Turkish houses and
khans. It was on this account particularly defenseless
against any organized assault. The population itself was
hardly a unit, and such cohesion as existed was found in
their common ties to their pastor. Some of the Armenians

lived by trade, in which Armenian did not hesitate to fleece Armenian; some by crafts, in which many of the folk were highly skilled. There were saddlers, and cabinet workers, and teamsters, and porters among them, but in and around Dilijan itself, no farmers, for the land had been pre-empted long before for the Turkish peasantry. On the whole, the Armenians were industrious and by far the most prosperous element of the town.

There had been, at one time, a great Armenian cathedral in Dilijan, but it had fallen into decay, with the decline of Armenia, and of it now the only vestige was the broken pieces of two baptismal fonts that protruded from among a heap of shards and broken brick near the Gumrick Khaneh. These two baptismal fonts could be said to be significant of the spiritual history of Armenia. One was of the dimensions of a man, crudely fashioned of basalt, and solid; the other was of marble, small and exquisitely carved, with many symbolic flourishes. The first was for the immersion of adult converts and dated from a most ancient past, from the days of the early Church, when evangelism was active and many converts were being made. With the subsidence of apostolic fervor the Church grew exclusive. Converts became rare, and one had to be born into the Church. The large font fell into disuse, and as the only baptisms were of infants, a smaller, more beautiful font had been executed.

In 1895, the only church in Dilijan was that erected by American missionaries. Formerly there had been a colony of these missionaries, and they had erected a spacious compound, a church, a schoolhouse and a clinic, as well as other buildings for their needs. Most of this work had since been abandoned, the missionaries having retired, resigned, or moved to more promising fields. The last of these, but one, had returned to America on the ground of his wife's health, supposedly impaired by the altitude of Dilijan. For the last thirteen years the spiritual responsibility for the Armenian community had rested with Amos Lyle, a long, gawky Texan in his forty-fifth year, a man who in appearance and attitude hardly seemed one gifted to shepherd a flock through a storm of disaster.

Amos Lyle was one of those pious, enthusiastic, hopeful apostles of the Christian gospel who have no conception of affairs, no capacity for organization and administration, who are other-worldly, absorbed in souls rather than society, in sheep rather than the flock. He had at one time been a cowhand on the southwestern plains of America, and he thought of his spiritual problems in the same terms he had used in handling his cattle. "As every cowhand knows," he once said, "it is the strays that give the trouble. The herd will look after itself."

This interest in the sheep rather than the flock, in straying heifers rather than the herd, was partly the result of his natural tendencies and his early life. He had an antipathy for organization and organized life; it may have been congenital, but it was fostered by the free, uncertain, routineless life of the plains. After leaving the range for the pulpit, and shifting his hand from the bridle-rein to the Gospel-book, this dislike did not disappear, but became more pronounced. His preference for what he liked to think of as the unfenced range of the spirit extended from his personal affairs to his concepts of society and his duty as a Christian apostle. It manifested itself in his utter improvidence, as the world terms improvidence. He lived each day as though it were his last—in his dress—which was nondescript, and in which the only concession to vanity was the battered, broad-brimmed hat he had worn now for thirteen years, and the Texas starred boots he put on for ceremonial occasions—in his food, his abode and his concerns. As for his food, he ate when there was bread in the cupboard; and when there was none he fasted. His abode was the extensive walled compound, erected by his predecessors, of which the walls and half the buildings were now in disrepair, the gardens weed-grown and the gates rusty on their hinges. His concerns were of the most diverse and unrelated sort, a variety of activities characterized chiefly by the enthusiasm with which they were carried on, the benevolence with which they were infused, and the reverence for God and His will by which they were inspired.

At one time, following an address he had made to a missionary conference, in which his zeal and his grasp of the mission task had made a deep impression, Lyle had been considered for ordainment as missionary bishop. He had declined the honor, with what was regarded by some as unappreciative remarks on the episcopacy:

"While I shall accept the will of God in this matter," he wrote, "I pray that He may take this cup from me. The world will be saved only as individual souls are saved, and souls are saved not by the episcopate but by the parish priest. I thank God daily that He has placed me where I may touch individuals, and I should count it a loss to be elevated to a post where I should deal with orders instead of persons, and policies instead of souls."

Amos Lyle was not ordained a bishop—his letter and a report of the manner in which he managed his own parish put the quietus on the very suggestion.

For thirteen years, therefore, with only one furlough, Amos Lyle had devoted himself, with steadily increasing enthusiasm, to the winning of souls to Jesus Christ from among the Armenian and Turkish population of Dilijan. Since the Armenians were nominally Christian, and since his predecessors had done yeoman work in proselytization, he had started out with a considerable flock. But the longer he preached the more the enterprise declined in its outward aspects: the extensive physical establishment erected by his predecessors fell into decay; the various guilds and auxiliaries, with the exception of his Sunday School, became defunct; the church roster had not been maintained, and Lyle at no time could tell how many members he had on his rolls. His financial accounts were impossible, and his formal reports, to the great annoyance of his mission board, were neglected.

Despite all this, Amos Lyle was a force in Dilijan; the Armenians with one accord looked to him as their pastor and shepherd; his preachings attracted large attendance; his Sunday School was thriving; and he wrote so many enthusiastic letters of an informal nature that his mission

board could never bring itself to reprimand him for his
failure to maintain his formal reports and accounts.

On the morning of this day in November—a day that
had dawned fine and clear, with no portent of the disaster
that was to occur—Amos Lyle had set forth upon a pastoral
call. His destination was the home of Emmanuel and
Miriam Verian, two young people for whom he had a great
fondness. The young woman had been ailing of late, and
Amos Lyle had suspected a cause which gave him great
rejoicing in his heart.

As he walked along he kept murmuring to himself, over
and over again, "Fear not, Mary: for thou hast found
favour with God. And, behold, thou shalt conceive in thy
womb, and bring forth a son, and shalt call his name
Jesus."

Amos Lyle was a bachelor, confirmed to his bachelor-
hood by his homely face, his harsh voice and ungainly
appearance, as well as by his tempestuous enthusiasm for
nothing but his Gospel. To him, the marriage state was
something mysterious and miraculous. A home—that is, a
consecrated home, where filial and marital love prevailed
—was a holy of holies which he entered with reverence;
and children were the angels of the Lord.

Amos Lyle had a conviction that children were the especial delight of the Heavenly Father, the particular objects
of Divine Providence. This might seem an odd belief considering the number of homeless children he was constantly picking up and bringing to his compound until he
could find a home for them, and the occasional foundling
that had been left at his gate since coming to Dilijan. But
Amos Lyle was not a logical man.

The Verians lived almost directly across the town from
the compound, in what was known as the "Old Town,"
and since not only the market streets and squares, but a
good deal of deserted area lay between, the distance was
not short. This gave Amos Lyle time for further contemplation as he walked along. From Miriam Verian, his thoughts
turned to Haig, the insouciant, half-wild urchin who
stayed with Lyle in the compound except when adventure

called him elsewhere. The boy had been back no ̶ ̶ ̶ was again growing restive, and Lyle had been ̶ ̶ ̶ him, with all the persuasion of which he had comm ̶ ̶ ̶ to content himself, learn a trade, go to school. Haig was one of Lyle's most perplexing problems, and the missionary spent many an evening in prayer and thought about what was God's will concerning his charge. It cannot be said that Lyle ever lost sleep over the matter, for sleep was always sweet and innocent with him.

There was also the letter which he must write to Dr. Coswold, pastor of St. John's in Philadelphia. Dr. Coswold had been greatly interested in the mission to the Armenians, and had offered to raise money for some purpose that Lyle might specify. Lyle had racked his brain for some purpose for which he could use money, but could think of none at the moment. His voluminous correspondence, all so earnest, so confident, so full of instances, so naïve in its appeal, brought him many offers like that of Dr. Coswold's.

Occasionally there were letters of inquiry, and Lyle had such a one on his desk now. An indigent scholar in a small Western university wanted Lyle to verify some dates and places and historical references: the scholar was doing research on a project, which he had not the funds to pursue in person, but which he hoped would establish his reputation and win him a better appointment. Lyle had already written him several long letters, but before he could answer the latest he would have to consult some of the Turkish mullahs of his acquaintance.

From consideration of this inquiry Lyle turned naturally to thoughts of the ancient past of this land, which contrasted so sharply with the newness and rawness of the country in which he had been reared. It filled him with enthusiasm to think of being in a land from which so much history stemmed—particularly so much biblical history— and where so many generations of men had lived and made their contribution to the stream of life. On the whole, however, he had little reverence for history. Ruins did not fill him with awe or with sadness. His attitude was not dissimilar to that of the Turks—themselves comparative

newcomers when the immensity of the past is considered—
who did not hesitate to use the stones from ruins as building blocks for their own constructions. Lyle had the long
view, but it was a view forward rather than backward, to
the future rather than to the past. The past to Lyle meant
only the firm hard rock into which one must sink a foundation in order to build a tower. The only message he read
in all the chronicles of the past was that the will of God
had gradually made itself supreme through the will of
man.

And finally Lyle, taking note of the cloudless day, the
warmth for so late in the season, and the golden sunshine,
thanked God again, as he did a dozen times a day, for the
privilege of being an apostle of the Lord in this land.

2. The Decree

AMOS LYLE had walked some distance, absorbed in his
thoughts, before he became aware of a strangeness in the
aspect of the town. The first thing he remarked was that
there were no children playing in the streets. This became
apparent to him as he passed the tanyard, where many of
the poorer Turks lived, and where their children could
usually be found playing a game with the knuckle bones
of sheep. Lyle always stopped and talked with the children, offered them lumps of sugar, if he had any, and told
them a Bible story.

Lyle wondered at not seeing the children, and he was
suddenly filled with alarm. The thought occurred to him
that there might be a plague, such as he had witnessed
in '82, the year he came to Turkey, when over half the
population had died. That had been a time of terror, a
trial that had strained Lyle's natural optimism—already
affected by the homesickness of his first year in the mission
field, as well as by the strangeness of his new life, and by

the squalor and misery he found—and had brought him to examine anew the sources of support to be found in his faith. Although Lyle had gained from this trial new strength to resist disaster, so sentimental was he about children that the thought of any suffering that might affect them never failed to quail his soul. And now the realization that he had seen no children in the street gave him a sudden somberness of spirit. This lasted, however, only a moment. With quick relief, he saw that the urchins had gone inside the wall.

"Why do you not play in the street today?" he asked one of the boys, Karim, the son of a porter.

"A policeman warned us to stay off the streets today," Karim replied. "He said there might be trouble."

Amos Lyle was so overjoyed at seeing the children that he did not think to ask what the policeman had meant. He talked to the children a little while and then went on to the *tope haneh*, the public square. Here he again became aware of an unusual quietness, something in the atmosphere that belied the clear skies and the warm, limpid air. The market place was usually crowded and noisy at this hour, but today it was like Sunday, when the Armenian shops were closed. He observed indeed that all the Armenian shops were closed, with the iron shutters drawn fast, and as he looked about him he saw almost no Armenians on the street.

Amos Lyle was puzzled, and tried to recall if he had observed anything like this before. He could not, in his thirteen years in Dilijan, but suddenly there flashed through his mind the remembrance of a happening during his youth in Texas—a lynching that had occurred in a certain town in which he happened to be, and to which he had been an unwilling witness.

A soldier had just posted a notice on the gray stone walls of the Ottoman Bank, and a knot of people were gathered around silently reading it.

"What does the notice say?" Amos Lyle asked of an old Turk who had just left the crowd, shaking his head and pulling at his hennaed beard. The man was Ibrahim Effendi, a broker of small ware. He lifted his downcast eyes heavenward, for he was squat and stooped and Lyle was exceedingly tall, and looked at the missionary.

"Who is this Hashim Farouk Bey, anyway; that comes to Dilijan like a desert wind, drying up the sweet water-courses of amity?" Ibrahim Effendi demanded by way of answer.

"What does the notice say, Ibrahim Effendi?" Lyle asked again.

"It says for all Armenian males upwards of the age of fourteen to appear at the Gapou this afternoon, at four o'clock. Trouble approaches like a two-humped camel."

"Does it not give the purpose of the assembly, Ibrahim Effendi?"

"All men are not blind, *agha*," Ibrahim Effendi stated insinuatingly. "Do you not know what has happened in other parts of Turkey? Can you not read the signs of the times? For what purpose was Hashim Farouk Bey sent to Dilijan, but to stir up trouble?"

There had been rumors of events in other parts, tales brought in by traders, of outbreaks between members of the Dashnak—the Armenian patriotic society—and members of similar organizations of Turks, as well as of repressive measures taken by the government against the Armenians. It was said also that in Van and Urfa there had been executions and wholesale shootings of Armenians. But traders loved to tell tall stories and exaggerate ordinary happenings into great adventures, to add to their reputations and the price of their wares; and there had been nothing either in the local papers or in those that arrived from the larger cities.

"Yes, I have heard of these things," said Lyle, "but this has been a quiet community. The people here are loyal and amicable. There will be no trouble here."

"You have not heard what I have heard," said Ibrahim Effendi, leaning over and whispering something in Lyle's ear that caused the missionary to start.

"Oh, no," he protested vehemently. "Such an idea is unthinkable. A concerted movement? No, no; this is no longer the age of barbarism. The Sublime Porte is an enlightened government. No, no, I say. You have been listening to fantasies. It is listening to such things that creates ill will and nervousness."

Ibrahim Effendi shook his head, dubiously.

"Then tell me, Lyle *agha*, for what purpose is the assembly?" he answered, with a shrug of incomprehension. "To read the Koran to them and convert them into Mussulmans? If for no other, then you should worry, seeing that you are commissioned to make us Moslems into Christians."

"Possibly a labor draft," suggested Lyle. "Hashim Farouk Bey has stated that he wishes to build roads, and that he would draft labor for the work."

"If no more than that, it is bad enough," replied Ibrahim Effendi. "Do you know what forced labor is like—when Armenians are called? I saw them building a wharf in Trebizond. Of ten that went down to the seaside, possibly two returned.

From reality Lyle sought refuge in his faith, which to him was a greater reality. It was not that he was afraid of realities of the earthly sort—it was only that he believed that the greater reality would subdue the lesser. He could meet realities when they occurred, but he could not contemplate possibilities. What Ibrahim Effendi had warned him of was only a possibility.

"But the governor is a just man, and will restrain injustice," he urged. "Hashim Farouk Bey is not the governor, but only the military commandant."

"You do not know this Hashim Farouk Bey. He is another of those wild men from Scutari who are not to be restrained."

Ibrahim Effendi spat.

"Let them stay on the Bosphorus, and drink their wine and eat their *pilaf* with spice, sleep with the Frankish women and dream dreams of spitting in the faces of the Frankish ambassadors. We do not need them here. We are at peace."

Ibrahim Effendi started on, and then turned and faced the missionary again.

"Lyle *agha*," he said. "I know you for a man of God, and though your God is threefold and mine is One, I respect your faith. For you, like me, believe in *Islam*—in submission to His will. But to submit to Hashim Farouk Bey, is that to submit to God's will? We must have no trouble here in Dilijan."

"God forbid that there be trouble."

"This Hashim Farouk Bey is a hot-head. Stronger wills must control his. Go to him and demand assurances. You are a Frank, and you dare to speak, whereas poor Turks like us cannot."

"But I am not a consul, Ibrahim Effendi," Lyle demurred. "Politics are not my concern."

He was alarmed at the thought that he should approach the authorities upon such a matter. The words of St. Peter weighed upon him, "Submit yourselves to every ordinance of man for the Lord's sake: whether it be to the king, as supreme; Or unto governors. . . . For so is the will of God." Lyle had come to Turkey to preach the word of God, to minister to the broken-hearted, to call men to salvation and the acceptance of Christ as their Savior, to teach love and long-suffering and faith, to tell men of the unsearchable riches of God's Kingdom. . . . He had not come to instruct the wise, to proclaim law to governors and princes, to mediate before an earthly throne.

"You do not understand affairs," urged the old Turk. "The times are bad. Horrible things fly through the air like *jinn*. A doom settles upon our country. In Stamboul, Abdul Hamid grows arrogant. He does not submit to the will of Allah, but listens only to the advice of upstarts and firebrands. Consider what is happening here. A new spirit abroad. Unrest increasing. Turks and Armenians quarreling. Trade stagnant. Beggary rising. Our province is ruined unless something is done."

The old Turk drew himself erect.

"But this is our province," he said proudly, "and not the Sultan's. We must have peace here. Go to Hashim Farouk Bey, and if he will not listen, go to the governor. Demand assurances that no rising against the Armenians will be countenanced. As you are a servant of God, go, like the Prophet Mohammed, and demand that the rulers acknowledge God and submit to His will."

When Ibrahim Effendi had ended and gone on, Lyle stood a long time in thought.

Hashim Farouk Bey, the commandant of the military garrison of Dilijan, was newly come from Constantinople. Lyle recalled what he knew of him. Hashim Farouk Bey was a young man—in his early thirties—with a sharp, decisive manner and the superior attitude of a man who is sure of his purposes. He was slight of build, with a narrow angular face, close-set eyes that were black as coal and brilliantly hard as two pieces of obsidian. His hands were delicate and graceful as a woman's.

Aside from Hashim Farouk Bey's outward appearance, which to Lyle signified nothing, Lyle recalled only that he was a difficult man to approach. He had met Hashim Farouk Bey at a reception given by the governor. The commandant had at first clicked his heels politely, and had made a remark about the great wealth and resources of America. But when he learned—from Lyle's conversation—that Lyle was a missionary who had not the slightest interest in wealth, had never possessed any, and indeed had come from the backwoods parts of his native country, he had promptly excused himself and had begun talking politics and international affairs with the German rug merchant.

Lyle had not had occasion to meet or speak to Hashim Farouk Bey since. The commandant was an energetic man, who was always to be seen drilling the troops of the garrison. This consisted of a small company of *gizil bashies*—red-fezzed and pantalooned gendarmes recruited from the hill Turks. Shortly after Farouk's arrival, however, additional troops had been brought in from Syria, a movement that had caused considerable consternation in the town. Hashim Farouk Bey had shortly explained that improvements in the military were necessary because of the international situation, and a little later, to calm the agitation, he had announced that road building would soon be started for military purposes.

Lyle's first assumption regarding the assembly at the

Gapou was that in some way it was connected with this project.

After a time, Lyle went up to the notice and read it for himself. The language was even more peremptory than Ibrahim Effendi had indicated, and it gave no reason for the assembly. Lyle stood in great perplexity. What should he do in the circumstances? He considered again the forebodings of Ibrahim Effendi, and again the injunction to render unto Caesar the things that are Caesar's. This was certainly an affair that "belonged to Caesar"—an assembly of citizens duly called by constituted officials. But did it not also concern God's children? Was it not something in which he, as pastor of the Armenians, might—nay, should—interest himself?

Lyle had been bred in the spirit of separation of Church and State, and he had an inculcated hesitancy about going outside his sphere. In the plains country of America parsons were one thing and sheriffs another. Like the stars that differ in glory, each shone with its own halo and never in the other's reflection. Their orbits were separate and did not cross. There were matters in which the final authority was the Bible, and places where a parson might go that a sheriff would be shot; but there were also affairs in which the sheriff's badge was the authority and a parson, if he meddled, might be lynched.

In casting about for guidance, Lyle recalled again the lynching he had witnessed. A poor Negro had been suspected of a crime. Passions had flamed. The sheriff had taken the Negro in custody—for his safety—and then as the crowd stormed about the jail, the sheriff had cravenly disappeared. On that occasion, a certain preacher—an itinerant evangelist whose exhortations had later brought Lyle to kneel at the sinners' rail—a mild-mannered, shining-faced man with a voice like a Hebrew prophet, had dared to climb the courthouse steps and assail the crowd for their inhumanity, and to plead with them for mercy.

He had almost been lynched with the Negro. . . .

Lyle thought of Elijah, who dared confront Ahab, and of Peter, filled with the Holy Ghost, standing before the rulers of the people and the elders of Israel. . . .

Lyle walked on slowly. He thought he would talk to Neshan Kovian, the moneylender, who knew all the Turkish officials and who was constantly receiving intelligence from distant parts. But the shutters were down on Kovian's shop, as on all the other Armenian shops. Garabed Khansourian, too, who was usually to be found in the coffee shops, talking politics with the *aghas* and *khans*, was not to be seen. The Turks themselves, whom Lyle encountered on the street, were lacking their accustomed cordiality. They eyed him resentfully, it seemed, or if they spoke, their words were short. Lyle's thoughts again reverted to the lynching he had witnessed. Just such an atmosphere had pervaded the streets when the rumors were spreading and the crowd was gathering—the heavy silence, the nervous, suspicious movements, the tension as of drawn revolvers. . . .

Lyle decided that Ibrahim was right, that it was his duty to make inquiry of the governor.

3. Affairs That Are Caesar's

THE governor of Dilijan was Bari Pasha, an indolent, complaisant old man whose chief private interest was his garden and whose only public interest was the maintenance of tranquility in the *sanjak*. Aside from a natural avarice, which his office of governor allowed him to satisfy without too great strain upon the public revenues, and which led him now and then to impositions upon the more prosperous element of the community—which included most of the Armenians—he was judicious in his administration. He lived in an extensive, ramshackle building of brick and stucco which was a palace only by designation, and whose many rooms—with the exception of those personally occupied by Bari Pasha, which were fitted

in becoming state—were empty, dust-filled and bestrewn
with fallen plaster.

When Amos Lyle was shown in, Bari Pasha was seated
in a square leather chair before an inlaid desk of Syrian
Damascus work, on top of which was an untidy array of
papers, blotters, inkwells, pens and Persian papier-mâché
pen cases. Hung on the governor's arm was a *tesbeh,* a
rosary of Baltic mottled amber, with ninety-nine beads,
one for each of the attributes of Allah.

Lyle stood on excellent terms with the governor, and
was frequently invited to the teas and receptions which
Bari Pasha was fond of holding. His attitude before authority was a combination of respect and outspokenness
which the governor liked, and often wished he could
emulate. Bari Pasha himself was never capable of anything
but indirectness, a political technique which thirty years
in public office had inbred in him, and he was constantly
amazed at how Lyle, without giving offense, could present
his views in a frank and unequivocal manner.

Bari Pasha never felt the master in any discussion with
Lyle; he experienced rather a delectation, an inner quivering of delight, at finding himself overborne by the superior
fervor and somehow unanswerable illogic of the missionary, much as he felt when he was being vigorously rubbed
and pounded by his masseur. But now, when Lyle began
to talk about the proclamation and his concern about the
assembly, he fingered his rosary nervously.

"Probably to read them some proclamation," he murmured. "No more, I'm sure."

Lyle, on his part, was as nervous as the governor.
While he had never hesitated stoutly to defend his faith
and his ideas of public and private morals in conversation
with the governor, the realization that he was now dealing
with a purely political or administrative matter filled him
with diffidence. Still, now that he had put his hand to the
plow, he would not turn aside.

"Your Excellency does not know?" he asked.

"The matter is in the hands of Hashim Farouk Bey. Will
you not have some tea?"

"You have no authority in the case?" Lyle respectfully persisted.

The governor was adept at dealing with ordinary men; he knew how to evade their questions when they became too direct. But Amos Lyle had made a point. Bari Pasha did not like to admit his impotence.

"This is such an inconsequential matter, and I was very busy. It's a slight inconvenience to call people away from their work, but—"

He lifted his hands deprecatingly, but the idea conveyed was helplessness. Bari Pasha found himself in a dilemma. He wished Lyle would go.

Amos Lyle's concern rose to anxiety.

"Your Excellency," he urged, his deep, cracked voice growing in resonance, "this is, I am afraid, more than the reading of a proclamation. I cannot help being reminded of the reports of what is happening elsewhere."

"Yes, I know. Exaggerations. As you can see for yourself, we have lived very peacefully here. A few deportations, but you must admit they were troublemakers. By the way, did you get all the information you wished for the American scholar? I have just received an illuminated manuscript of the renowned Sheikh Abul-Hasan which might interest you."

Amos Lyle ignored the digression.

"You have been a good governor, Bari Pasha," he said solemnly. "Everyone knows that. You wish your people well. But one in your office should have more than benevolent purposes. You are a man in authority and accountable to God for the people under your hand."

Bari Pasha gazed through the window into the courtyard where some laborers were removing tulip bulbs from the soil. He wondered why he had not retired from public office, with all its exactions and annoyances, to spend his days in his garden. This fine weather foreboded an early freeze, and there were many things he should be superintending. He hated cold weather, not only because of the garden, but because it started twitches of rheumatism in his legs.

Bari Pasha recollected suddenly that Lyle, while he

had threatened him with God's wrath, had not mentioned
the American government, and felt relieved.

"You are mistaken," he said thoughtfully. "I can assure
you that I have had a long talk with Hashim Farouk Bey.
He wants to build a road to Trebizond. He needs labor.
Assad Khodja says that this volume which I mentioned
contains many marvelous and never-before-revealed tales
of the Seljuks."

Lyle surmised that the governor knew what Farouk's
plans were, and that he had not revealed what he knew.
The thought horrified him.

"It would be a great sin, Bari Pasha," he said, his voice
trembling with earnestness, "to maltreat an innocent and
helpless people. A sin contrary to the law of Islam and
the teachings of the Prophet, and even more sinful by
Christian doctrine."

The governor sighed.

"These matters of high politics are a mystery to me," he
said. "Why must they disrupt the peace of a province to
settle their quarrels with the Franks?"

"Can you not give undertakings that the Armenian
people will not be harmed?" Lyle asked.

Bari Pasha drew a large red handkerchief from his
pocket, and removing his red silk fez, mopped his brow.
His hair was thin and scrawny on top, from constant confinement under the tight fez, like grass that has lain under
a board, hidden from the light. With the fez removed,
he looked like nothing but a pudgy, senile old man, with
neither character nor purpose.

"These army hot-heads—there is no telling what they
will do," he groaned. "Now, when I commanded a corps
—but times have changed. . . ."

The reference to his own early days as a commander of
troops awakened memories of a different man from what
he was now—young, vigorous, prompt in decision, courageous in action. In those days, Bari Pasha reflected,
battles were won by personal courage and spirit, and not
by a calculated superiority of men and equipment. These
new army men fought with machines rather than men,
and were inspired by hatred rather than by courage and

patriotism. They were insolent, self-assured—contemptuous of old men like himself. Yet the old ways had their virtues, old men had been heroes once. . . .

A dormant fiber in his character stirred and roused him to action. Bari Pasha arose.

"But I have the police," he said firmly. "I assure you —I swear by my head—that the police shall be restrained."

The police, to which Bari Pasha referred, were such an insignificant corps in Dilijan, compared with the troops, that the force of Bari Pasha's undertaking was lost on Lyle, and he left the governor with a sense of defeat. He passed through the long corridors, giving upon the empty, debris-littered chambers, suggestive of nothing so much as discarded shells from which life and vitality had vanished, and came into the streets, now even more deserted and premonitory than when he had passed along them earlier in the morning. They gave the impression that the town had suddenly been abandoned, or that the plague had broken out again, when people kept inside fearful lest death at any moment knock at their doors.

But though Lyle felt defeated, he was not in despair. The shock of the morning, when he had momentarily imagined the plague, and his relief at seeing the children at play, had strengthened him against a second blow. He considered a while, and resolved to see Hashim Farouk Bey. Praying inwardly for wisdom and guidance, he made his way to the Gapou.

The Gapou was the barracks of the troops and the headquarters of the military commandant—an ancient building. the outer wall of which had at one time been part of the outer fortifications of Dilijan, and because of the subsequent decline of the city now lay at some distance from the inhabited parts of the town. A great Roman arch, a gateway in the ancient wall, adjoined the barracks, and gave the place its name of Gapou, or Gate. Through this archway could be seen the yellow roofs and walls of the town. sloping gently up the valley. They lay so peaceful in the sunshine that Lyle wondered for a moment if he were not making a straw man of his fears, allowing the rumors and Ibrahim Effendi's admonitions to lead him on a wild goose chase.

Hashim Farouk Bey received Lyle with frigid politeness, standing, his hand thrust delicately between the buttons of his tunic.

"It is always an honor to receive a call from an American," he said in English, with more sincerity than his icy, clipped words conveyed, for he secretly envied foreigners, and particularly tall men. "But I must regard the subject of your interest as an impertinence. You are not a consul, no? You have no official status, no?"

"No. I have but a deep interest in this people which gives me ground to speak. I have been their pastor for thirteen years."

"You have been their pastor for thirteen years?" replied Hashim Farouk with ill-concealed sarcasm. "May I tell you, my dear *Mister* Lyle, that our Sultan, His Majesty Abdul Hamid, has been their father for twenty years. Since he ascended to the throne they have been his children, whom he has cherished as father and protector. And for twenty years, base, insidious forces have sought to wean his children from him, to plant the seeds of dissension in his garden, to cultivate hatred and enmity among the peoples of his empire."

Farouk's eyes narrowed until they seemed almost to emerge from a single socket. Beside the gaunt Lyle he seemed like a reed—but a reed that was made of steel.

"It is such representations as yours, coming from the consulates and embassies of the interested Powers, that have compelled His Majesty to set his house in order, to bring his wayward children to obedience, to recognition of him as their rightful lord—rather than the embassies, consulates—and missionaries. For twenty years His Majesty has been complaisant and indulgent; he has promulgated reforms and granted concessions. He has granted to the Armenians courts of appeal and a voice at his elbow, repeal of taxes and land reform, government in their own *sanjaks*. Yet each new act of graciousness is greeted as a sign of weakness; like greedy children they demand more; they wish not only foreign ways, but foreign tutelage."

He paused, for an instant, to give emphasis to his words, but without allowing Lyle time to interpose a remark, he went on, in his clipped, sharp voice:

"The time has come for a reckoning. His Majesty's patience is exhausted. From indulgence we turn to chastisement. Our wills are unshakable, our purposes resolved. The Armenian question is now to be solved, once and for all.

"For," he added, in a tone that rose in intensity until it was like the vibration of a taut wire, almost a scream, while his hand gripped at his tunic until the knuckles were white, "we Turks are still masters of Turkey."

"And now, my dear *Mister* Lyle," he concluded sharply, "I must bid you good day, for I have many things to occupy my attention. Another time, perhaps, and we shall have opportunity for a longer chat."

Amos Lyle left the commandant with an awareness of impending tragedy, awful and engulfing. His knees shook as he walked; he could barely stand. It seemed that he could hear the beating of wings, and that the heavens opened, and the four horsemen of the Apocalypse appeared riding, clad in their raiment of disaster, toward the town of Dilijan. He felt his own utter impotence to challenge these organized forces of evil, and the prayer burst upon his lips, "O God, be merciful to me a sinner for all my shortcomings, and for my transgressions."

But yet, of the nature of this impending tragedy Lyle had no inkling. Neither the governor nor the commandant had stated that thus and thus was to happen. The mood of despair evaporated; the four horsemen, who had momentarily filled his vision, passed, and in their stead, he seemed to see the face of God, like as to nothing but the cloudless sky and the blessed sunshine, and his spirit returned. He took cheer. "God is our salvation and strength, our refuge and strong fortress. Do ye my father's will."

Not far from his compound, playing in the dust of the street, was a Turkish urchin, black-eyed, with cropped hair. His father was a saddler. Lyle knew the father, knew the child. He stopped and spoke to him for a moment, then went on his way, no longer dispirited, but cheerful.

4. A Household

IN the bedroom, just off the paved courtyard of their small house, Emmanuel Verian sat dressing for his appearance at the Gapou, while Miriam his wife, striving to control her feelings, was helping him. In the courtyard a number of pigeons, which Miriam was accustomed to feed, strutted about, preening themselves and cocking their heads toward the door; the afternoon sun, still above the wall, shone in warmly, and was reflected in iridescent colors from their plumage. The house was on a quiet street, next to the extensive walled gardens of the wealthy Murad Bey, and no sound from the town penetrated. It was quiet here, save for the turbulence in Miriam's breast.

"You will want two pairs of socks," she said mechanically, trying to keep her thoughts on the moment. "It will be cold in the mountains."

"Yes, two pairs."

Emmanuel had already dressed in a woolen shirt and undershirt, and thick, warm *shalvari*, or baggy trousers made from homespun. He was a well-set young man, inclined to heaviness, with rosy cheeks, wavy brown hair, and soft brown eyes. He was a teamster by trade, a poet by nature.

"Will you be gone long, do you think?" Miriam asked falteringly, while she went to the drawers, built into the wall.

By the drawers stood a small piece of furniture which Emmanuel had made recently, had fashioned carefully and exquisitely of cured walnut wood—a crib for their baby, though its arrival was yet some six months away.

"Not long, I hope," he replied. "The last time—but that was five years ago—we were kept a month before being relieved. But some—those with families—were let off sooner, for a few *lire*, and allowed to go home. The officers were good fellows. I have no doubt that I shall be back in two weeks."

Miriam kneeled and opened the drawer. Slowly she felt among its contents, and finally, after some time, drew out a pair of socks, a pair with red and blue threads knitted into the tops, a pair she had knitted the summer before and which had never been worn.

"Two weeks!"

She put her hand to her hair as though to arrange it— a gesture to conceal her emotion.

Emmanuel Verian had assumed that the assembly at the Gapou was for a labor draft, as was the general rumor. He was one whose apperceptions were broad rather than sharp, and he had not attempted to read any further meaning into what he had heard.

He looked up at his wife, beheld her large, dark eyes upon him, but he saw in them no anguish or pain, but only love. Impulsively, he stood up and gathered her into his embrace. He held her a long time.

"What is that *gazel* from Hafiz?" he asked finally. "Recite it to me, so that I may taste again the honey of your voice."

Emmanuel had met Miriam three years before in Persia, where he had gone with a caravan. He had wooed and won her, and brought her to Turkey against her parents' will. In her childhood she had learned many of the Persian poems and often recited them for Emmanuel, adopting the liquid, melodic tones of the Persian in the recitation. Her anxiety crept into hiding in the marrow of her bones; she smiled, embarrassed at her husband's adoration, her lips curling, in a way that made Emmanuel adore her the more, to show her pretty white teeth; then with her eyes upon her husband, expressing all the passionate love with which her heart was overflowing, she began the poem, "*'Agher an turki shirazi . . .'*"

> *"Sweet maid, if thou would'st charm my sight,*
> *And bid these arms thy neck enfold;*
> *That rosy cheek, that lily hand,*
> *Would give thy poet more delight*
> *Than all Bokhara's vaunted gold,*
> *Than all the gems of Samarcand."*

"Ah, that was splendid!" he exclaimed, when she had finished. He drew her again close to him. "Some day we shall go to Persia again, shall we not? But there will be three of us then."

He feasted his eyes upon Miriam's ivory face and dark hair.

"Oh, I hope it's a girl, so that she may look like you!"

Emmanuel was quite foolish about his lovely wife. Miriam was more reserved than her husband, but her passion ran quite as deep. She seldom spoke, but her large, brown eyes were expressive of her mood, which was sometimes contemplative, sometimes—though rarely—sad, sometimes fiercely joyous, but never merely gay, always passionate and warm.

"I can never get over thinking of the day I first came down into Shahran," continued Emmanuel. "It was early spring, and the passes were still blocked with snow. But in Shahran, the almonds were in blossom, fretting the blue of the sky with tender tracery; the air was warm, and the sunlight like heavy cream. That night I heard the *bul bul* sing, and I knew that good fortune was in store for me—"

"Emmanuel, you will not leave me for long, will you?"

The words burst from Miriam's lips in a cry of anguish.

"Why, not long—not long, I'm sure," protested Emmanuel, surprised. "Perhaps I'll be back this evening, who knows? That would be odd, after I've dressed for a long journey."

Miriam was crying now.

"I saw Pastor Lyle today," said Emmanuel, soothing her and stroking her hair. "He had planned to call today. He wanted to know how you were, and he was overjoyed when I confirmed the news. He hopes it will be a boy."

"What did he say about the notice?" Miriam asked.

"He said he could learn nothing. He was on his way to see Hashim Farouk Bey. He hoped that it was only to read a proclamation to the Armenians, but he said we should be prepared for whatever God wills."

"God wills!"

"Pastor Lyle said that if I should not be able to get home tonight you are to come to the mission and stay with him. I wish you would."

"Pastor Lyle is a good man. Next to you—" But Miriam could compare no one with Emmanuel.

Silence fell upon them. They sat together, in each other's arms, for some little time, watching the pigeons in the court and the shadow of the poplar creep up the wall, making the most they could of each minute, lengthening its duration by watching its passage, knitting their souls together so that they should not separate, however far apart their bodies might be carried.

After a while it came time for Emmanuel to report at the Gapou; he arose and buckled on his outer garments, kissed his wife good-by and went out.

After Emmanuel had gone, Miriam sat a long while staring at the wall, trying to comprehend what this absence might mean to her. It was not the first, of course. As a teamster, carting loads to the nearby villages, Emmanuel had been away for two or three days at a stretch, and once or twice he had gone on longer journeys, when he was away for as much as a week. But these absences had been growing more and more infrequent. During the first months of their marriage, separation had been supportable by the novelty of their new life; but the longer they lived together, the harder it became to part even for a day. Emmanuel had finally given up all business that took him out of town. Though it meant some loss to their income, they preferred to sacrifice their comforts to the greater necessity of their companionship.

Emmanuel and Miriam were in that stage of married life when they required no other interest but each other. They lived very much to themselves. Later, no doubt, they would become more sociable, but few demands were now made upon them, for neither of them had relatives in the town. Miriam, having come from Persia, had no acquaintances here; Emmanuel's parents had come to Dilijan when he was a small boy, and they had subsequently died.

The house itself had demanded much of their time after their marriage. It was an old house, which they had acquired cheap; it had thick, musty walls and a sagging brick floor. Emmanuel had relaid all the brick, and had burned and whitewashed the walls, so that it was now bright and dry and airy. He had also made cupboards and shelves and chests of drawers, which Miriam kept, like the rest of the house, in immaculate state. Most of the objects in the house were Emmanuel's or Miriam's handicraft.

Miriam's blurred eyes were staring at the long chest of drawers which Emmanuel had fashioned, three drawers of which were already filled with baby clothes of Miriam's making. Emmanuel was proud of this particular piece and Miriam never polished it without running her palm over the surface to feel the almost imperceptible indentations left by her husband's slips with the plane. She loved these little imperfections, which gave her a sense of the character of the will that had struggled with the obdurate wood, just as she loved the little imperfections in her husband's character that gave her a sense of the quality of his love —his forgetfulness of the little delicacies of sentiment in the abruptness of his passion, his moodiness which he could not always conquer, his inability to consider a matter—like this assembly at the Gapou—either logically or conclusively.

As Miriam's eyes came to a focus, and with it her thoughts, she was reminded of her work—a blanket of soft wool for the baby's crib—which she had started on a new loom Emmanuel had made for her. She still had some time before the light would fail.

Casting aside her heavy thoughts, she rose slowly and started about her duties.

5. The Execution

When Emmanuel Verian arrived at the Gapou, a considerable number of Armenians had foregathered along the wall. Some of them he recognized—Petros Asganian, a dealer in foodstuffs, from whom he bought provender for his horses; Byranik Vasoon, a teacher in the school; Gregorian, another teamster, and others. They were all quiet, and nodded to him silently, as men do when they are gathered for a funeral. Some others were gathered in little groups, talking in low voices and casting anxious glances at the soldiers. These—a company of them—stood a little distance away, at ease on their arms, silent and indifferent, while their officers, who formed another little group, smoked cigarettes and talked quietly.

All seemed tranquil and orderly. The afternoon rays of the sun, golden upon the walls and upon the dust of the ground; the haze in the autumn air; the roofs and walls of the town above, laced with shadow and sunlight; the silent gathering before the Gapou—all suggested arrested motion, silence, peace, like a fresco on the walls of a church.

A few latecomers arrived, saw the crowd along the wall, and quietly took their places among them, or sought out friends with whom they might converse in an undertone. Someone wondered when the reading of the proclamation would begin. Another asked, in a quavering voice, if the work would be hard. This was a consumptive-looking lad whose chin was still downy.

"Hush," someone cautioned him. "It will be only the reading of a warning."

Time crept on, and there was no movement. It was now past four o'clock. The soldiers still stood at ease, and the officers continued to smoke their cigarettes. The Armenians gathered closer, and uneasiness began to show itself

27

among them, in their nervous glances, in their whispered
consultations. "Surely we will not be marched tonight," one
ventured.

"Hush," was the repeated admonition. "They might require a short march—to Kara Keliss possibly." This was a
nearby village.

The sun nodded toward the mountains. The roofs and
walls of the town grew nacreous and pink and the shadows
lengthened from the row of poplars by the road. A fitful
breeze kicked up a little whirlpool of dust that went
eddying by, saucily enveloping the officers, so that they
coughed and spat, and then, unwrapping itself from them,
hurried away across the ridge toward the mountains.

On the slopes of the valley, below the town, one could
see the Turkish peasants laboring among the vineyards.
The crop had been abundant, and the heavy clusters
sparkled, even at a distance, like garnets in the sunlight.
Earth and sky seemed to lie under a blessing. The rolling,
fruitful valley, the silent cloud-splashed sky overhead, the
town, slumbrous on the slopes, all seemed to speak of
a harmony of existence in which man and nature dwelt
in the bosom of a protecting god.

Finally, as though some secret button had been touched,
setting off an automaton, the officer in charge stepped
forward toward the Armenians. This officer was Hashim
Farouk Bey. He moved lithely, but the grace of his movement was concealed by a military precision that suggested
long drilling in the manner of the German manual. When
he was midway between the troops and the Armenians
he raised his hand for silence. Then, with a voice that
was controlled—quiet, precise, firm, beautifully modulated
—he commanded the Armenians to form in a double line
facing him.

The men quietly obeyed.

When the Armenians stood before him Hashim Farouk
Bey surveyed them all, as a schoolteacher might survey his
class, motioned to one or two to align themselves more
accurately, and finally, when they were standing to his
satisfaction, he drew forth a document, opened it meticu-

lously, so as not to tear any corner of it, and began to read.

This was the proclamation which the Armenians had expected to hear, but its contents were something not the most fearful imagination had anticipated. After the proper invocation to deity—"In the name of God, the Compassionate, the Merciful,"—and salutations to His Majesty the Sultan and Caliph, and to others of lesser rank, it continued,

"Whereas the military court sitting in Dilijan, and acting on express authority of the Imperial War Ministry, finds the existence of treasonable acts and acts destructive of the safety of the Empire, all attributable to persons of the Armenian race and faith; and whereas, because of the mendacity of the people of this faith and race, it is impossible to come upon the immediate culprits; and whereas all are implicated and guilty, the military court sitting in Dilijan condemns the Armenian male population upwards of fourteen years of age—"

Consternation broke out among the Armenians. Long before the commandant came to the sentence, they knew what their fate was to be.

There were over a thousand Armenians standing before the wall. The troops did not number more than a hundred and fifty and were equipped with single load Martin-Peabody rifles. Had they chosen to act, many of the Armenians might have made good their escape. It was not that they were lacking in courage. For centuries the select troops of the sultans—the janissaries—had been recruited from among their race. Neither were they lacking in the vitality from which all growth proceeds, for they had maintained their race and tradition and faith through centuries of oppression. Yet they offered no resistance. They seemed, indeed, incapable of resistance. At such times as this, when both spirit and mind are frozen, it is training that mechanically determines action. Turkish schooling had produced its results. For four hundred years the subject Christian peoples of Turkey had been forbidden to bear arms. The profession of fighting had been reserved exclusively to Turks and to other Moslems. The Christians had been compelled to assert their spirit in other ways, and they had, perhaps, come to find their strength in other ways. The rock that turns away the arrow is no less to be reckoned with than the arrow.

And so, now, the Armenians gathered here had no will to resist this officer, who represented the majesty of the Sultan and the authority of the Sublime Porte. And the commandant, with the contempt of the warrior for the civilian, dismissed any idea of resistance on the part of the Armenians and went about the matter as though it were of no more consequence than the execution of a single individual.

The reading of the sentence completed, Hashim Farouk Bey stepped back quickly and sharply issued an order to the soldiers. The soldiers came to attention, raised their rifles, and trained them on the Armenians.

Emmanuel stood in the second line, his head rising between the shoulders of the two men in front of him. When the order had been given to fall into line he had obeyed mechanically, doing as the others did. Emmanuel himself was elsewhere. His body had arrived at the Gapou, but his wayward thoughts, like a dog following his master, had been roving hither and yon, sniffing at this sight or that reverie, and hurrying back at intervals to his house to see how Miriam was. His thoughts were now at home, secure from the scene at the Gapou, pleasantly and comfortingly dallying with his wife. He was thinking that Miriam might be at the loom, or possibly in the court, feeding the pigeons. He could see her now, calling to the pigeons to perch upon her finger and shoulder, while she fed them. . . .

The command to the soldiers was like a sharp tug on the leash. His thoughts came hurrying back to the Gapou, but unwillingly, only half collected. He looked up and saw the row of rifle muzzles, like so many black beads, trained upon the men. The muzzle directly before him had a face stuck on top of it, one eye closed in a squint, the other open, and lying upon the gun barrel like a hazelnut. . . .

There was a moment while the commandant waited for the soldiers to take aim before he gave the order to fire.

For that instant all life, all movement, ceased, as though the sun stood still and nature had suddenly frozen. With the effect of a camera shutter opening upon a dark plate, in that moment Emmanuel beheld the entire scene in all its form and color, in clear, precise detail—the delicate violet haze over the mountains in the distance, the pink feathered clouds that brushed their summits, and the valley below splotched with the brown of plowed fields and the green of vineyards. Even the evening lark was not omitted in this picture; he saw it poised in mid-air and heard the song that seemed to float, thin and clear, upon the atmosphere.

But precise and vivid as were these objects of earth and sky, even more precise and vivid was the black point of the rifle that was trained upon Emmanuel. Upon it everything seemed to converge, as the lines of a picture all converge upon the perspective point, the vanishing point of infinity toward which all things are irresistably drawn. Emmanuel himself felt drawn along upon one of these invisible lines, as by a magnet, against which he had no resistance. He was powerless to struggle, as though under a hypnosis that congealed every faculty of his mind. He could neither think nor act. In a moment a puff of smoke would burst from that point and at that same moment a sharp something would strike his chest, and then the shutter of the camera would close. All the colors of the sky would fade, all the things which Emmanuel had known and loved—his home, his wife, all the poetry of life—would disappear in a twinkling, and all would be darkness, a void into which he could feel himself already sinking. . . .

On either side of him were Emmanuel's friends and neighbors. They were outside of the visible picture, but Emmanuel could feel their presence. They too did not move. They too stood transfixed by the rifle points bearing upon them. Over the entire assembly hung that same spell of bewitchment, as though all nature stood still and all movement had ceased. . . .

A leaf from an elm tree along the wall, one of the last clinging to the bare branches, fluttered down to earth, before Emmanuel's eyes, like a butterfly settling upon a flower, breaking the spell.

The commandant spoke.

"*Atesh!*" (Fire).

The word was abrupt, incisive, like the quick explosion of a rifle. Almost at the same instant the man on Emmanuel's right crumpled in a heap and a clap of thunder rolled across the valley. The man at his left began to thresh his arms, screaming in agony, and to stagger toward the soldiers. From the corner of his eyes, Emmanuel saw some of the men at the end of the line make a break for the valley.

The commandant shouted another order, and as the Armenians, now galvanized into action, began to run in every direction, the soldiers loaded and fired, at will, shouting and killing, firing shot after shot at the fleeing Armenians, firing volley after volley into the heap of slain and dying. The air was filled with screaming and shouting and the cries of the dying.

Above all this pandemonium Emmanuel could hear the trickle of a stream. He was suddenly thirsty and he wondered where the stream came from. Turning his head, he saw blood flowing in a rivulet beside his arm. He realized now that he was no longer erect, but lying among a heap of the slain. Over his head roared a vast tumult. . . .

Was he dead, or dying? Emmanuel did not know. He had been hit, perhaps. Or he had fainted and fallen. . . .

After a while the shouting stilled, and the rifle fire died away. Some of the officers stood among the heap of the dead and dying, watching for signs of life. Where a body moved or stirred, an officer fired a revolver.

Presently an officer stood over Emmanuel. The body that half covered Emmanuel was quivering and the limbs were moving convulsively. The officer pointed his revolver and fired. The body shuddered and was still. . . . Emmanuel dared not breathe.

The sentence of the military court having been executed, the dead were abandoned where they fell. Night came, and the soldiers were released to partake of the loot and rape of the Armenian quarter for which the massacre was the signal.

At the Gapou the dead lay under the stars, upon the soaking earth, in heaps of mangled and bloody flesh. Now and then when a cold breeze touched the still warm bodies, a faint stirring would disturb the silent heaps, where life still clung, reluctant to depart, and quivered protestingly, and in the stirring some buckle, or button, or strand of glossy hair would catch the starlight and cast it back to the sky, a solitary beam winging toward heaven, as a memento of the occasion.

Some three hours after the massacre, when the jackals were beginning to howl and gather near, and from the Armenian quarter flames were arising to light the sky with an orange incandescence, one of the bodies on the field moved, struggled free, and began to crawl away. It moved, belly upon the ground, propelled by knees and elbows, in a reptilian manner, like a lizard, hugging the earth, as though to lie prostrate were its natural state rather than to stand erect, as though it were only by abasing itself and identifying itself with the very soil that life might continue. Was this the body of a man, housing an eternal, godlike spirit, that crawled now like a worm, a creature upon whom the seal of degradation had been placed, a creature that was of no account in the eyes of God or among the habitants of the earth?

This object crawled; though it had survived death, alone among all those who had foregathered, it was unable to stand erect, for the spirit of manhood, which is the only force that could now make it stand erect, was gone. But though that spirit was gone, not all the attributes of its character had departed. Within this crawling body still clung love, and beneath love—far submerged—faith. In the feeble light of consciousness there flickered faint images of a home and someone loved, and toward these it crawled.

The figure reached the edge of the town. A wall, dark and friendly, rose before it. A hand came in contact with its rough surface; the fingers gripped the bricks and the figure drew itself erect.

The object was again a man, a man with attributes and qualities. This man had an individuality; he was an identity among the creatures of the earth. He had a name: his name was Emmanuel Verian. He had a home, and a wife, and an unborn child. Toward these he struggled, with shaking knees, with trembling hands, with frozen blood and uneven breath.

As he crept along in the shadow of the wall, he heard sounds. He listened. From a distant district of the town, where lay the Armenian quarter, arose a mingling of shouts, screams, rifle shots, and the crackle and susurration of flames.

Emmanuel paused. The faith-inspired vision which had supported him dissolved into a horrible image. The thought arose: he could not go home. Death and destruction raged there, as it had raged at the Gapou. Miriam would not be there. She was dead.

Where should he go? What was he to do?

Emmanuel, who only a moment before had found his feet, sank again to the earth and began to breathe convulsively.

Presently, however, he rose to his feet again. The vision of his home again passed before his eyes. It was obvious to him, however, that he could not go far. His strength was gone. The conviction that his home was gone, that Miriam was dead, made effort hopeless. The will to live was ebbing fast. Despair, more powerful to kill than bullets, had taken possession of his soul. Before he had gone a hundred yards, Emmanuel collapsed and fell into a gutter.

After a while a figure passed along the street, slinking in the shadows like a prowling animal, short and squat like the form of a beast: it was the boy Haig, roaming the streets for such excitement as he could find. He saw Emmanuel, approached him stealthily, saw who he was, and spoke to him.

"Emmanuel," he whispered.

A shudder passed over the man.

"Emmanuel," the boy whispered again. "This is no

place to be lying. The soldiers will find you here. Come with me."

Emmanuel stirred.

"Where?"

"To the compound. Everyone's there."

"Everyone?"

"Most everyone. They have been coming all day, ever since the rumors got around. It's safe there. Pastor Lyle won't let the soldiers in. He has put up a flag."

"Is Miriam there?"

Haig hesitated.

"There are so many—" he began, and then seeing Emmanuel's look, added hastily, "Yes—yes—she's there. Of course. Everyone."

"Then help me to my feet."

With the boy supporting the man, the two set off for Amos Lyle's compound.

"You're not lying to me, Haig, about Miriam?" Emmanuel asked.

"By St. Gregory," the boy swore.

Emmanuel paused, and his hands gripped the boy's shoulder convulsively.

"Now I know you're lying," he groaned, and gave the boy a shove. "Go away, you liar. Go away and leave me alone."

Emmanuel started off, staggering, in the direction of the *tope haneh.*

"Please come, Emmanuel," pleaded the boy, running up and tugging at his arm. "You'll see. Please come, Emmanuel."

Emmanuel stood still. Stupor came upon him, and in a daze he allowed himself to be piloted along.

Presently they came to the Rumeli Chai. This was the dry bed of an ancient watercourse, along which the Byzantine troops had once crept to take the city from the Turks—whence its name "Stream of the Romans." The bed of the stream was now a wagon trail for carters. Emmanuel recognized it, and sitting down in the gravel, refused to go farther.

"No, I shan't go," he muttered. "Miriam is not there. Let them kill me."

Haig was in perplexity. He would have willingly carried Emmanuel by main force, but the slope of the gully was too steep.

The compound was, fortunately, only a short distance away.

Leaving Emmanuel where he was, hoping that he might not wander off in his stupor, Haig raced to the gate and knocked frantically.

Lyle opened the gate.

"Haig, where have you been?" he expostulated in exasperation at finding the boy outside the walls. "Come in here. Don't you know you'll get hurt running around like this? Come in."

To Lyle's knowledge, Haig had been in the compound not an hour before. He surmised, in increasing annoyance, that Haig must have climbed the wall.

"Yes, pastor, I'll come in. I just wanted to see—but Emmanuel's down there, and I can't get him any farther."

"Hurt?" exclaimed Lyle, coming out of the compound and shutting the gate behind him. His righteous wrath subsided.

"I don't know. He can hardly walk. I don't know why. And he keeps wanting to go home. He acts like one drunk."

"Show me where he is, and thank God you have come to no harm."

"Hurry," urged Haig. "I saw some soldiers crossing the *khiaban*."

Together they found Emmanuel wandering down the trail of the gully.

"Emmanuel!" exclaimed Lyle, putting his arm about the man. "God be praised!"

Lyle helped Emmanuel up the gully and into the street that led to the compound.

"Pastor Lyle," Emmanuel whispered, "Haig is a good boy, but he will not let me go home. I must see Miriam."

"I have told him, again and again, pastor, that Miriam

is safe, but he will not believe me," protested the boy, nudging Lyle.

"But where, if not at home?" moaned Emmanuel.

"At the compound," urged the boy.

"At the compound? Ah, yes, she was to go to the compound. She is at the compound, safe, is she, pastor? Tell me the truth. Tell me the truth."

The words were like a lariat about Lyle's throat. He gasped:

"No, Emmanuel, she is not at the compound. Haig, we must tell the truth. Miriam is not at the compound. I went for her, shortly after dark, but she was not there."

"Dead," wailed Emmanuel, softly. "Dead. I knew it. I knew it. Oh, pastor, dead."

Emmanuel staggered drunkenly into the street, now illuminated by the late-rising moon.

At that moment a party of *gizil bashies* appeared at the bottom of the street, their red fezzes like bloody heads in the moonlight.

"Emmanuel!" called Haig from the shadow of the wall. "Save yourself. The soldiers!"

But Emmanuel staggered on into the center of the street wailing, "Dead, dead, dead."

The soldiers carried heavy packs of loot upon their backs. They were singing an erotic ditty,

"An houri, *so the Prophet says,*
Will dance for me with star-like toes . . ."

Lyle stepped into the street, and caught Emmanuel's hand in a vise-like grip, and drew him into the shadows.

"Come quietly and stay within the shadow and we will reach the gate before they see us," he whispered.

Emmanuel allowed himself to be drawn along by the missionary until they had almost gained the gate. Suddenly, with a violent wrench, he broke away and started running, staggering, crying as he went, "Dead, dead, dead."

"*Armeni,*" shouted the soldiers, and before Lyle could run to the rescue the rifles had barked, and Emmanuel crumpled to the earth. The work of execution begun at the Gapou had been completed.

"Miserable servant of God that I am!" cried Amos Lyle in agony.

The boy Haig had had the greater wisdom. Emmanuel did not die by a Turkish bullet, but by the destruction of his hope.

6. The Sanctuary

INTO Amos Lyle's compound had crowded upwards of two thousand helpless, frightened Armenians. The first— the foresighted ones—had come early in the morning, and had prudently arrived with belongings, which they had brought in carts, on donkeys, and on their backs. As the day wore on, and the premonition of disaster increased, the movement to the compound had become less and less a thoughtful precaution, and more and more a wild, abandoned flight—women hastening through the streets, babies in their arms, children clutched by the hand; old men doggedly shouldering what few possessions they could; a few young men and married men who had dared to ignore the order of assembly at the Gapou sneaking along the shadows to avoid detention.

Suddenly, toward nightfall, the movement had ceased; the soldiers had taken possession of the quarter and had cut off escape. All who were found in the streets were shot; those who clung to their own walls found the doors battered down, the men shot, the women struck down or dragged off for unholy purposes. Of those who had lived that morning, over half were dead before the sun rose again.

As for those within the compound, what was their situation? They were, for the moment, safe. During the night, parties of lustful and vengeful Turks kept appearing at the gate, knocking and threatening to break in, and occasionally firing a few volleys at the thick planking; but they did not trespass. Lyle would plead with them, argue with them, answer them firmly, defy them. They would go away, come back later, again go away, never quite daring to molest the property of the mission.

But beyond physical safety, what did they have? What did this Amos Lyle have to offer these people for their defense, for their sustenance? There was the compound; by treaties and by the capitulations it enjoyed inviolability, but this was his to offer only by the fortuitousness of circumstance. By the same fortuitousness there were several buildings, now in ramshackle state, which would serve to protect most of the refugees from the cold of the night. As for food, Lyle had none, or practically none; but enough had been brought in by those with foresight to keep off starvation for a day or so. What else?

The people in the compound were in a state of fear; at first anxiety, it was now terror. At every pounding on the gate, the terror increased; it approached frenzy. To Lyle they looked as father and protector, possibly to some extent before, but now implicitly. In his hands they placed their fate.

To meet the various and urgent needs of these people Lyle had but one resource—his religion. The people were drawn to him, and he was their only stay. His only stay was his faith.

Though these people were a community, a community is something seldom realized in fact. They had come in singly and in groups; they now stood about singly or in twos or threes. There was little intercourse among them. Fear—the malady that attacks the connective tissues of the spirit and leaves the soul standing alone and unsupported—had dissolved the ordinary ties and interests that lead people to converse.

Lyle had gone about among them, talking to them, comforting those that were silently sobbing, soothing the whimpering children, calming fears, restoring quiet to troubled spirits, engaging the people in conversation, until finally they were gathered together in little groups and beginning to feel reviving hope and solidarity.

When Haig had knocked at the gate, Amos Lyle was talking to a little crowd that had collected around a fire in the shelter of the gatehouse. The story of perils escaped is an anodyne to misery, and Lyle had been telling these people about a tornado from which he had once escaped. His listeners had heard the story before, for he had told it many times in his sermons. It was one of his most vivid memories, and was the experience, in fact, that had convinced him of God's especial providence for him, and had prepared the way for his later conversion and entry into the ministry.

The tornado he had witnessed had appeared suddenly out of a heavy, heat-laden sky, in the form of a sagging raincloud, had brought a breeze, which had increased in violence, and had become a black funnel racing across the plain, destroying everything in its path. Amos Lyle was in town at the time, loading a chuck wagon. The cry had gone up and down the dusty street, "Cyclone coming!" and men, women, children, dogs, horses, had begun to run about in uncontrolled fright. There was no escape. In a moment the wind struck; the air was filled with flying objects, indistinguishable as to form or color, and with the most excruciating sounds, like the whinnying of horses and the bellowing of cattle in a stampede, the roar of hail and the sound of breaking glass. Amos Lyle, standing beside his wagon, had fallen flat on his face. When the wind passed, a moment later, the wagon was gone, the store in which he had been buying provisions, ten minutes earlier, was gone, and what was left was a mass of splinters, wreckage, tin cans, and in the center, on top of an up-ended showcase, a display card of some biscuit maker, untouched except that over it hung, neatly suspended, a necklace of sausages.

The core of the tornado had passed straight down the street. Of the town's population of some five hundred persons, a third were killed, another third injured. Among those who survived unscathed was Amos Lyle. Later, while riding herd under the stars, Lyle thought a great deal about this mystery—of some being taken, and some being left—and he gradually became convinced that he had been preserved for a particular purpose. . . .

Now, in telling the story again, Lyle sought, as always, to impress the same conviction upon his listeners.

"Trust in God," Lyle had adjured. "We cannot say what the morrow will bring forth, but the power to still the tempest is His. Remember the glorious words of Our Master, spoken to his disconsolate disciples, 'And ye now therefore have sorrow: but I will see you again, and your heart shall rejoice, and your joy no man taketh from you.' Whatever they may do to us, we have our Redeemer and Comforter, and we know that He liveth. The powers of evil now press straitly upon us, but remember again the words of the Lord Jesus, 'Be of good cheer; I have overcome the world!' "

It was at this moment that the knocking on the gate occurred.

When Lyle returned, the mood of hope and confidence that he had engendered had evaporated; it had been, to these people, like the light that sometimes flares in the northern sky, illuminating for a moment the frigid darkness of the winter's night with bands of ethereal color, but then subsiding and leaving again the frigid darkness. The Armenians had heard the firing in the street, and now their mood had mounted to frenzy, their overwrought imaginations conjuring all manner of disaster.

"The Turks are coming. They will kill us all," a young woman, Marta Hovasian, was moaning. Her face was blotched with terror, and in the light of the fire it looked bloated and yellow like a pumpkin.

Lyle himself was no longer in a condition to comfort them. His hands were still warm with Emmanuel Verian's blood; it was growing sticky on his fingers. Lyle had rushed to Emmanuel the moment he fell, heedless of the soldiers, intending to bring him inside; then fearing the effect of the sight upon the people, he had carefully deposited the body near the wall.

"No, Marta," Lyle forced himself to say, all the time thinking of Emmanuel lying there outside the wall, "just two or three hungry fellows looking for a little excitement. See, they have gone by."

"They have gone, but they will come again. Why did they shoot?" she continued to moan, swaying back and forth.

"Yes, whom did they kill?"

A woman who had been holding a sleeping baby to her breast rose and began to walk around, hugging the baby as she did so, but staring all the time into the fire with a vacant look, like one hypnotized.

"They have shot my Mattios," she said, and kept repeating, in a monotonous, chanting voice, "they have shot my Mattios. Yes, he escaped the massacre and was coming here to take me home, and they shot him outside the gate."

"No, no, Mattios was not shot," spoke up the boy Haig, protestingly.

"Then who was shot?" came the demand from half a dozen throats. "Who was shot? Tell us."

But Haig remained silent.

Lyle looked at these people with compassion, and the injunction "Comfort ye my people" kept going over and over in his mind. But he needed comfort himself.

"You won't let the Turks take us, will you, pastor?" whimpered a slim, pale youth, Hohanes by name, who had disregarded the order to report and had fled to the compound instead.

"They are horrible, horrible, horrible," began Marta Hovasian again, and kept repeating the word "horrible" with rising inflection until it became an eerie, heart-rending scream. She who was the wife of Mattios went up to Lyle, hugging the baby, but extending her fingers and pointing to Lyle's hands.

"They have murdered him," she said accusingly. "See, you have blood on your hands."

The terror of these frightened women was spreading, leaping from person to person, as a fire in a crowded tenement block spreads, leaping from roof to roof. Unless something stopped it, the whole compound would be in a pandemonium in which they might suffocate and kill themselves by the very fury of their fear.

Lyle closed his eyes and lifted his head.

"O Father, Father, in heaven," he prayed, "give me what to say to these people. Help me to comfort them."

As if in answer, his mouth involuntarily opened and from his throat proceeded words. In his large, none too pleasant voice, he shouted, "Glory be to God!"

His voice drowned out all other sound by its very size and forced the crowd to silence.

Again words issued, in a raucous shout, like that of an old-time evangelist, "Glory be to God for this great deliverance."

There was a cart standing nearby, in which had been brought certain household gear. Lyle climbed into the cart and stood erect, full in the light of the crackling flames of the burning brushwood.

"Glory be to God for all his wonderful mercies," he cried loudly, raising his eyes toward heaven and lifting his arms.

The murmuring and the wailing died down before the piercing voice, the challenging words.

Amos Lyle did not pause, but keeping his eyes uplifted so that he could not see the crowd, he suddenly dropped his voice to a murmur, so that only those nearest him could hear it and others had to strain to catch his singsong,

" 'O give thanks unto the Lord, for he is good: for his mercy endureth for ever.

" 'Let the redeemed of the Lord say so, whom he hath redeemed from the hand of the enemy;

" 'And gathered them out of the lands, from the east, and from the west, from the north, and from the south. . . .' "

Then suddenly bursting forth again, like the trumpet of an exultant angel awakening the earth, he shouted, pealingly,

"Glory be to God who loves us all!"

He punctuated his last gloria with a tremendous clap of his hands.

The response came in murmured "amens" from various quarters of the courtyard.

Amos Lyle had by nature all the arts of a camp-meeting evangelist. His religious expression was primitive in manner. Rites, litanies, and liturgies—these played little part in his worship, which was rather one of deep emotional mood. His God was not One to be approached through intermediaries, or propitiated by rite and made splendid by ceremony. He was Someone very intimate and personal, a God who hated sacrifice and preferred a clean heart. Not all the people with whom Lyle dwelt appreciated this approach to deity; the Armenian Church is one of the most ancient, and its rites among the most splendid. The Armenians of Dilijan, though they had ceased to pay reverence to the old faith, had not forgotten its forms, and Lyle's direct, simple services had often, in times past, been repugnant to them. This, however, had made no difference to Lyle; he was too absorbed in his faith and too full of enthusiasm to be disturbed by, or to be aware of, criticism. Fortunately, there were those who liked his homespun religion and were affected by his emotional ecstasy. It was these who now responded and carried the others along with them.

At the sound of the "amens," Lyle lowered his eyes and surveyed the crowd.

"That's right, brethren," he exclaimed. "Praise the Lord. Praise the Lord. Blessed be the Lord Jesus Christ."

He continued to shout, coaxingly, exultantly, in a great swinging, throbbing voice:

"Lift your voices in praise to God. Sing like David to His glory. Praise the Lord Jesus Christ."

He began to sing the Armenian words of the hymn:

> "I love him, oh, how I love him,
> And how the Lord Jesus loves me . . ."

A few quavering voices took up the words, others joined in, and music began to well forth as a balm to suffering, as a long wall reared against despair.

When they had finished the song, Amos Lyle continued, without a pause,

"The Lord God loves us; He has preserved us. Like the children of Israel, we are under the protection of His wing; the wicked Pharaohs shall be harmless to us, and we shall pass through the Red Sea to deliverance. The will of the Evil One can prevail only so far. The strong arm of God resists him. Only trust in the Lord God. Believe that He will save you, and He surely will, for His arm is long, and His might is great. Remember how He saved Daniel from the jaws of the lions. Remember how He delivered the Hebrew children Shadrach, Meshach, and Abednego from the burning, fiery furnace. Remember how He delivered David from the Philistines, so that David sang,

" 'The Lord is my rock, and my fortress, and my deliverer;

" 'The God of my rock; in him will I trust: he is my shield, and the horn of my salvation, my high tower, and my refuge, my saviour; thou savest me from violence.' "

Lyle's words, and the words of the Psalmist, and Lyle's impassioned faith, all had their effect: as he recited the psalm some joined in, then others, until all those in the courtyard were united in praising the Lord and His Name.

When the psalm was finished, a respectful, prayerful silence fell upon the company, while they waited upon their pastor.

"And now, my brothers and sisters in Christ," Lyle concluded, "the day is done. Night's cloak, spread for our rest, enfolds us. Tomorrow, by God's will, we have a new day, a new sun, a new earth, a new soul, a new strength, a new task. Let us take our rest now and, like the wise virgins of the parable, keep our lamps trimmed for the coming of the bridegroom."

He lifted his hands, still stained with Emmanuel's blood, and pronounced a benediction.

Lyle had re-established the authority of the spirit among his people. One by one, in compliance with his injunction, they settled down among the carts, the gear, or around the fire. Though sleep came to few, shortly the compound was in comparative quietness, awaiting the morrow.

7. Miriam Verian

WHEN it grew late, and Emmanuel did not return home, Miriam Verian concluded despondently that he had been taken on a labor draft to some distant place.

She did not know precisely what labor drafts meant; she had only heard them spoken of casually by Emmanuel. They did not have them in the part of Persia in which she was reared. As she went about her evening duties her thoughts dwelt, in their loneliness, upon that land she had left. It was a peaceful land, a romantic land where the disturbing, uprooting influences of the West had never penetrated. There had never been, in her own memory or in the recollections of her people, any troubles between the Armenians and Persians. Men worshiped the One God, known as Allah, or the triune God of Father, Son and Holy Spirit, and lived side by side in contentment. As to what the differences were between these two concepts of deity Miriam had never been quite clear, for she was passionate rather than believing, loving rather than devout; she was aware only that there were differences between the mode of life of her people and the mode of life among the Moslems, and that she intensely preferred the Christian mode.

Miriam loved her own country. Her native town of Shahran, which was somewhat smaller than Dilijan, lay in a luxuriant valley among the Savalan ranges. In the watered fields and gardens of their slopes grew a variety of products for the use of man—both wheat and rice, as well as barley; among fruits, the apricot, the apple, the pear, and the quince; of vegetables, almost every sort known to the temperate climate. As for flowers, the gardens were ablaze with them from the last frost of winter until the first frost of the next. The roses, in particular, grew in abundance, and from their crushed petals were confected such things as the precious *attar*, or fragrant oil, and sweet preserves to eat, and the delectable drink known as rose *sherbet*.

How peaceful, how contented was the town! Characteristic of its spirit were the scribes and mullahs who were always to be found seated along the wall in the sunshine, drowsing one another with their tales from the poet Firdausi and wise sayings from the Koran; the dimly lighted bazaars, where the brass workers hammered at their anvils, and the rug merchants spread their wares for the veiled ladies from the *harems*. Miriam could see the rugs even now, gleaming like jeweled plaques in the half-light, and the queues of passing donkeys, the caravans of lumbering camels, the evening light reflected through the arcade, glinting upon the turquoise blue dome of the mosque. . . . These, and a thousand other scenes, came back to her in a fleeting moment of nostalgia and loneliness.

Yet she had given them up—these and her home, her father, who was a teacher in the Armenian Academy of Shahran, her mother, her three sisters and two brothers—for Emmanuel. From the moment she first saw Emmanuel she had been willing to give them up, to surrender them irrevocably—as she had done in marrying without permission—so intense was her love.

Though Dilijan was in many respects like Shahran, there were vast differences of degree, as she had quickly discovered. There was, first, the difference in the atmosphere. The quietness of Shahran was undisturbed. There were not so many foreign wares to be found in the bazaars as in Dilijan; almost every necessity or even luxury was made locally, from the printed cottons, known as *galamkars*, and the felts used for headwear, to such things as the illuminated copies of the Koran, the glazed tiles, the tooled leather, and the blown glass. The occupation of mind and hand in such activity satisfied the people and gave them a contentment which was not apparent in Dilijan, where foreign articles were beginning to arouse new desires and corresponding unrest and to create a disturbance of the local economy. Miriam remembered that in her first year in Dilijan there had been hunger and murmuring among the weavers as a result of the arrival of a caravan load of cheap cotton and woolen cloth from the European mills.

Though Dilijan was remote, the restive, urgent spirit of the West had begun to penetrate. It was manifest in such things as the demand for foreign goods and foreign culture, the discontent with the old ways of life, the insecurity of occupation arising from the competition of foreign trade and the shift in demand, and finally in the political aspirations of the Armenians aroused by the democratic philosophies that were spreading eastward.

The people here were different also. The Turks, though Moslems like the Persians, were less imbued with the spirit of Islam—of submission to the will of God—which characterized the placid, easy-going Persian. They were a stern, assertive race, vigorous and military in manner, more abrupt and uncompromising in their attitudes.

Miriam never looked at a Turk but with uneasiness. The men filled her with an irrational dread. She realized that this was not Christian of her, and Amos Lyle had often chided her on her timidity—quoting Scripture to his purpose—but she could not help it. The tales which gossipy women told with such delectation and adornment, of Turkish abductions and rape, filled her with horror and counteracted any good impression made by the kindly acts of which her husband was the frequent recipient. Murad Bey, their neighbor and one of Emmanuel's customers, had been very generous to them, and had given them most of the plantings of their garden, but often as he rode down the street on his prancing horse, she never looked at him; and when Emmanuel spoke praisingly of him, she would remind him that Murad Bey was, by reputation, a sensualist and a libertine.

As for the Armenians, they too were different: they were more commercial, less contented—possibly because their status had always been less enviable than that of the Persian Armenian, possibly because they had been in closer contact with the commercial influences of the West. Their faith was less vigorous: in Shahran there was an

Armenian church of the ancient, orthodox faith, where services were held in all their gorgeous ritual. In Dilijan this faith had disintegrated, and it was kept alive only by the ministrations of the missionaries, of whom Lyle was the only present representative.

But for all that, Miriam had found something precious in Dilijan, something she would not have surrendered. This was her house and home and life with Emmanuel. In Shahran, she would have had to fashion her married life according to the wishes of her parents and relatives; their influence would have always been present. Here, because Emmanuel also had no close ties, she had been free to create such a home as she and Emmanuel desired. This was their own, and theirs alone—the product of their joint spirit and will, the reflection of their own personalities and moods, their own contribution to the beauty and loveliness of the world.

Miriam recalled Emmanuel's advice that she spend the night with Lyle if he did not return. Emmanuel did not like to leave her alone when he was absent, and she had on other occasions gone to the compound. Though there was nothing of comfort or convenience at Amos Lyle's to equal what she had in her own humble home, there was Amos Lyle, who had about him the same independence of spirit which she passionately asserted, and Miriam had learned to love him on this account.

Miriam had eaten her supper, in a half-hearted, negligent way, barely tasting the food, hardly knowing what she had prepared; and she was now setting the washed dishes away in the cupboard. It was dark and she lighted a lamp. Through the thick walls of their house came a distant murmuring. Miriam did not know what it was, or what it portended, but she grew uneasy and thought that perhaps she should go to the compound.

She listened again, and it seemed that the murmuring increased. As best she could tell, it came from the Armenian quarter.

Miriam carefully put the house in order, first setting away the loom upon which she had been working, then closing all the drawers and cupboards and ranging the ottomans along the wall, pausing once or twice to wipe away a speck of dust or to examine some little object that Emmanuel had made. She wanted to talk to Lyle, she felt the need of his enthusiasm and comforting hopefulness, but she found it hard to tear herself away from her house.

Finally, after much dawdling, Miriam thought that everything was in order and that she must go. She latched and barred the windows and the gates of the courtyard, and then, remembering the pigeons, opened one of the windows and scattered some bread crumbs for their breakfast. Finally, she drew on the long street cloak she wore when abroad, which concealed all but the round of her face, and stepped on to the outer threshold. Here she paused again, hesitant, considering whether she would find it more comforting to be with Amos Lyle or alone in her house.

A light flared above the dark line of the walls and illuminated the sky. At the same time the murmuring again increased.

The idea struck Miriam, like a lash, that an uprising against the Armenians might have broken out. Her dread of the Turks mounted like a flame. Hastily closing and locking the door and drawing her cloak about her, she started for the compound.

The direct route to Amos Lyle's house lay through the bazaars and across the public square, but in going there Miriam usually avoided the market streets out of modesty, passing instead by the longer way of the Armenian quarter. Now, however, she felt that her safety lay in the darkness of the covered passages.

The entrance to the bazaars lay at some little distance on the right; to reach it she had to pass down a long walled street that had scarcely any doorways along it: behind these walls lay the extensive gardens and closely guarded *harem* of Murad Bey, one of whose great houses adjoined her own.

Miriam Verian had not gone far, walking as silently as possible, keeping to the shadow of the wall, when a man appeared out of the night, mounted on a horse.

Miriam hugged the wall to avoid being seen. The man rode by, saw her, turned, and spoke.

"Where are you going?"

The voice was direct, though not unkind, and commanding, with the manner of one who rides while others walk.

Miriam, in terror, was mute.

"Who are you?"

Still Miriam could not speak.

The man reined his horse nearer.

"I know you. You are Miriam, the wife of Emmanuel Verian, whom he brought back from Persia."

"Let me go, please," panted Miriam, crouching against the wall.

"You cannot go. They will kill you."

"No, no," she pleaded, looking at him with the look of a deer at the hunter. "Let me go."

"Do you not understand, *hanim*? They are killing all of your race. Come with me."

Miriam grew frantic.

"No, no," she pleaded, looking at him with the look of

"You will be killed, or worse, if you go. Do you not know me? I am your neighbor, Murad Bey."

Miriam Verian was incapable of comprehending the situation. She was by nature emotional rather than logical, and now she was overwhelmed by a flood of visions and imaginings.

A question burst from her lips, an agonizing, beseeching cry, "Where is Emmanuel?"

Murad Bey, looking down upon her from his horse, saw that upon his answer to this question depended her response to his will.

"Emmanuel is dead," he said abruptly, and repeated, "Emmanuel is dead." He added: "They are all dead, all that assembled at the Gapou."

Miriam stood for a moment, uncertain. Then as the force of these words sank in upon her, the weight of terror became insupportable. She stared glassily; her limbs gave way, and she sank to the ground.

But swiftly, before she had quite fallen, Murad Bey had

reined his horse near, and leaning over, with a powerful arm had lifted her into the saddle.

His horse responded to the pressure of his knee, and with Miriam in his arms, Murad Bey galloped on to his gate.

When Miriam Verian awoke it was morning. The glorious sun that had set the evening before upon the massacre of so many of her race was shining through the window, beneficently, as though nothing had happened to disturb the serenity of the world.

Miriam was lying on a long ottoman, clad in a Turkish negligee of fine silk embroidery, and warmly covered with a fleecy white blanket of fine cashmere wool. The room in which she lay was large and opulently, though sparsely, furnished. On the floor was an immense Kashan carpet, overlaid with smaller pieces of fine Kerman weave, and on the wall several others, of silk weave, were hung as draperies. There were no pictures, but several framed arabesques—verses from the Koran—and one wall was studded with bits of mirror, to give a magnificent, jeweled effect. The wall adjoining, which faced toward the garden, was occupied by four French windows, leaded and partly filled with an arabesque design in colored glass.

On a tabouret of inlaid Damascus work, standing beside the ottoman, within reach of Miriam's hand, was a silver bowl filled with fresh fruit—grapes; figs from Smyrna that had journeyed to Dilijan partly by railway, partly by camel back; apples from Trebizond; dates from Iraq; and plums from Urmiah. Beside the bowl was a vase, also of silver, heavily etched, containing water, and two or three napkins of heavy damascened silk.

Miriam Verian looked at all these things woodenly, as though she were an automaton, a dressed and bedecked doll set on a marionette stage. The past did not obtrude upon her; memory mercifully had withdrawn from the chambers of her mind; she was a doll, a doll that talked and walked, that could eat and sleep, but could not think.

She was such a doll, no doubt, as might amuse some *harem* master.

Presently Miriam Verian grew hungry. She saw the fruit, and her hand mechanically reached for it.

After a little while two serving women entered, bearing caldrons of water, both cold and steaming hot, and fresh garments.

Silently, with fixed eyes, as though the springs of volition were unwound, Miriam allowed herself to be bathed. But when she saw that the garments they had brought for her to wear were not her own, but the garb of a Turkish lady, some remembrance of the past returned—not a definite image, but an awareness of an earlier life, when she had been undefiled. She regarded the garments for a moment, and then buried her face in her hands, and sobbed convulsively.

The serving women looked at her silently, compassionately.

Presently she ceased weeping and allowed herself to be dressed.

After the women had gathered up the towels and spread the ottoman, they sprinkled the room with rose water, and then said,

"Murad Bey wishes to see you," and added, to indicate the character of Miriam's standing, "He will come here."

Murad Bey came in. He was a handsome man, in his early fifties, of medium height, inclined to portliness, yet active and muscular, with a round, fair face, smooth save for a heavy mustache. He was dressed now in European clothes, that is, striped trousers and frock coat, but with a red fez upon his head.

He bowed.

"Miriam Verian, *hanim*," he said softly.

Miriam's terrified, tortured mind could summon but one defense.

"I am with child," she uttered slowly, mechanically.

"Do not be afraid of me, *hanim*," said Murad Bey, gently. "Pray sit down while I talk with you."

His voice was reassuring, and he addressed her respectfully as *hanim* (madame).

Miriam sat down heavily.

Murad Bey began to apologize for his rudeness.

"I am your footstool, *hanim*. But I was alarmed. Terrible things were happening. I could not bear the thought of your—going to—a dreadful fate."

"What has happened?"

There was in Miriam's question no curiosity, no courtesy, no responsiveness of any sort. Her words came volitionlessly.

Murad Bey told Miriam, by indirection, bit by bit, hint by hint, what had happened.

"Emmanuel is dead—may Allah give him rest—but you are not without those who care for you. I have seen you many times, *hanim*, and though we have never spoken, I have observed you to be a woman of virtue, intelligence, and imagination. Women like you are seldom to be found among the people of our Faith, which, though it has the Prophet, has not the Virgin."

Murad Bey came and stood above Miriam, respectfully, his hands thrust into his sleeves, like an embarrassed servant.

"I have long wanted one like you in this household," he said softly. "Now that the fate which Allah has ordained to each has bereaved you of your husband, your friends and loved ones, abide with us. Instruct our women in your graces; light our courts with the splendor of your movement, our chambers with the paleness of your hands, and our hearts with the smile of your face."

Miriam shuddered, and tears coursed down her face.

"Is not the glade welcome to the fleeing gazelle?" Murad Bay said, persuasively. "There is peace in our household, Miriam *hanim*, and you will be safe from all harm."

"I belong to Emmanuel," moaned Miriam, "and I shall not believe him dead until I see his body."

She broke down, crying, "Emmanuel, Emmanuel, Emmanuel."

"You would like to visit the scene and see for yourself?" asked Murad Bey in astonishment.

Without knowing what she did, Miriam nodded her head in assent.

The thought of Miriam looking upon the dead and mangled bodies horrified Murad Bey. He looked at Miriam in pity and perplexity. Finally, he said,

"Then I will have a carriage ready and Jafar will accompany you."

Jafar was Murad Bey's eunuch, a Negro who had been bought by Murad Bey twenty years before and had served him ever since. In his company, and dressed in Turkish apparel that veiled her completely, and seated in a carriage that likewise was enclosed and curtained, Miriam Verian was driven to the Gapou, to the wall where the dead lay.

Overhead, in the still brilliant and calm sunshine, vultures were circling, and other carrion birds: the air was full of them, silently wheeling, on black pinions, black as despair, inevitable as remorse, not to be frightened or driven away, awaiting their moment with the patience of fate.

A silent, curious crowd of onlookers hovered around the field of dead, filling their sadistic appetites with the sight as the carrion birds would later fill their craws with the flesh. There were also some pious ones—Turkish women, shrouded in black and veiled, whose custom it was, for their soul's salvation, to attend death and bewail the dead of whatever creed or race. Their wailing now rose on the air, as though it issued from the unwilling soil that supported the dead.

A few Turkish soldiers stood guard, indifferently, standing at a distance to avoid the stench that was beginning to rise.

Slowly, at a distance and then nearer, Miriam, accompanied by the eunuch, passed up and down the line.

Jafar had been instructed by Murad Bey what to do should they find the body of Emmanuel: it was to be brought—after the soldiers had been quieted with money— to Murad Bey's house, where it might be interred in accordance with Miriam's wishes.

But they did not find the body. Gradually, the truth dawned upon Miriam that it was not there. The cry rose to her lips that had been spoken first by another Mary, a plaintive, piteous cry of despair and abandonment,

"They have taken my lord, and I know not where they have laid him."

8. Hashim Farouk Bey

ABOUT the time that Miriam Verian was making her visit to the scene of the massacre, Hashim Farouk Bey was breakfasting with the governor. He had just learned that nearly half the Armenian population of Dilijan had escaped the sword by taking sanctuary in the compound of Amos Lyle's mission, and his fury was such that he choked on his coffee, spilling it down his neck and upon the collar of his tunic, burning his throat.

Hashim Farouk gave vent to a violent oath, becoming purple-livid at the throat where the tunic fitted tightly, and then, because he was an officer bred in the tradition of discipline, he recovered his composure, apologized for his carelessness, and dabbed at his tunic with his napkin.

"The Americans are too officious," he remarked, softly, as he took up a cluster of grapes. "Though they profess sanctimonious intentions they interfere more with our affairs than all the chancelleries of Europe."

He picked off a grape, large and purple like a plum, broke it in two, extracted the seed with a little silver coffee spoon, and put it in his mouth.

"But this Lyle must release them."

"Lyle is a difficult man," sighed Bari Pasha. "I am afraid you will have trouble in persuading him. You start to lecture him, and before you know it, he is lecturing you—not severely, but with such a stream of instances, examples, and adjurations—both by God and by Allah—that you can hardly get a word in on a camel. And when you have him in a corner, he disappears through the wall like a *jinn.* Logic is nothing to him. All enthusiasm, great projects—but, like me, no execution."

Secretly Bari Pasha was relieved that so many of the Christian population had escaped. His olfactory nerves were sensitive, and it seemed that he could smell in the air the corruption of the slain. The smoke and flames of the burning houses had thrown him into a torment; from the window he could see wraiths of smoke still ascending from the quarter; and he thought of the flames of hell. He was terrified lest they reach him—despite the Prophet's promise that the legs of him who died in *jehad,* in war against the infidel, should not be singed.

The fact was that the governor's peace of mind was gone: Bari Pasha loved flowers and poetry, and to see the children smile at him in greeting as he strolled in the avenue attended by his secretaries and thumbing his amber rosary. Flowers would still bloom for a while, but it would be a long time before children again smiled in the streets—or anyone for that matter. Suddenly, poetry had become as tasteless as dried pomegranate. The governor longed for the old days when Turks and Armenians lived in peace together and the only occasions of friction were those caused by love—when some Turkish gallant wooed an Armenian maid too passionately, or when an Armenian lad dared to look beyond the veil of the *harem.*

No greater contrast could be imagined between the senile, comfort-loving governor and the young commandant Hashim Farouk Bey. The one represented the old; the other, the new. Hashim Farouk Bey was the embodiment of the pragmatic, scientific philosophy with which the European world—or certain elements of it—was so enamored at this period; he knew nothing of poetry and flowers and smiles; he had been reared in the metropolis of Constantinople in an atmosphere of politics and large affairs, and among a class of Turks that associated with Europeans and prided itself upon its Western "culture."

Bari Pasha had never been outside of Anatolia; his only contact with the West had been during the war with Russia eighteen years before, and he felt a superiority to European culture that is proper for the believer in the

Koran as the perfect manifestation of God, proper for the descendant of those valiant warriors who had subjugated the most renowned empire of history, who had harried Europe to the walls of Vienna, and had captured and made as their capital the fairest city of Christendom.

Hashim Farouk Bey, on the other hand, had gone to Europe as a student; he had mastered several of its languages, and he had acquired a taste for its culture. He had attended scientific and philosophical lectures and had learned, at secondhand, of the great philosophers of Europe—Descartes, Leibnitz, Hegel, Spinoza, and Hobbes—and of the lesser ones, Schopenhauer and Nietzsche, who were setting mankind aright as to what men should believe concerning God and man and morals. He had not grasped all that he had been told about their ideas, but he had caught certain phrases and scraps of ideas that had made a great impression upon him and had seemed to open new vistas for the imagination. Hashim Farouk had become quite convinced that Mecca was not the center of the world, which in fact lay somewhere off the earth among distant nebulae and stars; and that the Kaaba, the great black stone kissed by every pilgrim to the sacred city, had not fallen there from heaven; he had become quite cynical as to whether heaven actually existed, and even doubtful as to God. If there was a God, His nature did not conform to any of the ninety and nine glorious attributes assigned to Him by the Faithful; but on that point the philosophers were not in entire agreement.

Hashim Farouk Bey had acquired some positive disbeliefs from the lectures on philosophy, but as for any positive beliefs—the philosophers had been most confusing. To Descartes, for instance, God was the Prime Mover of prime matter. This was explained to mean that the universe was a machine—a machine that worked automatically in accordance with foreordained law, in which there was no compassion, no hope, no love. Leibnitz had expressed it more clearly—"The universe is a clockwork of God."

These philosophers were not only at odds with religion as revealed by the Prophet Mohammed, but as revealed by their own Christ. Hashim Farouk Bey remembered well—for it was useful information—the words of Spinoza, quoted to him, "To believe that God became flesh is as absurd as to believe that a circle can be made into triangles and squares. Between God and man there is as little connection as between the constellation of the Dog and a dog, the barking animal."

Hashim Farouk Bey had found nourishment in the pessimism of Schopenhauer and in the masterful, vigorous concepts of Nietzsche. From them he had learned, as a matter of dogma, that there was no pity, nor softness, nor remorse, nor love in the mechanism of the universe: it operated by law and logic and force—beautifully or fantastically or horribly, as one saw it—but with that same contempt for human hopes or desires or fears as a locomotive on a track or the great looms and spinning wheels in the cotton factories of Manchester.

Along with such concepts as to the moral order and the place of man in the universe, Hashim Farouk Bey had acquired, paradoxically enough, an intense patriotism for his own country and an inordinate conception of its destiny. Just how his country or his people could have any other destiny than that which would be ticked out by the "clockwork of God" or emerge from the mill of the universe, or how this destiny could be affected by his own will in the matter, were aspects which he did not try to resolve; but this too was as characteristic of the Europe of his day as the philosophers themselves. For all Europe was in a ferment of nationalism, of races and cultures and nations seeking to realize their aspirations. In Germany, not so many years before, a dozen different races employing the Germanic tongue had been coalesced into a nation; in the Italian peninsula, even more diverse and contrasting races—ranging from the blond Lombards to the dark-skinned and Asiatic Sicilians—had been bludgeoned into a common nationhood. At the same time these heterogeneous nations, that loudly proclaimed their "national" destinies, were inciting the division and dispersion of other races that had lived side by side for centuries under a common sovereignty. In the British Isles, the Irish were clamoring for their national rights, while the government of the Dual Monarchy—itself a conglomerate of races—had been endeavoring to wean from their loyalty to the Sultan the Bosnians and the Bulgarians; while England, France, and Russia were giving aid and comfort to the Christian minorities of Anatolia.

Hashim Farouk Bey had returned to Turkey imbued with the doctrines of the scientific schools and by the nationalistic spirit of the times—full of admiration for European culture, intensely hating its political manipulations, and convinced that Turkish sovereignty was imperiled. With the arrogance of his race, he was convinced that Turkey was for the Turks; that the minorities were barriers to national unity; and that they should be dealt with in a purely scientific fashion, that is, simply as chemical elements of an amalgam that were to be burned out with fire. In this light, faiths and traditions and ancient associations were only delusions to be exorcised; regard for humanity was only mawkish sentiment; pity was a personal weakness to which the strong man should never be subject.

The thought, now, that the Imperial policy was to be thwarted by a single missionary occupying a bit of ground made inviolate by treaty, that the Armenians, safe within the walls, could flaunt their defiance of him, caused Hashim Farouk's wrath to rise uncontrollably.

"Who is this Lyle to refuse to surrender these subjects of His Majesty?" he asked, as his neck again grew purple and the veins stood out. "If he does not surrender them, we will burn them out."

"I am afraid that the flames might run farther than you anticipate," replied Bari Pasha, fingering his napkin nervously. "We have no pretext of legality to touch the mission. We must admit, I am afraid, that within the compound the people are as safe as in a mosque or as holding the saffron tail of the Sultan's mount."

Though by his age and by custom respect should flow from the commandant to him, Bari Pasha felt impotent and slightly inconsequential before Hashim Farouk Bey. Hashim Bey not only carried things along by his positive, confident manner and by his air of logic, but he had, as well, the sentiment of the Porte and the governing clique behind him.

"We will not break in upon such hallowed territory," replied Hashim Farouk, curling his lip. "We will just toss the firebrands over. Let them protest to the fire."

Bari Pasha's horror of flames rose like a gorge in his throat, and he squirmed uncomfortably on his thick ottoman.

"But I am responsible for fires," he protested.

"Tut, everyone knows that fires occur, and that Turks are afraid of fire. What Turk would dare set a blaze? Besides, you have no fire apparatus. Even in Stamboul, fires break out and rage to the very walls of the embassies. We will burn them out."

"But why not leave them alone?" reasoned the governor. "They will not dare molest our people now. You have done a decisive work, and its effect will remain."

"They must be destroyed," said Farouk bitterly. "I hate the race. They are like Carthage to the Romans. The Ottoman Empire will never know peace as long as a single Armenian is alive. As long as one Armenian lives, the Powers have a pretext for threats and demands. And so they must be destroyed."

Bari Pasha knew nothing of Carthage and Rome.

"No, no," he quavered, "I cannot consent to fire."

His eyes were popping at the thought, and he imagined he could smell the odor of burning flesh. He drew himself up in dignity, and added,

"And I am the governor."

Hashim Farouk Bey bowed his head slightly in obeisance. He broke another grape, and the clear, amber juice ran through his fingers.

"Yet they must be broken," he said, as he extracted the seeds and deposited them on a plate. "If not by fire, then some other way. They must be broken as I break this grape."

Bari Pasha was relieved.

"No doubt of that," he assented. "They must be broken. But unfortunately, like your grape, the seed remains."

He chuckled affectedly, nervously, at the witticism. It

was a bright simile, he thought, a poetic simile. He would
remember it. "The seed remains though we crush the
fruit." That was better, he thought. Even better was, "The
fruit is soft, the seed is hard."

"Yes," said Hashim Farouk Bey decisively. "It is true
that the seed remains, but it is also true that the seed will
not grow without water, and that men do not live without
food. We will starve them out."

Bari Pasha blanched. A great lover of food himself, the
thought of hunger terrified him almost as much as fire.

"Yes," repeated Farouk Pasha, letting his sharp, intellectual eyes fall upon the governor in a slightly superior
manner. "That will be quite legal. Forbid all intercourse.
There are innumerable excuses. Quarantine, for one. A
plague is feared. They will soon grow hungry, and wander
out, like sheep from an overcropped pasture."

Bari Pasha did not dare protest further. What the commandant proposed was within his legal authority and instructions. He could, if he wished, issue an order forbidding all commerce or intercourse with the Armenians, and
place a quarantine upon the compound. . . .

Hashim Farouk Bey discovered, however, that the quarantine he imposed was ineffective, that his orders were
being frustrated. The Armenians were not starving. In
some way they were obtaining food. Hashim Farouk complained to the governor, who had control of the police.

"There are traitors among our people," he said bitterly,
accusingly. "Someone is providing those people with food.
Turks who have no love of their country, who prefer these
provokers of sedition and disunion to their own kind, who
wish to see our Empire under the heels of the European
Powers, our glorious Sultan kissing the hand of their ambassadors and meekly granting concessions and monopo-
lies to their commercial travelers.

"It has come to this pass, Bari Pasha," he continued,
"that our race, before whose exploits the people of Europe
trembled in the days of Suleiman and Omar, is now considered among the most insignificant among the peoples
of the earth. Do you know what we are called? 'The Sick

Man of Europe'—we, the Turkish race, than whom there is none more virile, more warlike. And all because we have, in times past, been gracious and kindly disposed toward this sycophantic, puerile, Byzantine remnant of an outworn and discredited people."

Hashim Farouk Bey continued to excoriate in this vein at some length, while the governor sat in silence fingering his rosary. When the diatribe subsided, Bari Pasha remarked,

"It is an old saying 'Money is like honey.' It is hard for men to resist the power of money."

"What do you mean?"

"I understand that among those who escaped to the compound is Neshan Kovian. Kovian is not poor."

Neshan Kovian was a wealthy Armenian merchant and moneylender.

"And Kovian, you think, has been able to buy food and bribe its way into the compound?" asked Hashim Farouk Bey incredulously. "And Kovian would spend his money to feed others than himself?"

"He is probably taking notes of hand from those who partake of the food."

"But the police?"—Hashim Farouk Bey knew without asking that they were amenable to bribes.—"Have you not kept them under surveillance?"

Bari Pasha shrugged his shoulders.

"The police are not well paid, and they have mouths to feed," he said.

The thought of his frustration was like bitter almonds in Farouk's mouth. He dared not trespass the compound; his government, beleaguered enough by protests from foreign embassies, had issued strict instructions to respect all properties of foreign nationals. And now that the refugees were obtaining food clandestinely—by connivance with Turks, nay, the very police—it appeared certain to him that his whole purpose would fail.

But Hashim Farouk Bey was a determined, even obstinate, young man, and the more he was thwarted, the more his determination asserted itself, the more vicious and malicious grew his intentions. What had been at first a coldly calculated matter of public policy now became a question of personal pride and resentment. Formerly he had despised and condemned the Armenians; now he felt toward them a black, malevolent hatred, a hatred that grew the more bitter the more he contemplated his frustration.

He recalled how Mohammed II had rid himself of the janissaries, how the Roman emperor Valerian had rid himself of the Goths, and Peter the Great of the *streltsi*. These were eminent examples from history; these sovereigns were written down as emancipators of their people, as courageous men who had been willing to violate their honor for the sake of a greater honor, to incur opprobrium for the sake of national security. Hashim Farouk told himself that for the sake of his own race and country, if not for the salving of his own bitterness, he could emulate their example. He would even better their example.

"Has the American Lyle been to see you again today?" he asked.

The governor sighed.

"Yes. He comes every day, pleading for his flock. And, of course, I am adamant and can give him no satisfaction."

Hashim Farouk Bey had resolved his mind.

"Then give him word that if they will agree to depart they may leave the country and go to Russia."

"That is a bitter choice," said the governor. "They will find it hard to leave the land where they and their ancestors have lived for so many generations."

Hashim Farouk Bey laughed cynically.

"Let them try the hospitality of the Tsar, who has shown such interest in their welfare. Let them find for themselves what peace, what welcome, awaits them elsewhere. They will conclude that Anatolia is a paradise by comparison, that the Sultan is a beneficent father by the side of this Christian potentate."

Hashim Farouk Bey did not contemplate these people passing over to the shelter of the Tsar. Between Dilijan and the frontier lay the range of the Ghulam Dagh, which the road crossed by a narrow, lonely pass. It had been none too safe in the past, and Kurdish brigands had on more than one occasion made it a rendezvous for forays upon passing pilgrims and caravans. In theory, the road was now safe, but if an attack should be made upon the Armenians as they crossed the pass, it would be easily attributable to brigands, and none would be the wiser.

Hashim Farouk Bey lit a cigarette, slowly, pleasurably. He wondered why he had not thought of the scheme before. It was so much simpler than the measures already taken, and so easily explainable in case of enquiries from the chancelleries and embassies. All he need do would be to station his troops among the rocks, out of sight, and when the Armenians passed through, give the signal. They would be in a trap. Not one of them would escape. . . .

"It is a hard choice," repeated Bari Pasha feelingly, thinking of what the town would be like when its most industrious population were gone. "Nevertheless, it is better than starvation."

He sighed.

"I will send for Lyle," he said sadly.

9. Murad Bey

MURAD BEY'S walls were of moderate thickness and of moderate height, yet to traverse them was like crossing astral distances to another sphere. Dilijan was one world: Murad Bey's household was another; what happened in the one was of no concern to the other. The household within the walls moved in its own orbit and was governed by its own especial influences. Like the world without, it had its joys and tragedies, its interests and pursuits, but they were of their own order, of equal range and intensity with those beyond the walls, but of a different quality. They were the affairs of the household, and sufficient to it; occurrences elsewhere—unless they penetrated the walls, and affected its inhabitants—remained vague and unreal. This was in accord with the ancient spirit of the *harem*,

a spirit that antedates Islam and the Prophet Mohammed
and was old in the time of Xerxes. Queen Vashti was con-
forming to its tradition when she declined to appear before the guests of King Ahasuerus. St. Paul was speaking
its ideals when he admonished the women of Corinth
concerning their demeanor.

What is the spirit of the *harem*, which encloses the affairs of a household in walls and reticence and secludes its
women behind the veil? It is various things according to
those that practice it. It is the spirit of the jealous posses-
sor, fearful for his possessions; it is the spirit of the strong
who subjects the weak to his needs and desires. It is the
spirit of ignorance that seeks to confine by walls and veils
that which a nobler spirit holds by bonds as fragile as a
sigh. But it is also other things. It is the spirit that hangs
the curtain before the altar, that covers the chalice with a
pall. It is the spirit that exalts the Virgin in the Christian
pantheon. It is the spirit of reverence for home and womanhood. The walls, the veils, the interdictions of custom—
these are the gropings of a culture in its effort to preserve
its most indispensable institution.

Murad Bey's household was extensive: Murad Bey was
pater familias to three distinct families, each with its own
matriarch, and he was grandfather to numerous progeny
by his several sons and their respective wives. Wives, sons,
daughters, daughters-in-law, and grandchildren, all dwelt
in one great household. It was a household of many houses,
with walls within walls—though they were walls of the
spirit—and *harems* within *harems;* in all, a vast establishment with many doors, to which only Murad Bey had the
master key; with many interests, often divergent and conflicting; with crosscurrents of love and jealousy and pride
and contempt; but all existing and finding their sustenance
within the enclosing walls of the *harem,* all submissive to
one dominant will and spirit, that of Murad Bey, and finding in that submission a tranquility that softened the
sharpness of strife and lightened the burdens of restraint.

This was all to Murad's liking and purpose: Allah had
gifted him with wealth and the art of acquiring wealth,
and he used his wealth as he saw wise. Where men of

substance elsewhere might buy pictures or yachts, or engage in new enterprises, Murad Bey preferred to enlarge his household. He never had too many children around him, either his own, or those of his sons, or those of his servants. His vast household and all its varied activities existed for but one purpose, the bearing and rearing of children, the perpetuation of the race as it flowed through the stream of Murad Bey's blood.

One of Murad Bey's sons was, like Esau, a hunter of game and a herder of flocks. He was forever roaming in distant places, in search of prey and excitement, but his family made their household within Murad Bey's walls, and Murad Bey was father to his wife, and father to his children. Another son was like Jacob, who tended the fields, and this son looked after Murad Bey's extensive estates and numerous villages among the Taurus. Still another son was a merchant in Dilijan, a respectable dealer in rugs and felts, shrewd and successful in his dealings. Yet another was a mullah and a doctor of laws, a religious but not an ascetic man; and another, finally, was government overseer of the post. All these sons made their households within the enclosing walls. All formed a widely ramified enterprise as vast and varied as some great corporation of the Western World, drawing its contributions from numerous sources, spreading its panoply over many pursuits and interests.

But for all that flowed to Murad Bey of wealth and comforts, of interests and affection, one thing satisfied him only; one interest—at once simple and inordinate—held his attention. His household was his appetite, and his taste was for women. His taste was that of a connoisseur, and like a true connoisseur he liked to collect about him the choicest examples to be found. And again, like a connoisseur, he was fastidious in his tastes; not the quantity but the quality was important. Moreover, he did not desire these examples for use, any more than does a lover of fine Sèvres china think of using a prize piece for his morning porridge.

Women such as Murad Bey could desire were rare: he had, by good fortune, found three in his lifetime—by good fortune, since he had had to accept them by reputation, not being exempt himself from the law of the *harem*. But as the Prophet permitted his followers four wives, Murad Bey had place for still another. For this fourth, he had long thought of Miriam Verian, and by good fortune again, Miriam Verian was now within his walls.

A week had passed since the affair at the Gapou. During this time Miriam had lain in a delirium, in the apartment overlooking the rose garden, inconsolable, moaning the name of Emmanuel, begging him to wait that she might join him. Murad Bey had called on her every day of this time, and had caused fresh flowers to be put in the vases, and music to be played for her in the early evening, when the lamps were lighted—one of his favorite concubines strumming quaint little melodies on a *zi-tar*—all to console her and drive away her grief; but without success.

It was when Miriam learned by chance, from a remark made by one of the serving women to another, of the survivors in Amos Lyle's compound, that hope returned and her strength revived. When Murad Bey called that day, she said to him,

"Emmanuel is alive and has fled to Pastor Lyle's compound!"

Murad Bey knelt down by the ottoman and patted Miriam's hand as though she were a child.

"Miriam *hanim*," he said softly, "your happiness, your health, and your trust in me are all that I desire. I have ascertained the facts. I would not deceive you, nor would I add to your grief. Emmanuel is dead. He was killed outside the compound, and he was later brought in and the rites of your faith read for his soul."

Murad Bey spoke with such sincerity, such earnestness, and such sympathy that Miriam was compelled to accept the statement. But some remnant of hope lived on.

"I wish to go to Pastor Lyle," she pleaded. "Will you not let me?"

"Miriam *hanim*, I shall not keep you where you do not wish to be. But I cannot let you go to the compound. Do you know what is happening there? Then I will tell you. Those people are starving, dying of hunger and disease.

Hashim Farouk Bey has condemned them to death, and since he is unable to take them by force, he has determined to starve them out."

"If Emmanuel is dead, then I would die with them," said Miriam doggedly. "What is life without him whom I love!"

She began to weep softly.

"No, Miriam *hanim*," Murad Bey repeated, "I cannot let you go. I would want you to go to your Emmanuel, but I cannot help you, for Emmanuel is not there. But Emmanuel's baby is here, and I want to see the baby safely born. It is the baby you must love now—Emmanuel's baby and yours. You must consider the life that is ahead, not the life that is past. You must try to get well, so that you may bear the baby, strong and healthy. Content yourself, Miriam *hanim*, until your days are fulfilled, and then we can consider the matter further."

These truths which Murad Bey spoke sank into Miriam Verian's ill, disordered mind with all their force and irrefutable logic, like a plumb line in muddy waters, and she came to the realization that she had no alternative. She was in a web from which she could not escape. Whatever the means by which he held her, whether by force or persuasion, or by the advantage of circumstance, she was under the will of Murad Bey. However much he might love her, as he declared, it was his will that was master, not hers.

But there was another will, another life, neither hers nor Murad Bey's—the life which stirred within her, and which possessed a will of its own. That life—that will—should not be subject to Murad Bey. Ah, that was it. Murad Bey was right: she must consider that life whose path lay ahead. She must try to get well, so that she could bear that life with a body healthy and strong. Yes, she must content herself until her days were fulfilled.

Toward the end of spring Murad Bey's household moved, as was its custom, to its summer retreat in the Taurus, where lay the numerous villages of which he was lord and from which he derived revenues.

Here Miriam was assigned a cottage of her own on a hill slope, with a garden below, and with a view of the majestic Taurus ranges beyond. Each day she received fresh milk and cheese, and dewy berries and wild honey, and warm fresh bread; and later, when her appetite improved, Murad Bey's own cook made for her such delicacies as the doctor prescribed for pregnant women—breast of chicken, cooked with raisins and currants and mild condiments, and served with platters of snowy rice *pilaf;* *sherbet* made with the juice of summer fruits, chilled with snow from the mountains; sweetmeats such as Miriam could never have dreamed of—*rahat lokoom,* or "throat's ease," candied almonds, *halvah* made of crushed sesame and sugar, and pastries flavored with honey and pistachio.

Miriam had never conjured in her imagination such sensuous delights of living. Who was she—the wife of a poor teamster, and a *giaour,* an infidel, at that—to be so sumptuously treated in this Turkish household? Abductions of Christian maidens were not uncommon, for the fact that Armenian women did not veil the face made them enticing to young men not privileged to look upon the faces of the women of their own race, and the belts of chastity, worn by women in medieval Europe, were still a customary defense against assault among Christian maidens of the Near East; but it was impossible to imagine that this consideration which Miriam was receiving was the usual lot of the Armenian woman abducted into a *harem.*

Miriam sat in the garden of her lodge early one summer afternoon—Murad Bey beside her—watching the sunlight play upon the distant slopes and upon the hyacinths at her feet, and listening to the murmuring of the water in the pool, and she wondered again at the providence that had so mercifully preserved her from death.

"God has been gracious to me because of my baby," she thought, "because He loves children."

If this were so, Miriam thought, then her baby should be very happy and be blessed of God throughout its life.

All this that she now enjoyed must be an omen of that happy future.

Murad Bey had expressed a desire to adopt the child. "If it is a son," considered Miriam, "should I not agree?"

Islam was a masculine faith, it was a virile creed, it made much of manhood. Its Paradise was for men. It might be better for a man to be a Moslem than a Christian. When they wished to extirpate the Christians, it was the males they killed. A son reared as a Moslem would escape that danger.

But if her baby should be a daughter? Miriam's lips compressed at the thought. She would die rather than rear a daughter for a Turkish *harem*. That lot she might accept for herself, as a sacrifice demanded by God, but she would not willingly surrender a daughter to such a fate.

"But why?" Murad Bey urged her gently, when she had expressed herself to him. "Do you not find that the women of this *harem* are treated with kindness, nay, with indulgence? They are not required to labor, as in Christian homes; they are shielded from the noisy and brutal life of the streets; their virtue is honored and protected. I have seen the Christian women in the Taxim quarter of Constantinople: it is not a pleasant sight. They drudge in offices and factories, and when they go on the streets they must paint their cheeks and lips to hide their weariness; they must compete for the attentions of men, like dogs for crumbs; they are treated with familiarity, and then with disdain. What is there about this Christian mode that you so prize?"

"Love!" replied Miriam fiercely. "Do you think I could have married Emmanuel, had our eyes not exchanged glances freely? Had I been a maiden behind a veil, what would have been my recourse? To wait until my father sought me out a husband—a man perhaps I had never seen, did not know, and with whom certainly I would have exchanged no word before the marriage? Or wait until some young man, learning that my father had such and such a daughter concealed within his walls, and hearing by rumor that she was fair, besought her hand?

"O God, God!" she exclaimed, and stood up in the vehe-

mence of her emotion. "Deliver my daughter from such a
fate, if so be I have a daughter. Give her that glorious
blessing of freedom which Thou hast promised to those
that are in Christ Jesus. Let her be a Christian maiden,
free to give her gift of love to him whom she freely
chooses."

She turned and laid her hand gently on Murad Bey's
arm.

"Forgive me, Murad Bey. You have been good to me.
You have made these days of waiting endurable. What is
it you want?"

Murad Bey was silent. Finally he spoke.

"I have wives, and sons, and daughters-in-law," he said
slowly. "Why should I desire a Christian woman among
my women? It is perhaps because you have something
that I have never seen before—this freedom of which you
speak. You are like a gazelle among the contented cattle
of the field, a soaring lark among swan. I would only look
at you, and watch you play, and bless the mysterious wisdom of Allah."

But Miriam grew pale, and Murad Bey, fearing again
that she might faint, did not urge his desire. Miriam's time
was indeed almost fulfilled when she should be delivered
of her baby.

It was one night the month following that her servants
were awakened by her cries, and before the midwife could
be summoned she had borne her child. When Miriam
emerged from her coma she murmured faintly, "Does my
baby live?" and when the old Turkish midwife, Fat'ma
Hanim, nodded, she smiled and slept.

The baby was a girl, and because it was a girl, there
was little jealousy among the women of the *harem*. Miriam
named her Sirani, after the Persian valley in which she
had spent her girlhood, and the baby grew like a blossom-
ing flower of the Persian oasis.

Toward the end of summer, when the baby was in its
fourth moon, Murad Bey again spoke to Miriam about her
future.

"It is well that the baby have a father," he said gently,
"and I would love her as a daughter."

Miriam hugged the baby to her.

"No, no, Murad Bey. She belongs to Emmanuel and me."

Murad Bey's eyes were pensive, sad.

"As you will. I have news for you."

"Yes, yes?" exclaimed Miriam eagerly. "Emmanuel?"

"No, Emmanuel is dead. But a remnant of your people have escaped."

"Where? How?"

"Into Russia. Hashim Farouk Bey laid a plot to kill them—he is a servant of *Shaitan*—but by the will of Allah some of them escaped. They are living, I have heard, in a certain village beyond Kars."

"Pastor Lyle? Did he escape?"

"So I have heard."

"God be praised."

"You have a regard for Lyle?"

"He is like a father to me."

They were again seated in the garden of Miriam's lodge, watching the sunlight play upon the purple mountains, now streaked with ocher and brown in anticipation of the end of summer. Murad Bey's household was preparing for the return to Dilijan, and his porters and servants were busy on the slopes, about the lodges, removing the shrubs, and buttressing the walls against the winter snows.

"This summer has been to me like one spent in the Gardens of Paradise," said Murad Bey. "There, our Prophet says, shall be *houri* with the face and form of women such as no man on earth ever beheld. Yet you are like such an *houri* to me."

"Would you like to go to Amos Lyle?" he asked abruptly.

Miriam's eyes blinded with tears at the thought. Her husband's last words had been, "Go to Lyle." If she had promptly heeded his wish . . . perhaps Emmanuel might never have died.

"They live in misery and despair, I understand," said Murad Bey, insinuatingly.

"I would go. Oh, yes, I would go."

"Then I shall arrange for you to go," replied Murad Bey quietly. "When we have returned to Dilijan, I shall set you in a carriage, and see that you are taken to Lyle."

He looked up from the ground at which he had been staring, across the valley and toward the blue ranges.

Never, it seemed to him, had the mountains been more gorgeous, never had the sunlight shone so opulently upon them.

"Perhaps," he thought, "this is but the foretaste of what is reserved in Paradise for those who show mercy."

Part 2

AMOS LYLE

1. The Plain of Bartzan

In 1896, the principal military outpost of the Russian Empire in the Caucasus was Kars fortress. Kars fortress and Kars province had formerly belonged to Turkey—they had been won during the war of 1878—and there was good reason to believe that one day Turkey might attempt to regain these lost territories. The Ottoman Empire was still one of the most considerable in Europe, with a frontier extending in three continents, and among those countries that bordered on Russia this Empire presented a military power only less imposing than that of Germany and Austria. Moreover, the truculence of the Turks in the face of the protests of the Christian Powers against the persecution of Christian minorities was creating difficulties of another sort for those Christian Powers which had Moslem minorities. In India, in Afghanistan and Turkestan, and elsewhere, Turkey appeared as a champion defending the interests of Moslems against Western imperialism, and the Caliphate had become a symbol of resurgent Islam. In the Caucasian provinces of the Russian Empire, particularly, there were Mohammedan minorities—Tartars, Kirghiz, Mingrelians—as well as Christian nationalities, especially the Georgians, who had never been willing subjects of the Tsar, and these peoples looked with satisfaction upon a powerful Turkey.

For these and other reasons, the Imperial Government

had decided upon the further strengthening of its key positions in the southern Caucasus. The chief of these was Kars. In 1896 new regiments were being despatched to this fortress, new military works were being constructed, the surrounding territory was being surveyed for its strategic values, and maneuvers were being held in all areas of possible military operations.

Among the officers newly assigned to Kars fortress was Captain Stepan Mikhailovitch Markov. Captain Markov was of a line that had been more successful in destroying than in procreating humanity, a line that had been better at managing brigades than households, and in winning battles than in wooing women: he was the surviving descendant of a once numerous family of Cossacks that had held large estates in the region of the Orenburg. As a result of the gradual disappearance of the other members of the family, without issue, title to most of these estates now rested with Captain Markov; but aside from the ancestral home near Varsova, Captain Markov seldom visited them, and certainly was little interested in their upkeep. He visited his Varsova place regularly, however, at holiday times and on leave, when he spent happy days with his lonely wife and son, but for the rest of the time he preferred the call of duty, as sounded by the bugle and the tympanum. Captain Markov had served with distinction on the Afghan frontier, and had endured the solitudes of a Siberian post without losing his good humor and the camaraderie for which he was noted. He was a handsome man, intelligent, and a good officer, of exemplary moral conduct—for the times and the service in which he was enlisted—and his only fault of character or manner was a cavalier and contemptuous attitude toward men of lower station, a somewhat arrogant faith in the military principle, and his philosophy of power. But these attitudes and faith and philosophy were common among men of his profession and times, and they blended so agreeably with the general coloration that his good qualities seemed to shine with added luster.

In May of 1896, Captain Stepan Markov, in command of a squadron of horse, was ordered to Toprah Kaleh for maneuvers. Toprah Kaleh, on the edge of the plain of Bartzan, some forty miles southeast of Kars, together with the road thereto, was one of the objects of the new military interest. The road to Toprah Kaleh, though now little more than a caravan trail, had been of importance in times past, and likely might be of importance again. Formerly, it had been a Turkish highway connecting with Erzeroum, Trebizond, and other cities of Anatolia. In still earlier times it had been an artery in the communications system of Byzantium and, before that, of the Roman empire. Although generally understood to have been built originally by Pompey, the Armenian savants at Etchmiadzin claimed it was laid out by the Bagratids who ruled medieval Armenia from their capital at Ani—though Ani, or rather the ruins of that ancient city, lay some miles off the present route. In any case, it was a natural strategic highway for an army invading the southern Caucasus from Turkey.

Since coming to Kars, Captain Markov had had a desire to visit the district, and particularly to inspect the ruins of Ani. Ani had been a city of considerable importance in medieval times, and among classic writers of that period its situation, from a military standpoint, was regarded as impregnable—a natural fortress, like Petra, or the Iron Gates of the Danube. A student of military history, Captain Markov had a curiosity to discover whether those ancient advantages still existed in this age of high-powered weapons and long range assault.

Fortunately there was an excellent camp ground at Dighen, on the edge of the Bartzan plain, north of the Araxes, and Captain Markov decided to allow his men a day in the chase, while he took the opportunity to make an excursion to the ruins of Ani.

Ani lay some fifteen miles away, on the bluffs of the Arpa Chai. Captain Markov set off at an easy trot, with his orderly, Jorki. It was a fine morning, with the sky cloudless save for the wreath that was beginning to gather, as it gathered every morning, about the head of Mount Ararat, beyond the Araxes.

Markov loved the mountains and the clear sunlit air of the uplands, and he was in a gay, careless mood. He looked across the Bartzan plain toward the great mountain rising solitarily on the earth's bosom, the more majestic because it was without comparison, and it set off his imagination.

"When the Tsar became lord of Bartzan," he remarked to Jorki, extending his arm to indicate the plain they were traversing, "he became the owner of the Garden of Eden."

During his tour of duty at Kars, Markov had learned a great deal about this Russian province, and it gave him a sense of satisfaction to tell Jorki what he knew.

Jorki removed his cap and crossed himself. Then he looked about him, scratched his cropped head, and wiped his chin on his sleeve.

"No," said Markov. "You will see no archangel Michael here, but there is good evidence of the flaming sword." He was referring to the naphtha springs of Surachany, near Baku, which he had once seen flaming in the night sky, ignited by lightning.

"But it's . . . it's not a garden. It's very barren," whispered Jorki.

"Nevertheless, according to tradition, it is here that the Garden of Eden was situated, or rather one pavilion of the Garden. The Araxes River is that third river of Paradise known as Hiddekel, 'which goeth toward the east of Assyria.' Not far to the south begin the headwaters of the Euphrates which is the fourth river of Paradise. . . . The other two I have forgotten. The Bible is dull reading, Jorki—what I have read of it. But I do remember that Ararat over there is the mountain upon which the Ark of Noah rested after the flood."

They rode on some miles until they came to an elevation, an extensive rounded hump on the plain. From here it was possible to look upon a magnificent panorama that shimmered and undulated in a patchwork of color up to the base of Ararat, and even then—for so gently does this mountain ascend above the plain that the vision is imperceptibly lifted to surpassing heights—onward and upward until the eyes encompassed the snow-covered and cloud-enwreathed summit of the great mountain itself.

At a distance probably ten miles to the east, clearly visible in the sparse air of the plain, there stood upon the horizon a dark mass of masonry, above which here and there arose forlornly a broken cupola and a shred of wall —all that remained of the ancient and mighty capital of Armenia.

But it was not the only ruin upon this desolate and abandoned plain. To the west, much nearer, was another crumbling stone heap which had been identified as a Greek settlement of pre-Homeric times. Ruins, it seemed to Markov, were everywhere. Even beneath this mound of earth on which they stood, there no doubt lay the ruins of a still more ancient past, ruins which the elements had mercifully covered with dust, which now had hardened into this hillock. "The whole world is a ruin," thought Markov, with an excess of mysticism and fatalism which was characteristic of his gay and easy nature.

As they descended the mound, they came to a terrain of rolling hummocks, coursed by little streams of fresh water. As they entered one of the gullies, they came upon what seemed to be the ruins of a village—a cluster of earthen huts, some fortified with stone and timber work, and a company of emaciated women and half-starved children. On the nearby terraces, ground had been plowed, and a sparse crop of wheat, green and tall, would be ready for the harvest soon. A few old men were about, herding sheep on the slopes, and some young men were working in a little patch of ground where vegetables were growing. Everyone was in rags, and wore a look of starvation. Markov saw the weary, frightened expression on their faces, and muttered,

"More ruins."

Captain Markov did not care to come near such squalor, but his way lay in that direction, and he was not a man to be turned from his course by trifles. As he drew near, he heard the sound of singing—but such singing as he had never heard before. It was religious music, though quite different from the majestic antiphonal chants one heard issuing from the churches and cathedrals of the Ortho-dox Russian faith. The music had a swinging, primitive, and marching quality, but was slower; and the voices, with the exception of one which seemed to lead the singing, were so quavering and cracked as almost to be offensive to Markov's sensitive ears. The dominant voice was that of a man, and it was booming, jubilant and decidedly unmusical.

As Captain Markov came up, he saw the singers—a group of people about a little rock platform, on which stood the man who was leading the song. The people were Armenians, Markov saw, but the leader was not. He was tall and gawky, wore a long frock coat, a wide-brimmed gray hat, very battered, and half boots, likewise worn and down at the heels, with a red star worked into the tops.

The singing stopped, and the man began to harangue the people. Markov did not understand what he said, since it was spoken in Armenian, but he got the drift of it.

"He is telling the people all about God," thought Markov, "and how Jehovah is looking after them."

Captain Markov smiled to himself at this nonsense, but being, after all, genial and tolerant enough of others' convictions, and finding also that he had a duty to perform, he respectfully dismounted and signaled to Jorki to do the same and waited patiently until the service was over.

But as Markov was contented to look upon this scene from superior heights, it was also apparent to him that those who were part of it were likewise contented. Markov was somewhat surprised to see how raptly these people listened to the preacher's words, despite their presumably empty stomachs. This surprise tempered the compassion he felt for their misery, a compassion which sprang naturally and easily from his generous, genial soul.

The preacher himself was more than contented. He was joyous—exuberantly so. He gestured and spoke like a man of limitless energy. His face radiated a vast and overpowering confidence. One would say that he had never laid an uneasy head to rest. Markov, for that matter, had never slept uneasily in his life, but he saw that there was a difference, though what this difference might be was a subject apart from his immediate contemplation.

There were other things the man suggested, but Captain Markov could not find the precise words to describe them. All he knew was that he felt slightly unimportant standing here in the preacher's presence. It did not annoy, but amused, him.

The preacher saw Markov standing in the background, and when the service was over and the group dispersed to go about the work of the day, he came over to him. He spoke first in Armenian, and seeing that the officer did not understand, addressed him in bad Russian.

"My name is Lyle," he said, "Amos Lyle. You must excuse my Russian. We have not been here long. But presently I will learn Russian. As the gift of tongues was given to the apostles at the Day of Pentecost, so will it be given me."

He extended his hand.

"And whom do I address?" he asked easily, though respectfully.

Markov responded in English.

"Stepan Mikhailovitch Markov, Captain in His Imperial Majesty's armed forces. At your service."

"I am very glad to make this acquaintance, Captain," said Lyle.

The missionary had a graciousness of manner which was innate, untutored, with the quality of naturalness found frequently on the frontier.

"Welcome to our village," he said. "We haven't christened it as yet, having come here only this winter, but when the first grain is gathered we expect to call it Bartzan, after the plain 'round about. But if your business is not urgent perhaps you will break bread with me. I have not yet eaten this morning."

Markov appreciated the courtesy and accepted.

Breakfast for Lyle was simple, consisting of black bread, toasted, and weak tea. He did not apologize, but he explained:

"We have little food now, but it serves, and we are thankful. But presently the windows of heaven will open. We shall have good crops and abundance with which to feed hungry mouths."

"You are very optimistic, it seems," remarked Captain Markov. "From all I can see, you are doomed to starvation. Nothing survives here. It is a land of ruins."

"You do not know the bounty of the Lord. The soil is good. The pasturage is excellent. It is good wheat land. This is evidently a dry year. Tell me, my friend, are you saved?"

"Saved?" asked the captain, startled.

"Yes, saved to the Lord? Are your sins washed away in the blood of the Lamb? Do you know the blessing of Divine Grace?"

"No one in my profession is ever safe," laughed the captain.

"When you have experienced the Redemption, you will feel safe in the jaws of hell. Nothing can touch you then," said Amos Lyle, earnestly, but with the joy of ardor lighting his face. "I too once lived in sin, and I was forever fearful. I knew no peace. But then I found God, or rather God found me—praised be His name—and I was saved. Now, whatever happens, I know that He is looking after me. Think well, and purge yourself of sin and let His face shine upon you."

"Well, are all these people here in this village saved, as you say?" asked the captain, a little uncomfortable.

"That I cannot say, as every man is answerable to God alone."

"Then I should say they are not saved, but lost, else they would not be suffering this misery."

"God's providence is boundless, and He may extend His bounty to whom He will—sinners as well as saved. But with what great assurance we live, knowing help is nigh! We may say with St. Paul,

" 'For I am persuaded, that neither death, nor life, nor angels, nor principalities, nor powers, nor things present, nor things to come,

" 'Nor height, nor depth, nor any other creature, shall be able to separate us from the love of God, which is in Christ Jesus our Lord.' "

This struck Captain Markov as so much twaddle. The man was an American, and it was interesting to see what these missionaries talked about, but he had had enough. He rose courteously, thanked his host, and then came to the matter of his business.

"Your people came over from Turkey, I gather."

"Yes," responded Lyle. "We have been saved by a great deliverance. God sent a snowstorm to deliver us, even as He sent a plague to deliver the children of Israel from Pharaoh."

"What nonsense!" the captain started to exclaim, but restrained himself and asked instead:

"How did this miracle occur?"

"We had been besieged in our compound for many days, growing more hungry, more destitute, but still praising the name of the Lord and trusting in His deliverance. A day came when it seemed that Hashim Farouk Bey had been touched by mercy, for we were offered permission to depart with our belongings, if we would leave the country, if we would abandon our homes and go to Russia. There was no other course, and we accepted.

"But the wisdom of God forewarned us, and we hastened our departure, going in advance of the day set, leaving at night by the Rumeli Chai—this is an ancient stream bed, sunk below the level of the ground, which we could follow without detection. We gained the mountains, and reached the pass of the Ghulam Dagh.

"It was there that Hashim Farouk Bey, having, like Pharaoh, repented of his graciousness, overtook us with his troops and fell upon us. We would have been slaughtered to the last man, but for the merciful intervention of the snowstorm. The snow confounded our pursuers, blinded their horses, and we were saved."

"But how did you escape the snowstorm?"

"By the grace of God. Many died from freezing in the bitter cold; but a remnant survived, and crossed the pass, where, on the other side, thanks be to God, no snow had fallen. And so we descended, by degrees, and came to this place where again we were blessed, for we found these huts which we have occupied."

The huts were the remains of a Turkish village, whose

inhabitants had fled from the wrath of the Russians in 1878.

And now Captain Markov came to his question, the official question he was obliged to ask as an officer of His Majesty the Tsar.

"Do you have a *ukase* to settle here?"

The question seemed to surprise the missionary.

"It is waste land, and what is no man's is the Lord's," he said. "We took it because of our necessity, as David ate the shew bread, as our Lord plucked the kernels of the standing grain."

"I am afraid His Majesty the Tsar, whom I serve, will differ with you there. This is his land, and you must have a permit to occupy it. Otherwise, you may be shipped out of here at any time by a band of hard-riding Cossacks."

"His Majesty the Tsar is a devout Christian, I understand, and he will no doubt incline his heart to the needs of these people. To whom do I apply for permission?"

"The governor at Kars. Go up to Kars this fall. Not now, this fall. The governor will be at maneuvers all summer.

"By the way," Captain Markov added, on an impulse, as he was taking his departure. "My regiment is well stocked, in fact, overstocked, and we could travel faster if we were not so loaded. I will send your people several barrels of provisions, if you like."

"That is good of you, very good of you. May God's blessing be with you."

"Then you don't condemn me as sinful?" smiled Captain Markov.

"Naturally not. It is not for me to condemn, but to call sinners to repentance. We are all God's children, but we all, like lost sheep, have gone astray, and the good shepherd is he who leads God's children back to the unsearchable riches of His love."

Captain Markov got away, and continued his visit to the ruins of Ani.

When he arrived at camp that night, he was tired from his excursion, and after giving orders to his lieutenant for the next day's march, and about despatching the provisions to the village, he went off to bed. He had spent a hard day riding around the ruins and studying their meaning from a tactical standpoint, and he was glad to be back in the comfort of his tent. All these ruins he had seen—including the human ones at Bartzan—depressed him. The thought occurred to him, and gave him a slight uneasiness, that one day Kars and St. Petersburg would be a ruin just as Ani. It might even occur in his day—so swift was the turning of the wheel of events. Ani, for that matter, had disappeared almost overnight.

This slight uneasiness evaporated, however, in the comfort of the tent. Captain Markov reflected on that. There was something very solid and reassuring about an army—about strong soldiers, well-fed and well-armed as these soldiers of the Tsar were. Captain Markov was very proud of his men, and drew satisfaction and a sense of well-being from the fact that their equipment was new and of the best quality. What a gulf, he thought, separated these well-shod, well-nurtured, well-kept men from those wasted, ragged beings down there on the plain!

He reflected on Amos Lyle, the missionary, and again the ludicrous swinging songs of the religious service filled his ears. The thought of Lyle made him think of his son, Pavil, now five years old—probably because Pavil's mother had the same sort of primitive ideas about religion as Lyle.

Pavil might be getting some of these sentimental notions about Providence.

He hoped not.

He wanted his son to be strong and self-reliant, to trust in his good right arm. That twaddle of Lyle's would make a man effeminate, though he had to admit there was nothing effeminate about Lyle himself.

He thought again of the solid comfort of his tent, and fell asleep.

2. Droh

AMOS LYLE was one who was direct and sympathetic in his approach to his fellow men. He never analyzed the conduct of others—he did not have the critical faculty— and consequently he never condemned. Logic, in his view, was not required of one whose eyes were fastened on God. Logic could in no case compass His qualities or His limits. God would cease to be God if we could analyze His composition, or define His qualities, or chart His kingdom and delimit its provinces and boundaries.

As with God, so with a human soul. To some, men are but chemical and physical combinations of elements to form bone, tissue, and brain cells, together with a mental switchboard that operates by impulses, either environmental or hereditary. To others, men are but units of a greater body, which they call the State, which is precisely organized and which functions according to a definite pattern and established law. But to Amos Lyle, man was a thing of infinite capacity, of infinite worth, a creature made in the image of God, and a partaker of divinity through Jesus Christ, a creature upon whom no bounds were set, for whom law had ceased to be—as St. Paul had said—and who was possessed of matchless freedom in the Lord.

To Amos Lyle, therefore, it made little difference whether men were alive or dead in the body, if they were "alive in Christ Jesus;" it made little difference, likewise, whether they were hungry or ate, were housed or lived under the stars, if their souls were saved. If men looked after their souls, God would look after their bodies. This philosophy was partly the result of his own background: his own youth had been one of hardship, so that hardship had become the norm of living. As a cowhand on a ranch, before he had become a minister and missionary, he had spent nights and days in the saddle, following the cattle, until it seemed more in the course of things to sleep on the ground with a saddle for a pillow than upon a bed. As for food, that came when it came, and stomachs waited. Yet Lyle had never considered this as hardship: it was the way of life on the range—every man on the ranch got his thirty dollars in silver every month, and keep, and that was being taken care of; that was good living.

But now these attitudes, which he still carried with him, were faced with a new condition. The remnant of the Dilijan Armenians who had escaped the massacre had found a home here in Russia, on the plain of Bartzan, in the abandoned huts and houses of what had once been a Turkish village. But they had no right or title to settle here. They were feeble and poor. They needed help of a material sort. Amos Lyle was faced with reality of a human order. Fervid as the spirit may be, hands cannot be lifted in prayer if they are manacled, knees cannot bend that are in stocks, eyes that are blind with suffering cannot see God. These people of Dilijan needed a protector, a father, one who could tell them when to plow and how to plow, how to build a house and to prune a vine, how to organize their life on an independent, self-sustaining basis; yet if there was ever a man unfitted and unprepared for such a task, it would seem to be Amos Lyle.

But Lyle realized the need, in his way, and his spirit was strong to the task. The first consideration was that of the official permit to settle at Bartzan, which Captain Markov had warned him must be obtained from the military commandant of Kars. Lyle thought that Garabed Khansourian or Neshan Kovian, or others among the elders and leaders of the community, should go up, perhaps as a delegation, to see the commandant. But one and all demurred. Khansourian would have gone—he was fond of show and political activity—but Kovian, the shrewd trader and banker, put his foot down on the suggestion.

"The Russians do not care for the Armenians," he said. "They will find occasion to insult and humiliate us. Let Pastor Lyle go instead. They will respect an American, and listen with attention to his pleading.

"But," he added, speaking to Lyle, "when you talk to them, impress upon them that we are a peaceful people, that we are obedient subjects, and, oh, yes, add that we pay our taxes promptly."

With these injunctions in mind, Amos Lyle set off for Kars.

With Lyle went the boy Haig, who had been mercifully preserved from the massacre on Ghulam Dagh by his own nimble-footedness in scurrying among the rocks, and who had become a favorite among the refugees for his cheerfulness, insouciance and general good spirits.

Haig was fourteen years old, or thereabouts, and he had been with Pastor Lyle now for five years. He had wandered into the compound one day when some workmen were making their infrequent repairs, had asked for food, received it, and presently had wandered out again into the streets. Later he had returned, and had continued to return, with increasing frequency, as his stomach, or need for clothes, prompted him, until he finally had attached himself as servant, messenger and general factotum. But he had never given up entirely his wayward tendencies, and he would, at intervals, disappear for as long as a week or two at a stretch.

Where he would go on these absences, he would never explain, but would laugh, or, growing very serious, would ask Lyle if he had ever been inconvenienced.

Since coming to Russia, Haig had been more attentive and docile—probably because it was a strange land, and he knew nowhere to go.

Lyle liked to have the boy around, not because of his services, which were none too efficient—though enough to suit Lyle—but because of his easy chatter, his independence, his good humor and urbanity, and because, in Lyle's eyes, he was a child of God.

Lyle had need of such a boy as Haig. His exuberant faith in the omnipotence, omnipresence and goodness of God was always on the verge of becoming a dogmatic fixation, and Haig's unpredictability was a constant reminder that the Father, in whose image both Haig and Lyle were created, was not always predictable.

It was late afternoon when Lyle and Haig arrived in the city of Kars; retreat exercises were in progress on the parade grounds, and a crowd jammed the edge of the field to watch the picked troops display their skill.

As they passed the parade grounds Haig's excitement became uncontrollable, and he begged the missionary to stay awhile.

Haig, and for that matter Lyle, had never seen such panoply in his life. Square after square of infantry passed, sharply in step, even of line, boots polished, rifles and bayonets glinting in the sunlight. Following the infantry came the cavalry, majestically mounted, uniformed in brilliant colors, galloping by with their standards flying, raising a cloud of dust; and then the machines of war, the heavy artillery with their caissons, and the lighter artillery—guns of all sizes and for all purposes of war. There were innumerable bands, it seemed, pealing their martial music until the air reverberated and the spine quivered; officers and gold braid galore; flags and bunting without end. To behold all this was to believe that war was the chief end and principal glory of mankind.

That night, in the caravanserai, to which Lyle went in preference to the ornate, smelly European hotel, Haig was full of questions.

"Where do they get those uniforms?"

Lyle told him.

"They don't have to buy them?"

"No."

"You can get all those clothes for nothing?"

"Yes."

"And a horse?"

Lyle nodded.

"You pay nothing?"

"Of course," Lyle said. "Sometimes you pay with your life."

Haig was ready with an answer to confound his pastor.

"I should say you pay with your life unless you are a soldier. If you would live, then you must learn to fight."

His answer, Haig saw, was not pleasing to his pastor, and he did penance by spending the rest of the evening attending to Lyle's wants, fetching hot water from the *toneer* for a bath, making the pallet down in the straw, loosening the blankets from the roll, and shaking them free from dust and spreading them. . . .

Some time during the night, they were awakened by a knocking. Haig was already at the door, talking to the man in rapid Armenian.

"He wants a doctor, pastor."

Lyle threw on his *aba*, the rough brown native cloak he wore in town, and came to the door.

He had long ago learned to respond automatically to these calls, and though he was not a doctor, he had learned something about simple and homely cures, bone-setting and the like. Also, while he was not presumptuous, he trusted in the Lord to supply his lack of knowledge and skill. Healing was for him as much a matter of the spirit as of skill, and only rarely—as in epidemics of fever—did he feel at loss as to what to do.

"What is the trouble?" he asked.

"A gunshot wound, he says," said Haig.

Either it was very serious, requiring urgent attention, or very trivial, not warranting calling a regular physician, of which there must be many in the city. This was, Lyle thought, something he might handle. On more than one occasion, during his ranch days, he had had to treat such wounds of cowboys too reckless or careless with their six-shooters.

The man entered. He was Armenian, but of a breed different from any Lyle had known in Turkey—tall, well built, and clad in the baggy trousers, embroidered jacket and beturbaned fez common among the Kurdish mountaineers.

"Can you come at once, *baroon?*" he asked.

"Right away."

Lyle hastily dressed, gathered together some clean linen from his luggage, and followed the man out.

Haig came along.

"*Baroon*, you will say nothing of this?" asked the man, as they went along.

"I try to understand things, and act accordingly. Has there been a crime?"

"Not according to our law and custom."

"Who are you?"

"We are the followers of Droh, and we come from Persia."

"And what do you do in Kars, if I may ask?"

"We pasture sometimes across the Araxes, when the grass is not good and we must wander far. We come to Kars to sell our rugs. But silence, now, if you please, *baroon*."

The man turned off the street and entered the bazaar. Though the street was illuminated only by the starlight which was reflected dimly by the yellow brick walls, the bazaar was without even this meager glow. Here, it was so dark that Lyle could not see his hand laid on the girdle of his guide. Residence in the East had however taught him certain methods of finding his way through these labyrinthian passages. He knew, for instance, that they had come to the silk bazaar by the smell of the cloth. In the same way he recognized the street of the brass workers, and that of the furriers.

They had passed the tobacco workers' stalls and had turned into a *khan*—a great open square where the caravans unloaded their cargoes. A light burned in one of the upper chambers of the surrounding warehouses. Their guide mounted the stairs, knocked on a certain door, which opened, and then respectfully standing aside for Lyle to enter, spoke the name "Droh."

Droh was a large man, with intelligent brown eyes, a smooth, ruddy brown face, and black curly hair. Like the man who had fetched Lyle, he was dressed in modified Kurdish fashion, but elegantly, with baggy trousers and a broad girdle of red silk wrapped several times about his waist and a shirt of fine linen heavily embroidered with red silk thread. One sleeve of the shirt was blood soaked.

"Thank you for coming," he said. "It's something that needed attention tonight, so that I may be on my way, but I couldn't ask one of the Russian doctors."

"I see," mused Lyle, as he set some water to boiling. "How did you know I was in Kars, and where to reach me?"

"Some of my men are stopping at your caravanserai."

Lyle washed the wound and discovered that the bullet had pierced the flesh, but had not gone through. Sterilizing a penknife, he prodded about until presently he located a piece of steel. It was only a matter of moments to remove it and dress the wound. When he had finished, he said,

"Now you must tell me what happened. Naturally, I will have to make a report to the authorities."

Droh's eyes flashed.

"The authorities already know about it. They did it."

Lyle looked at him understandingly and said nothing.

"Colonel Vronsky was killed tonight," the tribesman announced in explanation.

"This is a very serious matter," Lyle said slowly.

"That may be, but not to Droh," said the Armenian, clipping the words.

"No?"

"I did not kill him, nor did any of my men. I merely stated the fact."

"Yes?"

"The colonel was drunk. He was drunk when he entered the *dukhan* where we sat drinking *araki*. The colonel began to play up to a girl who served him. Someone shot him. That is all. But they attempted to arrest us. Because we are Armenians. We knew nothing, had done nothing, and so we simply refused to be arrested. Arakel was killed, and I was struck."

Haig had been listening in tense excitement. Now he burst out:

"How did you refuse to be arrested?"

Droh glanced at the boy, and a smile of pride overspread his face. This was the kind of attention he liked. He lifted his shoulders ever so slightly and answered,

"We threw a few benches, knocked down a few soldiers and even—cut a few veins."

"Oh!" gasped Haig.

"You should be a tribesman," nodded Droh. "You have the stuff."

"You are returning to Ararat?" spoke up Lyle. He was concerned about the interest which the tribesman aroused in his boy. He was also deeply disturbed about the larger problem of race relations which the situation created, and about his mission with the commandant.

"Yes."

"Then you should stay there. The city is not for you. You shouldn't have been drinking *araki*. It's bad for you. When can you leave?"

"At once."

"Then do so. Your arm will stand travel, and I must report this in the morning. By then, I hope, you will be well on your way."

"Thank you for your service. How much do we owe you?"

"You owe me nothing, but you owe God many prayers for your sins and for His protection. Good night."

3. Haig

HAIG was not to be found the following morning, and Amos Lyle set out for the fort alone—first leaving word with the keeper of the caravanserai that upon his return Haig should await Lyle's coming.

General Vorishoff, commandant of Kars fortress, received the missionary courteously. When Lyle entered he was seated at his desk, a sheaf of blueprints spread before him, architectural drawings of a new ammunition dump that was to be constructed. On a long conference table were other blueprints and maps of the surrounding territory. At the end of the room stood a console table on which a samovar was kept always humming for use during the general's many conferences.

"Sir," said the general in good English, rising and bowing quickly and stiffly from the waist, "be seated. You will have some tea with me? I am glad to see you."

"Thank you," said Lyle, and took the glass handed him by the orderly. From the window he could see the construction work that was going on. Excavations were being made for gun emplacements, and huge granite blocks, rough-quarried and slung between solid cart wheels, were being rolled up to be set into place for foundations.

"The international situation is tense," said the general, who observed Lyle's glance out of the window, and was agreeable to conversation. "The old concert of Europe is breaking up. Treaties mean nothing, and so we have to prepare. We are building a war power that will be the equal of any in the world. When we finish here, Kars will be the Gibraltar of Southwestern Asia."

Lyle was perplexed. He knew little about international politics.

"But what is the quarrel with Turkey?" he asked. "Surely it is not because of the Armenians."

"Oh, no, not the Armenians," sniffed Vorishoff contemptuously. "It is the European situation. Von Tirpitz is determined to create a German sea power. Four years ago, you recall, we entered into alliance with France. France and England are drawing together. Last January the Kaiser threw a bomb toward London when he sent his telegram to Kruger, and the windowpanes in all the chancelleries of Europe are still rattling from the explosion. Germany has been courting the Porte with sugar and spice and all things nice. And the Turks still think of Kars as theirs. And so you see how the wheels revolve."

The general paused, then added:

"But with Kars rebuilt, our southwestern frontier is safe. We will have no worry from this quarter and can release troops for Galicia and Poland. It is all provided for in the War Plans worked out by the Imperial Military Council.

"But what can I do for you?" the general asked.

The affairs of a little, poverty-stricken village of refugees on the empty plain of Bartzan might have seemed insig-

nificant after such world-sweeping discourse, but not to
Amos Lyle. He told the commandant, respectfully but
movingly, about their flight from Turkey, their settlement
at Bartzan, and their hopes for a new life under the
Russian aegis.

"It is an abandoned village, formerly inhabited by
Turks," he concluded. "We have rebuilt the houses, enough
to accommodate every family, and this spring we put out
fields of wheat and turnips. We already feel at home there
and, if we are permitted to remain, I am sure that this
barren plain will in time blossom again like a garden."

The general lighted a cigarette, leaned back in his
chair, closed his eyes and inhaled deeply of the smoke.
Then, allowing it to fill his mouth and nostrils as he
spoke, he asked, contemplatively,

"Where is this plain?"

"It is about forty miles from here, in the general neighborhood of the ruins of ancient Ani. The Araxes touches
it, and across the Araxes Ararat begins to rise."

"Good pasture land?"

"Yes, excellent."

"Empty land?"

"Yes, practically so. A few nomads graze their flocks
there."

"Good hunting?"

"I have seen a good many bustard, a few deer. There
are no wild pig or brush game that I know of. But then
I am not so well informed on these matters as I once was."

"You mentioned Ani. I had also heard of it from Captain Markov, who is the scholar of the fort. What is there
about it so interesting?"

"Ani was the capital of the Armenian Empire in the
tenth to the thirteenth centuries. It has been a ruin since
it was captured and despoiled by the Mongols in the
thirteenth century."

"It must have had considerable strategic value."

"Values in military strategy have no doubt changed
marvelously in the centuries since Ani was a stronghold,"
replied Lyle, who for all his simplicity was not obtuse to
the drift of the general's questioning.

"There are eternal verities in war just as there are in religion," replied the general with a slight condescension. "But tell me, the people whom you have brought over —without permission, I gather—they are Armenians, are they not?"

"Yes."

"I am from the Baltic, and have not met many of the race. What sort of people are they?"

"They are like all other of God's children," said Lyle simply. "They have capacities in any direction they are given opportunity. They love their homes, their children, and—most of them—their Lord. For chastity and domestic virtues, they are exceptional. I have never been among more interesting or more hopeful people."

"Yes, yes," said the general a trifle impatiently, "I am sure of that. But are they good soldier material?"

"Their courage under adversity is inspiring, but they are not warlike."

"How would you characterize them physically?"

"A robust people, inclined to shortness and stockiness, but of all degrees of feature and stature, since they were anciently a mixture of Semitic and Aryan stock; not the most handsome of God's creatures, nor among the homeliest. Their complexions are fair and ruddy, their features even, their hair usually wavy, and brown or black."

"What is their temperament?"

"Of every variety. Artistic, industrious. . . . Very shrewd, but many are quite simple. Placid rather than nervous; good humored; often introspective and sensitive."

"Do they make good subjects?"

"In Turkey, until Abdul Hamid came to the throne, they were well regarded. You will find that most of them have read, and treasure, the words of St. Paul, 'Let every soul be subject unto the higher powers.' They are, accordingly, obedient to lawful authority. They are clean; they believe in good works; they love justice and righteousness."

"That seems to be a very good recommendation," nodded the general, pursing his lips judicially. "As rulers of empire we must be like Romans, tolerant of all races and tongues and creeds. For like Rome we rule over the children of Ham as well as the children of Shem and Japheth. We deal with Semites and Mongols, with Lapps and Letts, with Poles and Permyaks, and Kalmuck and Kirghiz. But the Armenians, from all I hear, are a hard people to deal with. They are to Russia what the Jews were to Rome—a stubborn people who resist the new and cling to their ancient traditions, contemptuous, in their great age, of us upstart Slavs, looking for a messiah who will restore their former glory. Only last night one of a band of Armenian mountaineers killed Colonel Vronsky. And then managed to escape. For these reasons we are not eager to have more of them."

"I have had an account of that affair, and while it is most regrettable, I am certain that upon investigation you will find the Armenians not wholly to blame," pleaded Lyle. "In any case, I beg you not to condemn a flock because of a few pied sheep, not to judge my case and the case of these Dilijanis by the waywardness of one or two men. Our people are quiet and well behaved, I can assure you, and desire nothing but to live in peace and forget their sorrows."

"What do you know of this affair of last night?" asked the general, ignoring Lyle's defense.

Lyle told him of the incident of dressing Droh's arm, of which the general made a memorandum, and then renewed his plea for permission for the Dilijanis to settle at Bartzan—a plea all the more fervid since he recognized the bad effect which the affair had had.

The general, however, had other reasons for not desiring the Armenians at Bartzan.

"They are too near the frontier."

"Too near the frontier?"

"Yes," went on the general, with illogical change of emphasis. "In case of war, we want a different breed of men near the border. Your Armenian is too peaceable. We want men who can fight if necessary. In addition, from what you say, it appears that the plain of Bartzan might be admirable maneuver ground for working out tactical problems."

Lyle was nonplused that his people should be objected to because they were peaceable.

"Yes, the Armenians are peaceable," he protested, "and I would not want them to become fighters. But there will be no fighting, I am sure of that. Still, if not at Bartzan, surely there is other land for them?"

The government had announced its willingness to receive the refugees from the Turkish massacres and settle them within the Empire. The value of the offer depended, of course, upon the good will and discretion of the officials down the line, among whom was General Vorishoff. General Vorishoff was interested only in maintaining the dignity of the Empire, and impressing upon those who sought its favor the importance of petition. Suppliants must show the proper reverence. They should tremble slightly and be duly appreciative. Favors should not be too quickly granted.

The general rose. He could think of no further questions or objections.

"I will forward the case to Petersburg," he said, solemnly, and then added with a gracious smile, "and the Bureau of Colonization will doubtless find land for you. Meantime, I presume you and your Armenians may occupy the village temporarily, until we get word from the Bureau."

Lyle left General Vorishoff happily, with confidence that whatever might be decided as to the settlement, his people would be taken care of. He felt that, thanks to divine care, their trials were over, and they might look forward to peace and contentment in this new land.

When Lyle returned to the caravanserai, Haig was not about.

Lyle was not immediately disturbed, for it still lacked an hour of noon, and Haig, he decided, was wandering about the bazaars. But when noon came and the lad did not put in his appearance, he became a trifle worried. It was barely possible, he thought, that Haig had lost himself in the city streets.

He dismissed the idea as preposterous, and opened his haversack containing the bread and white cheese of their lunch. He broke off a piece of the cheese and then broke this in two, laying the larger portion aside for the boy. Then he took his cup, dropped in a pinch of tea and took it to the public samovar to fill it with hot water. He returned and, holding the cup in one hand, the cheese and bread in the other, he sat down on a curbstone in the shade.

But his appetite faltered. Two or three times he got up and went to the gate to look out. Once he started at a voice and looked around. A boy playing about the caravanserai was running and shouting greetings to a teamster entering the gate—perhaps his father. Lyle wistfully watched the meeting of the two.

He was now plainly worried. He had hoped to get started for Bartzan directly after noon, and Haig had so understood. He could not finish his meal, and wrapping up the bread and cheese again, laid them away. He walked again to the gate and looked out. The keeper of the caravanserai was standing there.

"You haven't seen my boy?" Lyle asked.

"Yes," said the man. "He went off."

"Do you know where he went?"

"I think to the mountains."

"The mountains? I don't understand," said Lyle.

"A mountaineer came by riding a horse and leading one with an empty saddle. He asked for you, and the boy came out. They talked. I do not know what they said, but the boy climbed into the empty saddle and rode off with him."

"He was a mountain Armenian?"

"Yes."

"What was the boy's mood?"

"He had been sitting where you sat, playing idly with some knuckle bones. This was strange for a boy, and so I went up and spoke to him. He wanted to know whether I had ever been to war. That I had, in the war against the Bulgars, when I was a subject of the Sultan, and I told him of our battle affairs. The boy seemed greatly pleased

and wanted to know more. I was still telling him tales—
most of them true—when this mountaineer came."

"Did he go off gladly?"

"It seemed so. We were in the middle of an adventure."

"Thank you."

Haig had gone off with Droh and his men.

Amos Lyle tried to comprehend the fact and grasp its
meaning, as he mechanically saddled his horse. What was
this desertion compared to the thousands of losses Lyle
had suffered this past year? What was this sorrow among
the many he bore? It is not the number of losses, or the
weight of sorrow, but their quality. One star differs from
another in glory, and to take Haig away was like taking
away the bright-eyed Mercury from the evening sky.
Haig, to Lyle, was the lamb for whose sake the good shepherd leaves the ninety and nine.

Haig had answered the call of adventure in his nature.
Lyle pondered that fact. Haig had gone off with the
tribesmen in search of something which Lyle himself
might have satisfied. For Lyle could be as virile and ad-
venturesome as these tribesmen, did he choose. He had
been such a free rider in his time; and he had ridden with
the best; he had broken wild horses to the saddle; he had
ridden into a stampeding herd, when life hung on his
daring and skill with his mount.

But he had given up this life deliberately for the meeker,
submissive life of a servant of God. He had, in so doing,
cast a cloak about his personality. It was not a drab life,
this career of preaching and homely ministering that had
been his day by day life now for fourteen years, but its
colors were on the underside, within, visible only to the
soul. Outwardly, no doubt, it appeared to many, as it had
appeared to Haig, colorless and monotonous.

He wondered why this was. Why did the Christian life
fail to appeal to the adventuresomeness of youth? Why
did the Church always portray its saints with sad-eyed
countenances? Why did it dim its sanctuaries with somber
light, sing solemn music, and recite its litany and pray
its prayers with mournful voice? The Master was a joyous man, and He had rebuked those who would put on

mournful face, "Can ye make the children of the bride-chamber fast, while the bridegroom is with them?"

Perhaps the Church had erred, Lyle thought, and perhaps he had erred by failing to understand the spirit of childhood. Christ had said, "Suffer little children to come unto me, and forbid them not: for of such is the kingdom of God. Verily I say unto you, Whosoever shall not receive the kingdom of God as a little child shall in no wise enter therein." Lyle wondered if possibly he had not thought of people too much as objects of salvation, and as sinners to be called to repentance, rather than as workers waiting to be called to the field, as apostles waiting to be despatched on the highways of Christian adventure. Was not Jesus one who called little children to him? And children are without sin, or at least, being young, their sins are not weighty.

Lyle considered again. Perhaps he had not learned how to deal with children on their own terms. That was quite likely. Sosnik, the midwife—who had borne eleven children herself—stoutly claimed that only one who has had children of his own can understand a child. But possibly, bachelor that he was, Lyle might yet learn the secret of childhood. God being his helper, he could.

Relieved by this self-examination and castigation, Lyle began to consider the larger aspects of Haig's running away, and to search for God's purpose in this loss—a purpose which he believed to exist in all happenings. By this time, Lyle had left the suburbs of the city, and was in the open country. Presently he had crossed the valley and ascended the ridge that lies to the east of Kars and passes through the northern suburbs of that city. From here he could see, in the distance, the great mountain of Ararat, bathed in colors of the afternoon sunlight.

This mountain was to Lyle a standing evidence of God's purpose that coursed through all nature. That it was the mountain upon which the Ark of Noah had rested he had not the slightest doubt. It was an historical fact which was confirmed by the very name the mountain bore among the peoples who lived about it.

By the Turks, it is called *Argi-Dagh*, or Mountain of

the Ark; by the Persians, *Kuh-i-Nuh*, or Mountain of Noah; and by the Armenians, *Massees*, or Mother of the World. If there had been a Flood, then this was the mountain. As for the fact of the Flood, the Bible was Lyle's sufficient authority.

As he looked at Ararat, it seemed to Lyle that he was standing in the veritable presence of his Lord. It filled him with an immense joy just to look at this mountain, to feel that as God had here spoken to Noah, so He might also speak to Lyle.

And thinking now of Haig, Lyle asked himself if he should not trust that God had His own purpose in taking the boy away, that He was leading the boy by His hand, as He had led Hagar in the wilderness. Perhaps Haig would return to him one day, in God's own time and for His own purposes?

Lyle thought of the Master's comforting words to Jairus, who believed his daughter dead, and made them his own, "The lad is not lost, but liveth."

As Amos Lyle's faith strengthened him against his loss, so it prepared him for his blessings. When he arrived home late the next day, Garabed Khansourian, who acted as spokesman of Bartzan, came to him with great news.

"Miriam Verian has come to us—risen from the dead, and bringing with her a child, a daughter!"

"I knew it! I knew it!" exclaimed Lyle. "Praise God for His bounty."

"You knew it?" asked Khansourian, perplexed.

"It is written that the Lord giveth, and the Lord taketh away; but it might also be written, 'The Lord taketh away, but He also giveth.' Where is she? Safe and sound? And the baby? Let us go see them."

And without pausing in his praise of God, he went into the house where Miriam and her baby were lodged, to welcome her and rejoice in her deliverance.

4. Elements of a Community

SEPTEMBER was drawing toward October, and no word had come from the authorities at Kars, either yes or no, as to whether the refugees might continue to occupy the land at Bartzan.

"What are we to do, pastor?" Lyle was being asked. "Do you think we can stay here, or will we be moved out?"

"It's good land, pastor. Very good wheat land," a farmer by the name of Ardeshir reminded him. Ardeshir was not of those who had lived in Dilijan, but was from Turkey, a refugee, who had heard of the settlement at Bartzan, and had come there.

The spring wheat crop had indeed been good, considering the late planting. A winter crop should do even better.

"But we must get the planting done before the frost comes," warned the farmer. "The seed must break and strike root before the cold sets in. Properly, it should be planted early enough to form a green field before winter."

Wheat had not been grown to any extent around Dilijan, the Turkish soil being more adapted to orchards and vineyards, but Neshan Kovian, the trader, had seen its possibilities at Bartzan and had procured the seed grain, the oxen and the plows by which the first crop had been put in—the fruits of which he, of course, shared. Wheat was an easy crop to handle; those among the Dilijanis who were townspeople soon learned, from the country folk, how to handle a plow, cut the grain, and winnow the straw; even the women, who of course constituted the great majority of the adult community, could help in the cutting and threshing.

There was something reassuring about the growing wheat. The quickness with which it sprang from the seed and covered the brown earth with a carpet of re-freshing green, grew tall and finally golden, it's heavy heads shimmering as the breezes blew over the field and ruffled the surface, all conveyed a sense of renewed strength drawn from the bosom of the earth. Here on the plain, so it seemed to the ever-hopeful Lyle, was made manifest the promise of God, given to the children of His creation, to the faithful Noah: "While the earth remaineth, seedtime and harvest, and cold and heat, and summer and winter, and day and night shall not cease."

Others were being attracted to Bartzan, refugees from other parts of Turkey, some of whom had drifted to the Russian cities but had found no welcome there, some to whom cities were strange and oppressive and who sought a home upon land that they might till, some who had heard of Amos Lyle and looked to him as a protector, some who had heard tales of free land on the Bartzan plain. The mere fact that here was a community, founded upon nothing, clinging desperately to life against im-measurable odds, winning the bitter struggle against winter and starvation, and at last surviving and creating a life of its own, had an immensely hope-engendering effect upon all those wandering ones who heard of it. They came, they erected huts, they planted little patches of vegetables or bought a few sheep, they added to the community. Bartzan had become a village, a community in the wilderness, self-sustaining, and nourished by hope.

There seemed but one obstacle to the growth of the village of Bartzan—the failure to receive the official au-thorization to settle there. The land was the Tsar's; the Armenians were merely tenants at will; it was possible for them to be evicted at any moment. Under such circum-stances, with what assurance could the seed be put into the ground, or walls and houses erected?

Neshan Kovian, like the financier that he was, was the first to show nervousness about the future. He grew re-luctant to make further advances to those in need.

"Unless the land tenure is secure," he complained, "credit is insecure. It rests upon contract, and unless men are assured of their property, contracts are like water."

He was stating an axiom of finance which was hard to refute. Yet it was one to which Lyle could not reconcile himself. This insecurity did not bother Lyle; "squatting" had been a common way of acquiring vested interests in the unsettled portions of the American West; many of the great ranch properties had been so acquired and the ownership was nowhere recorded in any book of public record. Lyle told Kovian, in simple terms, how the ranchers had made fortunes by pre-empting the free land and occupying it for their purposes without public right or title.

"But were they not driven from their possessions, to their great sorrow and loss?" asked Kovian.

"Eventually many were, and some were confirmed in their holdings, and occupy them to this day. But what eventually happened is of little concern, for all men are tenants of the earth but for a season, and must be prepared to surrender their habitation when it is required of them. They occupied the land, and used it for its natural purposes, as the Lord has commanded us, speaking first in Genesis when He gave man dominion over the earth and the beasts of the field, and bade him be fruitful and multiply, and again through His son Jesus, in the parable of the talents.

"God has brought us to Bartzan, and while we must be subject to the higher authorities, I take it that we may use this land until it is required of us, so long as we do not misuse it. And I am confident that if this land should be required of us, God will prepare us another habitation, even as He brought us to this, and that with patience we shall be gainers rather than losers."

"Possibly," assented Kovian, noncommittally. He did not agree with the missionary's view, but he was under great debt to him, owing him for the refuge at Dilijan, his life and all his possessions.

"Nevertheless, I shall go up to Kars again shortly, and make further enquiry in the matter. Meantime, let us trust in the Lord."

Kovian did, under Lyle's exhortations, continue to lend or advance goods on credit. His advances were moderate in amount, but in Bartzan, as in the great commercial centers, a little display of confidence among the leaders is like a little leaven in a great mass. Others, without asking, assumed that there had been a change for the better in their circumstances, and confidence rose.

Neshan Kovian was, for all his interest in personal profit, a vital force in the Bartzan community. He was the economic organizer. As Amos Lyle provided the spiritual sinews, so Neshan Kovian provided the material. Kovian had prospered in Dilijan, and he would prosper in Bartzan. Amos Lyle had observed this quality and had, at times, given it thought. He had wondered whether prosperity was a sin, whether it were possible for a man to gain much property without sins, such as injustice, exploitation and avarice. But he never came to a conclusion, partly because his mind was too occupied with other things to analyze conduct, more because he did not pass judgment on people. People had to be self-convicted of sin, or convicted by the Lord, not by Amos Lyle.

Of Kovian, he could say that he had never observed him in practices that were contrary to the ethics or customs of the community. His word could be trusted. Moreover, he never exacted the last kopek in a transaction. He was not ungenerous, but contributed as liberally as anyone to charity and community needs.

As to whether his transactions, even though ethical, resulted in his enrichment at the expense of the community, Amos Lyle could say that on the whole Kovian's affairs had brought added wealth not only to himself but to others. Thus he had provided the seed grain for the first harvest, going to Kars and bringing back a cartload, which he had doled out, taking promises in payment, redeeming the promises later at the equivalent of double. During the summer also he had brought good ash and walnut—timber being scarce at Bartzan—and had had Mattios Masghian, the lame carpenter, make looms which he sold for a portion of the cloth to be made from them. He had also fetched spools of fine cotton thread of English make from the Kars bazaars, and had encouraged the women to resume crochet work, an art for which the Armenian women were famous; and taking the product and selling it, he had made excellent profit both for himself and the makers.

As Neshan Kovian directed the fiscal affairs of the community, so the political organization rested with Garabed Khansourian.

Garabed Khansourian was from Dilijan, but he had not participated in the flight. He had been, at the time, in Tiflis, attending a convention of a benevolent society of which he was a member, and had come to Bartzan on learning that the survivors from Dilijan had settled there. Khansourian had no relatives left, but he had a strong sense of community kinship, and preferred to stay by those of the Dilijanis who had survived, than go elsewhere. At this time he was not so ambitious politically as he became later.

Khansourian was a plump, ruddy-faced, affable and intelligent man in his early thirties. He had not married, being one of those who are too busy directing community activities to organize that simplest form of community organization—a family.

Shortly after Lyle returned from Kars, bringing his hopeful news that the matter of the permit to settle at Bartzan would be decided shortly, Khansourian had come to him with a proposal.

"Don't you think, pastor, that we should have a mayor?" he asked. "We are a village, and things will be better ordered if there is form and government."

This, again, was something of which Lyle would never have thought, oblivious as he was to material necessities, but it was characteristic of Khansourian. It was he who, in Dilijan, had fomented the idea of a cemetery park, and had organized a committee to solicit funds for landscaping it; he who, when anyone died in poverty, had organized the collection for funeral expenses. It was generally supposed that in such instances, Garabed Khansourian retained a share for himself—a *mudakhil,* as the Persians say, a tenth part or more—but, if so, it was in accordance with a well-established custom, a prerogative that was the servant's in buying for the household, and the governor's in remitting the tax collections to the capital.

"I think the idea of a mayor is splendid," agreed Lyle. "I think also, of course, that we should have a school. Children, I have observed, are happiest when they are learning."

"By all means. One of my first acts as mayor will be to start a school. In fact, I shall preside over it myself and I already have a teacher in mind."

"Who is that?"

"Miriam Verian. She is very wise, you know, versed in the Armenian, and knowing as well the poetry and literature of the Persians, renowned among all peoples. The lamp of imagination illuminates her discourse, and she is, to boot, tender and sweet of disposition. But she grieves over her dead husband too much. Emmanuel was a nice fellow, but rather simple, and never mingled much. It is my belief that as we live in a society, we must mingle with our fellow men."

Amos Lyle smiled understandingly. Emmanuel, it was true, had never mingled much. He had been quiet, poetic by nature. Amos Lyle thought that if Emmanuel was not one who had lived much with men, he was one who had lived with God. Still, Amos Lyle, who lived very much with his fellow men, could understand Garabed Khansourian's viewpoint.

Garabed Khansourian was duly chosen mayor at a meeting of the people following the next Sunday's services, and from that moment Bartzan became an organized community. Shortly afterward, the school was started, with Miriam teaching the small children.

5. Conversation

EARLY in October, Amos Lyle again went to Kars to see if he could obtain the official authorization for the Armenians to settle at Bartzan. Garabed Khansourian thought it becoming that as mayor he should accompany Lyle on this trip, as the official representative of the village, but Neshan Kovian, who avoided public position, and was usually taciturn, again opposed it.

"Lyle can handle this better," he said sourly. "We are not a people who can deal with the Russians as equals, and they may decide that if Bartzan warrants a mayor, it should have a Muscovite."

Khansourian saw the wisdom of this, and Lyle went alone.

General Vorishoff was occupied and could not see Lyle, and asked him to talk to his adjutant. The adjutant, an elderly colonel with thin, highly-brushed iron-gray hair, tight-fitting uniform and a monocle, professed to know all about the situation, and assured Lyle that while he could say nothing definite at the moment, he would most certainly have further word in a fortnight. It was obvious that the adjuant knew nothing about the matter, not even that it was something awaiting decision by the Bureau of Colonization, and Amos Lyle left in perplexity and in sadness. It was apparent, from the general's attitude, that the matter of the villagers at Bartzan was one of infinitesimal consequence to the government of all the Russias, whose eye, roaming its frontiers on five seas, could not bring itself to focus on something so insignificant as one little village.

Lyle consoled himself with the thought that if Bartzan had escaped the attention of the bureau at St. Petersburg, at least one eye was upon it, the eye of the Father who, with all His concerns throughout the universe, yet beholds a sparrow's fall. . . .

On his way through the fort, thronged with officers and men, caissons and artillery rumbling through the streets, wagons with supplies, porters and peddlers, and women of ill repute—who were not forbidden entry to the grounds during the day—he encountered Stepan Markov. The officer recognized him and hailed him.

"Well, my old friend of the plain who is so concerned about my soul," he addressed Lyle jovially, but cordially, offering his hand. "What brings you to this citadel of power and wickedness? Concern about your flock of Armenians, I suppose?"

"I am glad to see you again, Captain, and to observe that my words, thanks to God, weigh upon your soul. There is always hope for the man who considers, even though he may take long in resolution. Yes, I have come here on behalf of my people."

"Your Russian has improved," remarked Markov admiringly. "You have devoted your time well in one direction at least. But you should learn to distinguish your military. It may be of some value later, for we military men swarm the country like locusts. I am now a major."

"Then let me congratulate you," replied Lyle, good humoredly. "I should have noticed that you are more thickly embroidered and be-gilt than when I saw you last, but I supposed that was because you are in the city, rather than in the country, where such things count for little, except to collect the dust of the road. Congratulations again."

"You can do better than congratulate me. You can drink to my health and future. Besides, I want to talk to you."

"Gladly, if I can propose a health with tea. I gave up drinking anything stronger years ago."

Major Markov looked at the missionary incredulously.

"Impossible!" he exclaimed. "First, how can anyone who has known the delights of intoxication willingly surrender them? Second, how in the name of all the saints do you keep up your spirits when you are low? How do you manage to stay out in all that misery without fortifying and regaling yourself now and then with a little wine?"

"As to the first," Lyle said, as they made their way

through the crowded streets, "I discovered that the happiest state of man is when he is in possession of all his natural senses, unimpaired and vigorous as God gave them to him. I used to drink a little on the range. Herding cattle in the cold, I would take a little whiskey straight from the canteen to warm me up. But I decided that it didn't help a great deal, and besides, I sometimes got a little befuddled, and my horse would have to bring me to the corral. I thought I should have at least as much sense as my horse; and then, I considered that if my horse could get along without a drink, so could I.

"As to the second. Sometimes I would take a little drink with the boys in the saloon, and since I never knew how much money I had, and was usually willing to stand for the drinks, I found myself always in debt, and that worried me and left me worse off in spirit than before.

"But what really decided me, as to both your first and your second, was the fact that I was converted. I learned that there is a stream of living water, that whoever drinks thereof shall never die, but have everlasting life, and I concluded to imbibe only of those waters for my soul's refreshment. And having decided that, and having discovered that these waters were magical in that property, I concluded that if they could refresh the soul, they could also refresh the body, and that I didn't need drink on cold nights in the saddle."

"Well, it is obvious that I am dealing with someone different from any I ever met before," said Markov humorously. "The nearest I can think of is a Mollocan—they're a sect of holy Russians who confine themselves to milk—but you don't resemble a Mollocan. I'll swallow the insult, and in fact do better. I'll have tea myself."

They entered a restaurant, done up in Byzantine colored glass and plaster and with massive pillars modeled after those in the Reservoir of a Thousand Columns in Constantinople, painted to resemble marble and arched over with round Roman arches. Latticework between the pillars formed little booths, which were lighted with lanterns of pierced brass. It was not a refined place, nor, on the other hand, rowdy; rather quiet, though the time of day may

have had something to do with that. A Russian waiter set
a steaming samovar before them, a teapot, cups and a plate
of *zakuska*—tidbits of dried and pickled herring, slices of
sturgeon, *pâté de foie gras*, caviar, pickles, relish and butter wafers.

"I want to know about this conversion," said Major
Markov, as he tested the strength of the tea, and then filled
glasses for Lyle and himself. Despite his talk about drinking, he was evidently as used to tea as to stronger drink,
and Lyle could not help admiring his outdoor look, his
well-set figure, his easy, commanding carriage.

"Tell me about it, won't you?" Markov asked.

The major had become gracious and kindly, as befits a
host.

"I am always glad to tell anyone about my experience
in finding God, if it is of any help," said Lyle fervently. "I
was a cowboy on a ranch in Texas when I was a young
man—"

"First, you must tell me what a cowboy is, and what a
ranch is like."

Lyle told him about the extensive cattle-growing enterprises of his country, to all of which the Russian listened
with the greatest attention.

"The Americans and the Russians have a lot in common," he remarked thoughtfully. "We both have a vast
frontier into which our young men may go and make their
fortunes. It gives a certain flavor to the national character
—and a certain affinity between the two peoples. Perhaps
that is why I like you."

He recovered himself, drank deep of his tea, and said,

"But I am leading you astray. This—this spiritual experience, as you may call it—is much the more important."

Lyle told him about the evangelist who had come to the
little Texas town and had begun "protracted meetings,"
and how he and certain others of the cowhands had ridden
into town on several nights—"chiefly to see the people, and
the pretty girls."

It was obvious, from the way Lyle told it, however,
that there was something else that had drawn him into
the meetings.

"My conscience was not easy," he said a little later in his narrative. "I felt as though something was missing from my life, felt as though I had a higher course which I was not following. I used to look up at the sky, when herding the cattle at night, and see the stars in the heavens, dipping down to the plain on every side, and I would think of the vastness of the earth and of the heavens, and wonder who I was, and feel terribly lost, and then ask whether I should ever understand who it was made all these majestic marvels."

A few nights' attendance at the meetings and Lyle had begun to see the way. The evangelist had a family, and one of his children, a twelve-year-old girl, played the organ while the evangelist, his wife, and his two smaller children sang. Lyle began to feel a desire to identify himself, not with the stars, not with the majestic works of God, but with His humblest: he wanted to be like this little girl, simple and childlike.

And then, as the evangelist told many stories of sinners repentant and joy found, Lyle became imbued with the glory of the Lord. He began to be filled with a great love for Jesus Christ. He felt that in Christ he had a comforter and a confessor to whom he might come freely and with knowledge that his sins would be forgiven, one who would fill his heart so full of joy that sadness could not enter.

It was the custom at these "protracted meetings" to sing while the evangelist gave the invitation, while he pleaded with obdurate sinners.

"I shall never forget that night," Lyle said, his face lighting with the joy of recollection. "It was the night on which I was born again, as Jesus said to Nicodemus. They were singing a song,

> " 'Just as I am, without one plea,
> But that thy blood was shed for me,
> And that thou bidd'st me come to thee,
> O Lamb of God, I come!'

"The congregation was standing, in song, and all over the tabernacle women were standing beside their loved ones—husbands, brothers, sons or neighbors—urging them, in the name of the blessed Jesus, to go up and offer their souls to Christ, while above the drone of the music, the pleading of the women and the 'amens' rose the voice of the evangelist, calling,

"'Come to Jesus; come and drink of the everlasting fountain. Jesus saves, oh, how He saves. Come, brothers! Come, sisters! Renounce your sins! Call upon the Lord, for His redemption is nigh! Come and be saved.'

"I responded to the invitation; I went to the altar rail, and kneeled and prayed. Immediately, it seemed, my load was lifted. I wanted to shout, I was so full of joy. I did sing, I shouted 'amen'; my soul was filled with a great joy.

"All this was not an emotional fervor, as you may think," he added, noting the look of amazement in the face of the Russian. "For some, no doubt, it was, for there were always numerous 'backsliders' after such a series of meetings, and sometimes a second series had to be held to bring to converted sinners the confirmation of Pentecost.

"After my conversion, I felt that I could not return to my old life. Not that it was not a worthy occupation; not that my new faith placed me above my fellows and the ordinary ways of living, but because I wanted to tell people about Jesus.

"The ranch owner, Mr. Scott, thought it was a good idea, and encouraged me to go off to school. I had had only elementary schooling, but he thought I could get a college education, as he said I was bright, and thanks to his faith in me, I did go to school, and got a degree after six years.

"Although," smiled Lyle, "Mr. Scott's encouragement may have been in self-interest. He let me have a hundred dollars and gave me more later, but said that it was worth it to him, as I had become so careless about equipment that I was better off the place than on."

Major Markov laughed heartily at this.

"Well, I can understand your Mr. Scott, for in the army they court-martial you if you lose a piece of equipment. Common soldiers are put on bread and water if they lose so much as a tin fork."

"Yes," commented Lyle. "I have observed that armies guard their equipment, but waste their men. But I may say in my own defense that I never lost a calf or a cow."

The Russian poured out more tea. Together they had nibbled most of the *zakuska*. He beckoned to a waiter.

"No," protested Lyle. "I have had enough, thank you."

"And you have never regretted your decision?" asked Markov ruminatively.

Lyle's eyes glowed.

"Never," he exclaimed. "I thank God every day that he has allowed me to come here."

"You never get homesick for your Texas plains?"

"Oh, yes, indeed," said Lyle. "I miss them very much. But always one is recompensed. There were, for instance, no mountains there, while now it is my privilege to live in the sight of one of the noblest mountains to be found in all the world. At least, so writers say who have traveled widely. There are few mountains like Ararat. Not until I had come to the East and looked upon the ancient hills of Turkey and, more latterly, upon Ararat, did I understand what the Psalmist meant when he said,

" 'I will lift up mine eyes unto the hills, from whence cometh my help.'

"Ararat is indeed a majestic mountain, a mountain of divine promise," he continued. "It is a mountain, Major, in the presence of which one cannot live without feeling the presence of God and His eternal promise."

"What is that promise?"

"The promise given unto Noah, and again to all his children through our Lord Jesus—that we are God's children, the creatures of His love, over whom He is continually watchful, whom He will no more destroy, but redeem to everlasting salvation. All faith, indeed, all mystery, comes to focus on Ararat, for it was here that God first covenanted with man. By that act the Omnipotent limited His omnipotence, the Eternal took cognizance of the ephemeral, divinity was joined with humanity, and man lifted up to God."

Major Markov considered this, and then remarked, with a piercing glance at the missionary,

"Do you ever have a desire to cross the Araxes and scale Ararat?"

The question took the missionary by surprise.

"No," he replied, "I am content to live on this side of the Araxes, to dwell in faith."

"That's where you and I are different. I am a Promethean. I could not live in the sight of Ararat a year before I had climbed to the top, and put my foot on its everlasting snows, and beheld the world from the heart of the mystery.

"But I have kept you long enough. There is just one further question I should like to ask you. You have spoken several times of 'souls being lost,' or 'in sin.' What I would like to know is this: how can a soul be lost when the eye of God—as you say—is upon His smallest creature? And how can a man be 'in sin' when man was created by God, and presumably whole and perfect? In the words of one of the Persian poets, 'Did then the hand of the Potter shake?'"

This was a question upon which wiser and profounder men than Lyle had stumbled. He seemed to realize this, and he paused before giving answer. He was too trusting to believe other than that Major Markov's question was sincere; he treated the officer as one earnestly desiring light, and he endeavored to give him the best light of which he was capable. The answer he finally gave was not in terms of the absolute, for he intuitively recognized that no question is ever asked in the absolute, but from the need of him who asks, and answers must be given in the personal terms of the questioner.

"I cannot answer for God," he said slowly. "Whether men are lost or in sin in His sight is something for Him to say. I only know that men, everywhere, feel lost and in sin. Some feel lost spiritually, some intellectually, some emotionally, some merely economically, and some morally. But all have a sense of being lost, of being uncertain of the path they follow, uncertain as to where it leads them in the end. And they lift their hands for guidance, and cry out for salvation, and seek a fold where they may be secure. It is to these that Christ—the Good Shepherd—offers His hand, His words, His love, His bosom."

"It has been kind of you to talk to me," said Major Markov, laying his napkin on the table, "and I have been much interested. This will be, I am afraid, our last meeting, for I am to be transferred shortly to Galicia. I am afraid, also, that I shall never climb Ararat and pierce the mystery, but some day, perhaps, my son shall. He is a promising Promethean."

They rose and went out. In the street they shook hands.

"But before I go," said Markov, "a word of advice about the *ukase*. Don't worry too much about it. I should say, forget it, and tell your people to settle at Bartzan." He laughed. "These bureaus, you know, are vast sleeping rooms, where cases and cobwebs collect and are disturbed only when the snoring begins to vibrate the rafters. Your case will repose in peace, and meantime your people can continue to plant and harvest, and be peaceful and multiply."

"Thank you for your good advice and encouragement," said Lyle. "And may God go with you and bring you eventually to His peace."

6. Growth of a Child

WHEN Miriam Verian's baby was sixteen months old she began to talk, and one of the first words she learned was "Amos." This was quite natural, for Amos Lyle came by nearly every day to see how Miriam and Sirani were getting along. Miriam would say, "Here comes Uncle Amos," and Sirani would come toddling to the gate, laughing and babbling. As the Armenian word for "uncle" was beyond her, Sirani learned simply "Amos."

This delighted Lyle. He would dandle her on his foot, his legs crossed, holding her two hands, or carry her about

on his shoulder, all the time talking to her as though she
understood every word he said, while Miriam would look
on in rapture and awe as if she could not comprehend
the fact that this wonderful, small being was her own.
Lyle involuntarily used English in talking to Sirani, and
the child learned that language along with her native
Armenian.

While Miriam was holding school, she kept Sirani in the
room with her, and the child soon learned to be very
quiet and amuse herself with bits of paper or blocks of
wood while Miriam was holding classes. The presence of
a baby in the room did not distract the children, as it
might have done in a more formally conducted school, for
the Armenians understood family life and its requirements, and Sirani's presence was the most natural thing
in the world.

At the age of two Sirani was drawing pictures in the
sand, or on paper when she had crayon and paper. These
were not mere markings, but meaningful, if immature in
technique: such things as a dog, or Amos—Amos distinguishable by the fact that the dog was equipped with a
tail—trees, Ararat, a house. When Sirani was four she
could make all the characters of the Armenian alphabet,
and at five she could read and write. At two, also, Sirani
could sing—that is, she formed her childish sounds into a
pattern of melody and rhythm that conveyed an idea,
though the idea was in harmony with her age and attain-
ments and was perhaps understandable only by others of
her own age. At four she could carry melodies that others
had created originally; this marked a growth of her technique, if it did not necessarily indicate a maturing of her
own idea. At four, also, she had a range of stories which
she had invented to fill her hours alone, or to entertain
anyone who would listen.

All this indicated, not that Sirani was an extraordinary
child, but that she was much as are all other natural,
intelligent children. If there was anything extraordinary
about her it was this: she was a child, not an immature
adult, as so many children are forced to be, either by
circumstances or by training.

Miriam never mentioned the tragedy through which she had passed, despite the fact that it was when she looked upon Sirani and saw her husband's image that these recollections obtruded most poignantly. Miriam never imposed her grief, or her personality, upon her child. Lyle, the only other person with whom Sirani came in daily contact, was of course of another breed; he could be in no company without its being aware of his personality, his vast cheer, and radiant enthusiasm. But Sirani would never learn from him of sorrow and repression and hardship.

Lyle's enthusiasm was never oppressive: he never dominated Sirani by insisting upon telling the child his stories, instead of listening to hers, by insisting upon teaching instead of learning, imparting his own wisdom instead of imbibing the deeper, simpler, more natural wisdom of the child. This was because childhood had assumed a mystical quality to Lyle; having never had wife nor children of his own, the begetting and rearing of children were mysteries of creation which he contemplated worshipfully. Since Haig's running away Lyle had begun to consider this mystery of childhood more seriously, more systematically if that could be said of one who was innocent of system in all things else; and when Sirani came, she did not become to him, as many children become, one who must helplessly accept the infliction of an elder's moods, but one of whom an elder should learn.

When Sirani was seven years old, she was left motherless. Miriam's death was not unexpected, nor violent, but a gradual fading, like a twilight that loves the day, yet welcomes the night and finds it comforting and sinks into it willingly. Miriam indeed was like a summer day out of its season, too brief, too poignant, too lovely to endure. Some months before her death she had talked with Lyle about herself, about Emmanuel, about Sirani.

"Sirani is a lovely child," she had said. "If I should go, what would happen to her?"

"She is in God's keeping, as are all His creatures."

"And so I think. And for that reason, I am not afraid to

leave her behind. She must live her life, be it long or short, active or quiet, and breathe her fragrance upon the world, and then she will join us who have gone before."

"You must not talk of going," remonstrated Amos Lyle gently. "The Lord still has need of you in His vineyard."

"I shall not go until He calls me, but I long to be with Emmanuel again, walking in the garden with him, holding his hand, and listening to his voice."

The passion of her desire to be united with her husband was hardly apparent in her face. It remained calm and pale, beautifully contoured, as always, without blemish or wrinkle, or strain; her dark eyes were calm; her hands, white, long, and delicate, were folded in her lap as she talked. Amos Lyle thought of pictures of the Virgin Mary he had seen, and it flashed over him why a large body of Christians could focus their adoration upon the Virgin rather than upon the Son.

"You do not understand this desire, Amos Lyle," said Miriam, "for your Master lives with you daily; but for me Emmanuel is gone. Though I trust in God, and believe that He will unite me again with my husband, yet Emmanuel is gone, and I do not know where he is."

In that instant, Amos Lyle caught an understanding of a great mystery, a mystery which to most men of strong faith remains always a secret. He understood how the women at the tomb must have felt when they found the rock rolled away and the body of their Lord taken away. Their lament was the universal cry of mankind, who, trusting in God, are in perplexity as to the meaning of His ways. "I know not where they have laid him." Though we strain to pierce the veil, he thought, it is not until death comes that many shall ever learn the secret.

"I am ready to go, not because I do not love life, but because it has given me all that it has to offer. Life has been very sweet. It gave me love, without which I would be nothing, and if I should cling to life, in preference to my love, both life and love would be worthless. When I go, I shall carry memories of the pleasantness of this world, of the golden sun, and the creeping mists of morning, the hyacinth in the garden, and the oasis in the desert, the mountains, purple and majestic, and the yellow plains, the cities I have seen, the affection I have known, laughing children, and the joy of having a child. All these memories I shall carry with me, and they shall be my heaven. For perhaps that is what heaven is, Amos Lyle, a state in which the beauties of the earth have been sifted of pain and ugliness and sorrow, a place in which we may walk with those we have loved.

"You do a good service, Amos Lyle, for by fixing the eyes of men upon their Heavenly Father you help them to realize the blessings and the beauties with which God has scattered the earth.

"As for Sirani, I would ask only one thing. Teach her, Pastor Lyle, to have no hate in her heart, and to love all sorts and conditions of mankind. I cannot forget that, though it was a Turk who killed my husband, it was also a Turk who saved me and protected me, while I was bearing Sirani, and who finally, out of his love for me, released me and sent me to you."

After Miriam Verian's death, Sirani came to live with Amos Lyle. For a moment, perhaps, Lyle was tempted to condemn Miriam for her willingness to forsake her responsibility to her child for the hope of reunion with her husband, but he quickly recovered himself, remembering that it was for God to judge, and that His ways are inscrutable.

He was, however, alarmed for some time over the responsibility he had assumed in Sirani. He who had lived alone for most of his fifty-two years—whose manner of living was one pretty much of catch as catch can, sometimes with food in the house, sometimes with none, clothes never hung on pegs, tables never dusted, lamps running low in the middle of the evening, bed never made, everything in fact disorganized—was no one to accept the meticulous routine that a child demands if it is to thrive. Routine is the easy condition of the child. Amos Lyle knew that. He had observed how quickly children adopt habit, how in those households where order was habitual the children

were peaceful and contented, and he was acutely aware of
his shortcomings in this respect.

Amos Lyle was not a creature of habit, and he doubted
whether, except by a miracle of God, he could ever become one. He himself had been left an orphan at Sirani's
age, and from that moment habit had disappeared from
his life. Whatever remained at the age of fifteen had been
extinguished when he became a cowhand on the ranch.
Herding cattle was a matter in which one consulted the
needs of the cattle rather than the needs of men; and human habits surrendered to those of the herd. Such things
as a regular bed, or regular meals, did not exist on the
range; even hot coffee was foregone for as long as forty-
eight hours at a stretch.

Still, Lyle thought, if one could lose his sense of habit
for the sake of a herd of cattle, he should be able to regain
it for the sake of a child. If he had ridden into the teeth
of a blizzard to bring in a freezing heifer, and had considered it only in the day's work, surely he could look after
a child, and not consider it a burden.

But Sirani was far from being a burden. She was, at the
age of seven, old enough to bathe and dress herself, and
attend to most of her wants. She required very little in the
way of attention. Moreover, she had radiant health and
vitality. Lyle's business consisted in calling on his congregation, visiting and preaching among the nearby villages that had grown up on the Bartzan plain, helping in
the field when the harvest was heavy, visiting the sick, and
of evenings writing a great number of letters. Sirani did
not interfere with these duties; after breakfast was over
she went to the school that Garabed Khansourian now
taught alone, and when she came home she rolled a hoop
with the other children or skipped a rope until Lyle's appearance. Supper was always light, food never being too
plentiful anyway, and then Lyle read his Bible for a time.
Formerly he read it to himself, after clearing the table and
washing the dishes; but now Lydia Kovian came around
each day to attend to that and to make the beds and to
wash Sirani's clothes. After supper, then, Lyle read the
Bible aloud to Sirani, and to Lydia if she had come.

Sirani would sit very quietly. Only now and then would she fidget, as when they were in the Prophets. Then she would find a bit of thread to play with, or she would slip down and begin to stroke the cat. After the reading, if it was still early, she herself would read, from some of the Armenian or Russian or Persian legends which her mother had collected for her, while Amos Lyle worked energetically at his letter writing.

Particularly did Amos Lyle learn from Sirani new things about the Bible narrative. To him the narrative of Genesis, the wanderings of the Exodus, the sins of the Kings, the admonitions of the Prophets, the story of the Gospels, all were surcharged with vast and oracular meaning. The people with whom these books dealt were not ordinary men in any sense, but majestic figures, speaking in strange tongues from heights above the day to day. This was no doubt because Lyle's acquaintance with Scripture began after his "conversion," when he was already grown.

To the child Sirani, the characters of the Bible were personages whom she might have seen here at Bartzan, personages superior perhaps to any she had known but essentially of the same fiber and mold. When they were reading of David's encounter with Goliath, Sirani remarked,

"I think David's mother must have been very frightened when she heard about it."

For a moment Amos Lyle was startled at this comment: he had visualized this battle as a titanic conflict of moral forces rather than of persons; he had never thought of the fact that David had a mother who, like all mothers, did not want her son to die in battle. He recovered quickly, however, and answered,

"Oh, I don't think so. His mother trusted in God, and knew that Jehovah would give victory to her son."

But later on, he began to show these childish questions more respect, and to discover that through Sirani's eyes he was beholding riches in the Scriptures that he had never considered before. And he began to understand more clearly a phrase which he had often used, "And a little child shall lead them." While God spoke to the nations in

the roll of the thunder, and revealed His face in the light-
nings, He also came into the hearts of men as a child steals
into a congregation, as Sirani came into Amos Lyle's life,
not demanding adoration but winning it by the power of
calling forth response.

And as Amos Lyle had looked to his God as a loving
father, so it was only after Sirani came to live with him
that he began to understand the depth and breadth and
unutterable wealth of meaning in that concept. If his own
power of affection could be so enormously expanded by
becoming a foster father, he thought, how great indeed
must be the love of the Heavenly Father.

7. Colonel Markov

THE year 1904—the same year in which was celebrated, on
the American continent, the centennial of the Louisiana
Purchase and a hundred years of peaceful occupation and
development of the Mississippi Valley—was marked in the
Russian Empire by widespread social and political disturbances verging on national revolution. In the country,
the peasants were discontented because of poor crops, low
prices, high taxes, and an oppressive landlordism. In the
cities, which were expanding with a lush growth of industrialism—the new talisman by which Russia hoped to
attain the cultural and economic status of the countries of
Western Europe—the proletariat were restless under the
growing conviction that the system of private capitalism
under which they worked was rapacious rather than benevolent, and that they were being exploited rather than
benefited. Among the tribes and subject races, also, resentment was rising against the Russian overlordship, the aristocratic Muscovite nobility, and the vast, complicated, and
unresponsive bureaucracy, centered in Petersburg, by
which they were governed.

Under the burden of prosecuting the war with Japan, in which ineptness and waste were everywhere revealed, the administration had broken down, and discontent welled forth in revolt and rioting in all parts of the Empire.

In the oil town of Baku, on the Caspian, conditions were particularly bad. The oil fields were rich, and new extractive and refining processes, along with the coming of the internal combustion engine and new uses for petroleum as fuel, had brought boom times, febrile activity, and prosperity for everyone except the oil field workers. The great concern was to drill more wells, to get more oil; work went on ceaselessly, day and night, under the most distressing conditions of human existence. Pay was good, but everything one bought with this pay was high, so that at the end of the week or the year, the haggard worker emerged exhausted, or maimed, with no more in his pocket than when he entered.

The inhabitants of Azerbaijan, the province of which Baku was the capital, were Tartars. They had occupied this land for some seven hundred years, settling there at the time of the great migrations from Central Asia in the days of Tamerlane and Genghis Khan. By long custom they were pastoral and nomadic; but with the industrialization of the area, they were gradually forced by economic pressure into the status of day laborers—porters, small craftsmen, and oil field workers. And as they gradually submerged, there rolled over them a new bourgeoisie attracted by the prosperity of the oil drillings—tradesmen, managers, bookkeepers, restaurateurs, and other commercialists. Chief among these newcomers were the Armenians, who, like the Jews in Europe, had formed a volatile element in the population as a result of the oppression of many years.

In 1905 occurred outbreaks against the Armenians of Baku and Azerbaijan, accompanied by rioting and massacres, indulged in both by Armenians and by Tartars, during the course of which the Balakhani and Bibi-Eybat oil works were razed by fire. The viceroy at Tiflis, to whom the representatives of the English and Swedish oil companies made prompt representations, was finally moved to action. Troops were despatched to the area.

The officer who had charge of these troops was Stepan Mikhailovitch Markov, now a colonel in rank.

One Sunday afternoon in August, Colonel Markov's intelligence staff received word of a concentration of Tartars at the Gara-agach *khan* on Alexei Varanoff Avenue above the Hotel Metropole, where they were being harangued and incited to march into the Armenian quarter and burn it to the ground. The leader of this mob was Baba Ibrahim, a fanatic mullah notorious for his Armenian antipathies.

Colonel Markov immediately ordered police guards stationed at all the side streets leading into Alexei Varanoff above the hotel, while he proceeded to the head of the avenue with a body of mounted Cossacks.

Before these dispositions had been made, however, the Tartars had already reached a pitch of frenzy and, led by Baba Ibrahim, were coming down the street just as Markov and his Cossacks appeared.

The iron shutters had been run down on all the shops in the street, as well as on the Hotel Metropole, but a crowd of the guests had gathered on the balconies of the hotel to watch the excitement.

When it seemed that a clash was inevitable, the women and most of the men among these spectators had withdrawn within the hotel. Remaining on the first balcony, however, was a small group which included two American petroleum engineers, an English company manager, a Greek who operated some freighters on the Caspian, and a Turkish military officer.

"This looks like it's going to be a good show," remarked one of the Americans, leaning over the balcony with only one interest in life, that of the satisfaction of his curiosity.

"It sure does," agreed his companion. "But I'll bet it isn't as good as a lynching. I saw one in Muskogee once."

The Englishman clasped and unclasped his hands.

"These things are terrible," he said nervously, while he continued to watch. "We never have any trouble like this in India."

The Greek, who could speak no English, was white with fear, but he dared not leave because of the greater fear of losing caste with the other Europeans.

The Turk likewise said nothing, but at the Englishman's remark produced a cigarette case, extracted a cigarette, and offered the case to the others, accompanying the offer with an expression that was between a smile and a sneer.

"Thanks," responded one of the Americans and accepted one.

The Englishman declined, as did the other American, but he, by way of explanation, pulled out a pipe and lighted it, all the while keeping his eye on the proceedings below.

The Tartar mob was densely packed. Most of the men were dressed in the half length *beshmeths* of workmen and wore felt skull caps, but the presence of many bare, shaven heads indicated their fanatic temper. By the mullah's exhortations they were in a state of religious frenzy, in which "death to the Armenians" would not only avenge their personal and social wrongs, but their faith as well, and win them entry into their Mohammedan paradise.

At the sight of the mounted men facing them, the cry went up "The Cossacks!" and some of those in the van fell back in dismay. At this, Baba Ibrahim, a tall, cadaverous Tartar, with a wildness of expression that was enhanced by a scar that extended from his forehead to his chin, began to cry, "*Wallah, wallah, jehad, jehad,*" and to move down the street waving his arms above his head like a prophet of old.

"And now for the whiff of grapeshot," remarked the Turk, flicking his cigarette ash, and moving ever so slightly to the edge of the balcony.

His manner was one of impersonality toward the proceedings. He regarded the affair with the air of a scientist examining a retort.

But the Cossack commander apparently was not disposed to be ruthless. The Cossacks had not unslung their rifles, which they carried across their backs, and Colonel

Markov had dismounted and was walking slowly forward
to meet Baba Ibrahim.

"Whew, that fellow's got nerve," whistled the first
American, as the colonel advanced. He was now in front
of the hotel, almost beneath the balcony.

The Turkish officer shrugged his shoulders.

"Very bad judgment, I should say."

Baba Ibrahim had paused, with arms upraised and
outspread, to suspend the movement of the mob, and
with staring, defiant eyes, he watched Colonel Markov
approach.

Colonel Markov called out,

"Baba Ibrahim *khodja*."

The mullah continued to stare, and Colonel Markov
spoke again,

"Baba Ibrahim *khodja*, I wish to speak with you."

Baba Ibrahim opened his mouth. For a moment the
words did not come, and then—

"Yes, Excellency, I listen."

Baba Ibrahim approached respectfully, while Colonel
Markov also advanced slowly. When they were together
Colonel Markov began to speak to him. The conversation
was brief, and in a tone so low that it could not be heard.

The parley seemed to turn out satisfactorily, for Baba
Ibrahim motioned his followers back and Colonel Markov
turned and started towards his men.

Before Colonel Markov had gone a dozen steps, however, a stone was hurled from the crowd, which struck
and felled him. The cry of *"Wallah, jehad"* rose from a
hundred throats, and in a mad stampede, the crowd began
to charge down the street. Colonel Markov staggered to
his feet and, whistling for his troops, sought to defend
himself with his side arms.

The Cossacks charged, shouting their war cry, and in a
moment they had established contact and were lashing
their opponents with their knouts. For a time the Tartars
stood firm, unflinching under the knotted scourge, pelting
the Cossacks with rocks, and defending themselves with
clubs and iron bars.

Colonel Markov was not to be seen. Either he had been

borne down, or was hidden in the mêlée. Deprived of his leadership the troops were fighting furiously but not intelligently. At one moment they had the mob on the go, and then before they could consolidate, the Tartars were collected in another quarter of the street, had regained their courage and were pelting and jeering the Cossacks. The fight would begin again; reinforcements would join the crowd, and the Cossacks would be at bay, overwhelmed, and forced to retreat.

The street was becoming littered with the fallen, borne down with the knout and hoof, lying with cracked heads and broken bodies.

"God almighty," groaned one of the engineers, while he kept his eye glued to the spectacle.

The Englishman and the Greek had retired, leaving the Turkish officer as their only companion. The officer's previous nonchalance had disappeared in a keen interest in all that went on.

"Where's the colonel—the fellow in charge?" asked the second American anxiously.

"He was picked up by one of his men and carried off to that side street yonder. Did you not observe?" responded the officer, from whose keen eyes nothing escaped.

"No, I missed that. Was he badly hurt?"

"Apparently."

The street battle had now been going on for half an hour. Horses and men were becoming wearied from attacking the apparently constantly renewed horde. Reinforcements for the troops were not coming up.

Finally, one of the sergeants loosened his rifle and began to fire. Up until now only the knout had been used. It had been in the nature of a police affair, a battle of fist and club and knout. The sound of rifle fire was signal for bloody work.

The rifles produced an immediate reaction. The mob fell back in a scramble for shelter. The troops were able to re-form their lines. The resistance of the mob had made the Cossacks furious, and now they turned to the rifle and revolver with blood lust and vengeance. Under the cruel assault the crowd began to melt, leaving dead and wounded everywhere. The gutters in front of the hotel were flowing red with blood.

In ten minutes—the three men on the balcony had hardly had time to take refuge from the fire—it was all over. Within a half hour the ambulances and carts and police wagons had picked up the dead and wounded, and the street cleaners were busy washing down the street and sprinkling it with lime. In ninety minutes the shutters of the shop windows were open, and the street was again busy with trade.

In the bar, whither they had taken refuge, the first engineer spoke to the Turkish officer,

"You'll have a drink with us, won't you? My name's Joslin, Tim Joslin, and this is Mr. Hopkins, Jake Hopkins. I didn't get your name?"

"Hashim Farouk is the name—colonel and military attaché of His Majesty's Embassy at St. Petersburg."

"I see. I suppose you're down here to see how the Russian army performs. Waiter!"

The waiter came up.

"What'll it be?"

"Thank you, but it is forbidden by my religion to drink. I will have a glass of mineral water, however."

"Well, there's nothing in my religion against drinking, thank God. Bet you got an eyeful on the balcony. I never saw so much cutting up in my life. Those boys are tough. They didn't seem to know when they were whipped."

"The Tartar is a good fighter. Naturally I would think so, since the Turks and Tartars are racially allied. But I must explain that I didn't come down here to see the fighting. A military attaché cannot go wandering over the country at will. I am on my way to Turkey, on leave, and I came down the Volga, through the Caspian to Baku, and will go tomorrow to Batum, and thence to Constantinople. It was merely fortunate that I had a chance to observe."

The waiter brought the drinks. The engineer who had been talking now examined his glass ruminatively, and followed this examination by a survey of the ornate French wall decorations. The bar was partly filled, and little groups here and there were discussing the riot with bated breath. No one except the Americans seemed willing to talk very loud, for fear of being overheard by secret agents of the Okhrana.

"I suppose, being a Turk," said the engineer, judiciously, "that your sympathies in this matter are with the Tartars."

"On the contrary, no. I think they acted very badly—very unintelligently, I may say. Naturally, also, I am on the side of law and order."

"I don't imagine you like the Armenians, from all I've read."

"Oh, no, you are wrong again," asserted Hashim Farouk, smiling blandly. He was obviously pleased to be in the company of foreigners of position—as he took these men to be—and flattered to have his opinions consulted. "The Armenians are a race of superior quality. They are a very intelligent people, very shrewd I should say, generally honest, and law-abiding. In every way, except in the matter of pugnacity and fighting qualities, they are superior to the Tartars."

"Then why in hell—excuse me, Mr. Farouk—but if you don't mind, would you explain why your people have been so interested in getting rid of the Armenians?"

"Partly because they are superior. They have become superior to their background, superior to their government. They have placed themselves under the protection of European powers, rather than trust to Turkish justice and equity, and so have given these powers excuse for interference with domestic affairs. But a larger reason than all—in my own eyes at least—is because they divide the Turanian peoples like a wedge. Some day all Turanians will be united, as all Russians, or all Americans are now, united under one caliph, from the steppes of central Asia to the Bosphorus. Then we shall have pan-Islam. But not until the Armenians are eliminated, for they lie directly between Turkey and Azerbaijan."

"That, I take it, is a pipe-dream of the long distant future—seeing as Russia still can wield a pretty big stick."

"Perhaps," asserted Hashim Farouk calmly. "Perhaps, also, we may both see the day. But let it go for mere speculation, as naturally a person in my position should not be fomenting subversive ideas in a friendly country."

"Oh, I understand you all right. Governments have to maintain appearances just like society matrons, smiling at each other but ready to cut the guts out of the other on a moment's notice."

The talk drifted off into other subjects in a cloud of cigarette and pipe smoke, and presently the Turk rose and bowed, and excused himself.

"An old windbag, if you ask me," said the engineer to his companion. "But I was curious to see what these Turks are like."

"I don't think he is a windbag," countered his companion. "If you ask me, I think he was dead serious. Struck me as a hard customer. Made me think of the time the Bolton gang held up a bank in Tecumseh. The leader was a fellow just like that—small build, hard as nails, eyes that were like knot-holes in a board fence. Knew what he wanted and to hell with the rest. I don't know much history, but I can guess that it was fellows like this Farouk that made the Turkish Empire."

"Yes, that Cossack officer was a different sort, come to think of it. He didn't want to hurt anybody. That's why he got down from his horse. I hope he wasn't badly staved in."

They continued to talk over their glasses until the afternoon papers were cried in the street, and one of the engineers went out and bought one.

"Let's see what it says about the fracas," he said, spreading it out. "Here it is, all over the first page. 'Bloody affair in Alexei Varanoff Avenue.' I can't make the rest out. Damn it all, they ought to get out an English edition."

"It says—yes—I can make it out," said the other. " 'Colonel Markov badly injured—not expected to live.' Something about last rites. Son being called from St. Petersburg. Paul Stepanovitch. Student in the Imperial Military Corps of Cadets. Expected by Moscow-Baku express. Poor fellow. Hope he doesn't die. That would be a shame—"

8. Philosophical Enquiry

THE people to whom Amos Lyle ministered were for the most part a simple people, with simple needs. Lyle himself was a simple man with a simple, direct philosophy. It was not often that his problems took him into the wider orbits of human relations, or that he was required to justify his philosophy in the broader arenas of intellectual conflict. Yet Amos Lyle had an able mind, and though it had been nurtured more by contact with people than with books and formal education, it was competent to face these challenges when they were presented. The first of these challenges had come from Major Markov.

Lyle's meeting with Markov had served to strengthen and clarify his thought, as much as it had served to implant new conceptions of life in the heart of that officer.

The second had come from Garabed Khansourian, mayor of the village, whose affability concealed his own intensity of spirit and passion of conviction. It was from an argument with Khansourian that Amos Lyle finally resolved, for himself, in material and pragmatic terms, the meaning of that lofty faith he possessed in God's guidance and purpose.

Garabed Khansourian was waiting for him, at his house, one morning when he returned from a walk in the village. The year was 1906. Lyle had been thinking of this anniversary year on his walk, observing with satisfaction what seemed to him to be the marks of progress that had occurred in the ten years the Dilijanis had been in Bartzan. He had talked with Mattios Masghian, the lame cabinet-maker, who still thanked God for his blessings, for the miraculous way he had escaped from Turkey despite his infirmity, and for his present strength and health. He had stopped at the little church that had been built in Bartzan, where he saw, with gratitude, a number of Armenian women, kneeling in silent prayer; and he had visited the school, and watched the children, Sirani among them, conning their lessons. All these seemed to Lyle to be the marks of God's grace and beneficence, and the signs of the spiritual fruitfulness of his ministry. There were, of course, things which he did not observe, since they were things which it was not his nature to observe, such as several empty houses, that had become vacant in the past year, and certain untilled fields, and numerous needed repairs in walls and streets. . . .

Garabed Khansourian rose when Lyle entered, and shook hands with the pastor. He was ill at ease for one generally so poised. He had been sitting in Amos Lyle's rocking chair—a type of chair unheard of in Armenia, and the wonder of the community, made for Lyle by Mattios when the cabinetmaker once had wheedled from the missionary his most secret wish. Lyle sat in it to read his Bible. Much as he cherished its comfort, he always looked upon it as slightly sinful, and justified himself by this pious occupation. Lyle thought that perhaps Khansourian was embarrassed at having occupied the rocking chair—it was now rocking violently from the abruptness with which the mayor had stood up.

"Sit down," he said, heartily. "It's for company, for such as don't get dizzy in it. I used to be in the saddle so much that it doesn't bother me. Gives me a feeling of being back on the range to sit in it."

Khansourian seated himself again in the rocker, uneasily, yet feeling that he should, that it was his due as mayor. There were really very few comfortable chairs in Lyle's house.

"You have done a wonderful job as mayor, Garabed," said Lyle. "I was just talking to Kovian, whom I met on the street. Kovian says he has a fair business now, the result of some new regulations you have ordered. I don't know what they are, but I know that your heart is in the right place, and that they are for the people's good."

Khansourian replied graciously with a few compliments of his own, and then, after a little while, brought up the subject of his visit. It concerned a move he was considering.

"I have become," he began somewhat uneasily, "a member of the Dashnak Society."

The Dashnak was a revolutionary organization whose object was the independence, or autonomy, of Russian Armenia, that part of the southern Caucasus lying south of Georgia and west of Azerbaijan. It was allied with similar groups in Turkish Armenia whose agitation had been one of the factors that had brought on the massacres. During the abortive revolutionary movement of 1905 in Russia, the Dashnak had been active among the Armenians and Armenian sympathizers in the cities of the Empire. As a consequence, many of the Dashnakists were now in exile, and the society itself had been officially banned.

Amos Lyle's kindly features became grave at the news that Khansourian was secretly a member of this outlawed organization. They grew more grave at what Khansourian now told him.

"At a meeting in Erivan recently, I was elected one of the secretaries. It means that I shall have to move to Erivan."

"That should be an important position, Garabed, to take you away from your people here," said Lyle thoughtfully, looking down at his gaunt hands, turning them over and over. "You have been mayor of Bartzan now for ten years, and Bartzan has prospered in the Lord."

"Yes, I may modestly say," replied Khansourian, his ease returning, "that as mayor I have done something to unite the people with a community sense. I saw that proper ground was chosen for the burying of the dead, that refuse and sewage were properly disposed of, that the children had a school—though I am quite embarrassed to speak of my abilities as a teacher, the great influence being that of our departed sister, Miriam Verian—God rest her soul— that games and dances were arranged for our holidays; in fact, many things."

"I do not know how we should have got along without you. Is this an important service, that you must leave us?"

"It is a call to a larger service. Of course, my work will

be known only to the elect, those who love our nation, and are willing to serve it in secret. The directors have agreed to find work for me in Erivan, to provide an appearance of occupation. I will be ostensibly an employee of a firm of cognac makers, while I will spend most of my time in organizing groups of Dashnak and cultivating an interest in our objects."

It was not Amos Lyle's custom to counsel his people on their worldly concerns or movements. He believed that in personal decisions one's conscience, and not one's pastor, should offer guidance. Whoever listened to the still small voice would hear presently, clearly and unmistakably, the will of God spoken. What was put into the heart to do was of God, and in accordance with His purpose.

But of recent years, the question of what attitude the Armenians should take toward their political and economic environment was more and more obtruding itself. The welcome which they had sought in Russia had not been forthcoming; they were in many ways little better off than they had been in Turkey. Particularly since the political disturbances of 1904 and 1905, oppression of the minority subject peoples of the Empire had increased, and the exactions imposed upon the Armenians had become oner-ous. It was clear that they lived under a hostile and un-friendly government.

Lyle could not but feel that this hostility was the result of the agitation that had been growing, among influential Armenians, for larger political freedom, either independ-ence or autonomy. The same situation was arising in Russian Armenia that had arisen in Turkish Armenia.

Lyle felt that he should speak.

"I do not think you are following the right course, Garabed," he said positively, turning his deep-set eyes directly on the mayor, "but I would not wish to persuade you otherwise, if you are convinced that this is God's will."

"Pastor Lyle," Khansourian protested, "you have given twenty years and more—soon it will be twenty-five years of your life—to our people; and so you must love them. But how can your ministrations mean anything unless and until our people are free? You merely stanch the wounds

that others inflict. Only when our people are free politically can their souls be free; not until they are independent will they be happy. They may go to heaven when they
die, but that release, that freedom you preach, is to be
found only in death. We must work to free Armenia, we
must look forward to the day when the Russian and Turkish lordship is overthrown, and then our Church, our
faith, will be free; then the hopes which are raised by our
faith will be realized. This is what I must devote my life
to, to making a free and independent Armenia."

Amos Lyle walked back and forth in the little room, his
head down, his gaunt frame bowed in thought. Finally,
he turned to the mayor, his hands clasped before him
awkwardly.

"Did I believe with you that the soul can be free only
when the body is free," he said earnestly, while his
knuckles turned from red to white under the pressure,
"the question remains, how will you achieve this freedom? Do you suppose that the Tsar, any more than the
Sultan, would grant independence to the Armenians—
which would mean surrendering also sovereignty over the
lands which the Armenians occupy—without a struggle,
in which blood would be shed, in which the young men
of the nation would give up their lives, while widows and
orphans would be multiplied, to weep over their dead?
And what assurance is there that such sacrifice would be
rewarded by success? The Turks and Russians, either of
them, have many times more soldiers than the Armenian
nation could possibly provide. They are, moreover, warlike peoples, who have placed their trust in force, and
force will prevail in any struggle that is pitched in that
arena.

"As for us, let us rather trust in the Lord God. Our kingdom, as Jesus Christ said, is not of this world, though it
may exist in this world, for it is above the things of this
world. Remember the words of the Apostle Paul, 'No man
that warreth entangleth himself with the affairs of this
life.' "

Garabed Khansourian arose and unbuttoned the top of
his frock coat so that he could talk more freely—he was al-

ways meticulous about his dress, considering it necessary to his dignity as mayor, and wore a long frock coat with velvet lapels.

"Do you mean to say, pastor," he asked, "that our nâtion must never hope to be independent, to pursue its own customs and ways and worship God in its own traditional manner? That we must never hope for freedom in our business, in our ordinary affairs, unless we give up our nation and become Russians? What does that mean? Utter extinction! Forced into ghettos, as were the Jews, forced to give up our language, and all its heritage of poetry and literature. Marry our daughters off to Russians, so that they have Russian names, ourselves convert our good Armenian names into guttural Russian! Who are these Russians, anyway? Who were they before Rurik the Viking made them into a nation? We Armenians have a lineage more ancient than the Jews. We have a great history. At one time Armenia extended over all that land from the Caspian to the Black Sea and westward almost to the Mediterranean. Our kings treated with the Roman emperors as equals, and the *basilei* at Byzantium sought our alliance in the wars with the Parthians. Our nation was the first to accept Christianity. Our king Tiridates accepted the faith for himself and for his people many years before Constantine raised the labarum over the Roman standard. When finally the Moslem swept over Anatolia, and Byzantium was overwhelmed, many of the Greeks accepted the Prophet Mohammed to save their necks. But we Armenians remained steadfast in our faith. An island of Christianity in a sea of Islam, for centuries submerged, cut off from all intercourse with our brothers in the West, but we remained true.

"Is this then the reward we must accept for this steadfastness, in this age of democracy and new liberties for peoples, passively to accept strangulation through Russification? No, no, pastor! We must resist, we must strive by all means at our hand to preserve our nation, by secret or open methods, and to hope for that day when the Russian power will collapse, and we shall again be a free nation."

"What you say is very logical and appealing," responded Lyle, his mental faculties rising to this challenge, "and I will not attempt to answer with logic, remembering that the Gospel was foolishness to the Greeks, greatest masters of all the logical processes.

"Once, when we had driven some cattle over into Arizona, I spent a day in climbing down the Grand Canyon of the Colorado. This canyon is very deep—over a verst—and, so scientists say, was cut by the river and rains, by many thousand years of slow washing of the water. But the strange part of this was that I picked out of the wall of the canyon, many thousand feet down, a sea shell, perfectly whorled as when it had been spun by the little creature whose home it once had been. The scientists explained that the rock layer from which I picked this shell, far down and covered over with layers of other forms of rock, had once been the floor of a sea. The land had lifted, the sea had dried up; what had once been the sea bed was now a plain, which after untold years became covered with a red soil, blown in by the winds. The land again sank, and again became a sea, again was lifted, and became the dry earth, through which a stream meandered on its way to the ocean. This stream became in time the river, its valley the canyon, and after millions of years from the time of its original deposit the shell was again uncovered to the light of day. How many other shells are there, waiting until they shall be uncovered, I do not know, but this one was uncovered. It had been buried no one knows how long, but God in His infinite wisdom called it forth, a moral perhaps for a doubting generation.

" 'There is nothing covered, that shall not be revealed,' said Jesus. All those that have been scattered shall be gathered together. Nothing that lives shall perish. Whatever is good and holy and true in the Armenian heritage will not be lost. It may disappear from our sight, but it is not gone, as Jesus was not gone from our midst when He ascended into heaven, as the flower has not gone when its petals are torn apart—for its fragrance has been breathed upon the world—as a song is not gone when the singer perishes, but lives on in the heart.

"Do we not err, Garabed, in seeking to preserve that which is visible rather than that which is secret and hidden from the eye? Do we not err, when we say, 'We have a church, therefore we have preserved our faith'?"

"But, pastor," interrupted Khansourian, "you yourself have devoted your life to ministering to Armenians, rather than to others; yes, even to a remnant of the Armenians, the survivors of a single community of Turkish Armenians. But there are other Armenians. Why have you felt that you should remain here if not to preserve on a small scale that which I wish to preserve on a larger?"

"I minister to the people on the plain of Bartzan because God sent me here. When the grain is white to harvest about me, should I go and seek another field? One can cut no wider swathe in a big field than in a little—that depends upon the length of one's arm. You can pick up pebbles only one at a time, whether on the seashore or on the plain, and you can save a nation only by saving individuals, and I have many 'round about me here who are not yet saved. And if I have devoted myself to one village of Armenians, it is not because they are Armenians, but because they are people, human beings, creatures of God, divine, immortal, all of equal consequence in His eyes whether here or at Erivan or in the larger cities of the world."

Garabed Khansourian rose to take his departure.

"You are very wise, pastor," he said. "I will think on what you say."

Garabed Khansourian did think on what Amos Lyle had said, for a month, but the conclusion of his thinking was a decision to go.

Amos Lyle spent many hours in thought, during the days after the mayor's departure, wondering whether he had said the right things, whether the position he had taken was sound, under any system of rational or pragmatic thinking. He was an American, but he tried to think of himself as an Armenian: he tried to think what a community of Americans would do under similar circumstances, overwhelmed by an arrogant and hostile culture, their cherished institutions threatened, their faith in democracy derided, their system of life built upon what that faith condemned.

Here was something for thought.

How would a community of Americans best preserve their faith in democracy and democratic institutions? To answer that question required an understanding of the essential elements of democracy. What were they? Bicameral legislatures? A division of political power among legislative, executive and judicial functions? The secret ballot? Representative government? Amos Lyle knew enough to recognize that it was none of these, that these were but the outward forms of democracy. He knew that tyranny, oppression, denial of human rights, could all exist in such institutions, as they did in certain large cities, in the industrial centers, and in certain rural areas where Negroes predominated in the population. A community of Americans isolated in Asia, in the time of John Adams, for instance, would have been foolish to fight for the retention of the political forms with which they had become acquainted, for those forms had been profoundly modified since the time of John Adams. Voting privileges had been widely extended, the form of voting had changed, the methods of electing the President, the uses of party organization, and a multitude of other changes had made the democratic forms of 1906 widely different from those of the time of the founding fathers.

Something remained, however, which also had changed, which had become richer and deeper with the passage of the years, which was distinct from the forms and institutions of democratic government. What were these?

They were the principles and spirit of democracy. How were these to be preserved?

Amos Lyle was convinced that they were not maintained by force and warfare. The imposition of democratic institutions did not necessarily make for democracy, as was apparent from the course of events in various European and South American countries that had adopted such institutions. Nor, on the other hand, would the denial, or destruction, of democratic institutions destroy the spirit

of democracy among peoples who had known its blessings. Democracy could live without institutions, but the
institutions were sterile without the spirit.

Moreover, the attempt to maintain democracy by force,
by pressure, by arms, was likely to lead to the destruction of the thing it sought to preserve. What is democracy,
if not respect for human dignity, for human individuality,
for the divine, creative spirit that resides in every human
being, however lowly? These things cannot be destroyed
by external force, for they are of the spirit, which no
sword can penetrate or cut. But they can be destroyed
when the spirit succumbs to the appeal to force to sustain it. For this force means the organization of human
beings under the will of another, and directing all their
aspiration, their individuality, their creative imagination
to one object, the development of a superior physical
force. An army is not formed to write poetry, paint pictures, sing songs, or create homes, but with one object
only, to overcome another physical force, to subdue human
beings. In this process all that democracy stands for—
respect for human dignity, brotherly love, individuality—
goes by the board. The more the democratic nations
make war, the less they remain democracies, but become
highly organized autarchies.

Amos Lyle, perturbed by his thoughts, his inability to
come to a resolution of his logic—which was taking him
farther and farther afield from his primary object, that
of determining what attitude he should take were he in
Khansourian's shoes—rose and walked out along the village street. At the end of the street the plain began, undulating toward the river Araxes and to the mountain
Ararat, which reared its snow-covered head in the distance. Upon its hoary but unwearied shoulders his spirit
had come to rest more than once, in these ten years that
he had been in Bartzan. He now gazed upon it, his eye
carried upward, until it wearied in surveying the heights.

A fantasy of mountain and vale, majestic and awe-
inspiring—heights of every form and shape, precipices
standing in silent and lonely grandeur, and valleys so
deep as to appear liquid and indistinct—a vast panorama

that confused the mind which attempted to grasp it at a single glance. And above all, dwarfing its nearest companion, the diminutive peak upon its shoulder known as Lesser Ararat, soaring high into a firmament, so clear as to impress the imagination with the sense of infinite space, towered the mighty summit of Ararat, a rugged and solitary dome of eternal snow, white like an old man's head, aged with experience and wisdom, wreathed in wisps of cloud like a halo, suggestive of divine peace and understanding.

Amos Lyle continued to think of Garabed Khansourian, and the profound problem his going to Erivan had posed. He had been thinking what he should do as an American, a member of a community of Americans, isolated, say, in Asia, seeking to preserve its traditions and culture. He had thought in terms of democracy, conceiving that to be the unique and precious gift of American culture to the world.

But democracy was not the gift of Armenia. This nation had not for a thousand years known political independence, or a political tradition. Certainly it was not political freedom that had preserved this people as a nation. What was it, aside from the unity and the cohesion given them by their faith, by their ancient Church, with its elaborate rites and highly organized clergy? The Armenian Church was, undoubtedly, a form of political organism, cloaking itself under the name of religion. But the authority of that Church had been sadly weakened in the course of the years, and for many Armenians the only thing left was their faith, which lived apart from their allegiance to the Church.

Was there something more? What were the elements of Armenian culture that deserved to be saved? Their arts, their handicraft? These were undistinguished, and of a bastard character, borrowed from Byzantium and Islam. What was genuine? Their characteristic architecture, for instance, had long since been borrowed by the West, and improved upon in the Gothic style of the Middle Ages. And having been adopted and improved, that was a fruit that had fallen from the tree.

What was the Armenian culture, the Armenian spirit,

that was worth saving, that made Khansourian's going to Erivan justified, that indeed justified Lyle's coming here from America, where there was so much need yet to be met?

Great beads of sweat broke out on Amos Lyle's brow, though the afternoon was cool, and the cooler airs of evening were beginning to fan his cheek. In the distance, the great, snow-capped dome of Ararat was turning pink in the evening light, but it offered him no answer other than the thought that the mountain had stood there, alone, aloof, majestic, as it had stood for so many thousands of years, long after it had served its purpose of providing a landing place for the Ark. Why had it been preserved past its time? Why indeed had Noah been preserved?

These questions seemed beyond Amos Lyle's depth. He was not a questioner, but an exuberant believer. He relied on God to give him directions, and he acted as he was intuitively directed, trusting that this inner wisdom was a wisdom planted there by God for a divine purpose.

But as Amos Lyle wrestled with these problems, he realized that he could not lay them aside without coming to a rational solution. Like Jacob wrestling with the angel, who would not rest nor relax his hold until he had been granted a blessing, so Lyle could not abandon this problem until he had received the answer. To do otherwise would be to stultify himself, to admit that he could not say for what purpose he ministered, or to what end.

Unnoticed, Sirani, now nine years old, came up to him and slipped her hand into his.

"I have been looking for you, Papa Amos," she said. "It is time for supper. You must be hungry."

"Yes, yes, so I am," said Lyle, taking her up in his arms. "Shall we go in?"

"My legs are getting so long that they almost touch the ground," laughed Sirani. "Before long, I shall be as tall as you."

"Oh, no, not so tall as I," he said, as he set her down. "But you are getting tall. We must be getting you some new dresses."

"But this one is all right, Papa. It is patched only a

little. The patches are pretty, aren't they? I like this one with the green and yellow in it."

But Amos Lyle was looking at Sirani, her long, spidery legs, very graceful for all that she was growing into the "awkward" age; her slim arms and long hands, her lovely little head, so round, so beautifully formed, the healthy wheat color of her complexion; her wavy brown hair upon her shoulders; her dancing eyes.

Lyle thought of her as the epitome of all childhood.

He thanked God that, since Sirani was destined to be motherless and fatherless, it was given to him to look after her—to him, who had never married, and had never experienced the great joy of parenthood.

While they walked home, Sirani continued to talk vivaciously about the hundred and one interests of childhood, while Lyle, listening with one ear, continued to think of the philosophical problem he had been considering.

Yet his thoughts kept reverting to Sirani, who was, after all, in the flesh and blood, a subject of thought far more fruitful than any abstraction. He thought of Miriam and Emmanuel, and their deep love for each other. In their devotion to the family altar, they were only like countless other Armenians he knew. . . .

This, he thought, with a dawning comprehension, was the answer that he had been struggling for.

What, after all, does any culture, or any institution of human devising, produce that is more wonderful, more sublime, than human beings? And how better to cultivate this product than by holy, devoted, kindly family life? Is that not the one institution, of all institutions, that is worth preserving? And what gift has the Armenian nation given to the world finer than its men and women, its children, and the homes that shelter them?

Whatever might be the final judgment as to the wisdom of Khansourian's course, Lyle's own philosophy was at last resolved. His course was clear. His task was to continue to minister to individuals, and to devote himself to the preservation of all that was lovely and good in the childhood of Armenia.

9. Death of a Community

THOUGH Amos Lyle did not know it, Bartzan was a dying community. The enthusiasm for the new homeland in Russia, which had brought a few years of growth and expansion of the population scattered in several villages on the Bartzan plain, had spent itself, and no new impetus took its place. Though the land was fertile, after a fashion, it was good only for types of crops unfamiliar to the emigrés. Moreover, title to farms could not be secured, for the Russian government had never given official permission for the Armenians to settle there. Another factor, perhaps, may have been the preference, or greater aptitude, for trade—particularly among those of the people who had lived in the cities and larger towns of Turkey—and the distance of Bartzan from the commercial centers of the Caucasus. Still another was the loneliness of the plain, and the desire to be identified with larger groups, a desire nursed by the feeling of security which a populous center gives, whether reasonably or not. There may have been other causes—a growing hopelessness on the part of the people and a willingness to surrender; a general dying out, or exhaustion, of the spirit of common purpose and racial unity, beaten down first, in Turkey, by outright persecution, and later, in Russia, by suffocation and contempt on the part of the dominant culture.

But Amos Lyle was not aware of this drying up. He never counted noses in his congregation: if one person was listening to what he was saying it made no difference that others were nodding. As long as there was one soul yet to be redeemed, his field was ample. He did not observe, therefore, that land that formerly had been planted was again in grass, that a lassitude was creeping over the people, and that various community activities were being abandoned. People came to bid him good-by; he felt their departure keenly, but soon not at all, for they were not gone to him. They were still in his heart, if not visible to his eye, and he frequently corresponded with them, for he wrote many letters, and his congregation remained as large as ever, if only in his thoughts.

It was not until Neshan Kovian came to him, to tell him that he was leaving, that Amos Lyle really awakened to what was happening to his people. This may have been because Neshan Kovian was going so far away. Kovian had come one evening toward the end of summer, as Lyle was working about some late tomato plants in his garden. The plants had become withered and weed-grown from neglect, for tending a garden was more an exercise than a pursuit to Lyle, and he would leave it for the smallest opportunity to talk. This garden was on the south side of his house, from which he had an unencumbered view of Ararat rising in the distance.

Kovian began by inquiring about the pastor's health, and then after a while he remarked,

"You write a great many letters, pastor."

"Yes," said Lyle. "Christ's community is world-wide, and while our work is here, we must bear in mind our brothers in distant parts. St. Paul founded the Church by his letter writing, you know."

"By writing letters, I presume you get contributions for your work," asked Kovian, who was always interested in the financial aspects of enterprises.

"No, Neshan. My funds come from the Mission Board. People make their contributions to the Board, which distributes them in all parts of the world where its work is carried on, as the need requires."

"I should think that you could get much more money by asking them to send their contributions direct to you."

"Then the work of other missions would suffer. The Board sends me enough. If more were needed, it would come. But people can remember us in their prayers, and their prayers are much more important than their money."

Kovian thought this over, and then said, "I have been thinking of going to America, pastor. Would you give me letters of introduction?"

Amos Lyle was without words. He stood looking at the tomato plants, and then ran his gaunt hands through his iron-gray hair.

"Going to America," he repeated. The word America awakened long-dormant memories. It had been eighteen years since he had been in America, twenty-five years since he had left America to make his home in Armenia. He had returned for his first furlough at the end of seven years on the mission field, when he was still stationed at Dilijan. He had been due to receive another furlough at the end of another seven years, but he had not accepted it. Those were hard years at Bartzan, when the little community was struggling to establish itself in its new home in Russia, and he had felt that his presence was needed there. When the next seven-year term was drawing to a close, the Board had written that its funds were low, intimating that Lyle, who had no family, might renounce his leave in favor of certain ones whose children needed contact with their native culture. Lyle had cheerfully agreed to surrender his third furlough. The fourth was not yet due. In the years that had gone by, America had faded in his memory. But now it all came back. He saw the great plains of the Southwest, undulating to the horizon, cut by the draws of creeks, hidden among the growth of elm and hickory and pecan; upon the higher ground the tall prairie grass, pink and feathery, and sprinkled with blue bonnets like lovely blue stars scattered upon the earth; and the great yellow fields of coreopsis in springtime. He saw the gorgeous Texas skies, blue as nothing else is blue, over which the clouds drove up from the south like white sheep herded across the plain. He remembered the call of the quail, which he had not heard now for eighteen years, but which came upon his ears as clearly as though it were yesterday; and he heard the song of the meadow lark rising above the prairie grass, and the night music of the mockingbird from a dark clump of mesquite.

He remembered his nights in the saddle, as a young man, herding the grazing cattle, with the sky overhead scintillating with a million stars, and the cool fresh wind from the distant Gulf upon his cheek, the contented lowing of the cattle and the sounds of the guitar from the distant ranch house.

The nostalgia that swept over him was like a sudden breaker upon a swimmer. In a second he saw the whole of Texas at a glance, smelt the dust of the plains in his nostrils and the odor of the saddle and sweating horses; and heard the hoofbeats upon the hard road, and his body swayed unconsciously to the rhythm of the canter.

He thought of the people he knew in America, and the thought awakened reminders of his own culture, of his own racial heritage. They were a free people in America, he thought, a happy people, a great people filled with thoughts of great enterprise, a people whose imagination was not limited by the boundaries of their country, but embraced the world. . . . They were a people of great hopes and great generosities, a people hospitable and tolerant and kind, a people at peace with themselves and with all mankind. . . .

His head lifted and Amos Lyle's eyes fell upon Ararat. In the evening sun it was glorious in the distance, majestic in its diadem of cloud, clothed with a raiment of light, its head in the heavens, the earth for its footstool. At the sight of the great mountain, that had come to be his companion and comforter in these latter years, his heart lifted, and he breathed deeply.

"America is a great country, Neshan," he said. "There is opportunity there. But God has walked in this land. It has been His garden from of old, and He loves it. Some day it will be restored as He would have it."

"For a long time I hoped so, pastor, but it is a useless hope. This is a pestilential land. God took His people out of Egypt, and it seems that He has also given signs that this land should be abandoned to the jackals."

"What signs do you see?" inquired Lyle.

"For twelve years now we have been expecting the official permit to settle here. Every year, every month, every day, of these twelve years we have been hoping it would arrive, dreading that the answer would be no, and that we would have to leave. How can one plant with

certainty that he will harvest? How can one build a
house when tomorrow he may be ordered out? I have
long wanted to bring in a millstone, which we could set
up by the stream and grind our grain; instead of having
every woman grind on her own stoop, to let the water do
the work. But millstones are heavy and expensive. If I
brought one in, I might have to abandon it."

"You worry lest we be ordered out," countered Lyle,
"but we have lived here for twelve years. Is that not in
itself a good sign?"

"I grant you that it is a good sign, pastor. But meantime the population diminishes. Four years ago there
were four hundred families here; today there are less
than two hundred. It's not alone the matter of the permit.
People everywhere are moving out of the village into the
towns. Town life is more attractive; it offers more interests and opportunities. I would stay on here, but you
can see, pastor, that there are fewer and fewer opportunities for business. To do business you have to go where
people are, because after all business is just traffic in the
product of people's labor."

"Then why not go to Erivan, like Khansourian," urged
Lyle. "At least, you would still be with your own people,
and I might see you sometimes."

"I thought of that," said Kovian. "You know I love you,
and all these people here, but I am a trader and a merchant, not a politician. Erivan is for politicians, and I do
not like politicians. It's more honorable, I grant, to be a
politician than a trader, but the trader is a man who
wishes peace, while all these politicians are hot-heads. If
they had their way, they would make more trouble for
our people. God pity the day if the country should ever
get in their hands."

"You would not, like Garabed Khansourian, wish to see
Armenia an independent country?" inquired Lyle, sur-
prised. He did not talk politics, and he had never known
Kovian's views before.

"God forbid!" said Kovian emphatically. "We Armenians are traders, or farmers, or, as with those who live
in the mountains, shepherds. For generations and genera-

tions we have lived under the dominion of other races, and we have lost whatever craft we may have had in government.

"It is because of such agitation that this part of the Caucasus is losing its attractiveness, that it is doomed to further decline. I am a shrewd man in a few things, and I can read the signs of the times. This whole part of the world is unsettled. God has set His face against it. No peace, no prosperity. That is why I am going to America—I with all my family."

"Well then," said Lyle, "if that is your decision, I will give you letters of introduction to various friends of mine. They are worthy people I have never met, but whom I have known through correspondence. God bless and prosper you, and I hope you will let us hear from you, as often as possible. When do you plan to go?"

"Within the month. I have been collecting rugs, choice pieces that are of little bulk but much value. The market for rugs is very good in America just now, and I shall sell them at good profit, and set myself up in business there. I speak fair English, don't you think?"

"Your English is very good, and you should have no trouble in establishing yourself."

Lyle's expression grew wistful. He added, a little awkwardly,

"Remember us at Bartzan, though, Neshan."

"Pastor, I shall see you many times before we go, but I shall tell you now that I, and my family, shall never forget you or our neighbors here at Bartzan."

"Perhaps your going will be bread upon the waters, which will return to us after many days," Lyle said hopefully, in parting.

Amos Lyle sat for a long time on the stoop of his doorway—as he had come to do—watching the dusk gather, watching the night envelop the plain, and the darkness rise, like dark waters, upon the slopes of Ararat until only the round dome was above the flood, glowing with a faint and rosy luminescence. Gradually the light faded from the summit, until a single pale ray was left, and then it soared away, like the dove leaving the Ark, to return again to the mountain top with the morning.

Amos Lyle felt a little hand slip into his. Sirani was again beside him. In the dusk her features were not distinct, but her large brown eyes were shining.

Amos Lyle clasped the hand and held it tightly.

"You are not reading tonight?" asked Sirani. "It is much past the time. I have been waiting."

"Yes, Sirani, I am coming in directly."

"I don't mind waiting. I am not sleepy, and I like to sit with you."

"Isn't it a little cool for you, child? Don't you want a shawl?"

"No, Papa Amos, I am quite warm. Don't you like to watch the stars? Kevsor has told me stories about the stars. I know the name of that one. It is Jupiter. People once worshiped a god named Jupiter. That was his star. Do you suppose that the Star of Bethlehem will shine again? That would mean that the Savior is coming again, wouldn't it, Papa Amos?"

"Yes, child. It probably would."

Sirani nestled closer.

"I heard what *Baroon* Kovian said. I feel sorry too that he is going. Avet is a wise boy. He taught me how to jump the rope and other games. But I will be here and will look after you, Papa Amos."

Amos Lyle smiled, while the strings of his heart were drawn tight with love for this little girl.

"I will remember that," he said, rising. "Yes, I will remember that. But shall we read?"

"Yes, Papa Amos."

They went in, and Amos Lyle lighted a lamp. The wick turned into a yellow flame that cast a soft glow over the whitewashed walls. The room was sparsely furnished—a refectory table of local walnut, poorly cured and uneven, but substantial, serving both for dining and study; two or three chairs of hewn wood, one of them the rocking chair which Mattios had made for Lyle; and a thick, comfortable rug of Armenian weave on the floor. The walls were bare save for the mezzotint copy of Hoffmann's

"Christ," the sole possession of Lyle's that dated back to his days at Dilijan—he had saved it by rolling it up and carrying it in his inside coat pocket—and a bookcase, three-quarters filled.

Amos Lyle fetched the Bible from the shelf, sat down and opened it. The place happened to be Micah, the fifth chapter. His eye fell upon the passage,

"And the remnant of Jacob shall be in the midst of many people as a dew from the Lord, as the showers upon the grass, that tarrieth not for man, nor waiteth for the sons of men."

Amos Lyle's eyes remained fixed upon the page until the words blurred, while his heart was flooded with the thoughts of God and His promises to His children.

Presently he said,

"Well, child, what would you like this evening?"

"Read about Moses breaking the tables of the law when he came down from the mountain and saw the people worshiping the golden calf, because the people had lost faith, and had forgotten how many good things the Lord had done for them."

Lyle turned to the passage, thumbing the pages slowly, reflecting on God's goodness in sending this child to him.

"Yes, that's a good story," he said. "We'll read that."

Neshan Kovian departed with his family and belongings, after paying all his just dues and taking in all that was owed him, early in October, after the greater part of the harvest had been gathered and debtors were in substance again and able to discharge their obligations.

He was greatly missed. The moneylender is frequently a popular person. In the case of Kovian, his departure left no one for the people to consult about the weather next year and what would be the likeliest crop to plant; no one to encourage—and finance—the outlay for an embroidered *aba* or a new kettle for the stove, before the harvest when means were scant; no one to give good advice as to how to use the proceeds of the wool or wheat crop, whether to use them to build new corrals or a

new roof for the house, or to lay them up in silver brace-
lets for the wife.

Lyle was a sympathetic listener whose advice was good
on any matter of spiritual importance, but not on these
affairs. He would never counsel going into debt. If there
was a need, and he had money in his pocket, he would
give without question, but he would have nothing to do
with notes of hand and interest, and many of the community would not accept aid unless they could repay
with interest. And though Lyle knew something about
the care of sheep and the growing of crops—in fact,
more than many at Bartzan—his knowledge could be
summed up by saying that he knew how to grow the
harvest but not how to spend the proceeds.

Neshan Kovian's going had, therefore, important reper-
cussions upon the community. Long languishing, it now
hastened to its extinction. Others followed Kovian's
example, though few dared attempt a migration as far as
to America, and within a year the already diminished
population of the village was further reduced by a half.

Such was the course of Amos Lyle's twenty-five years
as a missionary—from ministering to a populous community in a sizeable town to pastor of a bare hundred
families in an anaemic village. Year by year, for more than
five years now, instead of increase there had been de-
crease. Gradually all the substance had wasted away.
Once a full granary, now a bare handful. This had been
the history of the Dilijan community; this apparently was
the history of the Armenian nation: gradual wastage,
gradual shrinkage, gradual extinction, like the buffalo of
the Great West, like the beaver and the passenger pigeon.

The following year, 1909, all speculation as to the future
of the Armenian community at Bartzan was peremptorily
cut off. The long-expected order from the ministry arrived, but it was not the permit that had been hoped for.
It was a curt order for all inhabitants of the plain of Bartzan to evacuate within ninety days.

Kars fortress, already formidable, was to be made impregnable. All the surrounding territory was declared to

be a military area, from which all aliens and minority peoples were excluded. At Bartzan there was to be established a great supply depot and reserve station, where horses were to be bred for the needs of the troops, and sheep to be grazed for military supply purposes, and huge granaries and warehouses erected for reserve stocks of munitions and food, and barracks for troops who would maneuver and train on great parade grounds to be laid out upon the plain.

The villages and farms on the plain were in the way of this program and they must be swept aside.

The order had been brought by a military courier, who had posted the notice on the wall of the church and, mounting, had ridden on.

It was Baghran Kevorkian, a malicious old man, a lover of evil tidings, and a chronic grumbler, who hastened to Lyle with the news.

"At last the end has come," he wheezed, panting from his haste. "Just as I have been saying."

"The end of what?" asked Lyle mildly. He was at his stable unsaddling his mare, having just ridden in from a nearby village.

"We're ordered out," exclaimed Kevorkian, and his eyes sparkled with triumph. "We're ordered out, just as I have been saying ever since we came here. You have been wrong, pastor, wrong for thirteen years."

Amos Lyle ignored the accusation, and went on stabling his bony mount, while he questioned Kevorkian about the notice. He understood Kevorkian, had tried, through the years, to win him, in a patient way, from his oracular, malicious conceit. He laid the blame not so much on Kevorkian as on superstition. Kevorkian had a cast in his eye, the result of a stone thrown at him as a child; instead of being looked upon as a physical misfortune, it was considered as a mark of Satan—he had the "evil eye" which the Sinful One places upon his own. Kevorkian had, as result, become an Ishmael, an outcast held to the community only by Lyle's insistent compassion. Kevorkian, on his part, held a grudge against the world. His resentment had made him a misanthrope.

But in this instance, Kevorkian only expressed the general mood of the remnant left in Bartzan. When Lyle walked down into the village, he heard others talking.

"We should have gone long ago," complained the farmer Ardeshir. "We should have known that the green pastures of Pastor Lyle's promises lay elsewhere. Instead, we have stayed and hoped, and trusted in Pastor Lyle."

He spat.

Ardeshir had prospered in Bartzan; that was the reason for his staying. He knew well how to raise wheat, and the Bartzan plain was good wheat land. Lyle recalled that it was this same Ardeshir who had come to Bartzan the first spring of their settlement, and had asked for permission to count himself as a Dilijani, that it was this same Ardeshir who had urged his approval of remaining after the authorities at Kars indicated their coldness toward the community.

Marta Hovasian, the harpy, saw Lyle approaching and turned to accuse him directly.

"Thirteen years, pastor," she wailed. "You were thirteen years in Dilijan also. It is an omen. Thirteen years."

Amos Lyle grasped the fact that this remnant that was left had not remained in Bartzan out of loyalty, out of their love for the soil upon which they had made their new homes, but because they had lacked either the courage or the spirit to leave, or because, like Ardeshir, they had found Bartzan profitable, and had clung to their stored-up goods.

Now that the order had come, few were sorry to leave. Bartzan had long since lost its attraction for the people. It had served its day as a refuge, and now it was willingly abandoned.

Some went to Erivan, some to Tiflis. Little group by little group they went, driving their donkeys laden with their goods, herding their flocks ahead of them, weeping a few tears with friends and neighbors on separation, but speaking hopefully of new friends expected in their new homes, or old friends to be rejoined, or of relatives whom they would meet.

Despite the willingness, the eagerness even, to place

upon Lyle the blame for this exodus, for their having over-
stayed their time, most of them came by to bid their pastor
good-by, and in their farewells Lyle read such genuine-
ness of feeling as to drive from him all memory of re-
criminations. He saw their going only as the dispersion of
his flock—his loved ones—and there were only love and
sadness in his heart, while his words to them were words
of comfort and hope.

Lyle was the last to go. When all had departed, he
loaded his own cart with his few books, the Hoffmann
"Christ," his rug, his pots and pans, Sirani's clothing and
his own few spare clothes, and finally his rocking chair.
Putting Sirani on the top of the heap, he spoke to the
mare and moved off down the road.

"Where are we going, Papa Amos?" asked Sirani, settling herself among the bundles.

Amos Lyle was a man whose spirits rose with disaster.
He could be sad at the loss of Haig, at the death of
Miriam, at the departure of Khansourian and Kovian, but
the loss of a community, the desolation of a people, the
end of a quarter century of ministry, these were events
that curved back upon themselves, like four-dimensional
space, that extended so far into anguish and despair that
they returned in hope and joy.

"I don't know, Sirani. It doesn't matter where I go so
long as you are with me," he exclaimed with attempted
joviality.

"Of course, I will be with you," reasoned Sirani. "But
aren't you sorry to see all our friends going away?"

"I can't think about them going away, child. I must
think of them coming back."

He paused, and his eyes dimmed, and he began to
croon, as he did when he was overcome with the fervor
of his faith.

"They will all come back one day," he began to re-
peat, half aloud, half to himself. "We will be gathered at
the river Jordan, we will all be crossing over into the
Promised Land, we will all be gathered around the Everlasting Throne to sit at the feet of the Lord God."

He was silent for a moment, and then said to Sirani,

"I must think of that, Sirani, think of the Judgment Day, when the children of God will all be gathered together. But just now, I have you. You are all that is left of the mighty host. Just you and me together, Sirani. But they'll be coming back. We'll all be gathered together like the sheep that are gathered together by the Good Shepherd, meeting under the wings of the Heavenly One. . . ."

Amos Lyle began to sing to the creaking of the cart,

"'Lord, I'm coming home, coming home—
Never more to roam . . .'"

Presently Sirani asked again,

"But where shall we go, Papa Amos?"

Amos Lyle lifted and squared his shoulders, and took a firmer grip on his staff.

"I think we'll go up to Kars," he said, as though the idea had just struck him. "We shall go up to that wicked city, as Jonah went up to Nineveh, and preach to them the word of the Lord."

He spoke to the mare and began again to sing,

"'Lord, I'm coming home . . .'"

Part 3

MARKOV

1. St. Petersburg

On Christmas Eve of 1913, a year in which most of the world was at peace, and the Russian Empire in particular was enjoying the blessings of quiet and prosperity, Prince Constantine Cherniloff gave a supper party at his palace on Alexander Nevsky Prospekt.

The prince occupied his palace only during the season, preferring, for the rest of the year, to spend his time in his lodge in the Caucasus Mountains, his country place on the Volga near Kazan, or in Paris. The palace was ample for the accommodation of his many friends—and their friends, and friends' friends—who gathered for his annual Christmas Eve party. It was constructed of white marble and stucco in the French-Romanesque style of town house; the rooms within were decorated in a variety of modes, to reflect the variety of moods of its occupant. Thus, the ballroom was Louis XIV; the library was like an English cloister, with dim lights, dark oak and leaded windows; the game room was French provincial—an enormous, beamed chamber hung with arms and hunting trophies, accoutered with billiard tables, card tables, roulette tables and easy chairs, and warmed by a great brick fireplace; there was also a chapel fitted with soft lights, an altar and a magnificent ikon of the Virgin, gold and gem-encrusted, for the prince's devotional moods—despite the fact that the prince was a confirmed atheist. There were retiring rooms past count and bedrooms done to suit the tastes of a Madame Pompadour; these, since the prince was a bachelor, were for his more intimate guests.

At ten o'clock the cotillion—the only formal proceeding in the prince's parties—was danced, led by the prince and an aged countess, distantly related to him, after which the guests were left to do as they pleased. Some danced, some gamed, some ate, some talked. Dancing was informal, without programs, and consisted of waltzes, two-steps, and the newly-fashionable fox trot, with an occasional square dance, and sometimes, for diversion, a Caucasian sword dance, performed by a team of Georgian dancers. Among the games were auction bridge and baccarat, with cards, dice, roulette, lotto and billiards, as well as fencing for some of the officers who toward morning liked to wear off their tipsiness by exercise. For the gourmets, the refectory was set with three long tables, linen-spread and covered with vessels, urns and platters of silver and china, containing viands of three distinct sorts. One table provided food of French cuisine—*hors d'oeuvres*, fresh vegetables *en casserole*, chicken *glacé* and chicken patty, snails, frogs' legs, bonbons, fruit, ices and coffee; another boasted food in the Russian manner—*zakuska*, or Russian *hors d'oeuvres*, coarser and more pungent than the French, *bliny*, sausages, venison, jellied boar's head, buttermilk, rye bread, meat balls in soup, meat cooked in cabbage leaves, roast pork, and samovars of tea. The third table offered food of Persian origin—platters of steaming rice *pilau*, and *chillau*, lamb bits on skewers, honey and chilled cream, melons, *baklavah*—pastry rolled with ground pistachio nuts and honey—*sherbet* and tea. The discriminating among the prince's guests partook of the French fare; the fastidious, of the Persian; and the gluttonous, of the Russian.

On a sideboard stood wines and liquors for the free use of the guests, and glasses of various sizes and shapes.

As for the conversation it was past cataloguing. The prince's guests loved to talk, whatever the subject, and the sounds of conversation rose above the clatter of dishes and popping of bottles in the refectory, above the clipping of cards and dice and wheels and billiard balls in the game room, above the music of the orchestra in the ball-room, all in a confused clamor, sometimes pleasant, some-times raucous, sometimes violent. This conversation ranged in subject from polite enquiry to graceful comment on art and politics and religion, to gossip, vituperation and violent quarreling.

A young lieutenant of infantry passed one of these con-versational groups gathered near the staircase, and im-mediately became the subject of conversation. Tall, erect, handsome, of splendid carriage and physique, and bronzed from recent service in the field, he was in appearance not greatly different from dozens of other young lieutenants in the room who strode about in immaculate uniforms and with the assured manner of apprentice Napoleons, talking brightly and grandly and giving wise opinions as to the course of empire; yet his manner was distinguished by certain differences. He wore an air of detachment, as though he were puzzled about something, and his glance was somewhat more deliberate, more penetrating and ap-praising, than is usually the case among young lieutenants in charge of troops for the first time.

It may have been the look in his eyes, fleetingly glimpsed by one of the women in the group, which led her to ask impulsively,

"Who is that? Don't I know him?"

She was a matron in her fortieth year, the wife of a railway manager and the mother of four children—one of those wives of Lot who cannot resist the backward glance at their youth. The question annoyed her hus-band, not because of his wife's curiosity over a handsome young officer, but because it interrupted what he was saying. He had been talking upon the way they managed the state railways in Russia, and his listener was a mem-ber of the foreign diplomatic corps. The diplomat had been paying the closest attention—which had pleased the railway manager—for the diplomat had been charged by his government with obtaining all information possible upon the efficiency of the régime, and of the railways in particular.

"He is Lieutenant Markov," said the railway manager, turning his head. "His father was Colonel Markov, who was killed in Baku. As I was saying, Your Excellency, we have no labor trouble on the railways. The men are well paid and contented, and besides, they know it is of no use to oppose the administration. We have the power in our hands, and we don't stand for subversive propaganda—"

"Oh! Colonel Markov!" interrupted the diplomat's wife. "We have heard of him, haven't we, Donald? It happened while we were stationed at Constantinople. You remember that Turkish colonel we met—Hashim Farouk was his name, wasn't it?—who told us of having witnessed the affair from a hotel balcony."

"Yes, yes," put in her husband, trying to quiet her. As a diplomat, he regarded it impolitic to pass confidences along to any but his foreign office. "He said something, but I gathered he was gossiping, as"—he laughed nervously—"we all do. Excellency, you say you have no labor troubles—"

"It was a sad affair," put in the railway manager's wife. "Colonel Markov was such a fine man. His son looks like him, doesn't he? Tall and handsome. I remember now. Someone told me that he is stationed in Turkestan, and was cited for bravery last year. Some battle with the Afghans."

It was now the railway manager's turn to feel uncomfortable—operations on the Afghan frontier should not be discussed with a foreign diplomat, even though the noise of an American fox trot from the orchestra stand drowned out half what anyone said—and he thought it best to continue the story about the Baku affair.

"It was a very foolish thing to do and amazed everybody," he said rapidly. "So unbecoming to an officer—so lowering to the dignity of the Tsar, if you understand what I mean—to dismount and treat with the leader of a mob. He should have charged the moment he saw them. Only one thing carries weight in this world, and that is the firm hand, the strong will. That's the way we rule the Empire. Superior minds, superior wills, superior force—that's the only way. Isn't that so? But the scandal was hushed up. The colonel had such a wonderful record, and such a fine family background. Besides, it does not pay to advertise these little weaknesses, these little evidences of sentimentality."

The diplomat murmured assent.

The railway manager's wife watched Lieutenant Markov disappearing in the crowd of the ballroom, vaguely wondering how many young girls would be sighing over him tonight, while her husband and the diplomat resumed their conversation about the management of large affairs.

Lieutenant Paul Stepanovitch Markov had moved to the other side of the room, where he stopped to speak with a group of junior officers of his acquaintance. They were just starting into the refectory for refreshments and invited him to join them, but he declined and turned towards the game room instead.

The orchestra leader was raising his baton for another dance. Not far away, a friend of Markov's, Alexei Petrovitch Dosti, was frantically gesturing to him behind the back of a fat countess. The countess had an ungainly, predatory daughter whom she was trying to foist upon Alexei, and when the tentacles of the daughter loosened, she would fasten her own upon Alexei. Lieutenant Markov had relieved his friend of this burden on other occasions. Alexei was again signaling for help. But now young Markov only waved cheerfully in greeting and sauntered on.

In the game room Count Luchensky was winning at baccarat, and talking of the stock market.

"I've made a million within the year on Anglo-Indian Tea," he was saying. "With the improved prosperity in Russia, tea-drinking is on the increase, and Anglo-Indian is in a splendid position to take advantage of its opportunities."

The count was a successful banker, head of a large savings institution in Moscow, a fat man, with flabby neck that fell in folds over his collar, and a pudgy oily face.

"You can do just as well in Armstrong Mining," commented one of the players, a little sourly—he had been losing rubles by handfuls—"and it isn't taking money out of the country. Armstrongs are spending millions in the Urals."

By some it was considered unpatriotic to invest in foreign shares. The thought also occurred to Lieutenant Markov that it was not proper for the head of a savings institution to be gambling at baccarat or on the stock exchange. Still, the count was very successful.

"What is your system?" inquired a third player.

"System itself," responded the count easily. "Organization. Organization of intelligence. I never make an investment without the most careful survey of all the factors —beginning with the properties themselves, then the management, followed by analysis of the market, and finally of the general economic situation. That is the basis of all successful investment—organized knowledge—and then the will, quick and alert, to decide the propitious moment. It's very simple."

Lieutenant Markov agreed with that, and his passing doubts disappeared. That was the way an army was run, that was the way successful campaigns were fought. He listened awhile longer, but as the conversation still turned on investments, rate of return, probabilities, and the like, all of which was slightly boring to him, he wandered back toward the ballroom.

He wondered if he should not go and relieve Alexei of his countess. The countess had a strong will, and if someone did not come to his rescue poor Alexei would certainly be married before the holidays were over. Alexei was lacking in that power of will and decision of which the banker had just spoken.

The party was growing more gay and noisy. In the refectory, dishes were clattering and breaking, the sound barely drowned by the noise of chatter and repartee. More guests had arrived. People jostled one another, apologized tipsily, or muttered damnations, and went on to other diversions. On the ballroom floor, a band of gypsy entertainers were dancing, and when they had finished, a sleight-of-hand performer—a Frenchman imported for the occasion—began to amuse the guests with his tricks.

Prince Cherniloff's tastes were catholic: he liked everybody, whatever his creed or profession or interest, so long as he was successful. Artists, bankers, poets, merchants, public servants, engineers, doctors—all were represented here by those who had advanced to the forefront. But it was obvious, of course, that not all were branded with the mark of success. How many personal tragedies and failures were represented no one could tell, for everything was covered with the gilt of achievement. Alexei, for instance, might be counted a failure: though he had won his commission, he seemed unable to win promotion. And if the countess did not marry off her daughter soon she could be marked down as a failure.

Lieutenant Markov remembered that he had not seen his host all evening, and went to find him.

The prince, a man of distinguished appearance and captivating manner, was in a little sitting room, ensconced in a huge armchair, surrounded by a group of young men who were listening to his discourse with the awed respect with which the students of the Academy may have listened to Plato.

Prince Cherniloff had himself been a success in several lines of endeavor. These successes had not turned his head nor made him arrogant, as might well have been the case considering his birth and position; instead, they had given him a refreshing philosophy and superior outlook upon life. He was interested in youth, and the possibilities of youth, and at his parties he liked nothing better than to get off in a corner with a group of young men and instill in them his views, enthusiasms and philosophy.

"Come in, Pavil," he said, cordially, as Paul Stepanovitch stood by the silken portieres that draped the archway. "I have just been boring these young men with my ideas. You know them, don't you?—Lieutenant Kirinoff, Ensign Kriensky—"

"I know them all," said Markov, waving to them. "Please go on with what you were saying, Prince."

"No, no, you must tell us about life in Turkestan. I read about your citation. Splendid work. I started to drop you a note, but a telegram that instant called me to Paris, and I had to leave everything."

"It was nothing. Just to encourage us on the frontier. Please go on."

"I was engaged in giving these young men a lecture on success," continued the prince. "You can go to the head of the class, while I resume."

Markov liked the prince. He had known Cherniloff, through his father, for many years, and the prince stood in his eyes as somebody to emulate. He chose a brocade-covered stool and sat down.

"Success, I was saying, is merely a matter of the will. By the power of the will we can draw upon the inexhaustible resources within, and drive our faculties—as well as command the faculties of others—to whatever heights we wish."

Markov had heard this philosophy before, and he was in hearty agreement. He relaxed comfortably while the prince went on:

"Do you suppose my pictures hang in the Galerie Moderne because I am gifted like Raphael or Matisse? No. I have no more talent than any other man. I simply willed that I would paint, and paint successfully. As you know, I took it up only some half-dozen years ago."

It was a fact that the prince had startled Petersburg society about that time by announcing that he was devoting himself to portraiture, and he had followed that announcement by what was characterized in the press as a "significant" exhibition of his work.

"I willed to paint, and I directed every faculty to that end. I took six-hour lessons from the best instructors in Paris; I bought the finest pigments and canvas; I slept in art galleries. And then I summoned my audacity—that was a profound effort of will, for you know I am a modest man—to announce an exhibition. I hired the most expensive salon in Petersburg, and filled it with champagne to attract the attendance of every critic and artist in town, as well as all the élite. This last was also possible because

I had long ago willed myself to financial success, the foundation for all other success."

At this moment, the sleight-of-hand performer finished his entertainment, to a burst of applause, and the orchestra started tuning up for more dancing. Some of the prince's listeners began to show uneasiness, and to glance through the archway to the young women on the opposite side of the ballroom, who returned their glances longingly.

The prince understood their dilemma, and dismissed them indulgently, with a wave of the hand.

"That's enough for one evening, young men. Now run and amuse yourselves."

Markov remained with the prince.

"Don't you want to dance, Pavil?"

"Later," Markov responded shortly. "I'd like to hear you out."

Prince Cherniloff nodded understandingly. Lieutenant Markov, he knew, was troubled by a dilemma, the horns of which were rooted in his past and had to do with his father's unexplained conduct at Baku.

The prince began by insisting on Lieutenant Markov's telling him about life on the Afghan frontier, at some length, while he interspersed wise comments and understanding, appreciative nods. Presently he brought the conversation around, adroitly, to the subject of Colonel Markov.

"Colonel Markov was a splendid officer, and a gentleman," he said fervently. He added, thoughtfully, "I have often wondered about that Baku affair."

"And so have I," said Paul Stepanovitch Markov, with frankness. "I have never been able to understand it. The colonel's conduct was so different from what I had known him to be."

"I can only conclude that he had a sudden access of compassion," said Cherniloff gravely.

"But why did he surrender to compassion?" asked Paul Stepanovitch. "He was a man of iron will. If it was compassion, as you say, it was not because he felt an overwhelming pity, but because of some logical, understandable purpose. I can understand pity, but it must be directed to a larger goal. I am confident that my father had such a purpose, but I cannot understand what it was that required a display of pity—such as to cost him his life."

"Compassion is a virtue worthy enough in a woman, a poet, or an artist, but one to be shunned by an officer or an administrator," replied the prince sagely and weightily. "I can think of no circumstances in which its display is warranted by an officer of the army."

"But there must be," protested Paul Stepanovitch. "My father was too wise, too devoted to the Tsar to allow personal feeling to enter."

The young man's eyes had lost their look of detached appraisal and were flaming with zeal.

"Like him," he continued, "I want to serve the Empire, at whatever cost, to whatever end, to death—only that our country may be glorious and powerful."

"That's why I think so highly of you, Pavil," responded the prince warmly, approvingly. "You have a sense of our imperial destiny beyond your years, and a devotion to your Tsar that is remarkable even among men who are implicit in their devotion. But it is the Samsons who have their Delilahs. We who are strong in courage, sure of purpose, must avoid ensnarements. They are subtle in their approach, narcotic in their effect. Such things as compassion, pity, remorse, regret, must be avoided like a plague. There is no strength nor power in them. They are negative rather than positive, and we must seek the positive. We must realize, Pavil, that there is only one force in all the world, the imperishable and indomitable force of will. All that man sees, all that he has created, is the product of the mind, working through will. It is the only law, the only God. We are Prometheans, who possess the sacred fire that burned once on Olympus, but is ash there now, since the departure of the gods to the nether world, and we alone survive, by means of that fire."

"I like to hear you say such things," exclaimed Paul Stepanovitch enthusiastically. "You have a faculty of stating truth in logical terms. What you say is compact, like an emblem on an escutcheon. It's something one can carry with him as a guide, as a reminder of his purpose."

He hesitated, and added,

"Perhaps the colonel should have had something like that to remind him."

The prince saw that his words had not entirely removed the doubt in his young friend's mind, and to fortify them, he continued, persuasively,

"Even by Christian theory, is what I've been saying not so, Pavil? Does not the Jewish God, to whom Christians pay tribute, tell man, in Genesis, to be fruitful, and have dominion over the earth? And if man have dominion over the earth, over what does this God rule? What else is there?

"One's course is to strengthen the will, to live by will, and to dominate. That is what the new German school of philosophy is saying, in cruder terms. It is by the will that the Russian Empire has been created, an empire of a vastness never known in history save for the momentary conquests of Genghis Khan and Tamerlane. We are a race of supermen, destined to control Asia and Europe, if we but keep our bodies strong and virile, our wills and intelligence alive."

Paul Stepanovitch showed by the light that glowed in his eye that he had been convinced.

"But come, Pavil, you should be dancing," the prince concluded quickly. "You are returning to Turkestan after the holidays?"

"Yes."

"Come and see me again before you go, when we can talk in peace. I shall probably be leaving here shortly, myself. They have been wanting me to go to Kazan as governor, and I have about decided to accept. The fact is I am a little bored with Petersburg."

The two men rose and went out, the prince toward the game room, Paul Stepanovitch Markov into the ballroom, where the orchestra was preparing for another dance.

All the while he crossed the floor, Paul Stepanovitch was thinking of poor Alexei, and his plight with the countess, and wondering if he should not help him out.

2. *Small Talk*

ALEXEI PETROVITCH and his countess were nowhere to be seen. Paul Stepanovitch had looked up and down the ballroom, and in the conservatory and refectory, and the other rooms where the guests congregated, but without success. Paul Stepanovitch returned to the ballroom. He was quite cheerful after his talk with Prince Cherniloff; and he felt like amusing himself.

He stood for a moment gazing at the long ballroom, with its plump cupids clinging to garlands all over the ceiling; at the enormous mirrors, set between marble panels along the wall to increase the already great effect of size; at the milling crowd, bejeweled and dressed in scintillating gowns and gold-embroidered uniforms; and then he strolled over to the wide marble fireplace, crackling with a Yule log. A group of officers and ladies was standing at one end of the fireplace, talking animatedly about nothing. At the other end, on an upholstered marble bench, sat a young woman, the Princess Irina Sabayeva, a friend of Paul Stepanovitch's of many years' standing, whom he had first known when they attended dancing school as children. She was gazing abstractedly into the fire. Paul Stepanovitch went up to her.

"A penny for your thoughts," he said to her, in English, a language over which they had struggled together.

The princess turned and smiled up at him.

"I was just thinking what a nice boy you are, Pavil, to come and take pity on me. *Maman* will be so upset that I am not dancing."

"You didn't see me coming," protested Paul Stepanovitch.

"Oh, yes, I did. I saw you in the mirror. Then I started looking into the fire so as not to scare you away. But now I've told you, give me the penny."

"How about a dance instead?"

"A dance? Is that all you can offer? I would rather sit with you somewhere—where *maman* won't be wondering why I am not dancing."

The orchestra had just started the waltz from "Eugen Onegin."

"You don't like to dance?" asked Paul Stepanovitch, as he piloted the princess through the crowd.

"Yes, but not to that. Tchaikovsky is too sad for dancing."

They passed through the ballroom into the library, which was comparatively deserted, dimly lighted by tall wax flambeaux and by the illumination that came from the great leaded windows that formed one side of the room. A deep, upholstered bench ran along the base of these windows, and sitting there one could look out upon St. Petersburg.

The Princess Irina Sabayeva led Paul Stepanovitch by the hand to this seat.

"Isn't the city beautiful?" she said, looking out the window.

Petersburg lay under a new-fallen snow, a mantle which became it as an ermine cloak becomes a beautiful woman. The snow, by the light of the street lamps, sparkled with a million scintillations and cast an aura of radiance over the city, through which stood out, darkly, masses of masonry, crenellated walls, towers and turrets and cupolas, and the black expanse of the Neva, flowing with slow-moving, as yet unfrozen, water.

Paul Stepanovitch gazed down the Prospekt, at the dark, solemn mass of the Admiralty, the clock tower of Peter-Paul Cathedral, rising above the fortress, outlined in snow, and the great equestrian statue of Tsar Peter, on its massive granite pediment, impressive and magnificent in its drapery of white.

To Paul Stepanovitch the city was more than beautiful. It evoked in him a sense of majesty, of magnificence, of power, of imperious will.

"I like Petersburg," Paul said simply.

"Why don't you come here oftener, Pavil?" Irina

Sabayeva urged, while she stroked the braid on his sleeve.

"I come as often as I get leave," laughed Paul Stepanovitch. "I should have gone to Varsova. I haven't been back for years."

"Why go there? There's no one there."

"Well, Sorkin is there, who manages the estate. Sorkin's remittances are what makes it possible for me to come here."

"I like you, Pavil. I've never known anyone I liked better."

Paul Stepanovitch responded by impulsively taking her hand. Then patting it lightly, he replied: "Don't you go thinking seriously of young officers—particularly those stationed on the frontiers."

"And why not?" asked the princess, earnestly. "Is life there so absorbing that they never think of women?"

"You know very little about the way we live out there. I can see that."

"Come, Pavil," the princess insisted. "What do you do out in Turkestan that is so important?"

"Does the defense of the Empire mean nothing to you?" Paul Stepanovitch protested.

He was puzzled at her seriousness. Irina Sabayeva was a pretty girl, with soft round features that concealed her sophistication.

"Roman legions guarding civilization from barbarians— that sort of thing?" she asked, with a shade of irony.

"Yes, that—but more, too. You make it sound unconstructive. We're building railroads and paving the way for trade. We're teaching the tribesmen to settle down and plow the land instead of grazing it. Soil experts are introducing new crops—cotton, for example—so that the Empire can be self-sufficient. Then we do a lot in the way of sanitation, too—persuading the natives to lead healthier lives."

"Maybe they prefer to be dirty," Irina Sabayeva said vehemently. "Perhaps they prefer to graze instead of till. Why shouldn't they be permitted to live as they've chosen to live for a thousand years?"

"Come, Irina," Paul Stepanovitch said persuasively.

"We're not going to let a few backward natives stand in our way. Women are such sentimental and illogical creatures."

"Well, women are half the human race," replied the princess in a hard voice. "And their opinion ought to be worth something."

"If we left such things to women, where would we be? I suppose you would like to be living in a *yurt*, clad in a horseskin, drinking mare's milk, and carrying tent poles on your back, the way our ancestors did before Ivan. I suppose you would like to be living in a marsh, roasting your meat over an open fire, never bathing, living in stinking ignorance, the way a lot of our people did before Peter the Great. By God, it's men that make a world, heroes like Peter, who had an unshakable will, a great purpose, a conception of imperial destiny—"

"Don't forget Catherine," Irina interposed.

"Catherine was no lady. But you haven't answered my question."

"About my preferences as to whether I would rather be the Princess Irina than the daughter of a feudal *boyar?*"

"Yes."

"All I can say is that I think all this talk about civilization and empire is tiresome. It may be important, but there are other things that are important, too."

"What, for instance?"

"You wouldn't understand."

"Am I so stupid?"

Irina Sabayeva looked at Markov sharply.

"Look," she said, turning to the window.

A procession of brown-garbed monks, with lighted candles, was passing along the street, in the snow, chanting an antiphonal hymn, on their way to solemn mass at the Alexander Nevsky monastery, at the other end of the Prospekt from the Admiralty. Lighted sleighs occasionally passed, the lamps looming in the distance like little moons, waxing and then eclipsed, as they passed, and casting a moving nimbus about them on the snow. The music from the sleigh bells mingled with the chant of the monks, and rose, muffled and gentle, to the panes of the window, where it was assaulted by the music of the orchestra within.

"Let us get *maman* and go to mass," said Irina, jumping down.

"But you don't want to leave the party so soon," protested Paul Stepanovitch.

"Why not? I don't care about parties. They bore me."

Paul Stepanovitch remembered suddenly that Prince Cherniloff's last remark had been that he was bored with Petersburg. This had puzzled him, momentarily, and then he had forgotten it, but now Irina, who was on the morning side of life, youthful, vivacious, with everything ahead of her, admitted to being bored.

"Why are you bored?" he asked.

"Don't ask me, Pavil. That's something else you wouldn't understand. Besides, it's Christmas Eve, which is reason enough for going to church. Come."

Paul Stepanovitch reluctantly allowed himself to be drawn along. They found *maman*, made their adieus to their host, and called their sleigh. A moment later, the music and the glitter of Prince Cherniloff's were only a memory, and they were gliding along the snow-covered avenue. They came to the bronze Peter, standing on its sixteen-hundred-ton pediment of granite—that had taken no one knows how many lives to drag across the marshes—where Paul Stepanovitch turned in the sleigh to observe again, as he had often done, the imperial features, the magnificent posture so characteristic of the great Peter. They drew near the Admiralty, where Peter had founded Russian sea power, passed the fortress, and were in front of the Cathedral of St. Isaac.

There were others who had left matters of lesser moment to attend the Church's celebration of the birth of its spiritual sovereign; a vast throng was gathered waiting to enter the cathedral, massed before the portals, standing in the courtyard, even in the snow of the street. As one mass followed another, there was a constant coming and going. People wedged their way in, and wedged their way out: officers in gold braid and ladies in ermine jostled lesser folk—clerks in the bureaus, tradesmen, old women peddlers, beggars and outcasts. The great bells were pealing in a symphony of crystalline sound, and high upon the cupolas and turrets the hundreds of golden crosses gleamed in the starlight of the night. From within came the sonorous chanting of the priests and acolytes and the music of the choir.

Led by Irina Sabayeva, who eagerly kept in the van, they finally pressed their way into the narthex, and then into the crowded nave, where people were standing in attention to the services, or coming and going, kissing the ikons and lighting candles before the shrines: finally they stood in the transept, in front of the sanctuary where the Liturgy was conducted. Extending the width of the church, and closing off the sanctuary, rose the *ikonostasis*, the great screen, of carved and gilt wood, covered with pictures, in heroic proportions, of Christ and His apostles. In the sanctuary behind the screen, hidden from the eyes of the people, as in a pagan temple, was the altar, where were enacted the mysteries of the faith.

The choir, in the transept, was singing the litany in response to the chanting of the deacon within the sanctuary. A clear soprano voice, that of a boy, reared a column of sound, around which the other singers wove the melody in enharmonic scale. The chant advanced, it changed in mode repeatedly, it rose into crescendo in which the rich bass and soprano voices mingled and separated like silver streamers in the wind.

"Oh, isn't this heavenly?" whispered the Princess Irina.

Paul Stepanovitch said nothing. He was not impressed by the service; rather he was vaguely uneasy, and wished he had not come. It made him think of his mother, whom he loved dearly, but whose faith he had been led to contemn, as something ignorant and pagan.

The portals in the *ikonostasis* opened, and the deacon, resplendent in sacramental vestments, entered the nave of the cathedral. As he advanced he chanted the Great Litany, the prayers for peace, for the Church, for the Patriarch, for the Tsar, for the city, for travelers and those in distress.

At the close of each prayer, the choir answered with the

propitiatory cry of the litany, the cry that is older than the Church itself, the cry that was sung in the temples of pagan Greece, that was raised by Prometheus on his mountain top to the avenging gods, the cry that is old as man's first sin and repentance, the cry of despairing mankind to its Creator,

"Kyrie eleison." ("Lord, have mercy.")

At each enunciation of the *Kyrie,* the congregation joined the choir; the words rolled over the throng like a wave, and reverberated in the vault.

Standing beside Paul Stepanovitch, so close that Paul could smell the reek of his perspiration, even above the expensive perfume wafted from the Princess Irina, was an old man, with rheumy eyes and bald, wrinkled head: his senile, wavering voice had joined in the response, filled with such ecstasy that Paul Stepanovitch wondered whether he merely enjoyed exercising his voice, or whether he felt that his sins would be forgiven.

Paul himself had not opened his mouth. Though he had attended mass innumerable times, he was not affected by it; or if he was, he experienced only a restlessness that he could not quite define. Though he had never tried to reason the matter out, it seemed slightly odd that mercy, which was not a quality appropriate in human affairs, should be appropriate with God. As justice, rather than mercy, was the principle on which empires were built, so justice, rather than mercy, should be the principal attribute of deity, the cornerstone of a spiritual kingdom.

The deacon concluded the litany and repassed the portals of the screen into the sanctuary. The chanting of the choir dropped to a whisper, then soared again as the bishop entered, accompanied by his priests—the deacon holding the book of the Gospels, the acolytes bearing candles.

The bishop was more resplendent than the deacon. He wore a long white alb—the symbolic robe of mockery—covered with a chasuble which was so stiff with ospreys of gold and pearls that its stood out from him like a tent, an embroidered maniple and a cincture signifying the fetters Christ wore before Pilate.

As he advanced, the choir sang, three times, in piercing melody,

"Holy God, Holy Strong One, Holy Immortal One, have mercy on us."

Before the assembled throng, a reader in the bishop's train sang the Epistle, the choir answered with a Gradual, and the deacon, having incensed the book, sang the Gospel. Then followed the prayers of the litany, and at each pause the choir repeated the reverberating cry for mercy,

"*Kyrie eleison.*"

Again the procession disappeared into the sanctuary, and while the choir continued to carry a song, faint and sweet as a summer wind, the bishop, the deacons, and the acolytes were robing themselves in still more splendid vestments in preparation for the Great Entrance, the exhibition of the sacred elements.

The Princess Irina was absorbed in the service, joining in the chants with the choir. *Maman* viewed the mass as one views a spectacle at the theater. Paul Stepanovitch thought: "How splendidly organized, how beautifully it is all directed."

Paul Stepanovitch respected the Church; it was an ancient institution, more ancient, and in many ways more powerful, than the Empire. An organization that could keep itself intact for so many centuries, adding to its wealth and traditions, constantly attracting new adherents, was something worth admiring. It was an organization that moved as smoothly and as precisely as any military unit; indeed, an army man might well study its methods.

Paul Stepanovitch wondered who the directing genius of this organization was. The Tsar was of course its titular head, but below the Tsar, as in the ministries, was some intelligence, no doubt, some directing genius who provided the will and purpose that made it function so admirably.

He glanced at Irina Sabayeva, and saw the rapture on her face.

The doors of the great screen had again opened and now, to the symphonic chant of the choir, and amid the smoke of censers, the bishop entered the nave with all his company of priests. His head was covered with a magnificent miter, symbolic of the spiritual dominion of the Church, encrusted with emeralds and rubies, and over the miter was draped a veil which trailed behind and was held by one of the acolytes. In the bishop's hand was a golden chalice, while the deacon at his elbow bore a thurible and the holy bread.

As the procession entered through the north door of the *ikonostasis,* the choir began the age-old Cherubic Hymn of the Eastern Church,

"Let us, who mystically represent the Cherubim, and who sing to the life-giving Trinity the thrice holy hymn, put away all earthly cares so as to receive the King of all things escorted by the army of angels. Alleluia, alleluia, alleluia."

The procession of the sacred elements went slowly around the church, and then retired into the sanctuary through the central, or Royal doors, which had not been used until now. These doors were now left open, so that the altar, the bishop and the deacon were visible to the assembly. While the bishop prepared the elements, and the deacon waved the sacred fan, the Ripidon, over the chalice, the crowd pressed closer and closer about the center of the nave in expectancy of the climax of the mass. The heat of many bodies grew intense; the air was filled with the mingled odor of perfume, perspiration, and holy incense.

Irina was chanting with the choir; her mother was looking on with a vacant, bored expression—an attitude which Paul Stepanovitch was inclined to share.

The voice of the bishop singing the prayers issued through the open doors and filled the cathedral, each prayer punctuated by the piercing chant of "Lord, have mercy," which rose in the air like the voices of the condemned in hell and re-echoed from the dome of the cathedral,

"Kyrie eleison."

At the height of the litany the bishop shouted loudly, "The Doors, the Doors. Let us attend in Wisdom."

At that same instant the doors of the *ikonostasis* were abruptly closed; and hidden from all vulgar and profane eyes, by the great screen of gilt and wood, the mass continued and the holy mystery was enacted of the transformation of the bread and wine into the flesh and blood of Christ.

At the elevation of the Host, a stentorian Gloria echoed through the edifice until it seemed that the chandeliers shook and the very walls trembled; a bell rang and it was answered by resounding peals from the belfry of the cathedral.

The moment was one of liturgical triumph. By the force of song and incense and gorgeous litany the Church had established its sway over the hearts of men. The vast throng was lifted in exaltation; people gazed with rapture, or awe, or peace on their faces. Some were singing, some were weeping with joy. For a moment, it seemed to Paul Stepanovitch that he too had been affected; he glanced at Irina and saw the tears that filled her eyes, and he felt compassion for her.

At home, where they had a few minutes alone, Irina Sabayeva asked,

"Why don't you care for mass?"

Paul Stepanovitch fidgeted.

"It's only a show, after all. I prefer a good regimental parade."

Irina Sabayeva looked unhappy.

"That's not a good answer, nor true," she said. She was speaking again in English; Paul Stepanovitch liked the language and she felt a greater intimacy with him in using it.

"Your mother, I've heard you say, was very devout," she persisted, in a strained voice.

"Yes, but I never knew just what all this meant to her. My father's ideas seem much more sensible."

"Are you sure you know what your father's ideas were?"

Paul Stepanovitch was silent. He was not sure. The inexplicable Baku affair still plagued him.

"You are returning to Turkestan?" Irina asked.

"Yes, very shortly. The corps are holding their New Year's party, and I must be back for that. It's something the soldiers have part in, and it disappoints the men if their officers aren't present."

"You are very thoughtful of your men, I see."

"Of course, that's the only way to build up morale. You must take care of your men, treat them fairly, and let them know you are a man yourself."

"I see. You take account of their susceptibilities and temperaments."

"Whenever possible, I do."

"But you never have compassion on them?"

They were silent for a moment.

"You will come and see *maman* and me before you go, won't you?" Irina asked.

"Yes, Irina Sabayeva," Paul Stepanovitch promised. He touched her hand soothingly. "Tell me, Irinosha, why you are so moody tonight. You didn't want to dance, and there were dozens of men who were waiting for you to look at them."

"Oh, the world's sad, and there is no hope for it."

"Nonsense."

"Do you really want to know?"

"Yes, I do," said Paul Stepanovitch seriously.

Irina Sabayeva drew her ermine cloak about her shoulders.

"Tonight is a night of rejoicing," she recited, "for the Lord Christ was born this night. But I feel no joy, only a sentimental exuberance. Much gaiety, much affectation of joy, but no joy. Much talk of power, but everywhere weakness: much assuming of confidence, but everyone afraid, in fear of losing wealth, or looks, or position, or reputation. Where is the Lord Christ tonight? Not in Russia."

The Princess Irina turned and faced Paul Stepanovitch fiercely.

"That's why I am sad," she exclaimed bitterly. "What

is a woman here? An adornment for men—a plaything, if you choose, with which they amuse themselves when they are tired of talking of wars and politics, and their successes on the Exchange, their exhibitions and their publishers. O God, Pavil, why are men such fools?"

She turned her head away, while her hands picked nervously at the little handkerchief of Afghan lace which she held. A slight shudder shook her frame, and caused the ermine to ripple.

"Would you like to know what Christmas really means?"

"Yes, Irina."

Irina turned and faced Paul Stepanovitch.

"I will tell you, and then you must go. But you will kiss me good night, won't you, Pavil? Good night and goodby?"

"Yes, Irina, good night, but not good-by. Don't be tragic."

Paul Stepanovitch kissed her dutifully, like a brother. When he had put on his great coat and buckled it, he said,

"Now tell me."

Irina led Paul Stepanovitch to the door. Then hesitantly, with her hand on the knob, as though she were preparing to shove Paul Stepanovitch into the street the moment she had finished speaking, she said,

"Men say that by the birth of Christ the world was saved. But they are wrong."

"Yes?"

"Yes. Characteristically, they interpret events to suit their own egotistic desires. By the birth of Christ Mary was saved, and this is the lesson of Christmas, for Mary is womankind."

She flung the door open with a gesture of anguish, and pushing Paul Stepanovitch on to the threshold, she exclaimed,

"Now go, Pavil, and while you are shooting Afghans, think of this, and you will understand why I am sad."

The door closed behind Paul Stepanovitch. For a moment he stood in perplexity, considering whether he

should ring and re-enter. He wondered if he had done
something to offend her, and what it could have been.

While he lingered in hesitation, trying to comprehend
Irina's mood and words, the light within was extinguished.

Paul Stepanovitch stood a moment, and then hunching
his great coat around his neck with a shrug of his shoulders, he went down the steps.

3. Disintegration

In the year 1917, Paul Stepanovitch Markov was a captain of infantry in a company, a regiment, a brigade, a
division, and a corps of the Army of Galicia.

The fact that he was captain of such and such a company, in such and such a regiment, brigade, division,
corps, and army, gave Paul Stepanovitch Markov a self-
assurance and sense of strength that were not justified by
the times.

The precision with which a soldier could be docu-
mented and tabulated in a military organization suggests
qualities which properly are not assignable to it. The
procession of rank, ascending upward in even gradation
like the steps of a monument—from private to corporal
and to sergeant within the company; from lieutenant to
captain, and thence to major, lieutenant-colonel and
colonel in the hierarchy of the regiment; and above that,
brigadiers, generals, marshals, commanders of corps and
commanders of armies—gives the idea of something firm,
impermeable, rocklike.

Above the commanders of armies was the imperial
hierarchy of dukes and grand dukes, culminating in the
emperor himself, Tsar of all the Russias, absolute monarch
of a vast portion of the world's surface and population.

Flanking the army and the imperial household was a
quasi-legislative body known as the Duma, drawn from

the leading citizens in all parts of the realm; above the Duma a cabinet of advisers to His Majesty; and supporting them an array of bureaus and offices and ministries which provided the administrative personnel by which the affairs of this great population and this vast territory were administered and governed. Below them, again, were provincial governors and administrators with their sub-bureaus, agencies, and administrations, extending into all parts of the country and touching the life of the people in its most minute activities.

Throughout this ramified network of administration coursed an independent system of contact and communication, a far-reaching nerve ganglion the center of which was in the seat of imperial power at St. Petersburg, the threads of which extended into every town and hamlet of the Empire. This was the Okhrana, or secret police, and its duties were to maintain the functioning of the whole imperial system by observation and control, and by more forcible measures.

So complete were the surveillance and the control of the administration that one could not move from one province to another without a passport and the *visa* of the police. Registrations were universal and of every sort, from marriage and births and deaths to personal movements and the transactions of commerce. Everything was within the province of the administration; everything was an object of administrative concern; everything was organized, knit together, welded together; everything faced toward St. Petersburg.

But the organization of this vast empire did not stop with the imperial administrative and political system. The methods of land tenure, the system of exchange and trade, even the Church itself—all bequeathed to the country by a still older and more pervasively administered civilization, Byzantium—were of the most highly organized character. The Church itself, whose temporal and spiritual head was likewise the Tsar, offered a hieratic system without parallel in history, extending from laity to acolytes and village priests, to bishops, archbishops, metropolitans, and thence to the Holy Synod, with brotherhoods and orders innumerable. The system of land tenure, in Russia proper at least, had, despite the emancipation of the serfs and the abolition of many of the feudal appanages, retained much of the corporate and feudal character inherited from Byzantium, particularly in the customs of land tillage and the legal system by which it was supported. As for trade, the life blood of material civilization, it was nominally free and capitalistic; however, a system of co-operative purchasing and selling existed in regard to many of the staple commodities, so strong and effective that of all the institutions of Russia it survived the Revolution the least impaired, and became indeed the model for much of the later program of socialization.

Such then was the organization of the Russian Empire; in brief, a system in which, in theory and largely in practice, the State was everything, the individual nothing, his activities organized, administered, supervised and policed to a degree beyond the dreams of the most extravagant doctrinaire of current times.

Surveying this structure from without, therefore—looking from its base up to the apex—it appeared solid, enduring, vital.

As everyone knows, this was not the case. The bureaucracy, vast as it was, could not reach everywhere. Great areas of territory existed unknown to St. Petersburg except as shadings on the map, great sections of the population lived and died and knew the Tsar only as a name. The bureaus subsisted upon themselves, they lived and died watching their own operations, administering their own administration. The country was not too vast to be administered by a single Intelligence, but the Intelligence that administered it was not equal to the task; its rules and principles were not those by which an enduring structure can be reared. A superior Intelligence was required, a new rule was needed.

By 1917, the whole vast system was in process of disintegration. A political revolution in St. Petersburg had overthrown the Tsar, and had toppled the apex of the structure. To many it seemed that a new apex, a new figurehead, carved in the forms of democratic systems elsewhere, was all that was needed. For a time it appeared that with this new apex, together with a purging of the central, inmost chambers, the system would continue. The nation was at war; with new buttresses, the outer walls, upon the frontier, would continue to withstand the battering of the enemy.

This also was a mistake. The system was crumbling at its foundations. The customs and attitudes and traditions upon which the system rested, the principles and moral sanctions which form the cement that binds individuals in their primary relationships, were dissolving. They would continue to dissolve, irrespective of the temporary forms the outward mass assumed, until they had disappeared into the primary elements of life; and not until a new catalyst was introduced, a new and more enduring Principle was established, would they begin to coalesce and crystallize and form a new structure.

Paul Stepanovitch Markov, like most officers of the army, had no conception of the events that were taking place in the Empire at large, and certainly no understanding of their meaning, During the three years of his active service before the outbreak of the World War, he had been molded and chiseled to his place in the military scheme, and he did not look beyond it. This early service had been in Turkestan, in the same post where his father had commenced his military career. The army had been supreme there, standing above the civil authorities, and it had an active responsibility in the administration of affairs. The troops were, accordingly, well provided for, with billets and equipment of the best. Pride of service ran high.

It had so happened that the Austrian front to which Paul Stepanovitch had been transferred at the outbreak of hostilities was one in which army *esprit* was maintained. Despite the terrible defeats of 1915, morale had not broken, and honor had been retrieved by subsequent successes. Of all the units of the imperial forces, the Army of Galicia had enjoyed the greatest prestige, and had maintained the highest morale. The officers were proud, the men obedient, the organization complete, the services of supply competent.

After the issuance of the famous *Prikas,* or Order No. 1 of the Petrograd Soviet and Socialist Committee, however, a change began to appear in the troops. Though this order to form committees of soldiers to take charge of military units was addressed at first to the Petrograd troops, and was actually without authority of the Provisional Government, its effects were immediate and widespread. It was a sign for the dissolution of the armies. On the Austrian front, however, it appeared to be disregarded. On the contrary, a vigorous offensive was launched, and during July substantial victories were won at Brzezany and at Zborow. These victories were short-lived, and almost immediately thereafter the same dissolution began that was taking place elsewhere.

This change was marked, in the units of which Paul Stepanovitch was a member, by a lassitude that permeated the whole organization. The soldiers became unwilling to accept discipline, the officers had no interest in enforcing it. The services of supply faltered, and rations were not received, or were found stale when received. Commanders could not get prompt replies to their communications to headquarters, and this made them apathetic. Everybody was becoming shiftless and lackadaisical. The appearance of a sudden and overwhelming offensive on the part of the Austrians did not help matters. Men seemed to prefer death or capture to a stiffening of their discipline. They no longer wished to fight, for they no longer saw anything to fight for.

Toward the end of summer, when things grew no better, and rather worse, General Bievsky, in command of the 14th Division, obtained leave to retire with his men to Slavinka, in the Kuban, in the hope that rest would help morale. But nothing would help now. The dissolution of the flesh had set in; all that remained was the agony of death, and death itself.

Of this fact, however, Paul Stepanovitch was unaware. The men of his own company were loyal to him, and to all appearance their *esprit* was excellent.

This was due to the fact that Paul Stepanovitch was an excellent officer. He was in appearance everything that one expects in a soldier—tall and robust, with a finely balanced head and steady blue eyes, a carriage that was at once easy and supple and dignified—and for that reason, if for no other, he would have been admired by his men. But his qualities of command were equally apparent in his personal characteristics. He was thoughtful of his men's welfare, willing to share everything they endured, skilled in all the arts of warfare, and more courageous, more bold than any soldier he commanded. Beyond this, also, he was a stern and strict disciplinarian. He required of them cleanliness, orderliness and obedience above the soldiers of any other company in the regiment.

Paul Stepanovitch, therefore, saw no signs of weakening morale in his own company, and could not understand the necessity of the retirement to Slavinka. Nevertheless, he saw that his men were embarked promptly and in good order, and when they arrived at the Slavinka cantonment, he saw that they were assigned quarters that were clean, dry and well located.

After a month at Slavinka, the troops of the 14th Division were in a greater state of disaffection than when they arrived. Actual dissolution of authority, however, began at the top. The division was grouped in three brigades, in separate cantonments on opposite sides of the city. In two of these brigades the commanding officers and their staffs had lost the confidence of the officers of the line, particularly the colonels. The colonels, when they wanted anything, ignored the brigade commanders, and applied directly to division headquarters. Presently, the colonels lost the confidence of company commanders, who had, in turn, discovered that the only persons whom the soldiers respected were their immediate officers.

Order was, in fact, rapidly resolving itself into its simpler elements. Soon the soldiers would respect only their corporals and sergeants.

In the third brigade, in which Captain Markov was stationed, command was still intact, but this very fact tended to hasten its collapse. There were no concessions from above, there was no crack in the wall by which the smoldering fumes could escape. When finally the pressure became too strong, the result was explosion. This explosion occurred one night early in September.

On nights preceding this night in September, in a low-raftered basement room, lighted by a single incandescent lamp, the preparations for the event, and the manner of its execution, were being worked out in all detail by the Marxist revolutionary group, or cell, of Slavinka. The exact day and hour alone remained to be determined; that awaited word from Party headquarters. Volynski, chief of the cell, who by day was stationary engineer at the Slavinka water supply works and head of the union of engineers, plumbers and gas fitters in Slavinka, was to be proclaimed chief commissar.

Volynski was an appropriate character for this post, a neat-appearing man in his early fifties with a sharp, decisive manner that contrasted strangely with the monk-like expression in his black eyes. He could be most kind, yet most ruthless; he was a fanatical patriot, who was convinced that the welfare of his country required the extermination of the aristocracy and the elevation of the working man to power.

Volynski was now reciting again the assignments, and the procedure of the revolt. Kolodin was to assume command of the army—he had once been a captain of infantry, had been court-martialed, and degraded for fraternizing with his men, and finally discharged from the service for his subversive influence. Tuchevsky was to be placed in charge of public utilities, all services of which were to be shut off at the moment of the revolt. Other assignments followed, and then the details of arrests and proscriptions.

Volynski began reading a list of army officers and aristocrats who were to be seized immediately the outbreak began—men who were stigmatized because of their tendencies, their associations, their birth, or their holdings.

"Krylov, lieutenant colonel, to be arrested by Comrades Zilinsky, Shulgin, Mudenko."

The men named held up their hands.

"You will probably find the colonel at"—he named a certain officers' brothel—"any time of the day or night."

"Gurgensky, major, to be arrested by Comrades Kirin, Khabalov, Grasov."

He continued to read off the names and assignments, giving directions in each case. Occasionally, there was dissent, or remonstrance, or modifications suggested in the arrangements. These were noted, accepted, or rejected. Finally,

"Markov, captain, third brigade, assigned to Kuchenko, Sherkov, Dubinsky. You will find Markov difficult to deal with. He is liked by his men."

Kuchenko—Vasili Kuchenko—whose name was read as assigned to Markov, blanched. Vasili Kuchenko was of that order of men who stand at the other end of the spectrum from the flashing leaders of affairs—a little man with bald head, pale bluish eyes, and the abject manner of those who have been beaten and kicked about all their lives—the epitome of all those whom the Revolution was designed to uplift. Yet he was not one who would willingly undertake a revolution to change his lot. How he came to be associated with such a resolute, iron-willed crew was a mystery to him, as it was to a number of others. He had been drawn unwillingly—hypnotically it seemed—into the Communist ranks by a gathering he had attended in company with the orderly of an officer in the company next to his, and under the spell of Volynski's fiery address he had allowed himself to be enrolled.

Vasili Kuchenko was Markov's orderly.

"But my officer," he faltered. "He is not bad. What— what has he done?"

The protest was not addressed to the presiding officer, but was a plaint that issued from his lips, directed to no one. He was startled when his neighbor, a burly railway porter by the name of Gestov, growled,

"He's the worst of the lot—the way his head sticks in the air, and he struts as though he saw no one except giants. I know him. I've carried his luggage for him. If you don't step along quick, he barks at you. Worse than any other officer in the brigade."

"He's never beaten me," protested Vasili, bleatingly. "Besides, he's only a captain."

"Yes, and his tips were always good, but I don't like to hurry. I'm a porter, a free man working my own business, and he orders me to step lively."

"And he has large estates, which he never visits, I've heard," put in Roschenka, a sharp-eyed Jew, on the other side of Vasili. "That kind is what has made the sufferings of the peasant."

The talk came to the attention of the commander of the cell.

"Markov is the son of that infamous Colonel Markov, who massacred the Tartars at Baku," he stated, precisely and methodically, like a machine clipping off bits of tin plate. "That is enough to mark him for execution. The name Markov has been anathema to the Party for years. Had it not been for Colonel Markov and what he did at Baku the Caucasus would have been free in 1905, and the Revolution not delayed as it has been. Captain Markov is his son and must be arrested."

Vasili Kuchenko, quaking at his temerity, subsided.

The reading of the proscription list went on. . . .

After the meeting was over, Vasili Kuchenko returned to barracks, but first he went down by the river for a little walk. His officer was not expecting him back that night.

The placid Kuban seemed to soothe his harried thoughts. Vasili had never been in such torment in his life. He had never been used to thinking for himself and making decisions—that had always been done for him—and now when he was trying to resolve his conflicting loyalties he found it completely beyond him.

Walking along the river shore he became aware that he was on a bridle path. It lay in a park reserved exclusively for officers. This reminder that he was on forbidden ground filled him with a spasm of terror, and he involuntarily crouched among the shadows to avoid being seen.

But in a moment he took heart, remembering the fiery speeches and promises of Volynski.

"Pshaw!" he exclaimed, but not aloud. "Why shouldn't I? I am as good as any of them. Soon we will all be free to walk here."

Vasili began to ruminate. Among the trees the river gleamed dully, like a silver platter. He thought, "When the Day comes, and I don't have to polish boots, and press my officer's uniforms, and run his errands, I shall get on a boat, and go as far as the sea. And then, I shall go—"

He knew nothing of geography, and he could think of no place where he would care to go. He had merely heard the phrase "go to sea," and it had caught his fancy. But now, forced to think where he would go, he realized, with another quiver of terror, that he wanted to go nowhere.

What would he do if his officer were to be killed? If all officers were to be killed? Then he should have no living, for officer's orderly was all he knew how to be. The thought of having to go into town to look for work frightened him: he saw himself driven from door to door, growing more and more hungry, more and more miserable. . . .

There was prestige to being an officer's orderly. One had respect from the tradesmen and the porters, when he announced that he was orderly to so and so.

Then, his officer, Captain Markov, was certainly one of the best of the regiment. Other officers' orderlies showed him respect: it was because they heard their officers' gossip, and this gossip was all to Captain Markov's credit.

Kuchenko, for that matter, adored his officer with the abject adoration of a dog for its master. This affection, obtruding itself in his thoughts, with the reminder that his lot had been cast, and that it had fallen to him to partake in the arrest of Captain Markov, caused his skin to ripple in horror. Sweat broke out on his brow; he thought it was from the walking, and he paused and wiped his forehead with his sleeve. The brass buttons on the cuff caught and reflected the starlight; as they passed before his eyes Kuchenko could see the double-headed eagles with which they were impressed.

Vasili stared at these tiny emblems of empire, and it seemed to him that the world was about to crumble . . . crumble about his ears . . . swallow him up. . . .

Vasili began to sob softly.

4. The Revolt

FIRING had commenced at the upper end of the cantonment around the officers' barracks.

Captain Markov was in his company office at the time. Rumors had reached him that the Slavinka Soviet was preparing to issue a *prikas*, or proclamation, to the troops to renounce the authority of their officers and to set up revolutionary soviets. To forestall such an attempt among his own men, Markov had accordingly been keeping his company under the closest surveillance. In order to be near his men, and keep them under better control, he had some weeks before set up a cot in his office at the end of the company barracks.

At the sound of the firing he called for his orderly.

Vasili failed to appear.

Markov unlocked the door leading into the company hall. The room was deserted. The event which everyone had been expecting was about to occur.

Paul Stepanovitch Markov had a very clear concept of what his course should be. During his six years' active military service he had matured in will and faculty. The indecision that had characterized his early years had seemingly disappeared. He was a veteran of the wars, with passions resolved, purpose set, will supreme, and faculties clear. He understood what was happening. He realized that he was facing the greatest crisis of his career, that his life depended on his conduct at this moment; but his confidence in his powers was high.

Captain Markov's face set in a determined line. He stepped to the arms closet, took out two automatics, strapped them to his waist and threw a bandolier of cartridges across each shoulder. Then he put on his great coat and cap, belted it with another cartridge belt and holster for a third automatic, which he carried in his hand, and stepped into the company street.

The night was dark and a mist from the river had muffled the street lamps so that they shone as pale feathery globes. At the far end of the street, up near the brigade headquarters, a red glare had appeared, and points of light, that might be torches, moved about in the mist. The firing had increased and was accompanied by shouting and confused noises.

Markov had hardly stepped into the street when his orderly ran up.

"Captain, where are you going?" Vasili whispered frantically.

Vasili was bareheaded, and his tunic was unbuttoned. The light from the street lamp fell upon his bald head, and it shone with a nimbus. His face was drawn in a paroxysm of terror.

"Where are the men, Vasili?" Markov asked calmly.

"They are on the parade ground, now."

Vasili's voice was trembling, and his knees shook.

"No officers about?"

"They . . . they have barricaded themselves in the lodge."

"Get to your quarters," Markov ordered quietly, "and stay there. Keep out of trouble."

He was fond of Vasili, who had served him now for four years.

"No, no, Captain, it's useless," Vasili was protesting, so frantically that his throat rasped. "The whole brigade is in revolt."

Vasili's hands were clasped, and as he looked up to his captain so much taller than he, his expression, as the light

from the street lamp fell upon his upturned face, was like
a suppliant before an ikon.

"To your quarters, Vasili," Markov ordered, now
sharply.

"They'll kill you. Oh, for the love of God, for the love
of St. Peter and St. Paul, Captain, don't go. They are determined to kill you, Captain. I love you. Don't go."

Markov moved on. Vasili put himself in the way.

"Captain, you must not. Run away. You will find boats
tied up at the wharf."

Markov swore.

"By God, Vasili, what do you mean!" he exclaimed.
"Do you think I can run away! Get to your quarters."

"Captain, please, I tell you. They have already taken the
general. They are going to attack the lodge. Flee while
you can."

"Vasili," said Markov, controlling himself, and speaking reassuringly, "you mean well. But we can't let this
go on. What will happen to Russia if soldiers who are
sworn to defend her turn upon their commanders? We
must keep our discipline. If you love yourself, if you love
your country, get to your quarters and let me go about
my work."

"Holy Russia is no more," whispered Vasili. "Everything
is gone, the world is up-ended. The men are mad. They
are killing .They love you, but they will kill you. It's revolution, don't you see—it's revolution."

Markov's anger mounted.

"Get out of my way, Vasili."

Vasili again put himself in the path of his officer.

"No. Captain, you must not go."

In his anguish he put out his hand and touched his
officer's sleeve. Enraged, Markov struck Vasili heavily
with his fist.

The orderly sank in a heap to the ground. Markov
looked at him, as he lay in a huddle in the street, and
strode on.

Through the mist came suddenly the muffled detona-
tions of a howitzer. Mingled with it were shouts and

screams. Then the ground brought the sound of pounding, running feet.

At the foot of the street, Markov stopped and listened, to ascertain, if possible, in what direction the soldiers were moving. At the same time, with soldierly precaution, he covered himself by moving over against the barracks wall. From where he stood, in the shadow, he could see Vasili lying under the street light, cloaked with a pale luminescence.

It occurred to Markov that he had given his orderly a terrific blow, and he wondered, for a moment, if Vasili could be dead.

Well, he reflected, other men would be dead, for he would not hesitate to kill. He would kill every man who dared oppose him. He would kill until his last bullet was gone. Long before, when he was considering his course in the event of a revolt, he had coldly resolved to do so, if it were necessary. And cold resolution was now buttressed by hot fury, the hot and terrible fury that overwhelms men when they charge in battle, making him tremble in every muscle.

And then the realization came over him that he would be killing his own men. These were men he had led in battle. Among them were survivors of the battle of Lodz, men who had fought with him at the Vistula. Some of them had slept in the trenches with him along the Dunajec, that first hard winter of the war, and some had marched with him in the freezing snows of the Carpathians. These men were his comrades; they were like brothers to him, or his own children.

And with that realization, obtruding itself at so inappropriate a time, a perplexity which he had long ago thought to have vanquished, rose again, like a ghost from the past, like a spirit resurgent from the grave. What was his purpose?

What would killing them achieve? He himself would probably be killed in the end, for the revolt was now past any one man's power to stem. But though he realized that defeat was certain, what else could he do? What if all men in authority accepted defeat without a blow? How else was order to be restored except through will and discipline?

The firing and the shouting were increasing. Markov thought he could hear the men running in his direction. If they came as a mob . . . Vasili lying there would be trampled.

Markov went back to his orderly. Vasili was still stunned, and was quivering spasmodically.

The current of pity, long confined in Markov, rose to the surface, involuntarily, uncontrollably, like the sudden impulse that leads men, in the midst of battle, at the height of their fury toward the enemy, to pause in a charge to give a drink of water to a fallen adversary.

He raised Vasili gently and dragged him to the shelter of the wall.

As he did this a party of soldiers appeared at the head of the street and, seeing him, shouted. Markov drew his second automatic, and with both hands gripping gun butts, he prepared to defend himself.

The men came on, running.

Having surrendered, if but for a moment, to compassion, the heart now took full control of the will. Markov stood in indecision. He could not bring himself to fire upon these men—his own soldiers. Neither could his mouth open for words. He seemed to be stayed by a sudden paralysis of will and muscle. In a moment they would be upon him, and overwhelm him. With each instant of indecision, his paralysis increased. Suddenly, horror overtook him. and he could feel the hair rising on the nape of his neck.

By a mighty effort, Markov shook himself free. But his will was gone; his well-matured plans had dissolved into nothing.

Without realizing what he did, or why, he turned and fled.

Where he ran, or how long he ran, he did not know. He must have turned down a dark alley, and eluded his pursuers, for they were no longer following him. But still he ran, mechanically, without thought or plan. He seemed to be running in a dream, a nightmare in which it was not he that moved, but the scenes about him: they flitted by in dark shapes, dark patches and light patches, unreal, ghostly. Every now and then he seemed to hear bursts of fire, as in a sporadic cannonading, and once, it seemed, his vision was illuminated by the flash of flame.

All sorts of images began to rise before his mind, formed of the gray buildings and the patches of light that were the company streets; they became the woodlands and meadows of his home in Varsova, the streets of Petrograd, the sand hills and deserts of Turkestan where he had begun his career as a soldier, the Carpathian Mountains where they had fought the Austrians. All sorts of sounds filled his ears—an orchestra playing a lively dance tune, then a funeral dirge, leaden to mark the leaden pounding of his feet, the roll of drums and the cry of bugles. . . .

Markov was running mechanically, and his thoughts were flowing mechanically, with the images passing through his mind like caissons rumbling through an unlighted street. But gradually they began to organize, and to become connected. He was, without having consciously so decided, making his way to the muleteers' gate, from which he would be able to pass to the cantonments of the first brigade. The purpose had formed in his mind to go there and arouse aid.

Yet that was impossible. If his own brigade had revolted, conditions were certainly worse in the other cantonments. The town, no doubt, was also in control of the revolutionists.

Suddenly, out of the darkness, a party of men appeared, directly in his path. Markov's eyes were blurred from sweat and the exhaustion of his flight, and he could not distinguish their insignia. He recognized only that the man in their lead was not a soldier, but a squat, thickset person in a black leather jacket.

Markov again turned and fled.

"After him," screamed Tuchevsky. "It's Markov."

The soldiers began pursuit, firing their rifles as they ran.

Markov was growing weary, and as his weariness increased, his terror of being taken mounted. His heavy automatics weighed him down and slowed his running. The men were gaining on him.

Other soldiers were joining in the pursuit; they were converging in his direction. Markov felt himself to be a hunted rabbit. His only advantage in this moment was the darkness.

There appeared before him, among the trees, a pallor that twinkled faintly with points of light. This was the Kuban River, and the pallor was the reflection of the star-lit sky and the lights of the city. Just beyond Markov was a sharp embankment that went down to the officers' park.

Markov ran, panting heavily, along the edge of the embankment, and came to the path that led down to the water.

If he could reach the wharf, he thought, he could take one of the skiffs and escape to the opposite shore.

He reached the water's edge and came to the wharf; here he scanned the water frantically to find one of the boats. But for some reason, there was none. Others, no doubt, had already taken them for the same purpose.

Markov's pursuers were now on the embankment above him. He could hear Tuchevsky screaming and barking orders.

Like a slinking dog, Markov crouched under the wharf to hide himself. He was standing knee-deep in water. He could hear his pursuers scrambling down the bank.

Markov glanced apprehensively at the river. It was a good verst to the opposite shore, which was visible only as a dark line along the horizon. The water was smooth and silent, flowing in the night like molten lead.

His resolution driven by fear, by resentment, by insane defiance of his pursuers, Markov determined to attempt to swim the river.

He hastily removed his overcoat, his arms, and his boots, wrapped the overcoat around the automatics, and waded into the stream. When he was in to his shoulders he dropped his bundle and let it sink. He felt the bundle settle into the water and touch his foot. He was now unarmed and defenseless.

Sinking into the water, Markov began to swim.

He was some distance beyond the end of the quay when the soldiers reached the river's edge.

"There he is," yelled Tuchevsky. "Hear him threshing the water?"

A volley was fired and the bullets struck about Markov and threw up little spouts of water.

The mist and the darkness now intervened to cut off sight of the swimmer and sound of his swimming. The firing ceased. . . .

Markov was a good swimmer, and a verst was no great distance to swim, but the current was treacherous and the water was cold, and Markov was already exhausted from flight and surrender to fear. He swam until he was exhausted, and then turned over and floated. The coldness of the water was benumbing and Markov felt himself being sucked down. He turned over and swam on his side. That seemed to rest him and prevent the current from drawing him down. His clothes clung to him and impeded his stroke. He managed to unbutton his heavy outer tunic and pull it off, though in doing so he sank and remained submerged until his breath was gone and he had to fight his way to the surface.

The thought flashed over him that had he been weighted down by his automatics, he would never have reached the surface. But the thought that succeeded this thought—that if he reached the opposite shore he would be without arms or defense—caused a fresh qualm of terror to pass over him.

Markov had now been swimming a long time, but the shore was still invisible. How far away it was he could not tell because of the mist that clung to the surface of the water. Perhaps he was not swimming in the right direction. He felt his strength ebbing, and he summoned all his will power to keep going. But a will power that made him a courageous commander, that brought him to the edge of the enemy's trenches, could not sustain him against the implacable elements. He beat frantically against the waters, and with this beating his last reserves of strength disappeared. The current was drawing him under.

For the first time in this awful affair, since his words with Vasili, his tongue formed words.

"O God," he involuntarily cried. "Must I drown? Give me strength!"

The answer to this cry of anguish was the appearance, out of the mist, of the dark bulk of a river boat. It was a broad-beamed tug, and it was bearing full upon him.

To Markov this boat was the bearer of death. The watch, if there was one, did not see him, and in a moment the tug would be upon him. At this new danger his strength revived, and he swam mightily, frantically, to get out of the way. He thought he could hold out no longer. He could hear the parting of the waters like the roar of a waterfall; the boat loomed above him like a falling avalanche. A horrible smell struck his nostrils, and his throat was filled with slime. He was sinking. . . .

The boat floated by, grazing him as it did so.

The boat went by, and then a raft or barge in tow, and another, all riding deep in the water. Markov was at the mercy of their wake.

The last one passed, and Markov felt a rope drag across him.

He clutched it and held on, and the rope dragged him down. He drew himself hand over hand until he could feel the side of the barge. His hands came upon an iron ring. He gripped it, and drew himself up. With a prodigious effort, he pulled himself over the gunwale and lay upon the afterdeck.

Exhausted, he stretched himself out and lay there, cold and shivering, until he slipped into unconsciousness.

5. Karim Agha

KARIM AGHA had been a boatman on the Kuban River for twelve years, loading his barges with timber and hides and grain in Kovel and floating them down to Bhargovensk, bringing the barges, less heavily loaded, with small ware, back up the river by means of a decrepit steam tug. Since the building of the rail line, which moved goods so much more swiftly, traffic on the river had almost died out, and what traffic was left fell to the lot of Tartar boatmen, like Karim Agha, to whom time was something static and who did not know that interest accumulated by the clock.

Nevertheless, because time was nothing to him, and because he knew nothing of banks and loans, and hence of interest, Karim Agha had managed to prosper, and to recoup some of the wealth he had formerly possessed.

Twelve years before, Karim Agha had been a well-to-do merchant of small ware in Baku. Conceiving that his trade and his morals were suffering from contamination with the Christians, he had become a Christian-hater, and a follower of the mullah Baba Ibrahim. He had partaken of the abortive revolt of 1905, had been arrested in consequence, fined the equivalent of all his property, and released on condition that he exile himself from Baku. Since that time, in the calmer atmosphere of the Kuban River, and among the silences of the water, he had had occasion to reflect on his earlier fanaticism, to consider anew the will of Allah, and to curb his impetuosity.

Yesterday Karim Agha's barges had been tied up at the Slavinka wharves. Before he had had time to discharge his cargo, however, all the porters had quit the wharf, and the iron doors of the warehouses had been rung down and locked. That night, while the streets were filled with the noise of rioting, Karim Agha, fearful that he might again be arrested, ordered the hawsers loosed, and the barges set into the stream.

It was now daylight, and Karim Agha's barges were well down the river toward Kharshov. Karim Agha himself was on deck inspecting the barges, one by one. Though he was an old man, with spindly legs and spidery fingers, he went easily along the hawsers by which the barges were held in tow, and climbed nimbly over the gunwales, disdaining the aid of the boatmen who accompanied him.

He reached the barge, and paused to look at the morning. The mist was clearing, and a golden sun was peering through the haze along the horizon. It was the beginning of a lovely day of autumn, a day rich with the air and sights of September. The broad river was placid and in the morning light its silt-filled water was a mirror that reflected the wooded banks and the mountains along the horizon. Karim Agha, thankful that he had escaped the disorders in Slavinka, thankful for the gracious morning, lifted his hands heavenward, and murmured the invocation of his Faith, "In the name of Allah the Compassionate, the Merciful."

He moved on, followed by his men, their loose slippers clumping noiselessly on the planking, until he reached the last barge. There he paused, as he beheld a shapeless form lying huddled against the stern gunwale.

It was a man, clad in the soggy tunic and trousers of the Russian army. The bare feet were white and watershrunken, the hands, clutching the tunic, were pale and bloodless; the face was like that of a corpse.

"How came that here?" Karim Agha asked.

"We know not," responded Gooli, his boatswain.

Gooli went up and looked at the figure.

"He is a Russian officer," he grunted. "Shall we throw him overboard?"

Like a flash of lightning, hatred and the remembrance of wrongs done him by the Russians at Baku illuminated Karim Agha's face. He heard again the sharp pounding of the revolver butts on the door of his shop in Baku, again he was peering in terror from his upper window, while his wife clung to his gabardine, looking down at the armed and uniformed soldiers in the street. He remembered how he had gone down and unlatched the door, how the soldiers had burst in and begun to wreck his shop, smashing jars and containers until the floor was littered with debris. They had said nothing, they had gone straight to the work, without asking his name or presenting warrants. He had tried to protest, had pleaded, had stood in front of his showcase—a recent purchase, which had cost him dear —but at this they had given him a furious blow that had sent him sprawling, and then with another furious blow they had smashed the precious glass into a thousand shivering pieces. . . .

After that they had arrested him, as he was, without so much as allowing him to put on his skullcap, without which no good Tartar appears in the street. Without showing him a warrant, they had dragged him forth and had lodged him in prison, a vile prison, full of stenches, where there was no water with which to wash before praying, a place full of Christian vileness. . . .

Karim Agha's wife and children had suffered miserably during his imprisonment. When he was released, he learned that one of his children had died. As for that, however, Allah had blessed him with another son to take the place of him who had died. . . .

All that, however, had occurred twelve years before. Karim Agha had in those years tried to forget, remembering that Allah loves compassion and mercy, remembering also that the Russians were masters, remembering that vengeance would be visited by vengeance, and that it did no good to complain against fate. . . .

In a monotonous, high-pitched voice, Karim Agha asked,

"Does he live?"

Gooli bent over the figure.

"Yes."

In Slavinka, yesterday, Karim Agha had been talking with Muli Hassan, the proprietor of the teahouse, who knew all that was happening, and all that was rumored to be about to happen. Muli Hassan had said there would be a revolt, a new revolution.

"Then," he had said, "Russian dog will eat Russian dog. Then we shall have our loads lightened. Then we can exact the vengeance which is ours by right."

"What should we Tartars do?" Karim Agha had asked.

"Burn, kill," Muli Hassan had whispered, leaning over to Karim Agha's ear. "Wherever you see a helpless Russion, kill him."

Ali Ashraf, a moneylender of Slavinka, whose ears could detect the fall of a coin in a pile of down, had overheard what Muli Hassan had said, and had warned, in a croaking voice,

"But where no one will see you. Eyes are everywhere."

Karim Agha looked about him. The day was clear and growing brilliant. From the shore one could see every movement on the barges. Eyes might at this moment be upon them. Or the Russian might revive, if they tossed him into the water, and swim ashore. That would be bad; that would bring its consequences. Besides, had not Muli Hassan said, "Russian dog will eat Russian dog"? Karim Agha could carry the Russian on to Bhargovensk, and then, since he was an officer, he would no doubt meet his end quickly enough. Or perhaps, later, when they came to the swamp flats, a better opportunity might arise to rid himself of this baggage. . . .

"Let him lie," he said.

He turned, and started forward, paying no further attention to the prostrate figure, but began to talk with his men about the shallows that lay ahead, giving directions about the manner in which they should be negotiated.

An hour later, Karim Agha was squatting, with his men, about a charcoal brazier, in the deckhouse of the tug, intent on the breakfast that was cooking on the coals, when he heard the sliding door of the cabin open. He looked up and saw the Russian standing there, his eyes bloodshot, his clothing wet and clinging to his flesh. He was swaying slightly and he gripped the door jamb for support. As Karim Agha looked up, the Russian pulled himself erect, and stepped inside the room.

"Good morning," he said.

Karim Agha said nothing, nor did any of his men.

"I shall be glad to eat with you," the Russian said.

Karim Agha went to the hatch and grunted loudly. A boy appeared, a Tartar lad of twelve or fourteen years of age.

"My father does not speak Russian," he said, haltingly. "What it is you wish?"

"I would like something to eat."

The boy translated.

Karim Agha looked at the Russian with the same impassive immobility he had shown at the intrusion. After a moment, he said,

"You may have something to eat."

Gooli spoke to him in Tartar, which Markov did not understand.

"Do you know what you do, sire?" he protested.

Karim Agha silenced him with a nod.

One of the men now removed some eggs that had been roasting near the coals, took some goats' milk cheese and rolled it in a strip torn from a large brown sheet of bread, and handed them to the Russian. There was tea but they did not offer it, unwilling to defile their utensils by allowing them to be touched by a Christian. The Russian drew a kopek from his soggy pocket and tossed it to Karim Agha.

"I have some money," he said, "and I will pay for a cup."

The men hesitated, glancing toward their master. Karim Agha's eye flickered in the affirmative, and one of them handed the Russian a cup.

Karim Agha asked, through his son,

"How did you come to be aboard?"

"I was swimming, when your boat bore down upon me."

"You swim with your clothes on?" Karim Agha asked. The question conveyed no curiosity. It was hardly a question, more a statement showing understanding.

One of the men stood up, and then another, and one of them moved nearer to the Russian. For his part, he glanced about the cabin, took careful note of its contents, and of the number of his adversaries.

"When it is necessary," he said shortly.

Behind him, standing against the wall, was an iron bar. It served no purpose that was apparent. He set down his cup, and took it in his hands, looked at it, hefted it—all with the manner of utmost casualness—and then set it down by his side.

"Those are military clothes?" continued Karim Agha, still in the form of an interrogation that was not a question.

"Yes. I am an officer in the army of the Provisional Government."

"Your name?"

"Paul Stepanovitch Markov."

Karim Agha, with a slight movement, put his hand to his belt, where he carried a short sailor's dirk. But his expression remained unmoved.

"Your father was an officer?"

"Yes."

"Stationed at Baku?"

"For a while."

Gooli, who had been crouching behind his master, made to rise, but Karim Agha again stayed him with a movement of his hand.

"When do we reach Bhargovensk?" Markov asked.

The question was repeated, before Karim Agha answered,

"In ten days, God willing."

"I shall remain with you until we reach that city," Markov announced.

At that moment the helmsman, in the fore part of the tug, gave a shout. The members of the crew hurried on deck, leaving Markov alone with Karim Agha and his son.

"What is the matter?" Markov asked.

"We are in the shallows," the boy replied, "and it may be necessary to pole."

They had come to the flats of Ashiev, where the river broadens and slows in its course, dropping its silt, which forms shoals and marshy islands. Great care was necessary to follow the current, which shifted among the shoals according to the height of the water. At this season of the year the water was low, and the shoals were especially treacherous.

They were among these shoals now, and it required the efforts of all the crew, lined along the gunwales of the barges, working with long poles, to keep from stranding.

Markov saw, as he went on deck, that despite the greatest efforts of the men the current was lazily but definitely carrying the barges among the reeds.

He laid aside his iron rod, which he had brought with him, and, picking up a pole, began to thrust into the water.

Karim Agha, standing in the tug, muttered to himself as he watched Markov.

By much effort, they succeeded in keeping clear, and getting out into the channel. A little later, however, poling had to be repeated, and again and again during the day. Late that afternoon, Karim Agha ordered the barges tied up in an inlet to avoid grounding during the night.

Next day the men had to pole again, and Markov again shared in the labor. Karim Agha watched him at work, from the deck of the tug, his slit-like eyes taking in Markov's every movement. Once or twice his hand rose to his belt, where the dirk was fastened, but on each occasion the hand relaxed its grip and returned to his side.

Gooli, who was like a shadow to his master's desires, noted this movement, and spoke to him privately, during a moment of rest:

"The Russian is awkward with the pole. Should he become unbalanced—"

Karim Agha gave him a piercing glance, and then his eyes softened in affection for his servant, and he said,

"It is written in the blessed Koran, in the Sura known as Sad, 'Judge therefore between men with truth, and follow not thy passions, lest they cause thee to err from the way of God.' It is not yet time for judgment, Gooli."

Markov's bare feet were beginning to bleed upon the planking. Karim Agha saw these stains of Christian blood on his boat, and called his son.

"Yes, father."

"Is there not a pair of *baboosh* in my chest?"

"Yes, father."

"Fetch them and give them to the Russian."

Markov accepted the slippers, touching his forehead to Karim Agha, in token of appreciation, and went on with his work.

The barges finally became locked in a shoal from which the utmost efforts of the crew failed to dislodge it, and Karim Agha gave orders to abandon further efforts until morning. That evening, one of the Tartars rowed ashore in a goatskin coracle, to obtain eggs and cheese from the peasants.

The next day the men all slept, and the river was silent save for the water washing among the reeds and the herons calling from the marshes along the shore. The sun rose and scattered its plumage upon the waters, became a blinding chariot in the upper sky, and sank in a field of flame, but that was the only movement in this autumn tableau.

While the men slept, Karim Agha, awake, was squatting in the cabin of the tug, staring at the glowing brazier. His face was immobile, as always, revealing nothing of the thoughts that went on in his little, weazened head, or of the emotions that filled his breast. Only now and then, when he stirred slightly on his haunches, did his movements give any indication that he had advanced a stage in his thinking, and was considering some new aspect of the subject he was pondering.

Karim Agha was trying, as the Koran had enjoined, to judge between men with truth, but the truth eluded him. For twelve years he had tried to forget his wrongs at Baku, in the knowledge that remembrance was futile, that vengeance would be visited with vengeance, and that he must accept his *kismet*. But memory had eluded him, as a dog eludes its master, and kept romping about in his mind to inflame him with resentment. And now truth eluded him. What was the truth of judgment?

Should he judge this man by the Russian God, or by the God of the Moslem?

The Russian God was a god of justice. If he judged this man with justice, his fate was sealed. Karim Agha could do no less than drive the dirk into his heart for the male-factor, and the son of a malefactor, that he was. Karim Agha was inclined to judge the Russian by his own god. The Russians were professors of justice—let him have justice. Vengeance for vengeance!

But his God, Allah, was not a God of justice. He was an inscrutable Being whose ways were above finding out, limited to no canons or rules. Of all the ninety and nine attributes of Allah, what were the two He loved most? Every Moslem repeated them—"In the name of Allah the Compassionate, the Merciful." Not "In the name of Allah the Infinite, the Just," not, "In the name of Allah the Righteous, the Unmoved," but simply, "In the name of Allah the Compassionate, the Merciful."

If he judged this Russian, Karim Agha thought by the injunctions of his Moslem faith, then he could not judge him at all. He must execute something besides justice.

"In the name of Allah the Compassionate, the Merciful."

That, of course, was not according to Karim Agha's desires.

He began to tell his beads, reciting the ninety and nine attributes of Allah—His justice, His wisdom, His majesty, His everlastingness, His truth—but all the time, the in-vocation kept recurring to him,

"In the name of Allah the Compassionate, the Merciful."

"Why this insistence upon His compassion, His mercy?" Karim Agha wondered in perplexity. Never before had he given the invocation more than passing thought. It was a phrase used by the devout, that was all. But now it stayed him like a magic circle drawn about him; it held his hand as by an invisible cord. Why, he asked himself again, this insistence upon Allah's compassion? Should He not have taken greater glory in having formed the stars, and compelling them to their orbits, and in having made the mighty ocean and the towering hills? Was not His majesty, which was like that of no sultan or tsar, but gor-geous as the flames of the evening sun, more to be adored than His compassion? What were compassion and mercy that they should stand so high upon the agate steps of the throne of God, above timelessness and spaciousness,

above dominion and power? Were they virtues so dazzling, so precious, that God should wear them as his particular jewels above all others?

Karim Agha's perplexity continued to mount, while he
thumbed his beads.

But of that perplexity nothing was revealed in Karim
Agha's face, which remained, as ever, passive and immobile, or in his telling of his beads, or in his posture, as he
squatted, unblinking, staring at the glowing coals of the
brazier.

6. Reverie

PAUL STEPANOVITCH MARKOV had come on deck to wash
and bandage his feet.

As he sat against the cabin house, in the sunlight, gazing
at the distant shore, Paul Stepanovitch fell to thinking.

During these past days his strength had revived, and
aside from his bleeding feet he was well and strong. The
hard work at poling had given him a delectable physical
weariness, a tingling and pleasant aching of his muscles
that made sleep quick and dreamless, hunger active and
wholesome; most of all it had driven somber thought from
his mind, had purged it, for the moment, of the vitiating
poison of reflection.

Gazing at the distant shore, upon the silent and static
world, he gradually lost consciousness of himself and of
where he was. The warm sunshine was a soporific; it fell
upon him like a golden down, fleecy and comforting,
shutting out the visible world. He drifted into another universe, removed by a vast and impassable gulf from that
which he had known. For a while that world seemed to
disappear, and he lived as a speck floating in ethereal
space, in the midst of an ocean of time, swimming in the
illuminated mists that existed before the world was made,

before its creatures had been called into existence. Nothing existed, save himself, neither pain nor sorrow, neither birth nor death.

It was a scene, and a moment, of which philosophers dream, when, divested of the concerns of material existence, freed from all considerations of time and place and duty, they may grapple with the problems of the Absolute, the reality of existence, the meaning and course of destiny. . . .

How long he sat in this reverie, Paul Stepanovitch did not know. Gradually, the physical world returned, obtruded itself upon this somnolence, not clearly, but like the dawn of a foggy morning, in which objects assume fantastic and portentous shapes, in which the mind struggles between sleep and waking.

This awakening was not pleasant. Out of the murk of returning objectivity appeared unhappy memories; scenes began to form out of the void that assaulted the peace of reverie and racked the soul.

Markov's eyes gazed from the rim of the gunwale upon the morning—golden and placid and peaceful—but they saw neither the wooded shores, nor the mirroring water, nor the opalescent haze of the distance. Instead, Markov saw himself facing the soldiers in the company street, saw himself turning and fleeing, saw himself cornered like an animal, with terror in his eyes, and finally plunging into the river, like a desperate rat driven from a ship.

Markov became fully alive, and he began to struggle with these memories.

He recognized that he was on a boat, that he was safe now, for a while. Yet it was not safety that mattered. The thing that mattered was to drive from his mind the remembrance of his cowardice. His task was to reassert his faculties, reassert the supremacy of his will. Once that was achieved, it did not matter what he had done, or where he was going; he could reverse the course, were it headlong toward hell.

To assert the will, yes, that was the supreme task with Paul Stepanovitch Markov. That was the key to every situation. The will masters the faculties and brings them under control; when the faculties are under perfect control, then, and only then, can the individual control others.

But he could not forget that he had been a coward, that he had soiled his honor in a crucial test. Though he momentarily succeeded in driving the remembrance from his mind, it still remained. It was like a grain of sand in the shoe, a mote in the eye, troubling him with resurgent doubts. He had fled. There was nothing he could do about that. He could not return. He could only continue in flight. That which he might have protected and preserved, had he remained, was gone, completely gone. One man has been known to save a battle. In Slavinka, the night of the revolt, one man might have preserved the brigade. Markov had had that opportunity; he alone of all the officers was outside the barricade, and in a strategical position to command the men. He had fled.

Markov was not so foolish as to assume that he might have stemmed, single-handed, the flood of revolution, or even have prevented the revolt of his brigade. But as he was convinced that order was the product of human will, so he was convinced that the revolt had come because of the decay of will.

The will, that was it. He must assert his will, and drive out these devitalizing thoughts, this memory of weakness, and instead draw upon his untapped reserves of power and vitality.

He grew restless. He rose and paced up and down the deck, but his restlessness increased as he walked, for he realized that however much he walked he was going nowhere. The boat was lodged fast in the river.

What was happening ashore? The wooded fringe along the water gave him no clue. The mournful cry of the heron did not explain. Had the revolt been put down? Or had it been successful? What was happening along the battle front? How could the armies hold back the Germans, the Austrians, and the Turks, if the troops in the rear were mutinying? Was the whole nation collapsing? If so, the land would be overrun with the foe, from the Baltic to the Caucasus—Ukraine, Finland, Poland, the Lettish provinces, Russian Armenia, all these rich lands won for the Empire in times past would be surrendered.

He must reach Bhargovensk and hasten to rejoin his army. This delay was preposterous. Time was of the essence.

Markov's nervous energy grew as he thought of these things. Finally, he could contain himself no longer. He went forward to speak to Karim Agha.

Karim Agha was not asleep, he discovered, but squatting alone in the deckhouse, staring unseeingly at the brazier. When Markov entered, Karim Agha opened his eyes slightly and, seeing who it was, summoned his son.

"How long will we be here?" Markov asked.

Azeem translated.

"I do not know," said the Tartar, simply.

"What are you waiting for?"

"For a rise in the river."

"At this time of year?" Markov asked in consternation.

"Only a rise in the water will lift the barges."

"But if the water doesn't rise?"

Karim Agha shrugged his shoulders.

"But you have cargo that is due in Bhargovensk."

"It will keep."

"Why do you not fire the boilers? We could set the tug upstream and get the barges off the bar in no time."

"We have no fuel."

This was a fact. The tug was along to tow the barges back up the river, and fuel would not be taken on until they started the homeward journey. Going downstream, they floated with the current.

"Put men ashore chopping down timber. We could bring enough aboard in the coracle to get up steam and pull the barges off."

"We will wait until the water lifts them," responded Karim Agha impassively.

"And when will that be?" demanded Markov impatiently.

"It is in the hands of God."

Markov looked at the Tartar in disdain. Karim Agha

wore an air of timelessness about him, as though today were one with yesterday, or a thousand years before. Age was the marrow of his bones; it nourished him like a blood stream.

"It is in the hands of God."

Such an attitude was revolting to Paul Stepanovitch Markov. If Karim Agha stayed here until the planks of his barges rotted, it would not be because of God, but because of Karim Agha's laziness or stupidity!

"Hands of God!" he expostulated. "Let us take things into our own hands."

Karim Agha was silent long after his son had translated the words. Finally he spoke.

" 'It is God,' said the Prophet, 'who sendeth the winds and uplifteth the clouds, and, as He pleaseth, spreadeth them on high, and breaketh them up!' Did we take things into our own hands, you would no doubt be dead by now."

"Why do you say that?"

Karim Agha avoided the question. An expression of pity came into his wrinkled, passionless countenance, as he said, softly,

"You are safe here. Ashore you might be killed."

A tremor passed over Paul Stepanovitch, a remembrance of the soldiers rushing on him at Slavinka.

"How do you know?" he faltered.

"The whole land is in revolt—a new revolution. They call themselves Reds. You are an enemy of the Reds, since you are in flight. Bhargovensk is in their complete control. I had it from Gooli, who went ashore last night."

The aplomb suddenly went out of Paul Stepanovitch. He turned abruptly and went on deck again, where he began to pace up and down in agitation.

Gradually, however, his spirit grew quieter; his mood of futility and frustration subsided; he stood and gazed upon the placid river.

No change had occurred in the landscape; all was as static and silent as a scene painted on canvas; only the herons continued to rise above the marsh, the sun to course through the limpid sky, and the water to lap with a barcarole against the planking. But a change had come over Paul Stepanovitch, the peace of resignation. And out of this momentary resignation of the will came a revival of strength and hope. He was safe here, he realized. In time, the water would rise; he must accept this delay, and meantime gather strength and reserves, and make his plans for what he should do.

Paul Stepanovitch again began to study the river scene. He watched the heron wading in the marsh, observed and noted the rich colors of the grass, and the hues of the autumn foliage along the shore. He began again to dream, lazily, of his boyhood days at Varsova, where there was also a river, and autumn foliage and autumn scenes. It was an experience he had not often allowed himself, this of reverie and reminiscence, but now he was living again his boyhood, at home with his mother, and recalling the happy parties and excursions when his father was home on leave. He thought also of his school days, and of the days when he was a member of the Imperial Corps of Cadets, happy, proud, elegant in the cadets' uniform; and he thought of the parties he had attended, of the ball at Prince Cherniloff's, of the Princess Irina Sabayeva. The princess, he had heard, had married Ensign Kriensky, who shortly afterward had developed an affliction of the eyes, and had been retired from service, and they were now living in Warsaw with their two children. Paul Stepanovitch wondered where Alexei Petrovitch Dosti was. Alexei had miraculously been delivered from the countess, and he and Paul had seen service together during the early war years; but then Alexei had been transferred, and Markov had lost touch with him. . . .

And so Paul Stepanovitch continued to muse, and partake of the peace of the river, soaking it up as a wick draws up the oil from a basin, growing comfortable, and relaxed, and ceasing to care how soon the barges would be freed. . . .

The barges remained lodged upon the shoal for seven days, at the end of which time a rise in the water came, apparently from some late rains in the upper reaches.

Three days later the church spires and minarets of Bhargovensk appeared out of the mist, and that night they moved down into the town, tying up at the wharves along the Tartar quarter.

Next morning Karim Agha sent Gooli ashore. Gooli returned after a while with a bundle, which Karim Agha handed to Markov. It was an outfit of civilian clothes.

"My father says you should wear them, lest your uniform cause you to be arrested," said Azeem.

Paul Stepanovitch was overwhelmed.

"Your father is very kind," he said to the boy.

"It is nothing. He does it for his *izzet*."

"His *izzet?*"

"I do not know what *izzet* is in Russian, but something like honor or merit. It is commanded by the Prophet to make gifts to the needy. By getting *izzet*, one comes to Paradise. It is for *izzet* that my father gives you passage and provides you with clothing. You are needy, and he is happy to help you."

Paul Stepanovitch cast his eyes over the tug, and the barges, upon which he had spent the past two weeks, and suddenly he was reluctant to leave. There was a peaceful quality here that he had never known before, and now that he was going, it seemed that he had allowed a precious experience to slip out of his life without appreciating what it meant. He felt that never again would such a peaceful interlude come to him. He would go now, to take his part in the violent affairs of his country, and he would never return: he would go down into his grave struggling, fighting, always in action and movement.

He went and changed into the garb that Azeem had brought—it was a suit of black broadcloth, very frayed, such as a clerk might wear—and returned on deck. He spoke his thanks to Karim Agha, who listened without a trace of expression in his face to reveal what his thoughts might be, and then, drawing a golden coin from his pocket, he spoke to Azeem.

"Tell your father that I hope he has acquired much *izzet* in this gift and in the gift of his hospitality," he said, and went up and thrust the coin into the boy's hand, "But since you gain no *izzet* by what your father has done, take this and buy yourself something that pleases you."

He touched his forehead in salute and went across the plank that stretched from the gunwale to the quay, while the boy smiled and waved to him.

7. Home

PAUL STEPANOVITCH MARKOV was going home. He was tired. It would be a tramp of fifty versts across country to Varsova, near where the family estates lay, but he did not mind. His weariness was of the spirit, not of the body.

Paul Stepanovitch had awakened to the fact that he was an outcast—worse, a fugitive. After traveling half the distance to Ukrasnova, his army headquarters, he had come at last to realize that such a journey was futile. The army no longer existed. Wild stories reached him now from every hand of what had happened: mass revolt, wholesale executions of officers, depredations upon civilians, the whole countryside in flames and riot. To go on to Ukrasnova was to go to certain arrest and execution.

Paul Stepanovitch had gone to Kazan, where he had thought to have friends highly placed in the administration, from whom he might seek counsel or take aid. In particular, he thought of Prince Cherniloff, who had been made provincial governor at Kazan in 1913, and who, Paul Stepanovitch understood, was still incumbent.

But the prince was not at Kazan. Paul Stepanovitch learned, by enquiry, that the prince was in Paris, that he had secretly left his post the summer before, on the excuse of taking a cure for rheumatism, and that he had fled abroad. Paul Stepanovitch was amazed. This was the man who had talked to him so eloquently of duty, and of imperial destiny, and of strength of purpose. And at the

first signs of trouble, he had cravenly fled! Paul Stepanovitch could not understand such conduct. It was incomprehensible and left him bewildered. If the leaders at the
top were abdicating in such an abject manner, he thought,
what could they expect of their subordinates?

But Paul Stepanovitch's thoughts did not rise to bitterness against Prince Cherniloff. It did not occur to him
that he had been beguiled to his own misfortune by the
prince's counsel. He had too many other things to think
about, he was too occupied in grasping what was actually
happening either to concern himself with the propriety of
other people's conduct or to analyze his own concepts of
life. He was trying his best to discover in these events
some underlying order or purpose. Everything was in
confusion. A soviet of workers was in control of the city,
and there were commissars of this and commissars of that.
They could be told by the way they raced about town in
big automobiles with armed guards perched on the running boards. And there were other manifestations the like
of which Paul Stepanovitch had never seen. Everywhere
were soldiers with red arm bands and guards, bulletins,
propaganda, speeches, processions, arrests, decrees, pro-
clamations, shops being opened, and shops being closed,
red bunting flying, bulletins, propaganda, speeches, processions. . . .

Who were these new rulers? From where had they
come? They were people Paul Stepanovitch had never
heard of. People thrown up to the surface, from an un-
derstratum of life which Paul Stepanovitch had never
known, like scum brought to the surface in a boiling caldron.

In this new order of things, Paul Stepanovitch realized
with bewilderment, there was no room for one like himself. The old world had been thrown down, like a Roman
temple, and he was like one of its polished stones, riven
from its place, cast down, of no use except in the place
for which it had been hewn, of no use except in supporting an established order.

Nevertheless, Paul Stepanovitch, who had no interest
in politics, but who loved his country and was willing to

serve any government that would defend the frontiers, had considered going to the Soviet officials and offering his services. It was Budenko, a Jew whom he had known in Krasnov, who forewarned him, and made him aware of his complete isolation from the new order.

"You are a Markov," the Jew had said, "and your father was concerned—I do not know to what extent, and I do not judge—with the massacre of the Tartars at Baku. The name has long been bitter in the mouths of the Social Revolutionaries."

It was this Budenko who provided Markov with a new passport, certifying that he was one Nicolai Gorov, and that his occupation was that of railway clerk, and it was by means of this passport that he had since been wandering about the town, looking for news, looking for friends, looking for an opportunity for service.

Markov detested going under an assumed name, and wearing a masquerade, as he called his civilian clothes, but he knew nothing else to do. Fear was again beginning to creep upon him, fear that he could not analyze nor dispel. All his props were being kicked away; he was standing alone, now, deprived of his rank, his associations, his place in society, his occupation and his purpose in life.

He was beginning to act a coward. He had decided to go to Petrograd, to seek friends there. At the railway station at Kazan, there had been an immense crowd, pushing and milling, and trying to get through the gates. Markov had wormed his way almost to the barrier, before he saw that he would have to pass the scrutiny of the Red officials. They were seated behind a table just in front of the gate, and no one could pass through until the officials had examined and stamped the passport.

When Markov saw the men with their red arm bands, he grew fearful. Though he had his passport certifying him to be Nicolai Gorov, railway clerk, he was afraid they might question him, afraid that something about him might arouse their suspicions.

"Ai, ai, why do you not go on?" a woman behind him complained. She was leading a child, who was well-nigh smothered in the press, and she had a basket on her arm.

"I am sorry," Markov muttered, pulling his cap over his eyes. "I cannot go on this train."

"You are not going?"

"No, I am not going."

"Then, please, *tovarish* [comrade], give me your ticket. I have no ticket."

"I have no ticket, either."

Markov was wedged in, and the press of the crowd was making the child whimper. Markov pushed with main force and opened a little space.

"Can you not see?" he exclaimed impatiently to those about him, "I am trying to get out."

"Then why did you come in?" growled a yellow-faced Finn.

"Give room," Markov cried. "You are choking this child."

"Yes, yes, we are all choked. Do not push."

"Give me your ticket, please, sir, or comrade—I have no ticket," pleaded the woman with the child. "I must go on the train."

"Who are you to push?" another demanded. "A commissar?"

One of the officials at the desk shouted,

"Quiet, back there."

A soldier began to elbow his way into the crowd to see what the trouble was.

Markov felt in his tunic for some money. He drew out a silver coin and some copper kopek that were in the pocket.

"I have no ticket," he repeated, "but take this, and St. Christopher help you." He handed the woman the coins.

"Oh, thank you, sir—or comrade. Thank you."

"Who is that?"

"A bourgeois, who scatters small coin and gold," sneered a man in a greasy black blouse.

The soldier was edging his way in, but Markov's generosity had opened a path, and he escaped to the outskirts.

He did not dare to attempt boarding a train until late that night, when the only lights were from the oil lanterns on the table, and he could pass muster in the darkness.

Gradually, Paul Stepanovitch had become accustomed
to considering himself as Nicolai Gorov, and to his frayed
black clerk's suit; but he was growing tired of this dis-
guise. He had no place to go, nothing to do, and his
money was wasting away. Like many another man who
finds his ordered ways upset, long before he reached
Petrograd he began to think of home and to long to go
there.

He would go to Varsova, and see Sorkin, the manager
of his estate, and get some money, and live in the old
house for a while. The estate was some distance outside
Varsova, a quiet, secluded place where one could remain
without notice or attention. He could stay there until
things settled down, when he could decide what to do.

Except for hurried business trips to see Sorkin, to get
money and receive an accounting, he had not been home
for ten years, since a year or so after his father had died.
There had been nothing to go home for, and he had been
busy at school, and with his absorption in his career, and
had preferred to spend his vacations at Moscow or Petersburg or Tiflis.

Yet he could remember his home, with precise and infinite detail, despite the passage of the years; and as he
trudged along from Khalinsk toward Varsova, the pictures returned to flood his soul with nostalgia.

The country surrounding Varsova had always been fine
agricultural land. When Paul Stepanovitch wanted to
think of something beautiful he used to close his eyes and
recall the many delightful prospects that were to be seen
around Varsova. There was the Dasta, a smaller river
than the Kuban, but to Markov's eyes more lovely. In
spring, when it was filled with rushing snow water, it was
a wild stream, as uncontrollable as a drunken soldier, es-
caping its bounds and committing depredations on the
neighboring land. But as summer advanced, it subsided,
and became placid and comely, its surface a burnished
mirror that reflected the mood of the skies rather than
its own, showing more clearly than the heavens themselves
the varied grays and blues of cloud and sky. In August,
when the world panted with the heat, Dasta was slum-

brous and veiled with a mist that clung to the surface, a sleeping woman lying under a diaphanous coverlet.

Other scenes of the countryside had always entranced Paul Stepanovitch, and he had loved to think of them, despite the fact that he was never moved to return to them. The view from the knoll on which the Markov house stood was one of rural activity—the activity that is not struggle but peace, the work that knows its reward, the labor that is the assurance of rest. From morning to night, during the months of planting and reaping, the pleasant air was filled with the creak of carts, the cry of field birds, the lowing of cattle, the neigh of horses in pasture. . . .

The picture was always one of variegated color. The brown squares of fields—the land was broad and strip farming was not practiced—alternated with the emerald green of the pastures and the deeper green of the woodlands. The seasons could be measured by the color of the fields. With the plowing, the brown would turn to black, and then—as the crops thrust their sprouts through the soil—to a brown covered with a patina of yellow-green, fungus-like, which would slowly spread and deepen to a rich emerald. And then, overnight it seemed, this emerald would fade and become a delicate yellow, and finally a rich golden color. Harvest, and the gold was stripped from the earth, and for a brief season the brown returned. Then, winter, when all the fields lay under a blanket of white.

There were, also, the fragrances of the earth which were unforgettable—the rich tang of the soil in plowing season, the scent of blossoms—for orchard crops grew in abundance—the heavy odor of the meadows when they were mown, the fragrance of fresh milk and golden grapes and ruddy apples.

As he walked along the road toward Varsova, Paul Stepanovitch recalled these sights, these sounds, these smells, and at each turn of the road he looked forward expectantly for them to burst again upon him.

But though by noon he had covered a good half of the distance, these pleasant scenes did not appear. On the contrary, it seemed that the farther he walked the more silent and lonely the landscape grew. It was nothing tangible that Paul Stepanovitch could place his finger on. At this season of the year, of course, most of the harvests were over—only the grape and late hay crops remaining to be gathered—and that would explain a certain bareness in the scene.

Yet there was something else—something which gave it all an eerie quality, as though he had passed into, and become a part of, a dead canvas, or a waxen panorama. . . . He could not say what it was.

His feet were beginning to hurt. He had walked rapidly since morning, with a quick military step, but the shoes he had bought in Kazan did not fit him, and were now beginning to blister his heels. He was wishing for some conveyance, when he heard a sound, and he knew what it was that had aroused this feeling of loneliness.

It was the absence of creaking cart wheels. Cart wheels always creaked in Russia, at least in his part of Russia. The peasants seemed incapable of learning the use of grease. It had been that way in the army. More than once a surprise movement had failed because of creaking artillery wheels. To the peasants, grease was too precious to use on a mere wheel, and when peasants became soldiers, they were still peasants.

All morning long, until now, Markov had not heard a single creaking cart. What did this mean?

The conveyance had come alongside. It was not a cart but a heavy four-wheeled wagon of a type common in that district of Russia, known as an *arba*. The horses were small and shaggy—powerful enough, but badly underfed. The driver, a taciturn peasant, stopped, and motioned to Markov to get up. Markov mounted without a word, and for some little distance neither spoke. After a while the driver asked, in monosyllables,

"You came from far?"

"From Khalinsk," responded Markov, with equal shortness. "I go to Varsova."

"So I guessed," the driver grunted. "You are a native here."

Markov started, despite himself. He wondered if the peasant had recognized him. Yet, he thought, why should he be afraid of recognition? He was annoyed with himself for the nervousness with which he had become infected.

"Why do you say that?" he asked sharply.

"Easy enough. You have the Varsova accent. It is different around Khalinsk."

Markov was relieved.

"You go about quite a bit?" he asked.

"I have lately. I have been trying to buy seed rye. It is already late for fall planting."

"Your wagon is empty."

"Yes, none is to be had. All the grain that is visible has been taken. Some is hidden, no doubt, by those who live out near the forests, but I don't think it will get into the ground. It will be eaten this winter, or sold by handfuls in the market. Prices will be high."

Paul Stepanovitch considered what this meant. To the farmer scarcity of grain was only a matter of price; with the soil beneath him, neither he, nor his kind, would starve. That would be the lot of those who lived in town. In time of peace it was the towns that seemed to offer security of livelihood, while the lot of the farmer always seemed precarious. But now it was the farmer who had security. Paul Stepanovitch shuddered at the thought of famine in the great cities of his country—Petrograd, Moscow, Odessa, Rostov, Tiflis—populated with their millions of his countrymen—these cities which princes and tsars of the past had taken their pride in building. What suffering would be theirs this winter if the farms were bare! And then next winter, if no grain was planted!

"But things can't be so bad," he exclaimed anxiously.

"Oh, no," the driver assured him. "I have a good crop of cabbage in kraut, and plenty of turnips buried. Raiders never find turnips."

He was an *inogorodnie*, a peasant owner, Markov discovered, prosperous in comparison with the general run of farmers. Around Khalinsk there was no grain; elsewhere the farmers had neither grain nor livestock, and some had no grain nor livestock nor cabbage.

Toward Varsova they came upon great patches of

grass and woodland that had been burned over. It reminded Markov of some of the ground the armies had
fought over in Galicia.

"What has happened?" he asked.

The peasant shifted himself on the seat and shrugged
his shoulders.

"I don't know. I stay on my farm, and only leave when
I go to market or someone comes to my place," he said,
as though he were reluctant to talk further. "The country
is full of armed people."

He halted.

"Are you a Communist?" he asked abruptly.

"No."

The peasant eyed Markov shrewdly. Satisfied that
Markov was not a Communist, he said,

"Well, they demand grain and provisions, and they do
a lot of killing. People are afraid to show themselves. The
markets are closed half the time. Business is at a standstill.
There is nothing you can buy any more."

He paused, spat, and clucked to his horses.

"However," he added, philosophically, "I don't mind it
so much. You save money when you don't buy in the
market, and you get fancy prices for what you sell. If you
know how to hide your stuff about so that it doesn't show,
you can get rich. When this thing settles down, I'll be rich,
rich enough to own half the parish."

When Markov got down, he wished the farmer success,
and went on toward his own land. It was late afternoon
when he finally reached the borders of his estates. A road
wound for a verst through the woodlands to the house.
The main body of his estate lay beyond, stretching for
some four versts along the Dasta River, and extending
back for half as far again. His grandfather's grandfather
had acquired it during the Napoleonic Wars, as part payment for military services. It had been waste land then,
but this old officer had taken a fancy to it had built a solid
gray stone castle down by the river, and had made it his
homestead. This great-great-grandfather had been one of
four brothers, all officers close to His Majesty, all of whom
had taken part in the repulse of Napoleon, all of whom

had been granted lands at the hand of the Emperor, all of whom, save the one, had died without issue. All of these lands had passed to Markov's line; some of them were richer and better situated, but Markov's great-grandfather, grandfather, and father had continued to make Varsova the homestead. Most of these heritors had—when they were not away with troops—devoted themselves to improving the land, developing the woodlands, nourishing and enriching the soil, draining the lowlands, terracing the slopes to prevent erosion, until finally the estate had become an example to the whole province. During the prosperous Victorian era, the stone castle down by the water had been supplanted in favor of a large frame house of English Georgian style. It was this house where Paul Stepanovitch had been born, and around which clustered his childhood memories.

Paul Stepanovitch pressed forward in eagerness, though not without premonition. He had seen no one during the afternoon, and usually all the roads around the estate were full of carts.

At the side of the road was a great oak tree on which he had carved his name as a boy. He was impelled to stop and look at it again—only a glance, to reassure himself— and then he hurried on. It was strange how ardently he desired to set foot upon his threshold, to sleep again in the room where he had slept as a boy, to thumb through the books in the library, and to see the portrait of his mother over the mantel.

He quickened his steps.

The gravel drive was weed-grown and the lawn was scuffed by horses' hoofs. Paul Stepanovitch wondered when Sorkin was last here.

The house was just beyond the bend of the road, hidden only by the trees that lined the drive.

Another dozen steps, and he saw the ground itself—the lovely knoll, with the grass sloping away from . . . his heart faltered . . . a mound of black ash, from which a few stumps of beams stood black and gaunt in the autumn air. . . .

Paul Stepanovitch ran forward, seizing a stick as he

went, and began to beat at the ashes, frantically, like a man possessed.

The ashes were dead. Not a living ember remained. Already, though this must have happened within the week, grass was beginning to grow in the rich moist ash.

But Paul Stepanovitch continued to claw in the ashes. Some remembrance, something surely, must have escaped destruction. . . .

Nothing.

The metal casters of chairs and beds, burnt and twisted, were all that remained of the wing in which he had slept. Some picture wire, but the pictures were consumed; the twisted iron of the chandeliers and brackets, the ruin of pots and pans that were in the kitchen, now scattered about the fallen brick of the chimney.

The barns had gone also, and the cattle had been driven off. Nothing remained but the land, the orchards, and the woods.

8. *The Arrest*

WHAT was happening to his beloved country? What were these forces that were sweeping across the land like a plague? What had happened that the people of the Empire should be turning upon themselves while the enemy was still on the frontiers? Had the Russian people gone mad? What had stirred up all this contempt for the glorious traditions of the past and the beautiful and symmetrical order which had been established for generations, this hatred of Russians for Russians, this mania for senseless destruction of all that was old and solid and lovely?

Paul Stepanovitch asked himself these questions as he plodded toward the town of Varsova. He was young enough, and resilient enough of mind that he was not hopeless. He did not look upon the Revolution as the final catastrophe of life; he might be able to adjust himself to this new order of things if he understood it, if he could in fact find order and purpose in what was happening, for order was the reflexive demand of his intellect. At the moment, however, there was no order in it—no purpose, no meaning, no system. It was all chaotic, disordered, unreasoned, a complete unfettering of all the moral and intellectual restraints that held the passions.

His country was at war. That was the final and most important fact. Formidable enemies threatened on their respective frontiers—the Germans, the Austrians, and the Turks. The fact of these enemies should have been enough to maintain internal discipline. The Empire must be preserved at all costs. After the war was over, then they could decide whether a change in the form of government was desirable, whether Kerensky or Lenin or some other person should become the leader. But now, there was the war, and nothing should be done to weaken the morale of the armies.

But all that was over. The armies had revolted.

The thought that the army was gone filled Paul Stepanovitch with an emptiness of soul and absence of purpose. The army—symbol of order, the embodiment of perfect system—was gone. What was there left for him?

He wondered what had happened to his colonel, that night at Slavinka. Stern, uncompromising, Colonel Kutepov, who used to make his regiment move with the precision of a ticking watch. Yet Kutepov had finally gone to pieces, and Markov and the other captains of companies had had to manage their men as best they could.

Yes, it had all collapsed. Where were order and method to be found? What did these revolutionaries know about order?

Paul Stepanovitch realized that he should not be going to Varsova. He might be arrested, because this army that had saved Russia, that had built Russia, that had provided the one idea by which an empire might be created, was hated, and as an officer he was an object of vengeance.

Yet he must go. He must see Sorkin, and find out what had happened to the estate, what his rights were under this new thing that called itself a government. He could not simply let go everything. Those were his lands; they had belonged to his father, to his grandfather—to his great-great-grandfather. If he was an outcast from this new society, could he not still live on his own land, and manage it as he pleased, and preserve, in a cup, as it were, a tiny flame of human order and purpose?

It was dark when he reached the town. In the public square a mass meeting was being held, and a man was speaking under the light of gas flares. Markov wanted to hear what he said. He must learn—and perhaps he could find out here—what the Revolution was all about. He had never before had to consider what men thought about or wanted who were without property, career or security. But he was willing to learn and here was an opportunity. He moved to the edge of the crowd, and listened to the words that drifted out to him.

"Comrades," the speaker was saying—he had before this laid the groundwork of what he was now to say—"this being the case, it is the duty of us, the proletariat, to assert our might, to assert our Promethean heritage."

Paul Stepanovitch strained his ears. He knew the story of Prometheus, and he wondered how this man would apply it.

"Who is Prometheus?" the speaker demanded. The speaker was a young man, not as old as Markov, with the pale face of an ascetic, and large black eyes that were lighted with the fire of ardor. He spoke calmly, however, with even, measured words.

"Who is Prometheus, if not the Russian proletariat? It is he who has brought the fire to the altar of Russia, and feeds the flames of our culture. Our proletariat is the chained Hercules, performing his twelve tasks at the behest of the gods. And who are these gods, that have chained Hercules, that torture Prometheus? They are the Tsar and the vested interests, the Church, the capitalist, and the bourgeoisie. They sit on Olympus, and laugh and drink their nectar, while Prometheus and Hercules lie chained.

"We have," continued the speaker, the surface of his

logic now broken through and flaming with little jets of
passion, "been chained too long, too much devoured by
the vultures of our stupidity and lethargy. Now we Prometheans are shaking off these chains, and asserting our godly
nature.

"Godly nature."

The young orator began to play on that phrase.

"Godly nature. Nay, we are gods. If there be gods, we
are they. Certain it is that there is no god but the people,
and we assert our godliness by the strength of our will, by
the assertion of our invincible will." He raised his arm,
slowly clenched his fist, and shook it to emphasize his
words. "By our will, and our will alone, shall be created a
new Russia, full of all those blessings to the people which
the former masters of the country have denied us—great
physical works, hydroelectric undertakings, machines to
till our farms as they have in America—factories and
ships, and shoes for everyone. All these shall we bring
through the invincible will of the proletariat, Prometheus
unchained."

The speaker paused while his dark, passionate eyes
surveyed the crowd, and shouts of approval filled the
square. Then he continued.

But Paul Stepanovitch was not listening. He was thinking of what the speaker had just said. How familiar it
sounded! Not the words, but the emphasis upon "invincible will." He squirmed uncomfortably as he thought of
these ideas coming from another young man like himself.
It was as though they had sat in the same school, listened
to the same schoolmaster.

And so, thought Paul Stepanovitch bitterly, it was in the
name of will that all this destruction was going on! All
this lust for blood and lust for power, this rebellion, this
disorder, arose from the exercise of will!

Who was this speaker, he wondered, that he should
distort the truth so viciously? He was a traitor to his upbringing. Why, it was by the exercise of this same Promethean will that the Russian Empire had been created—by
the will of those invincible patriots and tsars of glorious
renown—Rurik, Ivan, and Peter, and Catherine. It was

human will that had created all the order that existed in the world, that had changed the tangled forests into arched and lovely woodlands, that had plowed the steppe and brought it to human obedience, that had tamed the beasts of the field so that they gave milk or drew burdens.

It was human will that had created society and social order, that brought stability and peace to households, and union to warring tribes, that created kingdoms, principalities and empires. Yes, it was human will, bending to the microscope, and to the book in dimly lighted chambers, resisting the call of the world of merriment and laughter outside, that had made and produced the physical inventions, the arts, the crafts, the science and the knowledge upon which human progress was founded. All those machines which the speaker talked about, which he promised the proletariat as the new dispensation—the locomotive, the electric dynamo, the automobile—all these were the product of human will of generations past. And it was human will that produced greatness and comfort in the world. By exercising its sway over the flesh, by subduing the evil within, by mastering the desires and the lusts, by resisting the temptations—of avarice, cruelty, ambition, meanness, sloth, and cowardice—had the will made possible the realization of the "kingdom of God" of which the priests spoke.

And now, in the name of human will, all this pleasant world, this universal order, the accepted ways of generations, were being overthrown.

"By the invincible will" shall these things be done, the speaker had said.

He was only aping what was being said by Trotsky and Lenin and the other leaders of the Marxist revolution—the will of the proletariat to power. And Trotsky and Lenin themselves were only echoing what they had heard during their exile in Europe.

All this was no more than what the Kaiser had been proclaiming for years—a "place in the sun," the "German will to power" to achieve the hegemony of Europe. And what the Kaiser had said was only what Tsar Peter had said when he determined to erect his capital upon the

Neva, and what Tsarina Catherine had willed when she determined that the Russian people should be heard in the councils of Europe. And kaiser and tsar, both were Caesars, and followed only in the tradition of the imperial Caesars of Rome, who had apotheosized themselves and exalted the *imperio*—I will—into a shibboleth, a creed, a cult, a religion, a universal destiny. "I will"—that had been the cultural and intellectual basis of European civilization. Though in name it worshiped God, and repeated "not my will, but thine, be done," in fact it worshiped the will of the ego—"I will."

And now, that "I will" was speaking its inevitable destiny. It was being swallowed up by its own creation. . . .

Paul Stepanovitch Markov's logic, hurried forward by the paradox of this appeal to will as a basis for revolution, had carried him far along roads of thought he had never traveled before. He saw in a flash the limitations of his philosophy, the bounds to his intellectual perceptions imposed by his belief in the sufficiency of the individual and the individual will, the inconsistencies and contradictions to which it led him. But though he grasped these things momentarily with his mind, his spirit was unprepared to receive them, and he cast them out. It could not be. He halted his thoughts sharply and gave heed again to the speaker.

The young man was now talking about God. He had begun a tirade against the Church, and the ecclesiastical system, which, in his view, had exacted from the workers their hard-earned money for the erection of churchly edifices, and for filling them with jeweled pictures, and for the support of a lazy, rapacious, parasitic priesthood.

Going beyond an attack upon the Church and clergy, the speaker began to revile religion itself, which he characterized as a fraud, without reason or logic.

"Christ taught meekness and subjection to a Higher Will," he shouted. "But why should we be subject to a higher will? What higher will is there than the will of man? There is no God. He does not exist. You can't prove that He exists. No scientist has ever found Him in a test tube, no astronomer searching the skies has located

Heaven. All this talk is a means of keeping the worker in subjection. The Tsar and the metropolitans and the capitalists speak, and what they decree is the 'Will of God.' No, my friends, there is no God. You are God. You are masters of your destiny. What cannot be proved by logic, or seen with the eyes, or tasted with the lips, does not exist. If Heaven exists, you will create it yourselves."

There was more of this, concluding with the well-known Communist slogan:

"Religion is the opiate of the people."

It struck Paul Stepanovitch again that what he was listening to was familiar speech, sentiments he had heard all his life, but not so abruptly or boldly stated. He himself had been weaned away from a devoutness learned at his mother's knee into an attitude of cold cynicism toward the Church which she had revered. He had not been aware of precisely how it had been done. Partly the work had been done by his father, who professed a superiority to what he termed the superstition of the masses, partly it had been done by men like Prince Cherniloff, who were arrogantly and intellectually atheistic.

Most of the intellectuals whom Paul Stepanovitch had known shrank from outright atheism. Since the titular head of the Church was the Tsar, and to condemn the Church was indirectly to condemn the monarchy, they would have shrunk from any such outright condemnation as "Religion is the opiate of the people."

Instead, they proceeded by a suave and appealing logic, which they molded about the anthropological theories of Darwin, and the dialectic materialism of Büchner and Moleschott. They intimated, rather than asserted, that the world was founded upon scientific principle and operated by immaculate Law that was subservient to no God, but was rather the essence of God.

It had been the appeal of this logic that had first led Paul Stepanovitch to question miracles, the fact of which his mother implicitly accepted, and with this questioning of miracles, gradually to dissolve the whole edifice of the faith she had inculcated in him. It was this logic that had made Prince Cherniloff's disdain of compassion so convinc-

ing. Law, since it was inexorable, as Law must be to be
Law, naturally took no account of exceptions: it was repugnant to Scriptural teaching in that it was built upon
statistical masses, and general forces, and reverenced the
movement of groups rather than individuals. It dealt, in a
word, with the ninety and nine, rather than the one. It
would indeed be a ludicrous Law that went running off
after the lost one, and let the ninety and nine shift for
themselves.

Paul Stepanovitch had learned more about this Law as
he had advanced in his studies, and had listened to lectures on physics, mechanics, and chemistry. Yet all he
learned was summed up in what this propagandist for the
Revolution was proclaiming: there is no God. Everything
worked by Law, that was precise and computable as a
problem in ballistics.

Paul Stepanovitch observed, without paying particular
attention to the fact, that a man not far from him, on the
edge of the crowd, was eyeing him closely. He was in the
black uniform of a seaman, with the orange and black
ribbon on his cap that identified him with the Baltic fleet.
It was these men, Paul Stepanovitch had heard, who had
started the Revolution by their mutiny at Kronstadt. Paul
Stepanovitch's thoughts were too absorbed, however, to
realize what this surveillance meant. He was trying, by
his every mental faculty, to cushion the shock he had experienced in discovering that everything the Revolution
proclaimed he had long ago accepted, that in outlook, at
least, he and the Bolsheviks were at one.

This was impossible, preposterous! That they should
use the same appeals and the same beliefs—the assertion
of the divine right of will, and the denial of deity—that he
had heard propounded by all his aristocratic acquaintances, that indeed he had accepted for himself, as justification for their destruction of the established order, was
something Paul Stepanovitch could not digest.

As he listened to the speaker, who continued to shout,
it all suddenly seemed quite clear to Paul Stepanovitch,
revealed as a flash of lightning reveals the chaos of the
elements. Paul Stepanovitch felt an overpowering sicken-

ing of the heart. He had been following a false ideal, had been bowing down, with the crowd with whom he had associated, to a Baal who devoured the children of men. Yes, it was suddenly clear that he had, all his life, since he had forsaken his mother's influence, been standing on the thin crust of a quagmire, and now it had suddenly cracked and opened, and was drawing him down into its murky depths.

This Law, which he had learned to accept, from professors and scientists and philosophers, was the law of the jungle; in detached, superior terms, the law of survival of the fittest. But the fittest was he with the strongest fangs, the greatest power, the shrewdest wit, the least pity, the coarsest sensibilities, the most vulgar wants. An Anglican clergyman, considering the miseries produced by the English industrial revolution, had first stated the principle; but he certainly must never have imagined what eventual shape and extension it would take. He had posed the proposition that as land is limited and population breeds unlimitedly, there must as a consequence be wars and famine to keep the population down, while the remainder are condemned to struggle with tooth and nail for what little the land produces. This theory of the operation of the universe had been eagerly accepted by the industrialists of the day and by the politicians and the writers who catered to the new industrial order, for it gave a plausible explanation of the ills of the times, and absolved them from any duty to remedy them. "It is the working of the law of population." And such an inexorable thing as a natural law could not be tampered with, lest it produce greater disaster than before.

And as industrialism grew, so the province of the Law grew. The machine, which was revolutionizing the customs of mankind, was a fit example of the working of Law. The machine worked by a natural law of physics; it paid attention to no man; if a child fell into a mill which it tended, the mill did not stop. Nor does Law stop. The Law, conceived more and more in mechanical terms, began to embrace all things—there were laws of art, and laws of society, and laws of mentality, and laws of politics, and laws of history, and laws of religion—all of them coeval, eternal and immutable. God was no more than Law apotheosized.

Wherever industrialism went went this new concept of the Universe. And as Russia, like all the other "backward" countries of the world, in the years that clustered about the beginning of the century, sought to overtake the more industrialized nations of the West, it had borrowed everything, accepted everything that would hasten the process, without critical examination or question. And so it had borrowed these intellectual conceits, and had taken them for scriptural truths, though they were repugnant to the mysticism and the ancient faith of the people.

It was these importations—this hasty industrialization, the adoption of the factory system of Europe, with all its intellectual garniture, unregulated and uncontrolled by those restraints and interdictions which the West was at last beginning to develop—that had precipitated the proletarian revolt. And now it was this same intellectual atheism and disavowal of God which had been used to justify the brutalities of the factory system that the revolutionaries offered as the principle of their new order.

Paul Stepanovitch perceived now the paradox of his own case. He could not accept the Revolution; it was too repugnant to his temperament; but if he rejected it he must reject the intellectual propositions which he had come unquestioningly to accept.

Paul Stepanovitch Markov had heard all he wished. He extricated himself from the listening crowd, and started toward the quarter in which Sorkin had lived.

"One moment."

Someone addressed him. It was the sailor with the orange and black ribbon on his cap.

"Your documents, if you please."

Paul Stepanovitch drew his papers from his pocket and handed them to the man.

"It is not necessary. I know you. You are Paul Stepanovitch Markov. You will come with me."

There was no point in resisting. The man was armed, and his comrades were not far away.

Paul Stepanovitch Markov went with him.

9. The Commission Extraordinary

THE principal agency of public control for the new revolutionary government that was extending with incredible swiftness throughout central Russia was the Commission Extraordinary for the Suppression of Counter-Revolutionary Propaganda—or Cheka, as it was known for short. Like many other of the revolutionary innovations, it was adopted from the old régime. The Commission Extraordinary was really the old Okhrana, the tsarist secret police system, modified and improved to fit the new necessities and the license of the times.

The Commission Extraordinary was the core of the revolutionary government established by Lenin and Trotsky; its organization had followed within a month after the Petrograd *coup* of October that had brought the party of Lenin to power, and it had promptly become an agency more autocratic than any other except the Red Army. In theory, the executive agency of the government was the Central Executive Committee of the Party; the Commission Extraordinary was merely one of its subcommittees. This was the situation at the top. Down the line, however, the local Commissions, or Chekas, were frequently independent of, and never responsible to, the local executive committees of the Party. The whole organization was an appendage of Moscow; it reported to the Kremlin and took orders only from the Kremlin.

In the provinces, therefore, with the raising of the Revolutionary banner, there appeared two governments on the scene—the Soviet, locally organized and reflecting to some degree local sentiment and aspirations; and the Cheka, independent, arbitrary, concerned only with the maintenance of the revolutionary power. The moment the Red Army occupied an area the Commission Extraordinary moved in to establish civil order, to combat counter-revolutionary propaganda, and to assure complete submission to the régime. The methods it employed to this end were hardly in accord with the enlightened purposes of the Revolution. By corps of informers and *agents provocateurs*, persons were accused, either upon rumor, suspicion, or founded knowledge, and apprehended. They were tried, convicted—or, rarely, acquitted—without calling of witnesses or hearing the defendant. Conviction was followed by immediate execution, "the highest measure of social protection."

These methods of social control were not, however, inventions of the Communists. The Communist Party simply adopted what they had already experienced with the tsarist Okhrana. Even the Okhrana did not originate them. They had been practiced with consummate skill in the French Revolution. And they were not new to the French revolutionaries. The French kings had been past masters in the arts of torture and punishment, and spying and intrigue, as means of maintaining the State. But beyond the French kings one must look to the Middle Ages, to the dungeons, the racks, the trials by ordeal, the burning pyres, of that period in history; and beyond that, to the imprisonments, the blindings, tongue removals, and castrations by the Byzantine emperors. Before that were the circuses and gladiatorial contests of Rome for those who defied the Roman state, and the proscription lists of the Roman consuls; and so on back and back into history. As far as one dare look, cruelty, torture, execution, spying, informing, intrigue, have been the means of rulers to maintain their power. . . .

As the Revolution spread and its fanaticism grew, the activities of the Cheka expanded and multiplied. Prisons increased without number. The number of the executed mounted into thousands, hundreds of thousands. Russia was in the grip of the Terror. . . .

It is not easy to comprehend how men whose purposes were high, who had offered their lives for their ideals, who had struggled with persecution and poverty and disappointment for a new social order in which they believed, men who had endured so much of intolerance and imprisonment and exile, should have turned, once they were in power, to the use of the same instruments by which they had been attacked, should have reverted to the same ruthlessness and inhumanity which they had opposed and condemned.

Vladimir Belinsky, for instance, who was head of the Kazan Cheka, and one of the most ferocious Chekists in all Russia, had been in his early days an ardent humanitarian, a sincere revolutionist, impelled by motives of patriotism and love for his fellow man. He had been, in his youth, a teacher of mathematics, slim, swarthy, angular and prominent of feature; at once solemn and friendly, and always with cookies in his pocket for the children on his street.

Belinsky had been impressed with the writings of Marx and Engels, had become convinced that a new world order would be achieved only by the emancipation of the worker and the establishment of a socialized state. He had joined the Communist Party, and for this had been exiled to Siberia. This experience had not affected his demeanor or his disposition; always, when others grew fanatical, he remained calm and judicial. If the new order was to come, it must come, he would say, as the result of the inevitable disintegration of the old; to hasten it by violence would destroy the very ideals and principles for which it stood.

When the October *coup d' état* occurred, Vladimir Belinsky stood high in the Party councils. As Kazan was a strong radical center, and supposedly enthusiastic for the Bolsheviks, a man of judicial rather than fanatical temperament was regarded as appropriate for head of the Cheka, and Vladimir Belinsky was selected. Being a humanitarian, he had promptly stopped the wholesale lootings and outrages, the breaking into homes in search of suspects and the executions in cold blood. He forbade all political arrests except on his own order and all molestation of people except by military police.

He also introduced decorum into the conduct of political arrests, trials and executions. Arrests were to be made at night, in order not to frighten the public by the sight of men under escort of armed guards. Examination of the accused was required. Established legal procedure of taking depositions was adopted: that is, the prisoner was questioned, his answers were taken down, and the document, signed by the accused, became a part of the record, and was used either in his favor or against him. Executions also were to be held at night—Belinsky regarded the public hangings of the old days as too brutal—and were to be handled by a method less painful and humiliating; that is, by shooting.

All these reforms, however, had results somewhat other than anticipated. Night arrests aroused consternation and horror: there seemed to be something especially sadistic in using for this purpose the hours dedicated to sleep and rest; and night arrests became one of the most terrifying methods of the Terror.

The use of depositions also proved abortive. Belinsky was an extremely busy man—as were most of the revolutionary officials of the time—and as he usually worked most of the night, he seldom found time to examine the prisoners until the early hours of the morning. At such hours the prisoners were frightened nearly to death, thinking they were to be executed before dawn, and they gave incoherent, stammering answers to questions. At such hours also, Belinsky, wearied from his night's labor, was irritable and impatient. The timidity of the prisoners was interpreted as recalcitrance. One night, in a rage, he ordered the prisoner to hold out his hand. Belinsky was smoking a cigarette. He ground the cigarette out in the palm of the prisoner's hand.

"Now, will you talk intelligibly?" he demanded.

The prisoner, livid, fell to his knees grasping his seared palm and began to babble. What he said no one knew. He talked, he talked endlessly, whether truthfully or not could not be told. But Belinsky had learned a new technique in extracting information. More, he had acquired a lust.

Being always pressed for time and torture being quick and effective, Belinsky began to adopt it gradually, at first in extreme circumstances, but soon on every occasion. From hot cigarette ends, he went to thrusting toothpicks under the nails and other more exquisite tortures which no one mentions. He oversaw the execution of many of the prisoners himself, and introduced some new methods which were aped by some of his admirers in other districts.

Fortunately for the people of Kazan, Belinsky did not last long. Overindulgence in bestiality resulted in a disintegration of his faculties. He began to suffer from obesity, from dimness of sight, and from obsessions. It was not known that he was ever tormented by the hosts of the slain—his conscience disintegrated also—but he had constant suspicions and moods. Formerly mathematically precise and logical, he now became superstitious. Omens and portents became an obsession. Friday was one of the hopeful days of the week for prisoners, for Belinsky would do nothing on Friday; when Friday fell on the thirteenth he was known to give pardons lavishly to propitiate his fortune.

His attention was easily diverted; like Nero, he would pause in the midst of deliberations to catch a fly; or he would imagine that lice were gnawing him, and would draw off his smelly boots and roll up his trouser legs to look for vermin. This began to disturb his colleagues, who were men of iron and did not hesitate to purge their own ranks when necessary, but since he was very efficient in directing the Terror he was not disturbed. His name spread and for hundreds of miles in every direction from Kazan—even south, it is said, on ships in the midst of the rolling Caspian, men trembled at its mention. Finally, however—within eighteen months after his assignment to the post at Kazan—he died of insanity.

At the height of Belinsky's power, the prisoners of the Cheka in Kazan were crammed into six separate prisons in various parts of the city. The smallest of these, but the most terrifying, because to be sent there meant almost certain execution, was the one in which the headquarters of the Cheka were located. This was the former mansion of one Count Rushtavelli, a leading citizen of Kazan in the old days, who like Prince Cherniloff had escaped to Parisian exile. The Cheka had pre-empted his palace for their own uses. The upper floors were gutted of their furnishings, which were replaced by pine and oak tables and chairs for the Commission's secretariat. The floors beneath the street level had been partitioned off into long cells, each of which would hold thirty to forty men, sleeping on tiers of shelves built against the walls.

This prison could not accommodate at one time more than five hundred persons; in a short space of time, however, it accommodated a great many more, for it was but a stopping place on the way to the grave, and many thousands passed through it on their last journey.

It was in this prison that Paul Stepanovitch Markov, following his arrest at Varsova, eventually found himself. En route here, he had been lodged in several of the Cheka prisons—at Varsova, at Tarsk—two prisons there—at Pultov, and finally at Kazan.

Paul Stepanovitch had hardly been thrust through the door into the cell before he was aware of a Presence like that of Satan. It was reflected upon the faces of the prisoners; it struck him head on like the hot fetid air of the cell. They were not living men who stared at him so vacantly: from them had evaporated all the attributes of personality, all the myriad qualities of character and spirit which exhibit themselves upon the countenance. All expression was gone, all color and animation, as the thousand scintillations and points of interest in a landscape are darkened by a thunder cloud. Here joy was erased and sadness written instead; vivacity was metamorphosed into stupor; where once was the light of hope was now the shadow of terror. All vitality was frozen: it was as though Paul Stepanovitch looked upon a wax museum, all pale and cast in attitudes of despair. None even raised a head at his entrance.

Near the window, which was a narrow aperture at the level of the street and at the ceiling of the cell, a man perched on the upper bunk and gazed stonily out into the patch of sunlight. Another, with long ringleted hair and the face of a poet, lay crouching on his bunk, his face buried in his arms; he moaned continually, but so softly that it seemed to come from without—the wind in the pines along the Volga, possibly. On the floor a monk, one of the *startsy*, knelt in prayer, as though there were nothing in existence at that moment but himself and God. A former merchant, who had been arrested because he had hidden some jewels, sat and gnawed at his nails. When Paul Stepanovitch entered, this man fixed upon him the look of a chained cat. There were others, in various attitudes and postures, but all with the lassitude of death in their expressions, the look of men for whom the tides of life were ebbing fast.

At evening, when the cell door was opened and bread and a caldron of cabbage soup was set in on the floor, there was a brief activity. The men ate, but shortly lapsed again into apathy and silence.

The air at night was vile, for the window was kept closed, but in the morning, on orders of an official of the Commission, it was opened and a few drafts of purifying oxygen were permitted to waft through. The room was swept and those who were fortunate enough to have blankets folded them at the heads of their bunks. All were then led into the yard for the sacred fifteen minutes of exercise and sunlight, and then back into the cell. Once an hour the jailer allowed those to go to the latrine who asked, but strict silence was imposed and any loitering was punished. During the mornings there might appear also a fleeting interest among the prisoners, and they would converse with each other for a few minutes, but as the day wore on silence again settled upon them, and brooding— destroyer of men more than war or plague—began again its vulture-like gnawing upon hearts and minds.

Every week—sometimes on several nights in succession— someone was removed from the cell and his place was taken by a new prisoner. For a few days this new face was like a lamp in a corner, lighted with some ray of hope, some reflection of inner fortitude, and then it would be extinguished, suffocated by the mere inertia of despair.

These removals were invariably late at night, when the men, drugged by the fetid air, were well-nigh insensible. The cell door would open; two guards would step in, go up to a certain bunk, and quickly but quietly awaken the sleeper. The prisoner seldom screamed at this apparition, for the effect of the confinement, or the manner of the guards, seemed to produce a hypnotic fascination. In the morning the space on the shelf would be empty, and the others would know that the Terror had struck down another victim.

10. Prison

PAUL STEPANOVITCH, being youthful and invincible, had prepared himself for the Kazan prison. The first day of his arrest he had adopted a definite regimen for his mind and body, designed to combat the influences of confinement. Though never in his life had he known imprisonment, he had often visualized the possibility of being taken prisoner of war, and he had prepared himself in advance for such an event.

He did not know how long he would be confined, or whether he would be executed or released, but he was aware of one fact: so long as he was kept in the cell, he lived; and as long as he lived there was hope, if he was prepared for what hope offers. If he kept his health of mind and body, he would not die in prison. Death lay on the other side of the door. To pass through that door might be the beginning of death, but it might also be the opportunity for escape. He must, therefore, keep body and mind alert for whatever happened. Now, as never before, his life depended solely upon himself, upon his nerve and nimbleness of body, and all these depended upon the mastery kept by his will over his faculties.

Yet, though he had prepared himself, he soon realized that he was in a situation different from any he had ever imagined. He was utterly alone and utterly dependent upon himself.

There had been times like this at the front, of course, when it was every man for himself, times when whether one lived or was killed was pretty much a matter of wit and physical vigor or luck. But even then, one was supported by comradeship. One didn't advance completely alone upon the Austrian army: there were men of your company to the right and left of you; men of your regiment beyond your company; and beyond and behind them, others—the artillery at the rear, and behind that the army reserve, the government, the Empire, and the solidarity of the Allies.

But all props were struck away now. No comrades, no organization, the Tsar gone, the army dissolved, the Empire corrupting and falling apart. Paul Stepanovitch could not bear to think of the last loss—that of his home—all the more acute from the fact that the place of his arrest was his own home town. He was utterly alone, and his life depended on no friend, on no one but himself, and on nothing but his own efforts. . . .

Paul Stepanovitch had been in the prison for a week before he began to feel himself being drawn into the depths of despair. He roused himself with a mighty effort, paced up and down the cell and swore to himself. The others looked on vacantly. Paul Stepanovitch was tempted to scream at them, to shake them, to shake the bars of the cell—anything for a diversion, anything to end this mortifying stupor, anything to break this deadly monotony. He would have started a fight—not because he was angry, or hated anyone, but merely to arouse his sluggish blood, to bring a spurt of vitality into those about him.

He surveyed the prisoners from his end of the room. The man near the window was still gazing out into the patch of sunlight, looking for his wife to pass; he with the ringleted hair still buried his face in his arms; the monk still prayed; and the merchant was again gnawing at his nails. The prisoners confined here were, or had become, creatures of a different sort.

What would he gain by shouting at them? The guards would run and order him down. No doubt they would think him hysterical. He would not give them that satisfaction.

He remembered his methods of handling soldiers, how he had kept them diverted during the defense of Vinshk, when they had been without relief for two weeks. That evening, he took some of the black bread and, moistening it slightly with the soup, made it into dough and fashioned it into chess pieces. Next morning, they were dry and hard. With soot from the kettle, taken off with a splinter, he drew a chess board on the floor of his bunk.

"Who will play this game with me?" he asked.

No one answered.

"It is a pleasant one," he said, as though he were speaking to children who knew nothing of the game. "It was brought from India. It was invented for an Indian rajah by a poor man who got a crown of gold for his reward. The pieces simulate an army and its captains. See, this is the tsar and this the tsarina, and these are *boyars* on horses and these are castles. . . ."

No one paid heed.

Paul Stepanovitch looked around him.

"Will no one play?"

The monk turned his head in Paul Stepanovitch's direction.

"Pray to God," he mumbled, in a voice that seemed to issue from a grave. "Submit your will to God's."

"Submit my will to God's!"

Paul Stepanovitch turned violently upon the monk.

"This is madness. What has God to do with this? If you would be free, assert your own will. Keep alive your spirits. The day will come when we shall see freedom."

The monk paid no heed, but began to recite, in an audible voice, the phrase he had been canting all these days:

"Lord Jesus Christ, Son of God, have mercy on me, a sinner."

The merchant was staring at Paul Stepanovitch with his unblinking, cat-like eyes, while he continued to gnaw his nails.

The low moaning, like a wind in distant pines, that issued from the ringleted-haired man became words,

"Oh, leave us alone, and let us dream. Leave us alone."

Paul Stepanovitch slowly set the chess pieces aside.

It was useless to do anything for these men. He and they

were going in opposite directions. He was trying to master
fate by a stupendous exertion of the will; they were doing
the same by a stupendous submission of the will. He
would keep alive by asserting his will to live; they would
escape death by dying first. To whatever narrow proportions their prison might be reduced, it was still large
enough for them, for they made it so by shrinking. Within
themselves, Paul Stepanovitch thought with disdain, they
were no doubt finding the green fields that lay beyond
these walls; within themselves they heard whatever laughter there remained in the world; within themselves they
found what peace and freedom life yet had to offer. It was
the old Russian way, the way of the peasants during the
days of serfdom, the ways of all the people when the
Mongols overran the country, the ways of the monks during the Dark Ages.

But it was not his way. He would live with his five
senses, by God or not by God. He would live until the
moment his heart stopped beating.

"Yes, I will play with you."

The speaker was a pale-faced young man of thin sensitive features, haggard brown eyes, narrow tapering hands.
He was hardly more than a boy. His voice was modulated,
but timid and strained.

"Good," said Paul Stepanovitch heartily. "Call my hand."

"Left."

Paul Stepanovitch opened his palm.

"Black. It doesn't look any different from the white, but
to mark the whites I have splinters thrust in the heads of
the pieces."

Paul Stepanovitch opened the game. He was an impetuous player, and followed his gambit by a furious
charge. The pieces fell before the onslaught, but the young
man was a cautious, conservative player, and for every
piece lost demanded one of Markov's in exchange. At the
end, by a sudden maneuver, he checkmated Markov's king
and won the game.

"Splendid," exclaimed Paul Stepanovitch. "Another?"

The young man's face lighted momentarily.

"If you like."

"I would. It's my turn with the black. Let's see if I can defend as well as charge."

They finished the game, this time to Paul Stepanovitch's credit, and played another, and another. The following day they resumed their play, and on the following. . . .

It was not until the fourth day that they learned each other's names. Names were of little consequence under the circumstances. Nothing was of consequence.

The only reality in their little world was time. It passed, and its passage was very real. It passed so slowly that it seemed almost to congeal, almost to become visible. Something was needed to speed its passage, to reduce it to the same terms of nothingness to which everything else in life was reduced. . . .

The young man's name, Paul Stepanovitch learned, was Gregory Fedorevitch Nekrasov, and he was the son of a former under-minister of the old régime. He was not a politician, but an artist and a writer. He had been arrested apparently because of some writings considered offensive to the Communists, which, in view of his father's connection with the tsarist government, put him down as condemned already.

They had not played many games before one of the prisoners, an elderly man, for whom the game awakened memories, moved over and looked on in silence. Chess is a game for silence, and it fitted into the moods of the prisoners. Others gathered around to watch, and then someone asked Markov how he had made the men. Markov showed him, and next day there were half a dozen sets and as many games in progress.

This was encouraging. Paul Stepanovitch now tried to organize a tournament. The players were paired off, and the opening games were started, but that night the elderly Mikhailovsky, who was by all odds the best player, was taken out by the soldiers and the tournament was interrupted, not to be resumed.

A few games were played by the others, but the spirit had gone, and the diversion was not strong enough to overcome the deeper mood. Only Paul Stepanovitch and

Gregory continued, by main strength of will, to forget their condition in the abstruse problems of the board.

One purpose was served, however. The company in the cell became acquainted; names were learned, and prisoners began to speak to each other. For a few days there was an atmosphere of camaraderie, and even a few quips were passed.

Every few days, however, one of the number was taken out, to what all knew was execution. There was no longer any pretense, even among the guards, as to what removal meant. Every time the cell door opened, some of the feeble and pathetic conviviality ebbed away; the newcomers did not restore it, and finally it had completely disappeared. It was as though each was again alone: the four walls of the cell had not contracted, but each prisoner had built about him a particular cell of the spirit, thicker walled and more impenetrable than the cells made by brick and mortar.

After a time—how long it was Paul Stepanovitch had no idea, except that winter was fading into spring—all of the original prisoners in the cell were gone except himself and young Gregory: of all the lamps that were burning when he had been brought here, his and Gregory's alone continued to flicker. The rest had been extinguished.

"It will be our turn next," said Gregory softly. He laughed soundlessly as he said this. His face was pale with prison pallor, and his large brown eyes loomed in their sockets like startled deer in a glade.

"Yes," said Paul Stepanovitch, gaily. "I'll throw dice with you to see who goes first."

They had long since alternated chess with dice, which Paul Stepanovitch also had fashioned out of bread dough, and which they had since thrown to the extent of many millions of non-existent rubles.

"No," said Gregory slowly, "for I should win. You would have to wait." His voice dropped to a confidential hoarse whisper, and he leaned over to Paul Stepanovitch and asked,

"Would you really like to save yourself?"

"Well, if it can be whole-skinned," said Paul Stepanovitch casually. "Not if it means becoming one of those castrates which I understand Belinsky delights to make."

"Oh, no, nothing like that," whispered Gregory. "Really safe, whole and sound. Would you?"

Paul Stepanovitch did not answer for a moment, but studied his companion's face to read his mood. Gregory was looking at him with wild, prophetic eyes, eyes that were full of promise, of pleading, of forewarning. His fingers were on his lips, which though normally red were now quite red and moist and trembling slightly. The fingers were loose, graceful, expressive, like the hands of the disciples in da Vinci's "Last Supper."

"Why not?" asked Paul Stepanovitch nonchalantly. He was fighting against that same tendency to delirium and fantasy to which Gregory, he suspected, had succumbed.

"Then you will; you may; you shall. I have had a vision. Yes, a vision. A dream, if you will. Prophetic dreams come to such as me. I saw the execution trench. It is on the edge of the forest. The soldiers line up. The prisoners line up. There is a moment! In that moment one may turn, leap down the embankment and disappear into the forest. It is night, one is easily lost. They will never find you. You are free!"

Paul Stepanovitch looked at Gregory long, and then smiled and laid his hand on Gregory's shoulder.

"That dream may be true, Gregory. But since you are to precede me it is meant for you, and you should make the escape."

"No, I shall not escape," said Gregory solemnly.

"And why not?"

"Why should I escape? I am a lost cause. I am of a lost race. We aristocrats have outlived our usefulness. Our day is done. The purpose that created us is no more, and the will to live is gone. I shall not escape. But you will. You have the purpose to live. I shall leave you the opportunity. Should I try to escape they would take precautions against another attempt, and so you would never succeed."

"Why do you say that your day is done?" Paul Stepanovitch demanded, growing impatient at his friend's passivity. "There is much to live for. You have an art, a skill, a gift to give the world. Why should you not live?"

Gregory only shook his head sadly, like an old man. He was in fact already senile, but senile from causes not connected with his imprisonment. Painfully Paul Stepanovitch grasped the fact of which Gregory was but the symbol: the universal fact that the old order, the order of things to which Paul Stepanovitch also belonged by inheritance and training, if not entirely by spirit, was dead.

He picked up the dice and shook them vigorously, as though he were shaking his soul out of its weariness.

"Come, let us play," he said.

They played until they had run the stakes into thousands of rubles and, when the soldiers entered with the soup and they had to hide the pieces, Gregory was far the gainer.

That night as they lay on their boards, Gregory turned over and touched Markov.

"Asleep?" he whispered.

"No, why?"

"You owe me one hundred twenty thousand rubles."

"Really? That's a lot of money."

"Yes, but I am going to wipe the slate clean."

"No. I will give you an order on Sorkin, who looks after my estates. He owes me that much or more."

"No, I cancel the debt—on one condition."

"Which is—?"

"That you do not laugh at what I told you about my dream, but take it seriously and prepare yourself for freedom."

There was something of a premonition in the boy's words, a desolation of pleading. Paul Stepanovitch felt compassion for him. Impulsively he leaned forward and took his hand.

Gregory clung to it, desperately, passionately, and drew Paul Stepanovitch toward him.

"Listen to me, Pavil," he whispered. "I need not live, because I have things here"—indicating his heart—"but until you have greater things in your heart, you must live."

Paul Stepanovitch gripped his hand.

"Yes, Pavil, it is for you, this vision," persisted Gregory, in the tone of a child generously forcing candy on a play-mate. "I love you."

Paul Stepanovitch's heart was bursting.

"I shall remember then, Gregory," he answered, through clenched teeth. "It is a bargain."

"Sealed."

"Good night, Gregory."

"Good night, Pavil."

Next morning Gregory Fedorevitch Nekrasov's place was empty.

Three nights later Paul Stepanovitch was awakened by a soldier and told to follow.

11. The Execution Field

It is possible to die by inches. Dying, indeed, may be a matter of the parts. It is possible for the arm to die while the body lives. It is possible for the soul to die while the heart still beats. It is possible for the body to die while the spirit lives. And it is possible for the attributes of person-ality to die while its essence lives on.

As Paul Stepanovitch stepped across the threshold of the cell into the narrow, dimly lit hallway, in company with the soldier, his heart began a sudden pounding of excite-ment. A tremor passed over him; his mind quickened with the flashing of a thousand distinct but disconnected images, with a multiplied speed of perception and apper-ception. In that moment of violent emotions and sensa-tions, as with Dostoyevsky, standing on the gallows just before his reprieve, something within Paul Stepanovitch died—and something, freed by the death of the part, lived with exalted flame.

What it was that died, Paul Stepanovitch did not know, as he did not, until long afterward, recognize the fact of its dying.

Among the images that flashed upon the curtain of Paul Stepanovitch's mind, the most vivid was that of Gregory Fedorevitch looking up at him, pathetically, pleading that Paul pay heed to the vision which Gregory had recounted. According to his vision, the execution field would be on a knoll near a wood; and Gregory had said that opportunity would be offered for escape.

Could it be possible, Paul Stepanovitch's beating heart urged, that the vision was true? That he might escape?

He became tense at the thought; blood suffused his face from the thumping and leaping of his heart; his spine tingled and his hands trembled. His nostrils sensed, through the damp, fetid air, the fragrance of the open country, the hills, and the plains, where his feet would go racing when he was again free. For a moment his spirit soared.

And then logic, the Nemesis of those who live by intellect, crept from the shadows and laid a cold, impersonal finger on his soul. It was preposterous that a man could see the future in a dream! One was a fool to be carried away by hopes so raised, at once so futile and false.

It was possible, of course, that there would be a knoll in a wood, for woodland and forest lay back of the city, on the hills above the river. To that extent the vision might accord with fact. But that would be a coincidence.

As for the rest, as for the chance for escape which Gregory had described, that could not be possible in any circumstances. It was Belinsky's practice, it was generally known, to drug the men before execution, so that they might not raise protest or attempt escape. Should one survive the effects of the drug, there would be the soldiers stationed about to prevent a break.

No, it was impossible.

Yet Paul Stepanovitch's heart, defying logic, continued to race, and his faculties were alive and ready for any chance. Logic cannot kill hope, which merely retreats into an inner recess, ready to emerge at the slightest opportunity.

At the end of the corridor the men were lined up by the guard. Paul Stepanovitch could only guess their num-

ber. It was murky in the corridor; the lanterns, hung on
pegs, illuminated faces here and there, and Paul Stepanovitch judged there were twenty-five or thirty besides himself. The air was close. There had been rains the last few
days, and the air was heavy with impending storm. No
one spoke; they were like dead men. . . . The only sound
that could be heard was that of heavy breathing, and the
occasional roll of distant thunder.

An official appeared, for whom the guard had been waiting. It was Belinsky himself, chief of the Cheka. He was
carrying a hurricane lantern, and he now walked down
the line of men, asking the name of each and checking it
against a list he held in his hand. The lantern swinging on
his arm threw a pattern of light and shade upon his face
that caused his features to assume grotesque shapes—the
nose now enlarging to exaggerated, bulbous proportions;
the eyes now glittering, now dark and cavernous; forehead
bulging and receding—so that he seemed to be an apparition rather than a man of flesh and blood. He had grown
portly, and the added flesh accentuated his bold features—
his bushy black eyebrows, heavy nose and wide nostrils,
curving thick lips, and the scar—the memento of his
Siberian exile—that ran straight and wide across his cheek.

He was dressed completely in black, from his black
leather jacket over a black satin blouse, to his black leather
trousers and boots.

"Your name?"

The voice that asked this question was soft and gentle,
the voice of a patient, rather weary schoolmaster speaking
to a pupil.

"Alexei Georgevitch Balasnov," the prisoner—a man with
flabby jowls and protuberant, frog-like eyes—gasped. "It
is . . . final?"

Belinsky did not answer, but checked the name on his
list and turned to the next.

But Alexei Georgevitch had begun to weep softly.

"Oh, please," he whimpered. "I have done nothing, I
love my country. Please don't send me. . . ."

Alexei Georgevitch had been a provisioner, who was
accused of adulterating food supplied to the Red Army.

"You mustn't take on," said Belinsky, speaking with tenderness and from the depths of understanding. "You are not going to be tortured. It will not hurt you."

Georgevitch's weeping subsided, and Belinsky continued down the line. "Your name?"

"Vladimir Petrovitch Constantine." The voice was firm, slightly defiant.

"Your name?"

"Boris Nicholeivitch Marishov." No defiance here, merely a tired unconcern.

There were forty of them, all told—forty prisoners who were to be released that night from their imprisonment.

The counting finished, the Cheka chief took the head of the line and led the way out the door into the court. A few drops of rain fell, and flashes of heat lightning illuminated the northern sky. The atmosphere was dense and heavy, warm almost as in summer. Belinsky glanced at the sky, and led the way up a short flight of steps to a great door.

The prisoners were conducted into a large, bare room, darkened save for a pool of light in the very center, that was poured in a blinding flood from an acetylene search-lamp rigged in the balcony. In this circle of light stood four rows of opera chairs; above them the motes danced and swirled in the glare; beyond, against a wall, dully reflecting the light, stood a table; on it gleamed a tray of surgical instruments. Near this table stood a man, a doctor apparently, ghostly in a white apron, his features outlined by the reflected lights—the thick nose, the bald clammy head, the eyes like a pair of schoolboy's marbles. He stood silent, erect, motionless, as the prisoners entered, but one looking closely at him might have seen the sweat starting from his forehead and collecting in dewy drops. There was no sound save the shuffling of the prisoners and the hissing of the acetylene searchlamp.

The prisoners were led to the row of chairs, under the rays of the searchlight, and gently told to be seated. There was no protest. The men obeyed, as though hypnotized. When they were seated Belinsky spoke.

"Comrades," he addressed them, using the brotherly greeting of the Communists, "a new day has dawned for

Russia. The people have asserted their unquenchable will; the proletariat of Russia are united in strength and purpose. The day has come when justice shall prevail, when the producers shall receive the goods they produce, when prosperity and peace and happiness shall dwell in the land. To bring this to pass calls for sacrifices. All of us have sacrificed for the Party. Further sacrifices are required. To this end I address you."

"What villainy!" thought Paul Stepanovitch. He wanted to scream, to denounce Belinsky. Such extravagant, impossible speech, to be addressed to condemned men as though they were attending a political rally! What fiendish purpose lay back of Belinsky's exhortation?

Belinsky, with a shrewd mastery of psychology and understanding of the subconscious streams, was now saying, in his soft, appealing voice,

"You have been taken in custody in the highest interests of the country you love. You are no ordinary men. You are true patriots. You love your country, as do others. Were you ordinary men you would have been ignored, as of no consequence, or shot down where you stood. Instead, you have been brought here, to the very center of the Red power, in order that we may study you and understand you, in order that we may determine, after full deliberation, what is best for you and for the Soviet State."

The prisoners received these words with apathetic unconcern. The long confinement, the days without communication or hope, combined with the sudden transfer from a dimly-lit cell to the beating glare of the searchlight, had produced in them a torpor of the spirit. The quiet, measured words of Belinsky served only to lull them into a deeper lethargy.

"After full deliberation a decision has been made. It is a decision with which you will agree. You can well realize the danger to the State, and the inconvenience and unhappiness to yourselves, if you were released. First, you have no friends. Second, you have no homes. Third, you have no place in the new society. The order into which you were born has vanished; the society which you knew is broken and dispersed. The ideals which you upheld have dissolved into a new ideal which you do not recognize. There is no peace for you here, no security, no refuge. All that lies ahead. You will find peace and refuge and your friends, but you will find them ahead, not behind you.

"Nor would you wish to return, should there be here and there a stray friend. What would be the result? You might struggle bravely. But why struggle when it is hopeless? A new order has already been fixed for a new generation. Would you again stir up strife among the people you love, and disrupt the order and well-being of our country by renewed civil war? You would not. The Soviet State answers for you. Like heroes, though execrated by the proletariat and unsung by the new generation, you shall pass from this scene like the gods of old as they descended from Olympus and passed into limbo before the new faith of the Church. You are prepared to go. The Soviet State declares it. You will go peacefully, quietly, without remonstrance . . . like heroes, like men, like Russians . . . quietly, without remonstrance. . . ."

Belinsky's voice sank and became soft, insistent, monotonous, the while he stood motionless, except for his eyes, which, from unmoving sockets, moved from one to the other of the prisoners.

The prisoners, under the searchlight, dazzled by its glare, warmed by its heat, looked steadfastly ahead, unmoving except for blinking eyes, in the most abject stupor. Had they known, at that moment, that freedom lay ahead, it is doubtful whether they could have been aroused. The acetylene continued to hiss, while from outside came the rumbling of thunder, which momentarily increased, and the rush of falling rain.

For the moment Belinsky continued to regard the prisoners; and then, with a slight motion of the hand, indicated to the man in the white apron that he should begin his work. The doctor came forward, cumbersomely, as though he too were under a spell. He moved to the back of the chairs, stood by each prisoner a moment, while with a hypodermic needle he injected a narcotic preparation into the shoulder muscles at the base of the neck. The prisoners accepted this passively. One or two raised feeble hands to brush the needle away, as though it were a fly, but when the fingers closed on the muscles and the needle pressed home, they no more than grunted slightly.

The doctor, emptying and filling the hypodermic, had come to Paul Stepanovitch. Paul Stepanovitch had been sitting like a man in a trance, but within him a mighty effort of the will was in progress. He had resolved that under no circumstances would he accept this opiate.

Circumstances, by whatever cause ordained, did not require this exertion of the will. As the doctor stood behind Markov the room was suddenly and blindingly illuminated by a flash of lightning, which was followed by a clap of thunder so loud and furious that it set the windows to rattling and caused the walls to tremble. The sudden crash so startled the doctor that he cringed and his muscles quivered. Even upon the others—the prisoners whom the pronouncement of execution had failed to rouse—this act of nature produced an effect as definite as upon the glass and stone. A sudden shivering and trembling passed over the whole company, not excepting the calloused and insensitive Belinsky. Indeed, Belinsky, in a superstitious fear, felt at his neck for the charm he wore there, to see if it were safe.

The thunder continued to roll and rumble, as though presaging another flash, and the doctor stood hesitant and expectant. Presently the thunder died away, but he continued to stand before Paul Stepanovitch, his needle in his hand.

"Come," said Belinsky, a trifle impatiently, relieved by the subsidence of the thunder.

The doctor started, looked at Paul Stepanovitch a moment in perplexity, sitting rigidly before him, and then passed to the next in line.

Paul Stepanovitch did not realize at once the full import of this incident. He only knew that he still retained his full senses and complete awareness of all that went on about him, while his fellow prisoners were already slouching in their seats not in control of their bodies. He was aware not only of this difference, but also of an increasing keenness of perception and motive power. It was as though suddenly he had risen to the surface after swimming under water, while those about him seemed to sink deeper and deeper. Belinsky, the doctor and the half dozen guards in the room, were in the depths. Paul Stepanovitch felt superior to them all. He felt as though he moved in clean air and sunlight, mentally and physically alert to everything that occurred.

This alertness, this keenness induced by nervous tension, brought with it cunning. He must accept his role, must, like the others, as they marched out, stagger slightly, gaze glassily, let his lower lip droop, with a trickle of saliva at the corners, and accept in stupefaction the coaxing and persuasive commands of Belinsky.

In the courtyard, a soggy drizzle of rain was falling. From eaves, overflowing, the water gurgled and swirled as it rushed down the drain pipes and collected in the gutters. The stone cobbles of the court were covered a good two inches with water that had no outlet.

Near the curbing were three large motor trucks, open, with high side-boards. A stepladder stood by the wall. One by one the prisoners were helped into the trucks, by means of the stepladder, with the greatest gentleness, as though they were semi-invalids, or decrepit old men.

The prisoners loaded, the soldiers mounted the running boards, bayonets fixed to their rifles, and the trucks started to the execution ground. The men were all water-soaked—the prisoners, Belinsky, and the soldiers. Regardless of the rain or the slippery, water-covered street, or the narrow range of the headlights, the trucks were driven at high speed, and roared through the streets like fire engines, swerving and careening while the prisoners, under the influence of the drug, rolled about like so many bags of grain. By the clock in a steeple, it was past two in the morning. It had been less than thirty minutes earlier that Paul Stepanovitch was removed from his cell. Within another half-hour the three trucks had reached the city limits and were following a macadamized road that led away from the river and mounted into the low hilly ground west of the city.

Far up among the low hills the trucks turned off the

paved road into a woodland where the ground was springy with the weight of many generations of leaves and humus. The rain did not beat so hard now, but fell straight, as through a sieve.

Presently they came to an open space, deep in the glade, dimly visible by the headlights of the trucks. They halted and the trucks swung around so that the beams of their lights converged upon the same spot.

Earlier in the day workmen had dug a long trench and the excavated earth lay in a muddy ridge alongside, marking its outline.

The backs of the trucks were now let down, and the soldiers got out and helped the prisoners down. Dumbly, like willing cattle, they allowed the soldiers to form them in a line before the trench. There was no protest, no outcry, no outbreak. Even he who had whimpered was now stupid and stolid.

The prisoners were lined up; the soldiers took their place some twenty paces away; Belinsky began to count the prisoners:

"One, two, three . . ."

Monotonously he went on. The lightning flashed, the thunder rolled, and the skies opened to a new deluge. Heedless of rain, as though he too were benumbed, as his faculties of pity and compassion were benumbed, Belinsky went on counting, oblivious to everything except his number.

He reached the end of the line.

"Thirty-nine," he exclaimed. "Have I miscounted?" And he began to count again.

"Thirty-nine," he repeated. "One is missing."

"Impossible, commissar," said the doctor, tonelessly. He was along to certify the deaths, and he was water-soaked and miserable. "How many were on the list?"

"Forty."

"You are certain, commissar?"

"Certain, by all means," said Belinsky, his voice even but with exasperation mounting momentarily. "But I will count them again, to be sure."

He got out the list, and holding it under the light of the

hurricane lantern began to count the names. The pouring rain soon had the paper streaked and soggy, but not before he had made the count.

"No," he exclaimed. "Forty is right. One has escaped."

The corporal of the guard, a nervous Lett, was in a panic.

"He must be in the woods, commissar. He can't have gone far." He shouted to his men, "Go search for him."

The doctor was quaking. He realized now that he must have omitted to give the injection to one of the prisoners, but he could not think which one it was. If the commissar should suspect him, he would join the next execution party as one of the condemned.

But Belinsky was thinking of nothing but his number. Thirty-nine was his most unlucky number, his unlucky three times his unlucky thirteen. This was horrible. He also began to tremble in fear.

Everyone was in a state of fear—the soldiers for having let a prisoner escape, the corporal for his failure to take precautions, the doctor for his negligence, Belinsky for his bad omen—everyone, in fact, except the prisoners who had most to fear. Under the effect of the cold rain and fresh air they were beginning to revive from the opiate, and were stirring with a sense of freedom and hope.

"Oh, this is bad, this is bad," muttered Belinsky, and fumbled inside his tunic for his talisman. The prisoners were nothing to him now. The only thing that meant anything was to ward off this bad luck.

"Thirty-nine!" he exclaimed, and began to swear furiously.

But swearing did no good. There were still but thirty-nine prisoners. The soldiers were threshing about in the woods, shouting and firing. That would do no good. If they found the man and shot him, there would still be thirty-nine. If they brought him back and restored the purity of the number, that would not elude the fact that thirty-nine men had stood before him, a terrible omen of ill luck.

Belinsky bawled to the corporal.

"Bring the men back."

The soldiers straggled back.

Belinsky stared at the prisoners. He must propitiate his luck.

Fortunately, Belinsky was master over the destiny of men. His was the power to give life as well as to take it away.

Among the prisoners were those whose faculties were clear enough to understand what was happening, and who long after remembered, in all its detail, this incomprehensible deliverance, this scene in which they were embers snatched from the burning, dead men released from the grave.

Belinsky had ceased his swearing, and an expression appeared in his face such as no doubt it had worn in those distant days before he had become involved in revolution, arrogant with power, and steeped in bestiality, in those distant days when he was a teacher of mathematics standing before his pupils. Fear had purged his spirit, momentarily, of its inhumanity, and the expression was one of tenderness and regard, the expression of a man whose spirit is sweet, whose life is blameless, whose interests are simple, whose intentions are pure. He looked at the prisoners with the look of a child in whom there is no guile.

"Put our comrades back into the truck," he said softly, compassionately, emphasizing the word of revolutionary fraternity—"comrades."

With no sign of amazement or question, the soldiers, who had long learned to accept whatever happens as ordained, conducted the prisoners to the trucks. They mounted; the trucks started and rumbled away.

At the edge of the city, the trucks were halted, and the prisoners set down.

"You are free men," said Belinsky to them graciously. "Go and praise God, if you have one, and serve the cause of the Proletarian Revolution."

12. Tiflis

THE year 1918 saw what seemed to be the inevitable collapse of the Russian Empire. Vast and fertile provinces that had been added to the original Muscovite dominion by Ivan the Terrible, by Tsar Peter the Great, by Tsarina Catherine, and by the bloodshed of their myrmidons, were being lopped off one by one. In Eastern Europe the Polish provinces, and Lithuania, Latvia and Esthonia, were invaded by the Germans and their cession to Germany granted by the dictated treaty of Brest-Litovsk. Farther to the north, Finland severed itself from the Empire, and to the south, the Ukraine and the Black Sea provinces were taken away by the Austrian armies. Farther south, the British, by a frantic dash through a neutral Persia, succeeded in reaching the Baku oil fields before the Turks, but the fact that Britain was a war ally did not mean that these rich territories were saved to the Empire. In the far north, an Allied expedition was beating down from Archangel, and in Siberia, Vladivostok had become the seat of a Japanese invasion supported by American, French and British troops.

While the borders of the Empire were thus being violated, within the country the land was being fought for between Communists, known as Reds, and various opposing forces known generically as Whites, supporting this or that pretension to government, and having nothing in common but their enmity toward the Reds. Geographical boundaries did not exist for these numerous autonomies. Here a city was governed—if governed it could be called —by a military junta or a single dictator; while in the villages just beyond there might be a peasants' soviet holding allegiance to the Red Government at Moscow. Another city might be under the Communists, while in secluded valleys not far away the local nobility might still be in undisputed possession of its manorial lands. Everything was confusion. Territories changed, became Red or White, and back again. It was not the land itself that suffered from these convulsions, but the people. The land was marred by war and destruction, but the land, left to itself for a few years, would cover its wounds with a blanket of fresh verdure, and would even restore man-made deserts to gardens. But for the people, things were being uprooted which would never be replaced. Old customs, old traditions, old beliefs, old faiths, were being destroyed. The loss of a custom may not seem a matter of importance to those whose philosophy it is to deride custom as a barrier to progress; yet customs serve mightily to ease the ways of life.

The abandonment—either by decree or by the confusion incident to war—of the custom of Saturday market and Sunday mass, the proscription by the Reds of the former modes of address in favor of *tovarish* (comrade) were to many a cataclysm as disturbing as a storm that washed away all the boundary marks of the fields.

The weariness of the spirit is a greater ponderable than weariness of the body. When the spirit is strong, the fields will be planted and the reaping done, even within sight of the battle lines. Such was the case among the peasants of France. But add the weariness of the spirit to a disorganization of markets, the interruption of communication, and the depreciation of money, and one has an explanation of the terrible famine that swept over Russia.

The will to struggle was gone. This weariness of the will, this tiredness of the spirit, was a universal phenomenon. Strangely enough, it appeared where the greatest hope should exist—in the countryside, where the means of sustenance were at hand, and where men had every incentive of custom and habit to provide for their own needs. It manifested itself in the abandonment of fields and the flight of peasants to the cities. In the summer of 1918, one could travel for a hundred miles over the rich plains of the Crimea and the Don and see scarcely a shock of wheat ready for threshing, or a furrow being turned, or a hay cart on the road, or a cow in the pasture.

The cities themselves, filled to overflowing with restless, migratory populations, had practically ceased activity, and it was a common thing for even the essential services of lighting, water supply, and street transportation to be disrupted for days on end. More common, of course, was the closing of factories, the emptying of shops, the dying of all trade.

Though the will to struggle was gone, struggle itself had not gone. In November of 1918, peace had finally come to the rest of the world, but not to that seventh of the world's land surface and its one hundred and fifty million people that make up Russia. The Indian levies of Britain returned to their peninsula and southern Asia was again at peace. The Moroccan troops of France returned to Africa; and that continent, where men had fought each other in remote jungle and lonely desert far from the arenas of Europe, saw peace once more. The Canadian and American troops began their homeward movement across the Atlantic and the Western Hemisphere was no longer even remotely involved in war.

But in Russia, war went on, went on over a million square miles of territory and upon a thousand fronts. Though the will to struggle had died, struggle went on. Men struggled and fought because there was nothing else to do. Death would have been preferable to struggle, but one cannot die without struggle. Even death itself has its price for release.

Toward the close of 1918, a few weeks after the day on which the guns ceased firing on the Western front, Paul Stepanovitch Markov boarded the train at Tiflis en route to Erivan and the Persian border. His intention was to cross over into Persia and from Persia to proceed, by way of India, to England and thence to America. His intention to leave his native country, and to go to America, were manifestations of Paul Stepanovitch Markov's condition and circumstances. He had wealth upon his person, a substantial wealth in diamonds and pearls, but within him there was a great poverty. He was ready now to flee, to give up the struggle—to give up country, home, what few friends might survive, desire, ambition; everything, in fact, but the desire to continue to breathe the air of the earth.

Upon his escape from the executioners at Kazan, Paul Stepanovitch had succeeded, after almost unbearable hardships of cold and hunger and nakedness, and adventures which would have caused the face of Odysseus to blanch, in reaching the Kuban, where he fell in with a band of desperadoes calling themselves Whites. This band, at the time, comprised well over two thousand men who were for the most part former officers of the Imperial army, landowners, nobles, professional men, and those who by conviction or for reasons of personal interest were opposed to the Soviet government. Its commander, Boris Korsakoff, was a man of unshakable courage and great tactical skill, but one who had only contempt for civilians, who was devoid of imagination, and lacking all political sagacity.

For some time the force made progress, conquering an area equivalent to half that of France, and setting up governments and administrations that professed to adhere to the ideals and principles, not of the Empire—for that was already dead—but of the Revolution as understood and enunciated by the Kerensky régime. These administrations did not survive, for they aroused no popular appeal, and no sooner had the army of Korsakoff moved on to other conquests than they crumbled from sheer lack of vitality and were replaced by soviets of workers and peasants.

As the Red star waxed and grew brilliant in the north, the strength and authority of Korsakoff's force progressively declined. The debacle of Korsakoff and his army was but the foreshadowing of the doom that was to overtake the other counter-revolutionary forces under Denikin, Kolchak, Yudenitch, and Wrangel. One by one the cities that Korsakoff had captured reverted to the Reds; in one pitched battle after another Korsakoff's army was decimated; the ranks were not refilled by new enlistments, for heart was not in the people for fighting; desertions further reduced their number. The remnant of Korsakoff's army, now no more than two hundred men, took to the hills, lived like bandits, carrying on guerrilla warfare against the Reds. Korsakoff himself was finally killed.

Paul Stepanovitch had remained until the very end, hoping against hope, but with Korsakoff's death all spirit went from the band; they became little better than outlaws. Paul Stepanovitch was unwilling to descend this low in estate, and he determined upon flight.

In one of the engagements, in which they had taken a small city, Korsakoff had, in order to revive the spirits of his men and to refill their depleted treasury, permitted looting. It was this instance of looting that filled Paul Stepanovitch with despair and eventually turned his thoughts to flight. It had also provided him with the means for flight. A short time later, in another engagement, one of the comrades, Vasili Sulevan, a cutthroat Cossack, was fatally wounded. Before he died, he spoke to Paul Stepanovitch, and drawing from his tunic a leather sack full of gems, he put them into Markov's hand as a gift.

Paul Stepanovitch accepted the purse, and tied it about his neck. When the remnant of Korsakoff's band had dissolved, he extracted one of the gems, a small pearl, which he sold to a Jewish trader for a suit of clothes and a bundle of paper rubles. He had heard that things were better in the Caucasus, that an independent Georgian republic had been set up and was now under the tutelage of a British army. He decided to go there. At this time he had not determined upon America. He still had hopes of returning to his own country when peace should come.

It was in Tiflis that Paul Stepanovitch's thoughts turned upon emigration to America. There was gaiety and an air of prosperity in Tiflis; the shops were open on the Golovinsky Prospekt; theaters and restaurants were brilliantly lit and thronged with women in sparkling dress and rouged faces, attended by men in cream-colored *tcherkess* and soft glove-leather boots. Street cars were clanging and crowded as they jolted past the Opera, the Namiestnik Gardens, and the vice-regal lodge. But it all had an air of unreality. It was like the hectic flush on the cheek of a consumptive. Could it be, Paul Stepanovitch thought, that here was a portion of his land, a corner of his Russia, that had come through war unscathed? If it had, then why and how had it escaped? Had the people here failed to bear their share of the burden?

Strangely enough, for one to whom wealth and luxury were not unknown before the war, and who had given little thought to the unfortunate peoples of his country, it produced in Paul Stepanovitch a strange uneasiness to see people so well-dressed, so sleek-looking, so obviously unconcerned with what was happening to millions of fellow Russians. It made him want to stand at a corner and shout to them, to cry upon them a vengeance, as the Hebrew prophets had done upon the unrighteousness of the children of Israel.

For the first time Paul Stepanovitch began to understand the meaning of the proletarian revolution, and what was its promise and appeal to ordinary men.

A person of shabby, but not beggarly, dress sidled up to him.

"Have you a cigarette, comrade?"

Paul Stepanovitch was standing on a corner of the Golovinsky Prospekt and gazing down the avenue at the Opera. The Opera was a building of great beauty, patronized in the old days by the nobility of Russia who resorted to Tiflis in winter. Paul Stepanovitch had attended the Opera once or twice in those distant days. He remembered the regal display of uniforms and gowns; the great gold curtain with the picture of St. George, the patron saint of the Georgians, slaying the dragon, worked in royal blue upon the gold; the crowd in the foyer during intermission; the great ladies and nobles munching sandwiches and swallowing beer with barbaric gusto—Paul Stepanovitch had since seen many a common soldier eat with more decorum—the sound of popping corks and insensate chatter drowning the glorious melodies of Puccini or Tchiakovsky that still rang in the ears. Then, he had accepted it all without analysis; he accepted these views, this social rivalry, this display of wealth, this grand and vulgar manner, as part of the accepted order. These were the people of worth; this was the institution of things which was the proper and ultimate product of the social evolution. Everyone of class in those days accepted the philosophy of evolution, and conceived that they were at the top because of natural fitness. It all seemed very cheap and gaudy now to Paul Stepanovitch. How little worth did a title confer; how little security really rested upon possession of lands and goods. The only ultimate value was that of self, the powers and virtues that resided within the individual, the qualities of personality, the strength of will. . . .

The voice of the man asking for a cigarette broke in upon Paul Stepanovitch's thoughts. He fumbled in his tunic. Yes, he had some cigarettes, he thought. He had bought a package that morning from a street urchin. He hadn't tasted a cigarette in over a year, and he had bought the package partly out of pity, partly to try smoking again and see how it was. The smoke had been bitter in his nostrils, either because he had lost his taste or because of the quality of the tobacco. He had forgotten whether he had thrown the package away, given it away, or still had it.

Yes, he had it. He handed it to the man with a *"pozhaluite"* ("Take it, please"), but with hardly a glance at him.

"Thank you, officer," said the man.

Paul Stepanovitch started.

"You mean to say—"

He was about to say "comrade," but remembered that this was not Soviet territory. Instead, he said,

"You are mistaken. I am not an officer."

The man looked at him shrewdly. He was thin and weazened, but not ill-fed. He had keen, feral eyes that one associates with police informers or gamblers.

"But you are undoubtedly of the gentility. One must look to the gentility for such generosity."

"Really?" asked Markov, with a trace of irony. He wondered what the man was driving at.

"Yes, generosity was the virtue of the nobility, for all their alleged faults; but I should add, since you deny that you were one of their number, and I should then condemn them, that this may have been partly because they had the money with which to be generous. But I must maintain that generosity was their virtue and that the spread of this new order of things will mean the death of that gracious gift to mankind."

Paul Stepanovitch was too weary for argument. He allowed the man to continue.

"Mark my words," the man said. "You shall see, in time to come, men more crafty, more grasping, more stingy, than the world has ever seen. Distribute the wealth of the world among the people—bah—the people are not ready to possess wealth."

He paused, drew out a flint and tow, lighted the tow with a practiced movement, blew on it until it was a coal, and lighted a cigarette.

"Why do you say that people are not ready to possess wealth?" asked Markov.

"Because the more they get the more they will scramble for," responded his acquaintance, inhaling the smoke with deep satisfaction. "Within a generation your self-denying Reds will be more land hungry, more imperialistic, than the worst of the tsars. When human progress is measured by the number of poods of grain in the barn, the number of shirts on the back, when the whole aim of government is to improve the standard of living, as they say, then unhappy is the outlook for Russia. In the old days it was not so; we had poverty, but what was poverty when we had the Church and the lighted candles and the thousands shouting 'Kyrie' on Easter eve? Take the silken stole from the priest and distribute it among the congregation, and what have you? Every man lustfully clutching a thread, and no stole for the priest. That is the result of your proletarian appeal! Generosity gone, everything gone; everyone scrambling for himself because the law and the gospel say that such is the purpose of living. . . ."

"That all sounds very nice," said Paul Stepanovitch, lightly, "but still you are mistaken. I did not give you the cigarettes from generosity, but because I don't like them."

"Ah, you belittle yourself, which is added generosity. Now your true bourgeois, who has found that he has lost his taste, might give a cigarette, but not the package. No. He would have said, 'I will keep the rest. Perhaps another will ask, and I will give and lay up double merit in heaven.'"

Paul Stepanovitch laughed outright, a thing he had not done in many months.

"Then, to justify your opinion and to show that I am generous, I will buy you a glass of wine."

"And in return, I shall take you where the best wine of the Caucasus is obtainable at a fraction of what the poorest sells for on the Prospekt. Follow me."

The stranger led Markov to a wine *dukhan,* tended by a Kirghiz, on one of the hill streets overlooking the Kura. The proprietor dragged down, from a tier of them lying dusty and cobweb-covered in the rear of this shop, an enormous oxskin. He untied a leg of this bloated creature and filled the glasses with tawny Khaketia vintage.

"Aside from this wine, which is the best the Caucasus affords," said the stranger, surveying the glass with delight and inhaling its bouquet, "there is nothing to live for here."

"Why do you say that?" asked Paul Stepanovitch slowly. "I thought you supported the aristocratic tradition."

"I do, but all that you see is only a shell. This independent nation of Georgia, that has risen so proudly and pretentiously from the Revolution, will be crushed like an eggshell the moment the Reds decide upon its conquest. That is why there is nothing to live for."

"You seem to account the Reds as very powerful."

"No, it is not their power—though theirs is the power of the devil—but our weakness. The people in office are the puppets of the English. The English cannot stay here forever. They have their troubles in Europe.

"All this business that you see in the shops is artificial. The Germans came in first, shortly after the so-called peace of Brest-Litovsk. But they had not army reserves sufficient to hold the country, and so they spent gold in cultivating good will, and in developing a Georgian army. They didn't last, and the English are here now, doing the same. They are paying out money because Britain can still fight with sterling notes if not with English soldiers. They think that by paying us we will do their fighting for them,

keep back the Reds and preserve the Baku oil fields to the
Nobel and the Royal Dutch-Shell interests, and the man-
ganese of Poti to the Rothschilds and Armstrongs.

"But we Georgians will not do that. We are nobody's
fool. Nobody is going to fight the Reds if they come in.
We are tired of fighting. Our English friends will quickly
leave. Then this business will dry up. It appears to be
something, but it is nothing. A small stone makes a great
splash in still water, and a few sterling notes make a grand
show when everyone is starving. But where are these sterling notes spent, that the British advisers pay out? In the
fancy shops along Golovinsky Prospekt or Pushkin Street,
in the restaurants and theaters. It is poured down from
above, but the thirsty soil absorbs it before it reaches the
roots below from which real prosperity springs. It's all
very gay here, but down in the lower town you will see
the misery multiplying and the dead increasing."

They had finished the glass of wine, and the shopkeeper
poured them another. Paul Stepanovitch felt warmed, and
his moodiness was mingled with euphoria.

"What would you propose, then, for a man in my situation?" he asked. "One who no longer has a profession, or
friends, or lands, or place, or hope or purpose?"

"Get out of the country, as fast as your legs can carry
you, would be my advice," said his acquaintance
promptly.

"That is nice advice," responded Paul Stepanovitch
ironically. "Elsewhere I would have even less of profession, no friends—instead, suspicious strangers—no land, no
place, no hope nor purpose. What good does it do to transfer the body?"

"Ah, but your very saying so shows that you are wrong.
You have a purpose, else you would not be so reluctant to
leave, and if you have a purpose, all these other things
will come—friends, possessions—such as you may have
need of—and position. That is the only advantage of place.
In another place you will be better able to realize your
purpose."

"I have no purpose except to keep a whole skin," said
Paul Stepanovitch bitterly.

"Ah, but you have."

"And what is that?"

"That I do not know. I am not so skillful as that in reading the mind, especially when you do not have it clear yourself. But it is there—I can sense it. Some trait in your nature—the pity, perhaps, which led you to offer me the cigarettes, that led you to buy them in the first place, that led you to invite me here—demands expression. Something in you has been covered up all these years, covered over by a layer of superficial logic—the creed of your caste, no doubt. But it boils and surges within you, and pounds for release. Search yourself, and you will find it, and when you find it you will discover that purpose which is stronger than your will to live."

Paul Stepanovitch gulped down his glass of wine and rose.

"Such damned twaddle as I never heard," he exploded. "You talked for a while like an intelligent man, and now you turn mystic, like a superstitious monk. Why, may I ask, don't you get away yourself? Why do you stay here? You, who are so full of wise ideas and understanding?"

The man laughed easily, without taking offense, and continued to sip his wine.

"Oh," he said, "very easy to explain. I shall get along here. I am like a light pea that always sifts to the top."

Violently, Paul Stepanovitch tossed a package of paper rubles on the table for the shopkeeper and strode out, leaving his acquaintance behind in the shop, sipping his wine.

After he had gone a way, Paul Stepanovitch felt sorry for his discourtesy. His sense of meanness and remorse increased the farther he walked, while his mood of bitterness with himself mounted. He wanted to get away from himself, to get away from this town, as far away as possible from this stranger, who might encounter him again, stand before him and accuse him for his discourtesy, for his faithlessness to his upbringing, and even, no doubt, harry him, like an admonitory apparition, with his talk of "purpose."

Paul Stepanovitch recalled his last conversations with

Gregory Fedorevitch, how this young man had gone to
his death with the same admonition on his lips, how
Gregory had been willing to surrender his hope for the
sake of the purpose which he thought he saw in his companion.

Without knowing what he did, or why, but with a sort
of mechanical volition, the way men struggle in the snow
without knowing where they are going, but struggle because they must go somewhere, Paul Stepanovitch made
his way to the railway station.

13. Two Children

THOUGH a rail line, substantially built in the old Russian
manner, ran south from Tiflis to the Persian border, service was now slow, uncertain, and frequently interrupted
by disputes between Georgia and Armenia. These two new
revolutionary states were never certain of the extent of
their sovereign powers and territories, and issues of prestige and national dignity—created by such matters as
diplomatic precedence, courtesies and amenities—were
promptly reflected in the railway timetables. The title to
the rolling stock of the railroad was a matter that was always a subject of debate. Since it had formerly belonged
to the Imperial government, it was, except when in need
of repairs, claimed both by Armenia and Georgia. Oper-
ating a train was, in fact, a procedure calling more for
diplomatic skill and finesse than knowledge of steam pres-
sures, gradients, and bills of lading.

When Paul Stepanovitch bought his ticket to Erivan, no
train had run for over a week. A great crowd had gathered
in consequence, many of whom had been waiting on the
platform, nestling among their bundles and baggage, for
days, hoping every moment that the train would move.
When Paul Stepanovitch arrived on the platform, how-

ever, the train had steam up and the bells were ringing, and most of the passengers were already aboard. They were in the vestibules, on the steps, sitting on each other's laps, perched on the roof.

The bell continued to ring, and more passengers crowded on. Paul Stepanovitch had found a bit of space vacant in the passageway and had settled himself alongside an Assyrian who was taking himself and his family to Mesopotamia.

A few, like the Assyrian, who had some means, were leaving the country, and upon their faces was the color of hope. But for the others, one wondered what lay ahead. They were going south, but for what? In the hope that things were better in Armenia? Yet the same train that took this crowd to Armenia had brought back a crowd, equally large, of those who were going north, driven by the same hope that was taking these south. Everywhere it was the same. Paul Stepanovitch had seen it all over southern Russia—a whole people uprooted, blown about, drifting, keeping to the herd like sheep in a storm. Even here, where the British were in control and conditions seemingly more prosperous, it was the same. Material decay, people fleeing from destruction, seeking another town, another village, another valley, where there was food, and peace. . . .

Toward two o'clock, after the bell had been ringing a good hour, the train finally drew out of the train shed, and started its creeping journey south. The road bed was in wretched condition and the rails sank in places under the weight of the train. On every curve it seemed that the cars would turn over, and spill their cargo down the embankment.

Late in the afternoon they reached the Armenian frontier, where another interminable time was spent while the frontier guards examined all the baggage and documents of the passengers. Because it was then dark, the train halted until morning, leaving the passengers to sleep as best they could curled up in their seats or on the ground around the customs shed.

The next morning they entered Armenia only to behold

a new desolation, which to Paul Stepanovitch was worse
than any he had seen. As they mounted the plateau the
trees thinned out, and the hills became bleak and barren,
and everywhere the aspect was one of abandonment. To
the natural frugality of nature was added the destruction
caused by war.

There, amid the stumps of hacked trees that marked
a patch of fertile ground, lay the ruins of an Armenian
village. It was like Galicia again, except that in Galicia,
where rainfall was more abundant, the vegetation soon
covered the scars from sight. Here, nature was not so
kind. The bones were left naked to the bleaching sun—
and the landscape was scattered with them.

Near Artof, a colony of refugees was encamped in
makeshift hovels of straw and tin. They were typical of
what one saw all over Armenia in that winter of 1918-
1919. What Russia proper had suffered, Armenia had suffered threefold. Following the disintegration of the Imperial armies, the Turks had broken in at the borders and,
repeating the shambles of 1895, had massacred and pillaged
wherever they went. Not until the threat produced by
the appearance of the British detachment under Dunster-
ville, which had beaten up from Mesopotamia by way of
Persia, had they halted their advance; and not until the
collapse of Turkish authority within the Empire and the
signing of the Armistice of Mudros, had they retired.
What one saw was the denudation and destruction produced by that invasion.

During the afternoon, as they crept across the plain,
Paul Stepanovitch, gazing moodily from the window, observed a mountain peak rising in the south, at first a nod-
ule of snow on the horizon, and then a rounded dome,
snow-covered, pushing itself above the rim of the plain.
The mountain caught Paul Stepanovitch's attention. There
was something affecting about the way it rose to view. It
was a solitary mountain: there was a look of loneliness
about it, as though all its companions had disappeared
under the horizon never to return, as though it had re-
appeared for a last searching look at the world before
it should again disappear, forever.

Though he did not know the name of the mountain, had never seen it before, Paul Stepanovitch had the singular feeling of being acquainted with it. He felt as one with it, as though they were invested with the same spirit, the mountain and the man, as though they had passed through the same experiences. Both were lonely, both set apart from the rest of creation—the man, whom the Creator had exalted above all creatures, and the mountain, lifted above the land. Both, by the rôle in which they had been cast, were condemned to loneliness. Both, because of their aloofness and elevation from the rest of life, felt the force of all the storms which swirl and rage through the chambers of the universe.

"What is that mountain?" Paul Stepanovitch asked the man next to him in the passageway—the Assyrian who was going to Mesopotamia.

"Ararat," said the man solemnly, with the air of an ancient Hebrew pronouncing the sacred *Jahveh*, name of God.

"Ararat?" asked Paul Stepanovitch.

"The same," nodded the man.

Paul Stepanovitch said no more. Of late he had grown very quiet. Never a loquacious man, he had sunk further and further within himself during these last years, either to find in quiescence strength for the fearful struggles to which the body had been subjected, or perhaps merely seeking, within himself, the solace and peace which seemed to have departed from the living world of movement.

As the train proceeded, the mountain grew larger in the south; it seemed to grow and swell until it dominated the horizon. In the evening sun the snowy dome was coral, and the broad flanks of the mountain, violet and misty, seemed to rise not from the surface of the earth, but from some different substance, an ethereal substance that was not like the cracked and wrinkled earth—aged and weary and worn out—but fresh and strong and full of youth.

It suddenly struck Paul Stepanovitch, watching the snow-covered peak as it towered higher and higher on the horizon, that the mountain had endured in spite of storm, that no doubt it owed its being to some vast convulsion of nature. If this were so, then might it not also be true of man? That he exists and finds his being in the convulsions of life, that in those very forces which are bent upon his annihilation he finds his strength and imperishable self?

"It's a beautiful mountain," said Paul Stepanovitch to the Assyrian. "Are there others like it in the south?"

"There is no mountain in the world like Ararat," said his companion, reverently. "It is the symbol of Armenia. They have it on the flag."

"That is interesting. Why is that? How high is it?"

"I do not know how high it is. But higher than all other mountains of the world. The Ark rested on Ararat. In Etchmiadzin they have a piece of the Ark."

"Come, come," said Paul Stepanovitch, to whom the superstitions of the ignorant were always somewhat annoying, "It's a wonderful sight, but don't let's spoil it by fairy tales."

"Do you not believe that the words of Holy Scripture are true?" asked the man incredulously.

"I don't know," replied Paul Stepanovitch. "I've never thought very much about them."

"You know the story of the Ark, don't you?"

"In a general way. I remember that in the army anyone who couldn't carry his liquor was called a 'Noah.'"

"Noah was not perfect. God did not save Noah for himself, but for the children of Noah—the children of God whom He loves."

"Do you think that God loves mankind?"

"Yes."

"What makes you think so?"

"If you knew what horrors we have been through—myself, my wife here, and our children! And now God is delivering us. We are safely on our way to Baghdad, where we have friends and relatives. God has saved us."

"How about all these others?" Paul Stepanovitch asked bitterly.

The Assyrian did not answer. What happened to other

men seemed beyond the range of his comprehension, a matter as unfathomable as the stars that were colliding in flames a billion miles away.

The train grumbled, slowed down and stopped. They were at a tank station—no more than a water tower, an outbuilding or two for railway supplies, and a short spur of track running out for a quarter of a mile from the main line. Beyond, the land swept bare and desolate for miles.

While the locomotive was taking on water, the passengers climbed out and walked up and down the track.

On the spur stood a row of armored cars, and flat cars loaded with tanks and pieces of artillery. The cars had been abandoned by the Russian army during its disintegration; they had apparently been standing there for months, and no one had attempted to salvage or protect them. The paint had peeled, rust had scrawled a cancerous growth over the metal sheathing, and here and there rain water, yellowed by the rust, had collected in hollows.

These decaying engines of war were to Paul Stepanovitch but another symbol of the decay of all things. The whole world was in dissolution; nothing would survive, all would vanish in the depth of despair and disappear in chaos. No ground was solid, no force was certain, no hope was sure.

Paul Stepanovitch walked out along the spur—out of a passing curiosity to examine the types of equipment that were rusting away. As he came near he observed a little fluttering under the trucks, a movement like that of a meadowlark when it wishes to lure the hunter from its nest. His interest aroused, he stood still and watched.

Two children, in rags, crept from beneath the trucks, where they had been hiding, and peered furtively about, like squirrels hesitantly emerging from their hollow. They were frail, emaciated, barefoot, bareheaded, clad in nothing more than bits of sacking. They were girls. One was about nine years old, the other not more than five.

The older child had a tin can tied about her neck by a length of string. She unfastened the can, and leaving the

other child, began to creep along within the shelter of
the cars toward the locomotive, all the time looking about
fearfully as though afraid of being seized. Water was running along in a ditch where the locomotive tender was
being filled. Reaching this ditch she scooped up some of
the turbid, yellow water in her tin can and then carefully
carried it back to her companion, who drank deep and
long. Then she returned and filled the cup and satisfied
her own thirst.

The thought of these children having to wait for water
until a train should pass, and fill the ditch with the overflow from the tank, sent a shaft of pity into Paul Stepanovitch's heart: it passed before his mind that there is no
more agonizing sight on a battlefield than that of a
wounded soldier in thirst, no more heart-rending cry than
that of "water."

He approached the children softly, and called to them,
using the affectionate diminutive *judikner*. The word came
to him out of his childhood, remembered from an Armenian nursemaid who had for a few years lived with the
Markovs at Varsova.

"*Judikner*, come to me."

The children saw Markov standing over them, and their
eyes were filled with terror. They stood motionless, frozen
by their fear; then, before Paul Stepanovitch could speak
again, they had darted away and crawled under the armored train.

Paul Stepanovitch kneeled down, so that he could see
beneath the trucks, and waited.

Presently he saw one of the children peering at him from
behind a car wheel. Emaciated and bony as the child
was, she seemed so soft against the hard metal, so full of
life against the utter deadness of the iron, that Paul Stepanovitch, until now touched by pity, was urged by a great
compassion.

He called again softly to the child, and held out his
hand.

Presently the children's fear subsided to timidity. The
older of the two edged herself forward a little way, and

looked at Markov, but hesitantly, ready to flee on the instant.

Paul Stepanovitch continued to coax. He was not insistent, but gentle and persistent. Gradually, the child came nearer. When she was within a few paces, Paul Stepanovitch, who could not remember ever having spoken to a child, knew intuitively what to say.

"My name is Paul," he said. "What's yours?"

"Asta."

"And her name?"

"Dina."

"Those are pretty names. Is she your sister?"

"Yes."

"Do you get cold staying out here?"

"Yes. . . . But I'm not cold now."

"I think you must be hungry."

"Yes."

"What do you like to eat?"

"Anything."

"Well, do you like *prianik?*" The Armenian word for *prianik* escaped him for the moment, and he used the Russian instead.

"I don't know. I never ate them."

"They are cakes, made with honey and butter."

The little girl looked at him stolidly. Her fear was gone, her thoughts absorbed by her hunger. Gradually, Paul Stepanovitch was subduing the child. She looked at him, and presently began to whimper:

"I'm hungry."

"Yes, yes, little one. I know you're hungry. And here's something for you."

Paul Stepanovitch drew from his pocket a piece of chocolate that he had bought in Tiflis for his journey. The fears of the child were overcome; she came forward slowly and accepted it. Paul Stepanovitch gathered her into his arms, and beckoned to Dina, who now followed her sister's example.

The children had never eaten chocolate before. Partly

because of this, partly because the starved stomach re-
volts at food, they only nibbled at it.

The train bell was ringing, and the passengers were
clambering aboard.

"Do you want to stay here?" Paul Stepanovitch asked.
He had been sitting on the end of a cross-tie, holding the
two girls within the crook of his arm, while he fed them
the chocolate.

"No," said Asta.

"Would you like to come with me?"

"No," said Asta.

"Yes," spoke up Dina, the younger, who, now that her
fear was gone and her hunger allayed, had discovered her
tongue.

Paul Stepanovitch did not try to persuade Asta by
promises of comforts. He sensed that the dignity of a child
is above such things, and that if they came with him, it
would be in response to the affection he felt.

"I don't have any house, but perhaps we could find
one," he ventured.

"We don't either," piped up Dina in her quavering voice.

"Then come, and we'll all find a home, shall we?"

Asta still hesitated. Finally:

"The black stuff is good."

"I'm glad. Then come. Let's hop aboard before the train
leaves us."

He took the children by the hands, led them to his car,
and lifted them aboard.

At first, and for some hours, Asta and Dina were very
quiet. They were still a little distrustful of this man who
had taken them up, almost before they were aware of it,
and had set them in a railway carriage full of so many
people. They had never been on a railway train, and besides, they were still numb from exposure and hunger. It
was fairly warm in the carriage, however, and Paul Stepanovitch still had in his sack a little food that was easily
digestible and served to palliate their hunger.

Gradually the children began to come to life, their

spirits to revive. Asta's short "yes" or "no" became sentences, connected discourse, and, after a time, a stream of chatter.

Bit by bit, Paul Stepanovitch pieced out their story. They had lived, with their father and mother and older brother, in a substantial stone house surrounded by its own fields, on the outskirts of a village, near Badan, close by the Armenian-Georgian frontier. A party of soldiers with red arm bands had appeared in the village and demanded billets. These were provided and the soldiers were quiet, but next day a rumor had gone round that the villagers were plotting to kill them. The soldiers accused the chief men of the village and promptly shot them. All the arms found in the village were then confiscated.

After a few days the soldiers left, taking with them most of the provisions that had been stored up against the winter. Two days later, however, they returned, passing through the village in hasty flight, and the following day the village was raided by a large guerrilla force of Turks. The Turks, finding nothing left to plunder, had gone through the streets shooting and killing all whom they saw.

The children's father had been shot by the Red soldiers. When the Turks appeared, the mother had seized the two girls—their brother was away in the village on an errand—and had fled down a ravine toward the hills.

"Then Mamma died."

Beyond that point, neither Asta nor Dina would say anything that yielded a connected story. How their mother had died, how the children had lived during the time between these events and his finding them, Paul Stepanovitch could never learn. He surmised that the mother had died from exposure or sudden disease—pneumonia probably—and he guessed, from the condition of the children, that they had been wandering about for months. There were references to a "cave," and their swollen stomachs indicated that they had been living on grass and roots.

Asta's eyes sometimes clouded, for no apparent reason,

and Paul Stepanovitch would know then that she was thinking of her parents. Asta, being the older, had a more vivid sense of her loss. In those moments, Paul Stepanovitch did not try to make her forget by distracting her attention—he knew, from his own experience, that the floods of memory are not to be dammed, but only channeled into fruitful fields—but gently he put his arms about her shoulders.

The plight of Asta and Dina awakened in Paul Stepanovitch latent powers and sensibilities that had long been slumbering, and his capacities for sympathy and affection expanded to a degree that he had never experienced. In a few short hours, he had acquired a new manhood, a new sense of care and responsibility that at the same time gave him a new confidence in his mental and physical powers.

After a while Dina grew tired, and her head began to nod against Paul Stepanovitch. He put his arm about her to make her more comfortable, and soon she was asleep. This she did with such naturalness that Paul Stepanovitch marveled at the ease with which a child can adapt itself to circumstance. Already Dina could sleep in his arms in confidence and contentment. She assumed, by right, that he would be a protector. As for himself, Paul Stepanovitch could not remember when he had ever held a child in his arms; he could but faintly remember when he himself had welcomed the protecting arms of another. These relationships of life, in which one finds strength in dependence on others, had been something which had been part of his experience, but they had been on a different level. The trust which soldiers put in their commanding officer was similar to this, yet very different. Soldiers rely on their officers, but the officers also rely on their men and find strength in their reliance. But a child depending upon a grown-up—what does a child offer in return?

There was much, he discovered, though not immediately. He wanted Dina to sleep and rest, and he arranged himself to make her more comfortable, while peaceful images that had long been absent began to return to his thoughts. The placid world of Varsova as a boy floated before him. He could feel his hand within his father's, as they walked along the river bank. He could hear the creak of the carts and smell the fragrance of the hay. . . .

Asta was still awake and looking out the car window.

"Where are we going?" she whispered.

"Why—" began Paul Stepanovitch. "To the south, of course."

Asta laughed.

"We are in the south now."

"But we are also in the north. We shall go farther south."

"I like you," said Asta.

"I am glad you do."

"When we stop again, Dina and I will get down."

"But why? Where would you go?"

"You see, you are going a long way, and you probably have a wife and little girls of your own. You want to go home and look after them."

"No," said Paul Stepanovitch, shaking his head slowly. "I have no children."

"But you have a wife?"

"No. I have no wife either."

"Then you have other things to do. Dina and I will get down."

"No, you will stay with me—for a while at least. I have no wife to look after you, and no home, but we shall find a nice place, where you can stay, where there are kind people, and other children to play with, perhaps, and—and—what else would you like?"

Asta thought.

"Naturally," she said, "I would like most to have father and mother again, but they are gone; and I don't know. I want Dina to stay some place where she can get food. . . ."

"Well, we shall see that she gets these things, and more, if they are to be had. Now, wouldn't you like to rest here in my other arm for a little while? When you both wake we will have our supper."

Asta smiled and presently both children were asleep, their heads in his lap.

Paul Stepanovitch, looking down upon them, began to consider this responsibility which he had assumed.

14. Train Acquaintance

THE flush of benevolence toward the children had begun to pale, and Paul Stepanovitch was finding them a bothersome interruption to his thoughts. He was not happy about the idea of going to America and he wanted to be alone with his problem. Dina's prattle annoyed him, and though Asta was quieter and more considerate, her very considerateness became an annoyance. She was respectfully attentive to this new friend who had offered his protection, was responsive to his mood, and when she observed that he did not wish to talk, she had gently nudged Dina to silence her. This only irritated Markov the more. It disturbed him that this child could penetrate the mask of his composure and see the conflict and doubt which he wanted to hide.

The fact was that these children aroused in Paul Stepanovitch a sense of his own inadequacy at the same time that they awakened distant, long-submerged memories of his own sheltered childhood. The combination of the two—the sense of insecurity and aloneness in a futile, disorganized world, and the remembrance, or the awareness, that there had been such a thing as security—stirred in him an intense, agonizing desire for some measure of security for himself. Yet it was a desire which he did not recognize; this yearning for peace was too submerged, too opposed to the surface, dynamic creed by which he professed to live, for him to admit it to himself. Paul Stepanovitch argued to himself that he was master of his destiny and sufficient for all his needs.

There were other streams of discomforting reflection that began to flow in his mind, as a result of these children. The fact struck him that some man had fathered them, that some woman had mothered them, that some man had possessed the courage, not only to contend against life for himself, but to bring a wife and children within the circle of his arm, within the walls of his defense. Some man had dared to accept the responsibilities of marriage, of support of a family, and though he may have failed miserably—leaving two children homeless in the world—his was a magnificent courage. It was a responsibility which Paul Stepanovitch, with all his philosophy of self-sufficiency and of the power of the will, had never dared assume.

Moreover, these children themselves had a courage which, by comparison, rendered his own as little better than cowardice. What were their weapons against the world? With a challenging audacity they turned their very weakness into strength. They were now going on a journey to a destination they knew not, with a man whom they had never seen before, and of whom they knew nothing, but with an implicit faith that was stronger than courage; and they went unafraid, confident indeed, and joyful.

When they came to Kutai, near where the line branches off to Kars, Markov sought relief from the children by climbing down and pacing the platform, on the excuse of getting some air.

One of the travelers spoke to him.

"You have two likable children with you. Yours?"

"No. I found them along the road," Markov answered shortly. "They may be likable, but I'm not used to children. I don't know what to do with them."

The man smiled understandingly. He was a plump, rosy-cheeked Armenian, with the affable, assured manner of a politician.

"I'm not used to children, either," he acknowledged. "We are men of affairs, you and I. We have never had time to raise a family. My name is Khansourian, Garabed Khansourian."

Markov resented being placed in the same category as the Armenian, and the reminder about never having had a family brought to the surface, for a troubled moment, the subconscious stream of his thought.

The man went on chatting, however, and presently Markov told him his name and the circumstances of his picking up the children.

"Children, children," sighed Khansourian. "They are so appealing, so full of loveliness and charm. I used to be a teacher of children, but larger duties called me. I am an Armenian patriot, an official of the Dashnak, and have devoted my life to Armenian independence. At last our work is crowned with success, and it is very gratifying, a wonderful thought."

"You are an official of the new government?" Markov enquired, taken by a sudden thought.

"No," replied Khansourian, embarrassed. "My work is in an unofficial, advisory capacity." He brightened, however, and added in explanation: "I find that I can render greater service without official ties."

Markov gave a noncommittal nod.

"Don't you think so?" Khansourian urged.

"One's service depends entirely on one's personal capacities and will, and not on position or rank," Markov said sententiously.

"That's right. That's what I've always said," beamed Khansourian, his assurance, momentarily shaken, returning. "Can you imagine what a wonderful thing it is to have one's life-long dreams realized, one's patriotic hopes fulfilled?"

He began to tell Paul Stepanovitch about the work, as a member of the Dashnak, which he had been doing during the years of the Empire, organizing societies, attending conventions, writing pamphlets, running the risk of arrest and exile, making frequent moves at night to escape the police, all for the sake of an independent Armenia.

Paul Stepanovitch looked at him unresponsively. All this enthusiasm, this talk of purpose and achievement, had an air of unreality about it. He himself had once felt such enthusiasm, but it was gone now. Everything was unreal—

most of all this enthusiasm. He was, in fact, very tired. . . .

Paul Stepanovitch wondered, momentarily, if all this talk his acquaintance was giving him was not just a little forced, whether it were not for effect, a whistling to keep up courage. It was apparent that this Khansourian was not an important figure among his people, and that Khansourian himself realized it, but he went on, just the same, pretending that he was, trying to make himself believe that his services were important. Paul Stepanovitch knew they were not, knew that the services of no man were essential, and that men delude themselves, for the sake of keeping their spirits alive, by telling themselves that they are needed.

Paul Stepanovitch had seen men like this Khansourian before—the kind who carry banners in a procession, and wave flags in a crowd, the kind who crowd around the dais but never so much as stand on its steps. It was this sort— Paul Stepanovitch suddenly realized—these people who are willing followers, who find a vicarious satisfaction in the triumphs of their leaders, rather than in becoming leaders themselves, that make great movements possible. It is not the leaders, with their fiery speech and flashing eye and self-assertiveness, but the masses who respond that produce great achievement. There are, in fact, no heroes. Heroism is a delusion. It is the froth that is thrown up on the crest of the advancing wave, but the real strength lies below, in the surge of the tide, or above, in the movements of the moon to which the tide is slave.

Paul Stepanovitch felt a pity for Khansourian, for his self-delusion, for the hopelessness of his life. . . .

He began to think about the children, back in the car. Khansourian sighed gently.

"But I sometimes wish I had raised a family," he remarked. "Children like those make one realize the sacrifices one makes in the name of patriotism."

He sighed again, this time a comfortable sigh of contentment, while his eyes took on the distant look of a man in reminiscence.

"Still, I think of Pastor Lyle, who has devoted his life to his faith, and he never took a wife. It's been a good

many years since I've seen Lyle. I remember that he opposed my leaving our town to go into this work; he thought
it a hopeless work. Yet I dare say we have succeeded more
nearly in bringing to pass the Republic of Armenia than
anyone will ever succeed in bringing to pass the Kingdom
of God.

"But there's an idea," he added with sudden inspiration.
"Lyle has a hostel, I am told, where he looks after or-
phaned children. Why not take your two charges there?
He's a wonderful man, a very good man."

"Who is this Lyle?"

"He's an American. He's been out here for thirty-five
years or more. Twelve or thirteen years of that time he
spent in Turkey; then he brought his flock over here during the Turkish massacres of 1895. I was one of the number. We settled at Bartzan. That's a plain south of here,
across the Araxes from Ararat. But after thirteen years the
community petered out. Lyle didn't have the qualities it
takes to hold a community together. No sense of organization, I think. I was mayor of Bartzan village during most
of that time. Then I was called to this larger work. It
wasn't long after I left that the village disappeared.

"Poor Lyle. I felt sorry when I heard about it. He went
to Kars then, where he continued to preach, but never
with much success. Kars was too worldly a city for his
simple soul. He didn't know how to appeal to the people
of the city. Since the Revolution, he has been justifying
himself by looking after orphaned children. I guess he
concluded that was the only way to get converts to his
views—to take them when they were too young to think
for themselves.

"But he's a good man," Khansourian concluded with a
worldly-wise appraisal. "You will find few better."

The locomotive bell was ringing and the passengers
were clambering back into the cars.

"How far is Kars from here?" Paul Stepanovitch asked,
as they walked back.

"Just a hundred versts from here. Beyond is the junction
station, which we should reach shortly. Of course, measured in time, it is much farther, for the train service to

Kars is even worse than here. They are manning Kars fortress with troops of the new Armenian national army, and most of the rolling stock is pre-empted by the military.

"Armenia is very short of equipment," he added sadly, and then brightening, "but that will soon be remedied. The people are throwing themselves with the greatest enthusiasm into the rebuilding of the country. Before very long we shall have railway shops and foundries and machine shops—everything, in fact, necessary to make us self-sustaining. The Allies, you know, will provide us with funds. They are behind us. The future of Armenia is assured."

Paul Stepanovitch was thinking of the hostel to which Khansourian had referred. The idea took hold in his mind. He became at once eager to go to Kars, even though it would delay his journey to America by some days. The thought of a shelter, a retreat, even though it would be for children, and not for him, met a response in the longing of his heart. It was as though one had said to an Arab wayfarer lost in the desert, "In such and such a place lies an oasis, where you may rest and quench your thirst."

"I presume this Lyle of whom you speak would be willing to look after the children?" he ventured.

"Oh, yes, no doubt of that. That's his nature. I have never known him to turn anyone away from his door."

Paul Stepanovitch felt called upon to explain, not so much for the sake of his acquaintance, but to justify himself in his own thought.

"You see," he said, "I am going to America. I am a Russian, and these children are Armenian. They do not belong to me. I have no responsibility for them. I merely offered to find a home for them."

"Yes, yes, I quite realize," put in Khansourian with an indulgent wave of the hand. "We are men of affairs. We deal with larger matters. How would national destiny be achieved, how would we have attained the independence of Armenia, if we had stopped to look after a few children? We must not be deterred by details. The larger outlook must prevail—don't you agree?"

"Yes, yes," assented Paul Stepanovitch vaguely, a little

uncomfortably. He did not quite agree, and yet he could think of no sufficient answer. It was what he had always heard, all his life. . . .

While Paul Stepanovitch had been walking up and down, the children had sat quietly, hardly daring to stir. As he climbed back into the car their eyes lighted with relief, but they did not move, nor speak, until he had seated himself beside them.

"I hope you had a nice walk," said Asta politely.

"We missed you," put in Dina.

Asta saw the gravity in Markov's face and nudged her sister.

"Did you really miss me?" Paul Stepanovitch asked, quickly, involuntarily. He felt an inner quiver at the thought that somebody missed him. It passed, however, almost as quickly as it had come, and he cleared his throat to tell the children about his decision for them.

"You would have more fun with some playmates of your own age," began Paul Stepanovitch judicially, in a persuasive manner. He found it a little hard to explain his plan.

"Perhaps," responded Dina dubiously.

Asta again nudged her sister. She herself had grown very solemn, as though she sensed bad news.

"There is a place in Kars where they look after children," Paul Stepanovitch began again.

"An orphanage?" exclaimed Dina. "I've heard of them. Mamma used to tell us about such places. They are not pleasant places for little girls, she said."

Asta now gave her sister a decided nudge.

"This place is very nice—that is, I understand so," said Paul Stepanovitch. "It is run by a very fine man—a missionary."

"Missionaries are nice people," said Asta politely.

Paul Stepanovitch was relieved to hear that.

The children made no further comment, which also relieved Paul Stepanovitch, for he realized that he had learned really very little about this Amos Lyle, or about his "hostel." He should have made a point of learning more. But even so, it was the only thing that offered, and what Khansourian had said suggested that the children would be adequately taken care of.

As for the children, they continued to say little, but lapsed into a timid quiet, as if they realized that their protector had lost his interest in them and was eager to be relieved of his responsibility. Paul Stepanovitch, for his part, sensed this change in them, but instead of it awakening a tenderness in him, it increased his moodiness and his bitterness. He had now no incentive to bind himself to the world about him, not even to hold the affections of two children who would have willingly lavished affection, had he so much as intimated that he desired it. And so he sat, stonily silent, between the children, but not seeing them, while they held to a timorous quietness, hardly daring to stir.

At the junction, he spoke to them, shortly.

"Here is where we get down to change to the train for Kars."

"Yes, thank you," Asta said, quietly, gravely.

15. The Shelter

THE condition of Kars province as it appeared from the open door of the boxcar which served for passenger accommodation on the Kutai-Kars line, was one of desolation, a land sterile and empty as a province of the moon. A journey across it was like a passage through a Dantesque landscape, in which all life had ceased, all movement had frozen, and the world was silent and cold. For miles upon the plain one traveled only to behold emptiness, decay, silence. Only one thing upon which Markov's eyes fell seemed to have existence and vitality: this was the mountain of Ararat, which, by the effect of the changing sunlight, shimmered enchantingly in the distance, now violet, now peach or rose, and always diaphanous, as though it were curtained by a veil let down from the heavens to keep it removed from the desolation that lay before it.

Kars itself was half in ruins. The walls of the suburbs were down, giving view to untended gardens and broken porticoes. The once substantial bazaars were now peopled with rats and dogs, with here and there a fear-haunted merchant bending over an almost empty case. During the Turkish occupation, practically everything that was without military value had been destroyed. And when the Turks retired they had attempted to destroy everything that was of military value. Fortunately, however, this retirement had been made in haste, and the forts and military buildings of the city survived, though sadly gutted. It was only around these forts, where the recruits of the new Armenian army were drilling, that signs of activity were visible.

An emaciated driver of a fiacre drawn by a scrawny, emaciated pony had taken Markov and the two children to Lyle's house. It was in the northern quarter of the city, in the hilly district where formerly the well-to-do of Kars had made their town homes. The house which Lyle occupied had formerly belonged to a wealthy merchant, but had been turned over to Lyle when the owner had fled the country. The house itself was large and substantial, but the latch on the door was broken, and one of the windows, where the pane was gone, was boarded up, with the boards half-nailed. The interior was clean and neat enough, but it was bare almost to shabbiness.

All this Paul Stepanovitch had observed with mounting concern. To take these two children into such a land was like exiling them on the sterile salt flats of Turkestan. The vision of a retreat, a refuge, which Khansourian's mention of a "hostel" had aroused, had disappeared the moment Markov crossed the threshold. There was no air of substance or management or cheer.

As for Amos Lyle, Markov was unprepared, despite Khansourian's intimations, for a person so unprepossessing. The Amos Lyle he met was a different Amos Lyle from whom his father had looked down upon, from his horse, twenty-two years before. The tall spare figure was now gaunt and cadaverous—a great scarecrow of a man who appeared all the more a scarecrow because of the clothes he wore. The Texas-starred boots, broad-brimmed hat and frock coat had long since been abandoned; Lyle was now dressed in a makeshift outfit of Turkish slippers, American trousers, Russian blouse—all neat and clean if incredibly ill-fitting—and over all a mohair *aba*, or sleeveless Tartar cloak. His deep-set eyes burned like lanterns in the hollows of his bony cheeks and forehead; his hair was white and shaggy; the hand which he extended to Markov was like a warm iron claw.

Still, Lyle had received him kindly, and the expression in his face and eyes, and in his cracked, booming voice, was enthusiastic and cordial.

Lyle had received Paul Stepanovitch as though he were expecting him, had not bothered to ask his name, but called him "brother"—"Come in, brother, what can I do for you" had been his greeting. He had spoken to the children as though he had known them always, had assumed that they came to stay, and had led them off, by the hand, to supper, bidding Paul Stepanovitch "rest himself" until he should return, when Paul Stepanovitch should sup also. Paul Stepanovitch had protested at this, but Lyle had insisted that of course he should stay for supper and spend the night as well.

The sitting-room in which Paul Stepanovitch was left was a small ground-floor chamber that formerly had been used as the servants' parlor. It was sparsely furnished, like the rest of the house that Paul Stepanovitch had glimpsed, lighted by an oil lamp, and the only wall decoration was a picture of Christ. Despite its bareness the room was neat, while the bareness was relieved by little touches of arrangement and decoration that indicated the presence of someone with a greater sense of taste than Markov's host exhibited.

Paul Stepanovitch was tired and sat down in what appeared to him to be the most comfortable chair. It turned out to be the most amazing chair he had ever sat in. The moment he had rested his weight in it, it tilted back violently and began to oscillate. Paul Stepanovitch extricated himself with a curse, and began, under his breath, to damn it and everything else about the house.

But his curiosity was aroused. Nervously and irritably he examined the chair. He observed that it was meant to rock. Lacking nothing better to do he tried it again, and after a while got the hang of it.

"This Lyle is a crazy sort of person," he thought, as he swayed back and forth, finding the chair more comfortable with each rock.

He began to study the lamplight, idly, as it rose in a V on the wall above the lamp. He became conscious of the picture that was illuminated by the V, of the calm eyes of the figure looking down upon him. This was a portrayal of the Christ different from any he had ever seen. Quite different from the bearded, sad-eyed, emaciated Christs of the ikons, this was the face of a youth, full of hope and vitality, of confidence and serenity, mingled with gentleness, understanding, compassion. . . .

Paul Stepanovitch's thoughts were on the point of focusing on something when he was disturbed by Lyle's entrance. Standing with Lyle was a young woman.

"My daughter, Sirani Verian," Lyle said. "Sirani, this is the man who brought us the two children—a true worker in the Lord's vineyard. I don't think I have your name."

"Markov—Paul Stepanovitch Markov," said Markov, rising and bowing.

The young woman, he recalled later, had met his look, as he spoke to her, with a curiously frank expression that made him wonder where he had seen the eyes before. He had the impression that he had already seen them, had been looking at them, but he could not recall where. Aside from that, and the remembrance that she was tall and beautifully proportioned—she wore a coarse woolen skirt and a knitted blouse that revealed the amphora-like curves of her body—he could not say just what she was like. There was a freshness, a vitality of youth about her: she would be barely in her twenties, he thought.

Lyle spoke to him.

"Markov? Are you, by chance, the son of Colonel Markov who was stationed at Kars?"

Paul Stepanovitch assented.

"I knew him," said Lyle, as he led the way to the dining room. "He is one of those who continue to grow in spirit after their bodies and careers are fixed. I had a great admiration for him. He suffered a heroic death for the sake of spiritual things."

Paul Stepanovitch slightly resented having this missionary pass judgment on his father and he did not respond. Neither did he feel comfortable when the missionary asked the Lord's blessing over the food, in a manner which, to one whose acquaintance with such things was limited to the formal and gorgeous military masses, seemed intimate, if not vulgarly familiar. This was of a piece with the missionary's addressing him as "brother," and referring to him as " a worker in the Lord's vineyard."

As for the meal itself, it was nothing more than a bowl of stew, black bread and margarine, and tea with a little sugar in lieu of dessert.

"How many children are you caring for?" Paul Stepanovitch inquired.

"I do not know," Lyle responded.

Paul Stepanovitch was astounded. Apparently the missionary did not believe in counting the children. He had, it came out, children living in half a dozen houses scattered throughout the quarter.

"I should think you would find quarters where they could all be brought together," Paul Stepanovitch commented. "It would be much easier to look after them."

Amos Lyle did not seem to get the import of the implied question. Sirani, her eyes upon Markov with that same frank, unembarrassed look, that was both understanding and questioning, spoke in her father's defense.

"Father believes that if we keep them in smaller groups they do not realize so sharply that they are orphans and homeless. We take our meals about, going round to the various houses, to help them feel that they have foster parents—or, in a way, uncles and aunts—who are interested in them."

Markov was in a critical mood, and he continued to

prod and dissent, with a seeming delight in exposing the flaws in the missionary's enterprise.

Lyle began telling about the good fortune of the day: the receipt of a supply of meat. During the night a herd of goats had wandered down the hills toward the fort and had thrown the sentries into alarm. The next morning the herd had been rounded up, but the soldiers looked upon them as an ill omen and refused to touch them. The commandant of the fort, General Bazian, had thereupon turned them over to Lyle for his children. The gift had come at an opportune time, for the larders were exhausted.

"You mean to say that you trust the feeding of these children to such chances and accidents?" Markov broke in with consternation. He was annoyed with himself for not having made closer inquiry before leaving two helpless children with such a man.

"God fed the children of Israel in the wilderness with manna and sent the ravens to Elijah, and Christ fed the multitude with a few fish and loaves," responded Lyle heartily, confidently. "I am certain He will not be unmindful of our need."

"I don't know about those instances," Markov replied, a little stiffly, "but this appears to be pure chance, and can you rely upon these chances to feed and care for so many children?"

"I realize that it is hard for those who have been brought up in a world of logic, dominated by the law of cause and effect, to realize the meaning of chance in the ways of God," Lyle said understandingly and without condescension. "But I have found them to occur so often and with such regularity as to have no doubt of God's merciful and constant provision for His creatures. Perhaps, in certain fields of human activity, men must rely upon the laws of certainty, but in others, where the laws of certainty have broken down, reliance must be upon the Author of law, rather than upon the law.

"The Church has existed many centuries upon nothing more certain than free-will offering, and the hazards which that entails. Indeed, it is when the Church loses its faith in the so-called fortuitous, and attempts to build bulwarks against chance—such as endowments and properties—that it loses its power and its spiritual values. It is like building the tower of Babel against a flood. The Church's strength lies in its material poverty, in the unseen storehouses of God, in faith in man, in faith in the response of men to the goodness of God."

"That may be true for the Church," said Paul Stepanovitch skeptically, "but this is a different matter. This is a practical situation. An army wouldn't think of starting a campaign with no commissary, no service of supply."

"And a well-fitted commissary would be of little use without an army of spirited, believing men," replied Lyle quickly.

He looked at Paul Stepanovitch so hard and so directly with his deep-set eyes that Paul Stepanovitch became uncomfortable.

"It is not so much about food for these children that we should be concerned as capable, interested people to help look after them," he added.

A little later, he asked,

"You are going to America?"

It was partly in the nature of a question, partly as though he were ruminating.

"Yes."

"I have often thought that America needs missionaries from the Old World, as much as the Old World needs missionaries from the New. You can do a great service in America, with your talents, your strength, and your good heart."

Paul Stepanovitch did not reply to this immediately. He saw Sirani's eyes upon him—questioning, he thought, a little fear in them, possibly, lest the conversation become dangerous. He felt that she understood what was going on in his mind. He was not going to America with the thought of rendering service. He was going to America for safety—personal safety and security.

"You may be right," he said, after a little. "It seems that Russia is a doomed country, headed for destruction. It makes one think that everything people live for is hopeless."

"Sometimes it seems that way," said Lyle quietly, "and then God revives our spirits, and we see clearly again, and we behold the wonderful mystery of His love, how full of hope life is."

"I fail to see it," said Markov moodily. "What hope is there for these children you are caring for? The world is dying. Everything is dying. If these children survive, it will be only to be killed off in their prime. It is all hopeless, I tell you. I once had great belief in the destiny of my race. I believed in Russia. But look at it now! Everywhere death and destruction."

Paul Stepanovitch had lost control of himself. It was as though the atmosphere of this house were too much for him, as though something within him, some involuntary part, was struggling to throw off these influences which ran so counter to his logic and the inculcated beliefs of his youth. He continued to talk, expostulate, protest, seeking to exorcise this influence that threatened him, fortifying his argument with instances and memories, and the horrible things he had seen.

Amos Lyle let him talk on for a while, and then when he paused, Lyle said, thoughtfully,

"Whether one should condition one's conduct according to whether one can see the ultimate results of that conduct is an interesting question. I doubt whether it can be resolved by logic. Certainly one must have some regard for the obvious consequences of one's acts. On the other hand, to avoid action because its consequences are not foreseeable is apt to lead to complete abandonment of action, program or purpose.

"In my youth I was a herder. It was a happy life, and I found a lot of satisfaction in watching over the cattle, watching them crop the range, watching the young heifers running about in play. Somehow, I never considered the fact that they were destined for the slaughter pen, that the only object of my employers in raising them was to ship them off to the abattoir when they should be grown. Perhaps I might have revolted at the thought and given up the life on that account. Perhaps I might not have, considering instead that all life is lived for the service of other life. What led me to abandon this employment was not revolt at the logical purposes and effects of herding cattle, but a desire to shepherd a higher form of creature.

"There is, on the other hand, a sect in India, the Jains, who regard life of whatever sort as so holy that they wear gauze masks over their faces lest their breath kill the miscroscopic life of the atmosphere. I cannot condemn them for these convictions, for undoubtedly they are living in accordance with the highest principles, as they see them, but I do not believe that logic need be carried to such extremes to justify our submission to God. Life on this plane would be without hope, and would cease to exist, since it is impossible to sustain even the life of the body without killing the cellular life of the tissues.

"We have been placed, by the inscrutable wisdom of God, on a plane of physical and material existence, and it is on this plane that we must work out our destinies, our salvation, and the will of God. We do not achieve salvation by escape, but by bringing this world into conformity with God's will. It must be assumed that we will err, which is another name for sin, and it is for that reason that we have a Mediator, by whom our sins may be washed away, our human imperfections erased, and we permitted to stand, pure and spotless, in the presence of our Maker.

"But I cannot conceive it to be a sin to rear children whose fate it may be to die early or suffer hardship. For me it is sufficient that these children live, and their lives are so precious that I thank God that He has given it to me to watch over them."

After supper they had returned to the little sitting-room, where Lyle, first asking his guest's permission, read the Bible and prayed, as was his custom. The conversation did not return to controversial subjects. Just what they talked about, Paul Stepanovitch could not quite recall, as he lay awake that night, staring overhead into the darkness. The last hour he had spent with the missionary and his daughter had somehow gone rather pleasantly. Whether it was the effect of the supper, which though scant was sufficient and warming, or the quieting influence of the sitting-room, which for all its bareness was not with-

out a soothing atmosphere—somewhat like the simplicity
of a monk's cell—or the manner of his host, Markov could
not say.

Lyle, he admitted, was, despite his peculiarities, sincere,
understanding and sympathetic. Lyle had not prodded
him about his beliefs and his past, as he had prodded
Lyle. Lyle had, indeed, shown a great considerateness in
avoiding any subject which might be irritating to his guest.
The War, the famine, the Revolution, none of these had
been mentioned. Lyle had talked instead about the customs of the country, its history, art and archaeology,
had told stories of his youth on the Western plains of
America. . . .

Lyle impressed him as a man who was curiously unaware of tragedy, either personal or social, as though
tragedy did not exist. Paul Stepanovitch wondered how it
was possible for a man who had lived through so much as
Lyle had, here on the frontier, feeling the full blast of the
war, to be so impervious to the import of circumstance.
. . . It seemed to him as though the man lived in a walled
compound of the mind—the way the prisoners of Kazan
lived—yet with a difference. Lyle's was a compound spacious enough for much to happen therein, of joy and activity and purpose, and it was one from which sorrow and
tragedy were excluded. It must be very comforting to
live within such a wall of the mind, Paul Stepanovitch
thought. . . .

Sirani had shown Paul Stepanovitch the way to his bed-
chamber, and had turned down the coverlet of his cot for
him.

Paul Stepanovitch had recalled that he had not given
the children a thought since Lyle had led them away. He
suddenly wondered how they were, whether they had
been fed and comfortably lodged, and whether they were
happy. He had asked Sirani about them.

"Asta and Dina are in bed," Sirani had replied.

Paul Stepanovitch had felt a little shock. The thought
that the children had been so decisively taken out of his
hands, transferred to hands that were more willing than
his, had given him a feeling akin to jealousy.

"I—I think I would like to see them again, before I go," he had said hesitantly. He had felt a little awkward in making the request.

"Why, of course you will," Sirani had assured him promptly. "But they are asleep now. They are at the Dobrunyi house. Andranik will show you there in the morning. You will probably want to sleep late, or I would take you there myself. I will be at the Dobrunyi house, and will show you the children."

"Thank you," Paul Stepanovitch had said humbly.

The Dobrunyi house—another of the old mansions of Kars—sheltered a group of girls ranging in age from six to twelve years. They were, Markov observed as Sirani escorted him about, all meanly clad, in odds and ends of garments, and looked underfed and in none too good health. Their clothes were clean, however, and the children themselves appeared in good spirits.

They found Asta and Dina already with a group, playing in the court. It was something like drop-the-handkerchief. Two older girls were standing at one side, as mentors.

At the sight of Sirani, the children stopped their play and with exclamations of delight gathered around her.

"Well, Lydia, your bruised knee is quite well, isn't it?" said Sirani, kneeling before one of the children and examining her leg, while she continued to talk to the others. "Hasmik, your brother will come this afternoon to see you. Arshalus, the next time I come I hope to have a new dress for you."

Arshalus, a round-headed little girl with pock-marked face, was in rags.

"Yeghsapet, I'm ashamed of you," Sirani reproved another gently. "Did you wash your face this morning?"

Sirani knew each one by name, and she had something individual and personal to say to each. The jealousy which Paul Stepanovitch had experienced the night before returned. He reminded himself that he had always been able to call every man in his company by his first name, although not many officers could do so. Out of this jealousy grew a resentful curiosity about Sirani.

She was obviously a girl who had never known the luxuries to which women of his acquaintance had been accustomed. He wondered whether she had ever yearned for jewels and furs and silks, such as the women who formerly lived in this house must have worn. Sirani was, he noted, admirably equipped by nature for such adornment —her limbs had a rounded fullness, her body was well-formed, her carriage was graceful and erect, her face had color and animation.

"How long have you been looking after children this way?" he asked.

"Oh, for a long time—ever since the War started, when I was eighteen—but never so many as this past year, since the Revolution."

"Don't you ever get tired of this?"

"Yes, often. I become completely exhausted. But a good night's rest soon brings me around."

"I mean discouraged?"

"Discouraged?" Sirani looked at him in surprise. "Why? What is there discouraging about children?"

"I mean, the hopelessness of it all?"

"Oh, the things you discussed with father? That's because you are tired. I don't think of those things. Or if I should get a little low in spirits, I come and play with the children. There's so much enthusiasm among them that it takes hold of you."

"Aren't there other things you would like to do? Travel, wear good clothes, go to a theater, or something?"

Sirani shot him a quick glance.

"Are you trying to make me unhappy?" she asked.

"Oh, no," Markov protested, coloring. "I just wondered." Sirani laughed.

"Naturally, I think of those things. I would like to see Persia. My mother was born in Persia, and she told me things about that country, when I was very little, which I still remember."

"Do you like the theater?"

Markov asked this last question in the hope of finding something in common for them to talk about. He was curious as to the mainsprings that kept a girl like this going.

"I have never been to the theater, but I like to dance."

"Good. Can you do the fox trot?"

Paul Stepanovitch pictured her, in lace and tulle, gliding across the floor at Prince Cherniloff's.

Sirani's large eyes showed perplexity.

"Fox trot? No, peasant and Caucasian dances."

Markov's anticipation fell. He thought of the sack of gems he wore inside his tunic, under his arm. He wondered if she liked jewels. Most women could not resist them—some would sell their virtue for them. He casually mentioned some of the famous collections he had seen.

"There used to be a shop in Kars," said Sirani, "that had the most wonderful jewels—rubies and pearls and emeralds and others—it closed just before the Revolution began. I was so sorry. I used to go by sometimes, with Papa Amos, just to look at them."

"Wouldn't you like to have some to wear?"

"Oh, they belong on lovely ladies and on ikons."

"What is the thing you would like most for yourself?"

"Some children of my own," Sirani answered with disconcerting frankness.

The remembrance flashed over Markov of his last meeting with the Princess Irina Sabayeva. Between these two women what a gulf lay, in birth, station and background; yet how alike their desire!

The recollection of the princess brought with it, incongruously it seemed, memory also of Gregory Fedorevitch, in Kazan prison, who had urged Markov to save himself while willing himself to die. The Princess Irina and Sirani, Gregory Fedorevitch and Lyle—what was there in common among them? Something which he seemed not to possess, nor understand, though he was vaguely aware of it.

Before he left for Erivan, Paul Stepanovitch felt it necessary to make some provision for the children Asta and Dina, whom he had entrusted to the missionary. He drew out his leather sack and extracted several glittering gems, some set and some unset, which he laid on the table before Lyle.

"The Good Samaritan, I believe, gave money to the host and promised to come again with more when that was spent. I can't say I shall ever be here again, but these"—indicating the jewels—"should be enough to provide for the two children for some time to come."

Amos Lyle picked up the stones and thumbed them for a moment, reflectively.

"No," he said, "I will not take them. Though these are precious elsewhere, they cannot be eaten. Where people want bread, not even stones like these will take their place."

"You mean to say that even with jewels you cannot buy bread in Kars?"

"Oh, I don't doubt one can. But I know nothing of buying and selling. These stones cannot be turned into bread. They may buy bread but only by depriving others of bread, both by reducing the available store and by raising the price beyond people's means. The children will share in what food is to be had—of that I am sure. I would rather have bread that is given—shared—than bread that I tore from the hands of others by the power of money."

Paul Stepanovitch was filled with incomprehension. He resented the missionary's superiority to what he offered, and wondered if Lyle were trying to insult him. He glanced at Sirani and saw that she was looking at the gems with wide-eyed wonder, and he recalled how, in the Faust story, Mephistopheles had tempted Marguerite.

"Well," he said with a shade of irony, "if jewels are of no value to you in exchange, at least they are still desirable for adornment. With your permission I should like to present one of these to Sirani in appreciation of your kindness to me."

He picked out a diamond ear pendant, one of a pair of which the other was missing—a beautiful piece, however, the finest of the lot, set with a large round diamond of flawless perfection—and laid it before Sirani.

Amos Lyle looked at Markov from his cavernous eyes, eyes filled with such brooding that Markov grew uncomfortable, and the thought flashed over him: "I have touched this old man, his sanctimonious surface will crack, and he will let fly at me."

But Lyle only said, in a very quiet voice,

"If Sirani chooses, she may accept."

Markov turned to Sirani and his face flushed, for Sirani's eyes had turned from the pendant to him, and her look was one that was full of understanding. She showed none of that eagerness for possession of the bauble which he had imagined she might.

"Would you like it?"

Sirani must have sensed the remorse in his voice.

"If you wish me to have it," she said very quietly, "I will take it—as a remembrance."

Markov laid the pendant in her hand.

16. Erivan

In Erivan, capital of the newly-organized Armenian National Republic, as in Tiflis, the hard kernel of reality had been coated with the nacre of a new enthusiasm, and misery hid its face behind the veil of hope. The cobbled streets resounded with the clatter of new infantry regiments, raised by the spirit of patriotism for the new nation; officers of the government, looking very important and eager, hurried from one errand to another in American motor cars; and makers of bunting, flags, and the famous Armenian cognac, were doing a prosperous business.

But the army was equipped and clothed and fed with surplus war stocks of the Allies; the government was supported by foreign credits; and the spirit of patriotism was fed by promises of the Allied statesmen. All these supplies and loans and promises were with an object, and that object was not entirely in consonance with Armenian necessities and security. The Allies needed a friendly territory in the Caucasus, a buffer between Red Russia to the north and the Asiatic masses to the south. Communism must not be permitted to spread southward into India and westward through Turkey toward Syria and Egypt.

Since the interests of the Allies were essentially political, rather than humanitarian, their gifts were spread within a narrow circle about the capital. Here food was to be had, if not in abundance; here was trade, and activity, and enthusiasm. Beyond this narrow circle of warmth and light spread the darkness of hunger and the cold of misery. The Great Famine, that had begun in the north, was slowly creeping over the land.

But in Erivan, as in Tiflis, and in a few other military centers, where the Allies had their representatives, there was still food and gaiety and hope.

Paul Stepanovitch Markov had reached Erivan in the latest stage of his journey to America. A train ran south from Erivan to the Persian frontier, and from there he would go to Baghdad and Bombay, where he hoped to dispose of his jewels. India, he had heard, was prosperous under the silver inflation.

Markov had first to see the British consul in Erivan, whose office was in Alexandrovsky Street.

An officer of the Armenian army suddenly crossed over and stood in front of him.

"Pavil!"

"Aleisha!"

The two men embraced.

Alexei Petrovitch Dosti was now wearing a bastard uniform of mixed Russian and British ancestry, which had been legitimated by the shoulder badge of a major in the Armenian Republican Army.

"This is too much for me, to see you here," he exclaimed. "Come, I know where we can break a bottle of cognac, and you can tell me what you are doing."

"It's plain enough what you are doing," answered Markov, with the assumed nonchalance which is the mask, or mark, of affection among young men. "You are managing to keep to your profession, even if it is with a two-kopek outfit. Where in the world did you get that uniform?

Was it necessary to kill two soldiers to get one suit?"

"You're just envious now, my dear Pavka," laughed Alexei Petrovitch. He had drawn Markov into a cognac shop which was filled with officers and cigarette smoke and black bottles on pine tables. "Here," he called to a waiter. "A large bottle, and *zakuska*."

"*Zakuska!*" exclaimed Paul Stepanovitch. "And so you eat well too?"

"Well, apologized Alexei, "it's not genuine Russian *zakuska*, but a makeshift, like this uniform. But still *zakuska*, or such as one can make from tinned California sardines, stale Greek cheese, and South American tinned beef, with some wretched sour cabbage for trimmings. You will see. And if you're hungry, it's good. Damned lucky you are to get it. That's from being in the army. You won't get it elsewhere."

"I see. You fight, not on a full stomach, but for a full stomach," Markov bantered. He was pleased to see Alexei again, and his spirits were high. "Where's glory, and medals, and all?"

"Oh, that will come. I'm all for this new government. It has a great future. Lord Bryce has been here, and we have British support to the hilt. But before I defend myself any more, you must tell me what has happened to you since— the spring of '15, wasn't it?—that we were billeted together at Kovarasnik?"

"It's a short story and soon told. Our men rebelled at Slavinka; I had a chance to make a run for it, and did, like a damned coward. In Varsova—that's where our house was —I was picked up, thrown into prison, where I stuck for God knows how many months, was taken to Kazan to be shot by the fiend Belinsky, and escaped because a clap of thunder frightened the old boy with the needle. I spent nearly a year with Korsakoff, but his outfit went to pieces, and now I'm on my way to America."

"Don't be another damn fool," urged Alexei Petrovitch, pouring out a stiff drink from a bottle which the waiter had set before them.

"I want mine well-watered," said Markov, as he reached hungrily for the platter of *hors d'oeuvres*.

"No, you don't want to go to America," Alexei Petrovitch protested, as Markov poured back part of the cognac and filled the glass with water. "What would you do in America? There's no place for a soldier there. Ha, ha. You go down the street in a uniform, and people ask, 'Where's the band?' Or they want to know what hotel you're a flunky for. But look at me. I'm a major. I never rated more than a lieutenancy before. Stay here and I'll get you a colonelcy at the least."

"I never heard that Armenians knew anything about fighting," said Markov.

The cognac was warming to the stomach, and the *zakuska,* despite its being an imitation, was satisfying. Markov was feeling very comfortable.

"That's just it," explained Alexei. "Armenians know nothing about fighting. They know nothing about administration. They have no political aptitude. Why should they know about government since they've not had a government of their own for how many centuries? But how they can make the money! Don't you see the possibilities? We will govern the country for them while they fill the treasury.

"Eventually, there will be a ministry open—war, navy, maybe. They are going to get some of the Black Sea littoral, Belikian tells me. He's minister for war. The Allies are bound to support us. Even the United States is behind us. I tell you, Pavil Stepanovitch, there's a future here. Believe me, you would be making a mistake to go off to America. I want to introduce you to Colonel Ajarian. You will like him—funny fellow to be a colonel—but don't mind that."

"Yes, I'd like to meet an Armenian colonel," said Markov. "I haven't laughed hard since you dropped your monocle down the bodice of the countess what's-her-name. God help him if he's as fat and as pompous as that old potato barrel."

Markov was, in fact, more than mildly interested in what Dosti had told him. The more he thought of it, the less he liked his decision to go to America. That country held nothing for him, and Armenia—well, it had once been part of Russia.

"Please don't form any preconceptions. He may disappoint you at first, but he's all right. I want you to like him. I would like to have you stay here."

"So I could help you out of your predicaments with dowagers, eh, Aleisha?" said Markov, laughing. "By the way, to whom did the countess get her daughter married off?"

"Boris Andrayevski finally succumbed. Poor Boris, he was killed after they had been married less than a month. The daughter, being in widow's weeds, then proved quite attractive, and Cherniloff took her off to Paris with him."

"Cherniloff! That damned ermine," Markov exclaimed bitterly.

"Why do you say that? I thought you were a favorite with the prince."

Markov was silent. He didn't know just why he had cursed the prince, except that he had fled the country, which he himself was now preparing to do. Yet the fact of that flight, after his brave advice to Markov, was like sand in the teeth every time Markov thought of it.

"You know I love you, Pavil," exclaimed Alexei impulsively. "I always have. You've done me many good turns. Don't you remember the time you got me transferred from under that old whoreson, Colonel Baratoff? If you never did another thing for me, I'd bless you to my dying day for that."

"Baratoff wasn't so bad. You didn't understand him. He believed in discipline, that was all."

"Discipline, hell! What he believed in was sadism. He tied his men up by the thumbs too often to suit me, put too many of them on bread and water, and used the lash too often. Everyone knew that it did no good—everyone, that is, but Baratoff. That's what was wrong with the army, and with the country. Too many Baratoffs. Too many stupid disciplinarians, using discipline as excuse for cruelty."

"I'll warrant you that we're not going to get out of this mess until we get some more Baratoffs, more who believe in order and discipline," Markov argued hotly.

"Anyway," said Alexei Petrovitch, "I'm glad you got me out from under him, and now I'm going to take you to my Colonel Ajarian."

Ajarian proved to be a short, stocky Armenian who gave the impression of having had more experience in handling silks and stuffs than rifles and artillery. Beside the handsome and precise Alexei Petrovitch, he appeared even more unmilitary than he was. For though Alexei's uniform was shabby and nondescript, Alexei filled it with broad square shoulders and alert, quick-moving limbs; but Ajarian slumped in his until folds formed on the chest and the cloth stretched across the shoulders, while his legs were too short for the trousers, which made bags around the knees and above the boots.

"I'm glad to meet you, Captain," Ajarian said in greeting to Markov, rising from his desk and thrusting out a pudgy hand, at the same time sizing up his visitor with a keen, appraising eye. As though he read Markov's hidden thoughts, he continued, "I'm not an army man by training, but I know some things an army needs. And one of them is good, competent leadership. I am interested in good officer material. But, I regret to say, good officers are rare. You Russians are excellent tacticians and strategists, and many of you are good organizers, but it takes a particular type of temperament to handle the Armenian soldier.

"Bear in mind that the Armenians, in general, have never borne arms. That was forbidden, you know, to those of us who were reared in Turkey. The Armenians who form the new army are not used to barrack discipline. You can't use on them the sharp methods practiced with the Russian soldier who has done his term of service while young, and more or less expects the same sort of treatment when he is called to the colors.

"I can tell from looking at you, however, that you are of the right type. I think you will find it interesting—challenging. We have a great task ahead, and it will be entirely on the shoulders of the army. The Turks are none too contented with the Armistice of Mudros, and when they have recuperated they will assuredly resent the Armenian Republic on their flanks. The Communists, also, will no doubt try to carry the Red Revolution into the Caucasus. We can offer you, I think, a good post—but it will be a hard post."

Markov liked Ajarian for his realism and his bluntness. He was interested, he said, in what there was to offer. Alexei Petrovitch was delighted. He left Markov with his chief, who was to introduce him to other members of the government and Markov would join him at his quarters that evening.

Through Ajarian, Markov met Belikian, minister of war, and Garchik, minister of economy, and Vartsoun, minister of communications. Among them all he found a great enthusiasm and a wealth of projects brewing. Garchik was going to establish great spinning factories to take care of the wool grown and the cotton that would be cultivated— cotton cultivation was a project that involved dams and irrigation of the desert tracts in the south—and cement mills to provide building material for the new cities that were to rear themselves throughout Armenia. . . .

Vartsoun had ideas for hydroelectric undertakings. He had been in America and had learned something about how such projects were created there by merely waving a financial wand; he knew something also about how these financial wands were waved, and he talked a great deal about debentures and indentures and flotations that were Greek to Markov. In fact, it all seemed slightly chimerical to him, but it was a new world that had been born out of the decay of the old, and while everyone acted slightly dazed, they were very sure of the brilliant future that lay ahead now that peace had come. . . .

Markov, though a little nonplused by these projects and schemes, was still interested in the career possibilities of the Armenian army. . . .

Incidentally, if he stayed here, he would not need the jewels he possessed. He had never felt comfortable about them since he had acquired them. Though he had come by them honestly, they were loot in the first instance, and he had received them from hands that had stolen them. That made him, Markov felt, something of an accessory after the fact.

The mere existence of jewels, he thought as he walked along toward Alexei's lodging that evening, was incongruous with everything he saw about him. Jewels were bright and full of life and color and brilliance. They belonged in a gaily illuminated ballroom, around the necks and on the arms and fingers of fair ladies, against lily white throats, flashing from satin and lace at men in gold braid and uniforms. What a contrast that picture was to the drabness here! The sanitation service had broken down and filth filled the gutters and permeated the air with a stench. Wraiths of human beings moved along the streets followed by wan-faced wretches begging a piece of bread.

Snow began to fall, as though gently to cover the death and decay of the city with a winding sheet, and to hide the misery of the world from sight; but it, too, was a mockery and a curse. For this first snowfall meant the end of the growing season, and the few vegetables that had been coming into the market would now cease altogether.

Armenia was to face a hard winter.

"So they have offered you a colonelcy!" exclaimed Alexei Petrovitch, delighted, when Markov had told him about the results of his interview.

He set a kettle on the charcoal *ojak* for tea.

"That's splendid. You will go right up the line, for you have genius. I've always said so. You know how to handle men. I wouldn't be surprised to see you minister of war eventually. You see, there's no nobility, no caste here, no seniorities, nothing to slow up your advance. Besides all that, I'm glad you'll be here."

He went to the cupboard and got out a loaf of black bread, a tin of canned beef, and another tin container of preserves.

"You don't mind eating here in the rooms, do you?" he asked. "I don't have much to offer, but it's of better quality than you can get in a restaurant."

"No officers' mess?"

"Not unless you're in the line. I'm attached to the staff. Supply service. And I can requisition what tinned goods I need."

"From where is the army getting its supplies?" Markov asked.

The water was boiling and Alexei put in a pinch of tea—stemmy and coarse and broken.

"The British have a supply depot at Batum. We order from them, and pay by drafts against balances in London which they have established for the government. Practically all of it comes that way. We have a large shipment coming down this week—flour and more tinned beef and lard, but also some chocolate and canned milk. Better quality, I hope, than this tea. We'll use part of it in barter for cabbage, of which there is still some to be had in the markets."

"Any of it go for relief of the starving?"

"Some, but very little. The army comes first. That's one advantage of being in the army, you know, and one reason why we have been able to raise troops to the colors. I'm afraid an Armenian wouldn't join up otherwise."

"There," he added, pouring out the tea and setting a platter of the tinned beef on the pine table. "That'll stay our appetites. I'm hungry.

"You won't find the Armenian an easy pupil," he went on. "They don't care much for fighting. I had some of them in my outfit in 1915, but I lost most of them. They were terrible as fighters—no staying power, no sense of what it was all about. But I think they'll do better now it's their own country they are serving."

"Yes, I'm sure of that," assented Markov, philosophically.

He had grown abstracted and, while Alexei talked on, he picked absently with his fork. Alexei noticed this and exclaimed, rising,

"Good God! Don't tell me it's wormy. It would turn my stomach for a week."

"No, no, it's all right. I was just thinking."

"Thinking!" echoed Alexei, re-seating himself. "That's damned odd of you. You gave me a scare. What are you thinking about?"

Markov looked up, his eyes squinted in thought, while he tapped the table with his fork.

"I'd like to know more about this shipment you spoke

of, Aleisha," he said, thoughtfully. "Do you suppose they would sell me a carload or two of flour and the like?"

"Sell you a carload of it! What on earth are you talking about? What would you do with a carload of supplies?"

"That doesn't answer my question, Aleisha," said Markov shortly, with some of his old military abruptness. "Can a carload be had for money?"

"Anything can be done with money. But I must say that the government is honest."

"I don't want it by bribery. Can it be bought honestly?"

"Well, they have sold some, but they don't talk about it. The government needs money. Its credits are good only for imports, but it needs money for local payments."

"To whom should one apply?"

"My colonel is as good as any. He is chief of supply. But what sort of crazy person am I to tell him you are, who is offered a commission but wants to buy flour?"

Markov thought a moment before answering. Then he said slowly,

"It's for another crazy person. There's an American in Kars who has taken in a mob of children, and has the crazy idea that he can feed them on cobblestones. The crazier part about it is that I took two children to him to keep, supposing that he had a real hostel. They'll starve before the winter is out if somebody doesn't look after them. And since I am responsible, at least for two of the children, I want to send them some food."

"A carload of supplies can't be had for a kopek, you know. It will cost a lot of money. Why be a damn fool and spend it? You're not responsible for the children in Armenia, nor for all the cracked fools that live in this world."

"I'm not being a hero to spend it. I have the money, and it cost me nothing. It was loot, and I want to get rid of it."

"Oh," said Alexei understandingly. "A penance?"

"Oh, damn it, no," exclaimed Markov impatiently. "I didn't take it. It was given to me. But I don't want it. I was going to use it to go to America. But since I'm staying here. . . ."

"You're really staying? That's wonderful. Then in the morning we'll see the colonel about the flour."

Part 4

SIRANI

1. The Feeding of the Mouths

SIRANI was seated in the large reception hall of the Baratouni mansion, the second of the houses occupied by Amos Lyle for his orphanage. The great room, on which still hung the red silk damask coverings and oil copies of Rubens' voluptuous ladies, was scattered with scraps and pieces of sewing, while squatting on the floor, among the scraps of cloth, were a score of Armenian women, their diadem-like headdresses bobbing up and down as they busily sewed and talked.

This was the "sewing circle" that gathered daily at the Baratouni house to sew clothes for the children. It had grown up spontaneously—unorganized—as the expression of the charitable spirit of the women of Kars. Many of these women were themselves destitute, many had families of their own who were meagerly cared for in these days, all of them were in the shadow of misery, but they knew of Lyle's children and they wanted to help.

Often, however, there was no sewing for them to do. One cannot sew without cloth, without thread. But today there was cloth, much cloth. Along the wall stood several unopened bales of army blankets.

Sirani had spoken to Lyle about the need for cloth. Winter was upon them, and most of the children were in rags.

317

Lyle had thought, and finally inquired, in a manner that indicated he knew nothing of these mysteries,

"Can you make garments out of army blankets?"

"We can make clothes out of anything that's flat," Sirani had assured him, laughing.

"Good. I think I can get blankets."

Lyle went to General Bazian, commandant of Kars fortress.

"Excellency," he said, "you haven't visited our children in some time."

"No," growled the general, genially, "and I don't want to. The last time I visited them it cost me two hundred cases of condensed milk and almost provoked a mutiny. I can't do anything like that again, Lyle. My men are short of rations now, and if I dare give you any more from the commissary, I'll be hailed to Erivan and court-martialed. That would be a fine reflection on the new Armenian Republican Army, wouldn't it?"

"I saw some bales of blankets being moved about the warehouses yesterday as I passed," said Lyle, ignoring the general's question.

"Don't tell me you want them," protested the general.

"Not I, but we have several hundred children who, Sirani tells me, are cold from lack of warm clothes. And several score women who like to sew for the children if they have something to sew. And Sirani tells me blankets can be worked up very nicely into warm garments. But I suppose that your soldiers will be needing them. They get cold stamping about doing guard duty, and the like."

General Bazian threw up his hands.

"Take them, take them. Only don't ask for the fort for your children. The government insists that we keep a few soldiers here, just for appearance's sake."

"It's very generous of you. I was sure that if you understood the need. . . ."

"Hang it all, it's your damn luck again. It so happens that the commissariat at Erivan has got mixed up again and sent me blankets when I requisitioned beef. And so if I give them to you, don't—for God's sake—come here wanting food. I'm serious. The troops are on half rations now."

And so, under Sirani's guidance, the "sewing circle" was making up the blankets into garments. Blankets were not the most appropriate material for clothing, and it took much skill and hard work to fashion them into garments for children. Sirani had got Lydia, one of the women, to help her in cutting out the patterns, designing a style of dress that offered the most economical use of the cloth.

But it was this same Lydia who now leaned over to Sirani and whispered, wheedlingly,

"May I not make one dress with a little piece of paneling?"

Sirani pressed her lips together. She had had to contend with these wheedlings before. All the women loved doing this work, but their irrepressible creative and maternal instincts made them want to do more than sew a plain dress.

"Not this time, Lydia," she replied. "Maybe later. If we put in panelings there won't be enough cloth to go around."

"What!" exclaimed Vanouk, a beldame who had been famous for her fine lacemaking in better days. "With all those bales—surely there is enough and to spare."

"The material is thick, you know," explained Sirani, "and it doesn't go as far as you might think. I have counted them all, and there will be barely enough for what we need."

Vanouk grumbled to herself, and went on sewing with her deft, quick fingers.

"There would be enough to go around," Marta Hovasian exclaimed, lifting her hands in protest, sharply, "if Pastor Lyle did not keep bringing in more children."

"Why, Marta," said Sirani, in a shocked tone, though she knew that Marta was talking for effect, "you don't mean—"

"Yes, I do. Where's the food coming from to feed so many? We could feed half of them, maybe more, but every day another arrives, or several. And they are always starved and have to be coaxed with the most delicate food we have. It's better, I say, to let a few starve than run the danger of all of us starving. That would be a sorry end, now, wouldn't it? To feed us all until within a month of summer and then starve us until we all died!

"I know," she asserted, raising her voice until Sirani became truly alarmed. "I am in the kitchens, and I see how little there is left. It's awful, I say. I don't know what we shall do."

And Marta broke into loud weeping. Sirani arose and put her arms around her and comforted her.

Marta's outbreak heightened the difficult part that was Sirani's. She understood Marta's fear, felt it keenly herself. How were they to care for this constantly swelling crowd of children? Pastor Lyle was like a Pied Piper; he never went through the streets without finding some starving child, parents unknown, to bring back to the shelter of his houses. His latch string was always out; and well-meaning persons—and others who wished to escape their responsibilities—would bring waifs to him with easy confidence that he had the resources with which to care for them. Throughout the province, and beyond, the word had passed that there was a man at Kars who looked after helpless children.

Amos Lyle never seemed to bother—at least he never showed any outward concern—as to how these children would be cared for.

This was the fitting and logical result of Amos Lyle's long practice of his faith. It was, to many, a preposterous and absurd result.

When Amos Lyle was asked how he proposed to take care of these children, he would answer, "God has sent me these mouths to feed, and I must feed them with what I have. When more is needed, I will look to God."

To Sirani, when she had asked how he had managed to get the blankets, he had replied, "God opened the heart of General Bazian, and he gave them to us."

Sometimes, when he was pressed for a logical answer, as he had been by Markov, he would reply by asking if the children were not better off with him than left in the streets. "Surely," he would say, "we should not abandon our responsibilities because we cannot see how we are to discharge them!" If inquiry persisted, his answer was dogmatic in its assurance. He would point to the fact that they were being fed. He would challenge his inquisitor with the statement that the best evidence that they would be fed tomorrow was the fact that they were fed today.

But few went so far with their questioning. Amos Lyle's forthright assurances, his abounding enthusiasm, quelled any attempt to assault his convictions.

But while the voices were stilled, the doubt and skepticism remained.

Sirani stood midway between these opposing views, a bridge over which the conflict raged, the conflict between Lyle's confidence and the fears of his helpers.

She understood her father's devotion and faith. She understood the depth of his logic, a logic beyond the reach of skepticism and doubt, that found its basis in its very audacity. She understood the depth of his faith. She realized that to doubt was to have faith of a negative sort, a disbelief that was a denial of human capacity and of God's providence.

But she understood, too, these doubts. Since she had come to live with Amos Lyle, she had known nothing but loving care and devotion. That did not mean, however, that she had always been provided for. Many times the cupboard—which had to yield only enough food for two— had been well-nigh bare. That it had never become entirely bare was owing to her frugality and the fine art of managing with small resources which she had acquired through necessity. There had even been times of comparative abundance, and at such times Amos Lyle had dispensed what he had with prodigal hand. And Sirani would watch their few belongings gradually disappear to meet this or that charitable need, at first with dismay and fear, but finally with passive spirit, hoping, trusting, that better times would come.

And now, with the end of the War, when girls of her age in other lands might hope for happier days, this new burden had been laid upon her.

Pastor Lyle was too occupied, too wrapped in his enthusiasms, too busy gathering in the waifs and pouring out his charity, to attend to details of management. Those duties had fallen to Sirani. When the first children were brought in, it was Sirani who took them and bathed them and prepared bowls of hot wheat gruel, and spread a pallet for them to sleep on.

She had not found this a chore; on the contrary it had been a happy experience. When more children began to come in, Amos Lyle sent other women to help her, women who had answered his call for volunteers.

It was not the hard work; it was the responsibility that began to weigh upon her young heart. It was the constant precariousness of it all, the constantly arising question— will the meal hold out? Will the cruse fail?

Twilight drew on, and the women laid aside their work for the day.

Sirani arose from her stool, tired. After the women had gone, she went over the heaps of completed garments. Much work had been done—but, alas for her well-conceived plan for husbanding the cloth, almost none of the women had followed the patterns. With irrepressible imagination, they had cut the cloth to suit their fancy—and their fancy invariably led to voluminous skirts for the girls and broad baggy trousers for the boys. In addition to this waste of good cloth, they had diverted themselves and satisfied their creative urge by applying bits of embroidery here and there. This last was not so bad—though it consumed time and delayed the work—but the waste of the precious cloth. . . .

Sirani felt tired, even discouraged.

She was being put to tasks for which her spirit was willing but for which her hands were too frail. There were hundreds of children; scores of volunteer workers; all this called for management and administrative experience which she lacked, and for which Amos Lyle knew not even the name.

Sirani thought she would take a little walk before going home, to stretch her limbs and clarify her thoughts. A heavy snow had begun to fall and it had grown bitterly cold since morning, but she did not mind. The blood flowed quick and warm in her lithe body—too quick, sometimes, for her own quietness of spirit. She drew her shawl about her, to keep the sticky wet snow particles from her eyes, and set out.

It was growing dark in the streets, and there were no street lights. Sirani walked and walked, and as she walked she forgot about the unfinished work, about the children still going around in cotton dresses and *shalvari*, about the wheedlings, and protestations and complaints of the women.

She began to think of herself.

This was a luxury for her, but it was also a luxury in these times to have a vigorous, young body that recovered quickly from tiredness, and could combat the cold and snow with warm, ebullient reactions.

She began to recite to herself a poem from the Persian which she had heard her mother recite many times, and which she still remembered despite all the years. It was one of the *gazels* of Hafiz, and the verse that Sirani most remembered ran,

> *"O happy hour! when I shall rise*
> *From earth's delusions to the skies,*
> *Shall find my soul at rest, and greet*
> *The traces of my loved one's feet:*
> *Dancing with joy, whirled on with speed,*
> *Like motes that gorgeous sunbeams feed,*
> *Until I reach the fountain bright*
> *Whence yonder sun derives his light."*

Sirani's mother, when she came to this *gazel*, had always dropped her voice and drawn out the words until they seemed to sing like the wind through bare branches in winter, and Sirani knew that she was thinking of Sirani's father, whom Sirani had never known. She had often wondered what her father, the Emmanuel who was the husband of Miriam, had been like. Though she was much too young to understand the passion and the longing that filled her mother's heart at thought of Emmanuel, she intuitively recognized it, and she imagined her father

to have been someone very wonderful indeed—the type of
man she would like some day to have for a husband. . . .

But this afternoon there was, for some reason unap-
parent to her, no sadness, no longing, in these verses;
rather, they seemed to convey the ardor of young love and
ardent hopes for the future.

For reasons that Sirani could not understand her
thoughts kept reverting, as they had reverted from time
to time, to the young Russian who had spent a night in
their house some two weeks before. She had studied him,
while they sat at dinner, drinking in his every look, his
every word, as he had talked with Amos Lyle, but she had
said little to him, and he had seemed to ignore her completely. The next morning, when he came to see the children, he had begun by asking her a series of odd questions
—did she like travel, did she like theaters, or dancing, and
the rest?—all of which she had answered to the best of her
ability, considering the way her heart was beating.

What had he meant by those questions? Was he merely
curious, prodding her, in his cold, superior way, as he had
prodded Amos Lyle? She did not mind his prodding, she
was too independent to care, but the more she thought
about it the more she was convinced that his questions
came not out of curiosity, but out of need. She felt sorry
for him, in an awed sort of way; she felt that there were
sorrows and tragedies and experiences in his life which
were beyond her comprehension, and which caused him
to assume, in her mind, incomprehensible proportions. She
felt that he was a man of great potentialities, a man as
yet unaware of his strength.

The diamond pendant which Markov had given Sirani
she had put away in her little box of treasures along with
her mother's wedding ring and bits of colored glass kept
from her childhood. She recalled how he had offered it
to her, in a moment of bravado, in resentment of her
father's having refused anything for the children. It had
been the first time Amos Lyle had failed to understand
a human need, and she had accepted the gift, at the risk
of creating a false impression on Markov, out of humility,
out of compassion for their guest.

The snow continued to fall in large white flakes, to envelop her, tu cling to her cloak like down. But the snow was not cold; on the contrary it was strangely warm and comforting.

Sirani had always felt herself enveloped with love—that of her mother, that of her father, whom she had never known, that of her foster father, and that of her heavenly Father. These loves, all of different colors and qualities, blended into one, like an aureate sunshine that warmed and nourished her spirit and evoked joy and gaiety. She now became aware, suddenly, of another sort of love, a love not like this, but more like the falling snow, which was cold, yet embraced her warmly, shutting out all sights and sounds but that of itself, which, though whiter than sunlight, fell upon her as lightly, yet pressed and clung, and demanded a response, aroused a quickening of her blood, and set her imagination soaring, her step hastening.

From a boarded-up window, through the cracks of which pale slivers of lamp-light fell and illuminated the falling flakes, came sounds of music and gaiety.

Sirani had not heeded where she was walking, and she realized now that she had come into the quarter of the town frequentel by soldiers from the fort.

For a moment she was dismayed that she should be in such a part of town. She started to hurry away, but the music, creeping through the cracks, held her. It was a popular Caucasian air, named, for no reason whatsoever, "Sylvia"—a rapid voluptuous melody to which the dagger dance was frequently performed. As she listened to it, Sirani's body began to sway ever so slightly to its rhythm. Her eyes closed, her lips parted, and she felt herself being caught and whirled by her partner—as she had seen it done in an open air fête, one summer before the War, when she was still very young. . . .

She roused herself and hurried home, counting herself fortunate that she had encountered no one.

As she drew near the house, Sirani saw some heavily loaded carts entering the courtyard. Snow covered the tarpaulins with which they were spread and glistened in the hollows of the withers and along the lean loins of the horses that drew them. A squad of soldiers accompanied the wagons.

Inside, a number of men were vociferating with her father. As she came in, Amos Lyle turned to her with relief.

"Sirani," he said, "will you talk to these men? It's about the supplies that have just come. You will know better what to do with them than I, and I have these letters to get off in the mail. The train is leaving tonight, and if the snow keeps up, another mail may not go for some time."

"Yes, father," said Sirani, obediently. Amos Lyle's letter writing was an important duty with him, next in urgency to his charity. He was always writing letters to people in America, letters about the work on the mission field, Pauline epistles in reverse order. Sirani understood this penchant of his, and as Lyle hurried out she nodded to the men.

She knew them all. They were cooks and stewards in the children's houses.

"I must have five hundred pood at least," broke in Byranik, almost before Lyle had crossed the threshold. Byranik was cook and steward at the Baratouni house, where Sirani had been working with the sewing—a short, dark Armenian with a benevolent but pugnacious face. "Five hundred pood at least. I have by far the most children, and they are, too, the most underfed."

"Five hundred pood of what?" asked Sirani. "I know nothing of this, you understand."

"The flour that has arrived! A whole carload! Don't you know?"

"Let him have the five hundred pood of flour," growled Arshan, pouting. "It's lard I need. There will be flour aplenty, but lard—of that I want my share. Do you know that unless we can get more fat on their little bones they will grow stiff and will crack, just like a piece of biscuit that is all flour and water!"

"Well, first, we must find out how much there is, all told," said Sirani, sparring for time. She had suddenly grown tired again and could not think clearly.

She had had these battles before. Every time a windfall

arrived she had to divide it up among these benevolently rapacious despots of the kitchen. If no more than a sack of potatoes, she had to count them out, one by one almost, and once—when there were very few—to split one in half to make the proper division between Byranik and Arshan. It was ludicrous, but pathetic.

"How much is there?" she asked.

"I don't know," spoke up Byranik again. "Wait until the Russian comes. He knows. All I know is that I must have five hundred pood. If there is more, do with it what you will."

Sirani hoped the Russian would make the division. This work needed the strong will of a man.

"Where is the Russian—who is he?" she asked.

"He's at the station, seeing the carts loaded, *hanim*. His name is—what is his name, Arshan?"

"Markov—yes, Markov, that's it. He was here before, he said."

"Markov!" exclaimed Sirani, and the blood rushed to her face.

"Markov, yes, Markov."

"Well," she said, "let us wait until Markov comes. He will know what to do."

2. Hostage to Fortune

PAUL STEPANOVITCH MARKOV was seated in the rocking chair in Lyle's sitting-room, wool-gathering. Outside, snow had begun to fall again, as it had been falling, intermittently, for the past week. Snow was everywhere, deep in drifts; the streets were blocked with it; the roads were closed; no trains were running.

Paul Stepanovitch did not mind being snow-bound; anything to postpone a decision was agreeable to him. He did not relish joining the Armenian army; he did not want to go to America; and the best thing in such a state of mind was a condition of affairs that made decision unnecessary.

It was comfortable here; time had passed noiselessly and unperceived; he was becoming rested; and he was beginning to feel like himself again—confident, strong, restless.

Relaxed in the comfort of the rocking chair—Paul Stepanovitch marveled again at the genius of the man who had invented it—his thoughts wandered contentedly. He ruminated on his school days in Petersburg, when he had been a member of the Imperial Corps of Cadets, thinking of the gay times he had had, the balls he had attended, the friends with whom he had consorted, the young ladies to whom he had paid indifferent attention. . . .

Those had been pleasant, insouciant days; but they were all gone now.

Markov did not regret their passing. That life, gay as it was on the surface, had never been satisfying to him, and he had been glad when he got his commission and was transferred to Turkestan. Since the Revolution, Petersburg had finally ceased to have even symbolic meaning for him. It represented a dead epoch, an extinct system, and he no longer had a desire to fight for it. That desire had faded when Korsakoff's band disintegrated, and died when Markov determined on emigration to America.

But now that the ideals and purposes of the old régime were dead, for what did he, Markov, live? He might have felt a great resentment in the loss of the years of his youth, fighting the Afghans in the deserts, the Austrians in the mountains, if he could conceive of a better object to which he might have been putting his energies and devotion. But there was none. His life gyrated around a vacuum or, at best, a small nucleus of self.

At the moment, this particle of self held his interest. It wanted rest and quiet to recuperate, to find itself again, and it felt very comfortable in this small, bare sitting-room. There was nothing here to distract one. Outside, the snow was falling softly. A pale light, of no intensity, illuminated a world of grayish white, in which nothing

was distinguishable except the snowflakes gently falling
past the window. Within, there was nothing to distract
the attention unless it were the picture of Christ hanging
on the wall above the lamp. Markov studied the picture
abstractedly and wondered where he had seen the eyes
and their expression before.

Markov recalled, for no particular reason, some hyacinth that had grown in a window box of his bedroom,
as a child, and that had looked in at him in the morning,
with a morning freshness and beauty.

And he began to think of Sunday mornings before the
War, and of their sabbath quiet, broken only by the pealing of the church bells. He recalled the quiet streets of
those mornings, and the worshipers passing through the
church enclosure, the girls in starched pinafores with
ruddy smiling faces, drawing their shawls about their
heads as they entered. . . .

He thought again of the hyacinth growing in the window box of his bedroom. His mother had planted it there
with her own hands and had tended it herself. . . . He
thought of his mother, as he remembered her, on summer
days, in starched peasant garb, seated on the grass, with
the Dasta flowing below, among the tall pine trees, and
the heavy, fleecy clouds drifting by overhead in the sunlit
sky. He heard again the creak of carts in the fields, the
lowing of cattle, and the bark of dogs. . . .

"Pavil, it is peaceful and happy here, is it not?" his
mother had said to him. "You will grow up—all too swiftly
to suit me—and be a man, and do brave deeds and have
many adventures. But nowhere will you find such peace
as here—at home. Yet peace is not here"—with her white
hand she had motioned toward the river and the fields—
"but here"—touching her breast.

Paul Stepanovitch had almost forgotten the words—
for even as a small boy he had been absorbed by the
desire of going off to war, like his father—and he had
even forgotten the occasion, the summer in which his
father had spent the whole season at home and everyone
was full of happiness. He recalled the words now, precisely
as his mother had uttered them, and they came to him,

not with poignancy, but quietly, as though his mother's spirit, entering the room with the pellucid light, were again speaking to him, reassuring him. . . .

Markov recalled his days on Karim Agha's boat, days that were also silent and peaceful, in which his spirit had been lulled to quiet by the placid waters and the motionless sunlight, and he had seemed to drift into a world of contented unreality. But then, his spirit, like that of an unwilling subject of a mesmerist, had rebelled, had struggled to assert its will, and had proclaimed its sovereign power to subdue all things. . . . And he thought, again, of Gregory Fedorevitch, and what he had said, "Until you have greater things in your heart, you must live," and of the monk, who had counseled him to pray to God, and submit his will to God's. But he had rebelled again from the thought of peace.

Now, Markov welcomed peace. Yet he knew that he wanted peace as a child unwillingly wants its bed. The moment he should find himself covered with its warm blanket, he would become restless and sit upright and seek to escape. . . .

The light had begun to fade from the window.

Markov recalled that Sirani was at the Baratouni house. He would go and see that she got home safely.

He found Sirani bending over one of the cribs, talking to its occupant, a bullet-headed, black-eyed baby of a year and a half who was gurgling over a wooden contraption that Sirani was dangling before him. Sirani did not observe Markov standing by watching her.

"Now, Tooni," she was urging, "say 'dog'."

The child only laughed and clutched the wooden figure.

"You big boy, you must learn to talk. You are quite old enough."

Some syllables issued from the little lips.

"There, that is splendid. Try again."

But Tooni was holding the wooden figure—it was supposed to be a dog with a tail that wagged—outstretched in his hand and was trying to say something to someone behind Sirani.

She turned and beheld Markov. Looking up at him from the level of Tooni, she seemed to be gazing into the face of a giant—a giant with brown eyes and an immensely broad forehead upon which the suggestion of a frown was apparent.

"Oh, I was just playing with the baby," she said, rising, confused and coloring. "I really should be seeing about the milk. It was thoughtful of you to include a supply of milk. The babies need it so badly."

"Oh, please, no," said Markov. "Won't you go on. I have never—I mean it was most interesting to watch you talking to the little fellow. Please don't let me interrupt you."

Markov's tone was abrupt, a manner of speaking that he had acquired on the drill field, and which occasionally reverted to him when he was uncertain of himself. Sirani understood, however, that he was trying to be pleasant, and she turned to the crib. But Tooni had sat down and was playing with the wooden dog. She watched him in silence, and then turning away she said softly,

"He is contented now, and we may as well go."

"Tooni is old enough to need toys badly," Sirani remarked as they went out into the hall. "And so I tried my hand at making something. Mattios lent me a saw and hammer."

Markov had been quick to grasp the division of labor between Amos Lyle and Sirani. He recognized that the burden of managing this enterprise rested upon the shoulders of the girl.

"You have a hard job," he said. "So many to look after. You bear up wonderfully."

"I probably wouldn't if it were something other than children. It is so much fun to be around them."

"Fun? How so?"

"When I am with them I forget everything that is going on in the world," she replied. "I suppose it's because they live in their own world—a world filled with fantasies and delightful things such as only a child can imagine."

"But aren't you being unfair to them?" responded Markov a little sternly. "Here, for instance, you make that baby a toy. But how about the others? Everyone should

be treated alike or you will have jealousies. You should no
discriminate. The only way you can manage people is b
absolute justice, which in this case—where food an
clothing and the like are limited—means absolute equalit
of treatment."

"That may be for grown-ups—soldiers, possibly—but no
for children," Sirani stoutly defended herself. "They do no
have a mathematical sense, and their spirit of generosit
is more developed than their sense of justice. What give
joy to one gives, by reflection, joy to all."

Markov grew warm to the argument. He could not, h
thought, allow himself to be downed by this girl.

"The fact that children do not understand justice doe
not mean that you should not execute justice," he said i
a tone calculated to quench any response. "Because a ma
is ignorant and cannot count is no reason for giving hin
short change."

"But what is justice?" answered Sirani. "You remembe
the parable of the householder who went out early in th
morning to hire laborers into the vineyard, and he agree
with some for a penny a day, and he hired others durin
the day, some at the third, some at the sixth, some at th
ninth, and some even at the eleventh hour, but to each h
paid a penny. And the Lord rebuked those who com
plained that he was unjust in making those who ha
worked but one hour equal to those who had borne th
heat and burden of the day."

Paul Stepanovitch was silent at this. He had a recollec
tion of the parable, but he had never given thought to it
meaning.

The snow had ceased to fall, and as they crossed th
court, Markov gave an appraising glance skyward.

"That drain pipe is broken," he remarked, pointing t
the corner of the court. "It should be repaired."

"I spoke to Mattios about it some time ago, but he ha
been so busy, and besides, I suppose he didn't think i
mattered."

"Drains are very important," said Markov gravely, goin
over and studying it in a judicial manner. "Yes, it shoul
be mended. As you can see, water will settle around th

foundation if it is not carried away properly. It breeds decay and bad odors, and sometimes disease. Once, in our barracks at Dostov, a whole company came down with malaria because of a bad drain.

"Of course," he added, to avoid what he thought might be a reflection on Sirani's management, "it isn't important at the moment, for no doubt this snow will hold for some weeks, but it should be attended to. I am not doing anything just now—until train service starts again and I can leave for Erivan—and I'll see what I can do about it."

"That would be very nice," Sirani murmured.

The next day Markov got some tools from Mattios and commandeered the services of a couple of men who helped in the kitchen, and in a short time he had not only the drain repaired, but the courtyard cleaned of snow.

The repair of the drain led naturally to other work, as Markov's reviving energy and restlessness drove him to find occupation. He excused his interest to himself on the ground that the whole organization offended his administrative eye and sense of order. The storage of the food, for instance, was entirely too haphazard; the bins were not tight and would draw rats. Markov got together those who knew something of carpentering and mended the bins.

Everywhere, of course, there was work to be done. Markov went from one task to another, gathering authority as he went. He began, before long, to introduce new organizational lines. He saw that among the volunteer helpers certain ones had capacity, and with Sirani's consent—he was careful not to assume direction in any case without consulting her and obtaining her permission—he put them in charge of units of the work.

Meantime, the weather abated, the roads were gradually cleared of the heavy snow, and a bulletin announced that a train would leave for Erivan.

Markov made preparations to leave Kars.

But before the train left for Erivan an event occurred which detained him and bound him to the work that Lyle was carrying on.

Word had gone about the town that there was food, in

quantity, in the houses on the hill, and a hungry crowd had collected.

Amos Lyle was in another part of the city at the time, holding a prayer meeting. Sirani, returning home, saw the people gathering. It was not a large crowd at the time, and there were both men and women present. They were for the most part quiet, and they respectfully moved out of Sirani's path to let her mount the stairs.

Probably they hoped that a food distribution would be made, which certainly would have been the case had Amos Lyle been there, for he would have given them the last pood of flour in the bin, trusting that before the morrow Providence would replenish it.

But Amos Lyle was not there; instead, Markov, who had been occupied in mending locks on the house.

Markov had observed the crowd collecting, and he had taken the precaution of double-bolting the outer door. It was he who undid the locks at Sirani's knocking.

"Why is the door locked?" Sirani asked.

"Did you not see that crowd out there?" Markov asked in reply. There was a frown on his face.

"Yes," answered Sirani, "but they're harmless. They're only hungry. I think we should give them some bread, poor things."

"Absurd!" exclaimed Markov. "To give them anything would only start a rush, and we'd be overwhelmed. They would break in and ransack the place until not a scrap was left."

"Really?" asked Sirani, apprehensively.

"Did you ever see a riot?" Markov asked.

"No."

Sirani had never known a person with the self-assurance of Markov, and she placed great trust in his words.

"I have sent to the fort for police protection," said Markov, as he peered down upon the crowd through the shutters. He was trying to be reassuring.

"Soldiers! Police!" exclaimed Sirani, thoroughly alarmed and dismayed. "Heaven forbid. No, Paul Stepanovitch, we must have no soldiers about. They might shoot and hurt someone, might even kill someone. That would be terrible. We must have no soldiers."

Markov looked at her incredulously.

"Better to have the soldiers than to have this mob break in and steal all our precious food," he said curtly.

"No, no. No soldiers. These people will go away quietly, after a while. We will speak to them, and explain why we can give them nothing."

"Would you go out there and try to make them forget their hunger?" Markov asked in amazement.

"Yes, we can explain to them about the children."

"They know that already," Markov answered cynically.

"But when you explain things, they see it differently."

Markov had no will to do such a thing, and consequently no courage. The recollection of how his father had met his death in just such a foolhardy manner mingled with the remembrance of his own personal debacle at Slavinka.

But Sirani was looking at him trustingly, and as he saw her eyes upon him, he knew that he must do as she would have him do. His lips set, he said,

"I will go out and speak to them, and you remain here."

He went to the door, followed by Sirani.

"The moment I am outside, bolt and double-bolt the door, and under no circumstances unbolt it. Do you understand?"

"I don't understand, but I will do as you say."

"Under no circumstances are you to unbolt the door, not until the last vestige of the crowd has gone. Do you understand?"

Markov opened the door and stepped onto the threshold. He could hear the bolts sliding behind him.

He was now facing the hungry crowd. He had formed no idea of what he should do, except that he should in some way keep their attention diverted until the police arrived.

"It's the Russian," he heard someone say.

"He will not give us food," said another.

This last inflamed him.

"No, I will not give you food," he shouted. "I cannot take food away from hungry children to give to you."

"He has food, and he refuses to give," a woman wailed. "And we are starving."

"Let us have some food."

A man started up the steps.

"Give us food."

Others followed. Yet there was no violence, no sign of weapons, clubs, stones or the other accompaniments of rioting. These people had hard, wasted faces that were set in lines of terrible desire, rather than fury.

"Stay back," commanded Markov.

"Can we have some food?" one asked piteously.

The crowd continued to press forward. Others were on the steps.

A blind rage took hold of Markov.

He flung himself upon the formost man and hurled him back down the steps. Those behind, against whom the Armenian staggered, fell back.

"Stay back," shouted Markov again. "You will get no food here."

It was a foolhardy thing to rouse a hungry mob and to stand and face them defenseless. In a moment they could have borne him down, torn him to pieces.

But it was a curiously apathetic mob. They had no sense of battle; but they had also no sense of defeat. In a moment, they were again upon the steps, pushing doggedly ahead, stubbornly, passively, like cattle huddling against a barricade.

Again Markov drove them down the steps; again they gave way; and again they advanced. They did not attack him, though they bore down upon him. Their only object was the door, through which they would reach food.

But now a heavy blow from Markov's fist had brought blood. He had struck one of these men in the face and had cut his lip. The man tasted the warm blood and stared in hurt surprise. It was as though he said, "Do you not understand? This is not play. I am famished and I want food."

Markov was growing weary with this repeated driving of the crowd; he looked warily about for a weapon. The mob was about him now; they were pounding on the door.

"Perhaps," the remorseful thought flashed through

Markov's mind, "I should have tried to coax them away with bread in the first instance. Now they will hammer in the door and take everything."

At that moment, however, the police appeared. Four soldiers headed by a slovenly corporal came up and began to send the crowd on its way, one by one, by laying hands on shoulders and gently shoving, but accompanying the shove with rapid expostulations. The respect for authority, the weariness of hunger, the hopelessness of breaking in, all had their effect. After all, it was only rumored that food was stored within. The mob finally dissolved.

Sirani washed the blood from Markov's bleeding cheek and bathed his bruised knuckles.

"I suppose I have made a fool of myself," he remarked sourly, "in not doing as you advised."

"We are not all gifted alike, Paul Stepanovitch," said Sirani sympathetically. "You do not have the gift of a honeyed tongue, but you did the best you could."

Markov felt rebuked, despite the fact that there was no condemnation in Sirani's words or in her tone. He wondered how much impression he had made on Sirani in these past days, just what her reactions toward him were. He needed something just then to salve his vanity, his broken self-assurance. The crowd had been pacified by the sight of a uniform. If that was the case, all the authority he had ever exercised as a captain in the Imperial Army had issued from the cloth, not from himself. He had been, then, only a rack upon which to hang a symbol, a scarecrow—no more.

But if there had been something more—the man behind the cloth—then how much manhood had he lost in these last years! A mere corporal had sent them away. A most unmilitary, undisciplined person, using no force but words, which had been sprayed upon the crowd like so much gas.

Sirani, young girl that she was, could have done as much.

"Why didn't you come out and send them away, then," he asked morosely, "if speech was all that was needed—a gift in which you say I am lacking?"

"Please, Paul Stepanovitch, do not misunderstand me. I wanted to come out, I was on the point of coming out, I would have come out—but you had forbidden me to."

Markov was secretly pleased that his wishes had carried such weight with Sirani, even to his own hurt.

"Besides," added Sirani, "I could not believe that harm would come to you."

"No?" asked Markov.

"No," assented Sirani. "In the first place, they were harmless. They meant no violence. In the second place, I believe"—she hesitated, then took courage—"you have something yet to do before it is time for harm to befall you."

"You mean, you think everyone has a destiny to fulfill, and will live until that destiny is fulfilled?"

"Possibly. Something like that."

"And what is mine?"

"I do not know, Paul Stepanovitch, but it is full of hope and promise."

A flicker of a smile lighted Markov's face, a smile of mingled self-disdain and self-conceit.

"You don't think I have acted the fool?" he asked.

Sirani's eyes filled with wonder akin to awed admiration.

"No, Paul Stepanovitch, on the contrary."

Markov did not leave Kars immediately, as he had planned. He did not feel that he could go just yet, for reasons partly connected with the assault on the house. Despite Sirani's assurances, he felt that he had not acted up to the occasion, that there were things which he might have learned from Sirani and Lyle about human nature which he had not learned. There was a secret. What was this influence over men that they, and even this corporal, seemed to possess, which he had lost? It was an influence and force which he himself had surely once possessed; but it was gone from him now, dried out of his veins.

There was also another consideration which he offered to himself for staying. He was convinced of the absolute necessity for a strong hand, if this enterprise of the missionary was not to collapse utterly. Here was need for him, and he resolved to stay on and see it through, at least to see it on its feet.

Had he not already invested much in this venture? He had provided the food that was now the object of attack, and he had the right to see that it went where he had destined it to go—into the stomachs of the children. Moreover, he had now shed his blood—a trifling amount, surely, but enough that it was a symbol, a hostage to fortune—in defense of the interests of these children.

He would stay for a while longer.

3. Back to Bartzan

THE winter relaxed its grip on Kars province. Train service was haltingly resumed with the capital. But Paul Stepanovitch Markov did not leave Kars. He was busy looking after the children whom Amos Lyle gathered in, and a thousand and one things concerned with the enterprise occupied his mind and body. Upon him now rested the management of the feeding, clothing and shelter of the children. At intervals the idea returned to Markov that he should go to Erivan and offer his services to the army, or resume his project of going to America, but the reasons seemed to lose their cogency, and the intervals between such thoughts gradually widened. He never announced his decision to remain; but it was not necessary. Amos Lyle assumed that he was staying and rejoiced that he had another helper in the vineyard. Easily and naturally, Paul Stepanovitch had become almost a member of the Lyle household.

The food held out, though it was again running low, and the clothing—made from the blankets obtained from General Bazian—sufficed, but there were shelter, shoes, personnel and many other things that required the attention of an able administrator. Shoes, for instance, had been the earliest and the most serious problem. To provide shoes, Markov had ransacked the leather shops of Kars and finally, at heavy price, had acquired a quantity of decaying goat hides. He had had them carted home, smelling as they did, had had them salted and retanned; and then assembling the men, he had found how many could wield a needle, and had set them to work making crude sandals and moccasins. It was very much the same procedure that Sirani had followed in the case of the blankets, but with this difference: Markov tolerated no variations. There was so much leather; it had to cover so many feet. It was cut in the most economical fashion and was used where it did the most good—on the soles. For the smaller children he improvised sandals made of heavy flooring felt taken from underneath the carpets in the Baratouni house. In the same way, Paul Stepanovitch took charge and reorganized the whole functioning of the enterprise, dividing the work into departments and assigning the helpers—according to their aptitudes—appointing some as cooks, some as nursemaids, and some as general workers and janitors. Everything that pertained to the physical care and well-being of the children, Paul Stepanovitch regulated, and regulated admirably.

Amos Lyle, who was never critical—judgment being the office of the Lord—saw all these things with admiration and joy. The young Russian was sent of the Lord, and what he did was right. Should it not be right—if he made errors—the Lord, who was good, would correct them.

But if Amos Lyle was eminently pleased to have Paul Stepanovitch around and if Paul Stepanovitch was finding new interests and new satisfactions in this work, it could not be said that Paul Stepanovitch was entirely happy. He was constantly aware of a strange mixture of contentment and restiveness in living with the Lyles. His body was contented; it felt a comfort and peace that it had never experienced before. But the atmosphere of the home was surcharged with something that gave Markov a feeling of inadequacy, of living submerged while those about him were floating in the sunlight.

"Am I overlooking something?" he asked of Sirani one

day. He frequently asked Sirani to accompany him on his rounds of the houses, partly because he was fond of her company, partly because he realized that she understood the temperament and needs of the children much better than he. Though she was a woman with a depth of sympathy that gave her understanding of his own complex moods, she was in many ways like these children—one who lived not merely in the sunlight of the surface, but in the sunlight and lambent air of the heights.

"Am I overlooking something?" he asked.

"The children need toys," Sirani answered promptly and emphatically. "I feel sorry that they have none."

"Toys?" exclaimed Paul Stepanovitch. "Isn't it enough to give them food and warm clothes and shelter? What else can they expect in a time like this?"

Sirani appeared shocked. Markov remembered what she had said when he had caught her playing with Tooni. Since then he had seen other bits of wood and knotted rags being hugged by various ones among the children, but had not realized that Sirani had been supplying them.

"Yes, toys," answered Sirani. "Why not? They need toys as much as they need food."

"But I have play apparatus fixed up in the courts," Markov argued. "That should keep them healthy."

"Play apparatus is different. They must use that together. Don't you understand that children are not all alike? Each one is an individual, just as you or I. They can't be reared all in the same mold, however much circumstances seem to force them together.

"I don't know how it is with soldiers," she went on. "I suppose that they can be made all to act uniformly in a certain way. But not children. Their minds are growing, and their bodies are growing, and just as their clothes must be changed and refitted to accommodate their growth, so must the other elements of their environment be modified. A baby of twelve months is immensely different from a baby of nine months."

Sirani paused, alarmed at the vigor of her wandering argument and hesitating whether to go on.

"Yes, I can see that," said Markov, shortly.

Sirani saw that Markov was offended, and she felt sorry that she had been so outspoken. Yet, it was an issue between them. Markov was turning everything into a regiment. She wanted to make him understand.

"Don't you see, Paul Stepanovitch?" she said. "They need exercise for their minds, something with which to express their individuality. We are all made in the image of God, and we are all creative, like God. And this creative spirit comes out, seeks expression. Some of the children find expression in one way, some in another. But all need tools by which to express themselves, for fashioning things and for the molding of their thoughts. The tool of the young child is a toy."

"Perhaps so," assented Markov, thoughtfully, "but I never found it so. When I was a boy, I used to have a mechanical train—it came from Germany—and stuffed animals and other things, but I never cared much for them."

Markov's expression and the thought of him playing with a mechanical train brought a ripple of laughter from Sirani.

"Oh, no, toys like that are not necessary, Paul Stepanovitch. Something very simple does just as well. Children have imagination. The little cut-out board I gave Tooni was a dog to him."

Markov looked at her in perplexity and then smiled ruefully.

"I don't know much about these things, I know. That's why I'm asking."

"Oh, I'm sorry I laughed."

"No, don't be sorry. It is so good to hear someone laugh. Laughter is precious here."

Sirani sobered.

"But don't you ever listen to the children laughing? Come and watch them play—the older ones particularly—and listen to their laughter. Thanks to you and father, they can laugh."

"Thanks to your father, rather. But I seldom hear them laugh. They become very quiet when I am around."

Sirani looked away at this, and then added, quietly,

"They become quiet because they respect you. Everyone respects you. They know what you have done to improve things."

"Yes, they respect me. That's the trouble. You too. You call me Paul Stepanovitch. Why don't you call me Paul, or Pavil?"

Sirani colored to her temples, but smiled happily.

"Oh, I would like to," she said impulsively.

They were on their way to the Baratouni house, by the road that follows the ridge. The weather was mild and they paused for a moment to enjoy the cold air and the warm sun. From where they were they could see the snow-covered peak of Ararat above the line of the nearby hills, on the eastern horizon. In the light of the afternoon, it seemed to be peering over the ridge like a benevolent but quizzical old man.

"I like to talk to you, Sirani," Paul Stepanovitch said. "These ideas of yours about toys and the individuality of children—they interest me."

"Then you should talk to my father, because I learned them from him."

"That may be true, for he's a wonderful man, and easy to talk to; but some of his ideas—well, they are above my head—they seem to have been drawn from some rarefied atmosphere, as though they had been drawn down from . . . well, down from the top of Ararat."

He pointed to the mountain, which was gathering a flame about its head, the reflection of the sun upon its dazzling snow crown.

"But with you, though you may have the same ideas, they have come to earth, where someone like myself can reach up and grasp at them."

Markov took Sirani's hands in his and looked full in her eyes.

"Sirani," he said earnestly, "will you tell me more about your ideas? Not now, but some time, and I won't feel offended if they—if they differ from what I have always held. Will you, please? I want to know more about you, what it is that makes you so gay, and so happy no matter what happens."

Sirani's voice mounted with a new-found power, with a realization that she understood Paul Stepanovitch and his need.

"Yes, Paul," she said softly. "I will tell you—as much as I can."

A few days after this conversation, Amos Lyle, on one of the rare occasions that he looked about him, found a number of workmen in a shed busy with a lathe and a band saw, busily at work under the direction of a cabinet-maker. Markov was standing by watching.

"What's all this?" asked Lyle, curiously, going up and inspecting the work.

"They are to be toys," explained Paul Stepanovitch solemnly.

"Toys?" exclaimed Lyle. "Let's see."

Paul Stepanovitch picked up one of the contraptions that was finished.

"I found that Hagopian knew something about toy-making and put him in charge," he said. "Here, this is a what they call a—a—what is this, Hagopian?"

"It's a monkey on a string," interrupted Lyle. "This is marvelous. And this, it's a pecking hen, and this—yes, the whole list is here—the things you see in an Armenian home. This is marvelous, Paul, marvelous! How did you ever think of them?"

"Sirani gave me the idea."

"Oh yes, Sirani. Of course. She always has more ideas than you can shake a stick at. When you come to think of it, children need toys as much as food."

In that moment, Markov knew why he understood Sirani, but did not understand Lyle, though both thought the same thoughts, and lived by the same faith. As he had intuitively stated it to Sirani, she brought her ideas to earth.

As if to confirm this discovery, Lyle laid the toys down, and dismissed the subject from further thought by saying,

"This is splendid. We're really creating a home for the children now. We have absolutely nothing to worry about."

"No?" asked Markov.

"Not a thing," added Lyle, with conviction. "I have some wonderful news. Can you walk along with me, while I tell you?"

Markov laid aside the toys they had been examining and went out with the missionary. The day was clear and sunny, with a touch of warmth that was a promise of spring.

"It is news," said Lyle, "of a wonderful regeneration of a soul, of a marvelous justification of faith. I have had a letter from Neshan Kovian."

"Neshan Kovian?"

"Yes, he was formerly one of our congregation—many years ago. When Kovian left us, I was sad. Kovian was a merchant, and I was afraid that his eyes were upon the riches of the earth rather than the riches of God. I thought that he should have stayed and kept his hand to the plow here, where his own people were. How mistaken I was! What a lesson it is to teach us faith! The Lord removed Kovian from our midst, and took him to America for His greater glory. But the Lord always justifies Himself to a measure beyond the reach of human faith. Just as, when the children of Israel complained of their hunger, He covered the earth with manna, so again His blessings are an unlatching of the windows of heaven."

"Yes, yes, it must be very interesting to see a soul regenerated," said Markov. He had work to do, and this evangelical talk was beyond him, much as he was trying to understand it.

"You do not understand?" Lyle asked, observing the shortness of Markov's responses. "Paul Stepanovitch, when you are saved, you will understand."

There was no rebuke in the missionary's words. He had grown in wisdom since the day he had said almost the same thing to Markov's father, twenty-three years before. Lyle was still thinking of Kovian's letter and continued, almost without interruption,

"Behold God's wisdom! Kovian prospered in America. He grew rich, blessed not only with worldly riches, but with riches of the spirit. He writes me that he has bought, and is sending us, a shipload of supplies for the feeding of the destitute in Armenia."

"A shipload! Good God!"

"But more than that. The Relief is coming into the Caucasus. The heart of America has been touched, and it is sharing its great wealth and blessings with our people here. Our prayers have been answered; the Lord has manifested His Holy Spirit, and the new day is at hand."

Markov took off his cap and wiped his forehead.

"It means then," he said a moment later, "that we will soon have all the means we need to care for the children?"

"Yes."

Amos Lyle's eyes were shining through lids wet with tears.

"Then," said Markov, "this is not so much a sign of God's virtue as of your own. It is the result of your own labors, of your own unquenchable spirit. Men have been challenged, and have been aroused by your faith. It is the response to goodness, of which you spoke, but it is your own goodness.

"But I have a plan," he continued in haste. "I have often thought of how we might care for the children if we had the means. You know of the supply depot at Bartzan?"

"Bartzan? Yes."

"It is unoccupied. I have talked to General Bazian, and the army does not intend to use it. Let us move the children to Bartzan. Where we care for hundreds here, there we can care for thousands."

Lyle grew thoughtful.

"But to put the children in barracks," he commented, rubbing the back of his hands. "You have suggested the idea before, the possibility of bringing the children together in one establishment, but it never seemed quite right to me. It would be more like a camp than a home. Keeping them separated in small groups at least preserves the semblance of a home."

"But there are very good reasons why they should be transferred," Markov said, "reasons that overweigh such disadvantages."

He went on to give his reasons—the problems of management that would be simplified; the facilities for caring for many more children than were at present available; the opportunity to grow food on the land and thus to become partially self-sustaining; the removal of the children from the confinement of the city; and the provision of space for occupation and recreation.

As Paul Stepanovitch went on giving his reasons, the missionary seemed to sink into a mood, as though he were oppressed by a weight.

"You have much to commend your project," said Lyle, "but—"

"But what, pastor?"

"I hardly know," the missionary said in a bewildered manner. "I hardly know. I have never thought much about the necessity of providing for the future. You see, I went into the ministry with the Lord's injunction to provide neither gold, nor silver, nor brass in my purse, nor scrip for my journey, neither two coats, neither shoes, nor yet staves. I have tried to live on that principle, and I must say that from my own experience I have found it works. I have never known want."

They had come to their own house. Lyle mounted the steps slowly, laid a heavy hand on the knob, and turned it. He opened the door, yet did not enter, but stood on the threshold, looking off into the distance.

Paul Stepanovitch had forced the missionary to consider a viewpoint as opposite from his cherished convictions as the missionary's were to those of Paul Stepanovitch. It was an issue which Lyle had faced before many times, but one that had never been posed in such insistent, challenging terms, that had never been so redoubtably defended as now. He was desperately trying to meet the challenge, to understand the viewpoint which the young man held, and to find a common ground between their divergent philosophies.

Paul Stepanovitch sensed that the missionary was in great perplexity, a perplexity as great as his own, and it gave him a sympathetic understanding of the man. For the first time, he began to feel a common bond with Lyle, and with this feeling came a humility. If this missionary, whose philosophy had been fixed through so many years of living—and old men do not adapt themselves readily —could struggle to understand Paul, perhaps he should make a greater effort to understand the missionary. Perhaps he had repelled men by his dogmatic self-assurance as Lyle had repelled him, at their first meeting, by his overbearing faith in what he believed. Perhaps it was in humility, rather than in confidence, that men find their common selves, and their common purposes.

Paul Stepanovitch thought of his mother's humility, and of the monk in the cell, urging him to submit his will to God's. . . .

"It is true," Lyle was saying, "that an expectant mother busies herself in preparing garments and coverlets for her baby, against its arrival; that the birds busy themselves with making nests. Such provision is God-given instinct. Perhaps what you are proposing is only this, on a vaster scale. . . ."

He paused, breathed deeply, and continued,

"Yes, Paul, you must be right. You have been sent of God and your wisdom is God-given. You have been a great blessing to the children. You are a new Gideon, while I, I am afraid, am an aging Moses.

"Bartzan has sweet memories for me. It was there that Sirani came into my life—the richest blessing of all. Take the children to Bartzan. Make them there a new community; found there a new city of the Lord; make a new covenant with God, in the shelter of Ararat—a city of children—children of God—"

A load seemed to have slipped from his shoulders. He began to hum, as he entered the house, a revival hymn of his youth, words of which came in snatches to Paul Stepanovitch,

"There is a land of pure delight,
Where saints immortal reign. . . ."

4: The City of Children

EARLY in April, the children whom Amos Lyle had gathered under his wing were transferred to Bartzan, and the founding of the "city of children" was begun by Paul Stepanovitch.

Paul Stepanovitch had gone to Bartzan while the ground yet lay thick-covered with snow, and had surveyed the condition of the buildings. He had come back enthusiastic about the opportunities, and early in March, when the weather had abated somewhat, he had gathered together the fittest of the carpenters and masons and had taken them to Bartzan to begin repairs and replacements, and to make all things ready for the reception of the children.

There was much to be done, but there was much to do it with. To begin with, there were the long gray stone barracks that had been substantially built by military engineers of the Imperial army. The roofs of these buildings leaked from want of attention; plaster and molding were falling; and much of the woodwork had been burned—from campfires which nomads had built on the floors; but otherwise they were intact. The great kitchens, especially, were in usable shape—if the removal of all small ware be discounted. There were great iron ranges, and kettles and vats; and even some stores of coal. More satisfactory still, from Paul Stepanovitch's new-found interest in education and recreation for the children, were the workshops—consisting of an immense building and sheds, with forges and anvils and bar iron and many tools and long racks of good dry lumber. It was Paul Stepanovitch's intention to train the older boys in handicraft, and the equipment would suit this purpose to perfection.

Spring settled upon the land with the ease and swiftness of a bird. Within a fortnight the snow had gone, and the Araxes, whose deep-cleft canyon lay a dozen miles from Bartzan, was brimming bank-full with rushing snow water. The land was ready for the plow and the new home was ready for the children. Paul Stepanovitch had busy days and nights ahead.

A spur of the Kutai-Kars line had formerly branched to Bartzan, but rails and spikes had been ripped up before the withdrawal of the Turkish forces. It was necessary, therefore, to cart the children a distance of some twenty-five miles overland. Carts were scarce, and even more scarce were horses and oxen to draw the carts, for most of the draft animals in Armenia had gone under the butcher's knife to feed a starving population. A few shaggy ponies had been located, but since Paul Stepanovitch had other uses for them the men and older boys volunteered to enter the harness. In this fashion—some trudging on foot, some in carts drawn by men and boys —in parties of hundreds and fifties, the children were taken on the last stage of their journey to their new home at Bartzan.

While this was going on, plowing and planting were in progress, for which purpose the oxen which Paul Stepanovitch had acquired were employed.

By June the great Bartzan depot again swarmed with human beings and resounded with human activity; but now children and not soldiers were housed, play rather than martial exercises echoed in the squares. Paul Stepanovitch had ordered the essential services with admirable precision and with the grasp of a skilled commander; the system which he had already introduced at Kars was rapidly and easily expanded. Those among the women who were skillful at baking were told off to the kitchens; and each was assisted by groups of girls, who alternated their kitchen duties with duties in the weaving shed or at the spinning wheels. This was a method which Paul Stepanovitch had conceived for training the older girls in the arts which he deemed to be the equipment of the housewife. Others among the women were put to looking after the sleeping quarters. But Paul

Stepanovitch did not follow the barracks method. Impressed by Amos Lyle's desire to maintain a home atmosphere as much as possible, he had had the barracks divided into rooms, each room holding a group of girls, and a bed for a woman who had charge and to whom the children were to look as to a foster parent. These he called "mothers," some being "mothers" of ten, some of twenty, and some of thirty. In this fashion, Paul Stepanovitch hoped to maintain the atmosphere of a home even though there were no parents.

In the same way, he allotted tasks to the boys, some to help the men at the plowing and gathering in, some to work in the carpenter shop, some at the mill. Picked groups he made "patrols," whose duties were to aid the younger children at their play, to see that they did not stray, and to act in general as guardians. For men were few, and the method of "mothers" for the girls could not be paralleled with one of "fathers" for the boys.

Paul Stepanovitch had been incessantly active all these days; by midsummer, however, he was able to relax a little and observe how this great family of children lived which had been brought together by Amos Lyle and was being cared for by their joint contributions. He observed with satisfaction how from morning to night the great barracks and squares hummed with the sounds of activity and joy—children at play, men at work, and women at their appointed tasks. Bartzan on a small scale had become a busy town.

There were vast differences, however, between this town and an ordinary town. In one of his letters written about this time to James Coswold, rector of St. John's in Philadelphia, with whom he had been in correspondence many years, Amos Lyle attempted to set forth the differences, as he saw them. "That difference which appears to me as most profound is this," he wrote. "In most communities that I have observed, affairs belong almost exclusively to grown-ups. They are run by grown-ups, and for grown-ups. All activity is directed toward the satisfaction of age. It is as though life found itself only in maturity, that it became precious only as it approached death, and grew wise and wonderful only as it grew senile.

"Furthermore, in the communities of the world, effort seems to center about the satisfaction of the vanity of age. Age, not sufficient unto itself, requires adornment, power, panoply and pomp. Its ego requires expression, and for this reason materials must be gathered together; even by those who are artistic and creative, substance is demanded, and the sacred door of the arts is open only to those who have attained maturity: indeed, maturity seems to be a criterion of artistic achievement.

"But children do not require habiliments; their glory needs no reflectors to enhance its brilliance. It shines of its own accord. They are not under the necessity of striving, for they possess all; they need not create, for they are already full and perfect. For what else is the creative urge but the necessity of restoring a lost perfection, of filling out that which is incomplete and imperfect?

"Age is voracious; it demands to be amused, to be adorned, to be humored. I can say this because I myself am beginning to feel the aches and pains of age, and find myself surreptitiously seeking out the rocking chair which Mattios made for me, though I had vowed many years before never to sit in it, in penance for my laziness. Age is vain and self-conscious and acutely sensitive to its inferiority. And so the energies of the world are devoted largely to satisfaction of its vanity and its pettishness, rather than to serving its legitimate needs. Theaters, clothes, automobiles, jewels, honors, office, and even war and monuments and great commercial enterprise—all these cater to the whims and wants and pride of age.

"But childhood demands none of these things. Being closer to the source of all life than age, and as yet undefiled, it is whole and perfect and self-sufficient. It demands nothing, for it is already everything—it is life, as God created it, pure and uncorrupted and full of the divine spirit.

"And so it is that there is joy at Bartzån, joy that is

inconceivable and past understanding except in the light of childhood. For there is suffering here; the children have been deprived of almost everything that is required for the good life elsewhere—parents, homes, comforts, security. But the spirit of childhood rises above these things; not impervious to suffering or unmindful of pain and distress, it is superior to them, and soars on divine pinions above the terrors of the world.

"Those who attend to the children partake of this joy. This is because their activity arises from a personal, rather than impersonal, interest. In other communities, for instance, commerce serves a social purpose, but this purpose is obscured and to many it is no more than a device for making money. Is this not because of the money mechanism through which the operations must pass before the results are finally realized? Money becomes a screen interposing itself between him who labors and produces and him who uses the product of the labor—a sort of reflecting screen in which the producer sees only himself reflected when he looks to discover the purpose and object of his work. In Bartzan this screen does not exist. Neither money nor trade corrupts the flow of necessary goods from the producer to the consumer. Those who work in the kitchens are those who eat the bread; those who fashion shoes in the sheds, or weave cloth upon the looms, see the shoes upon the feet of children and the cloth upon their backs. The change counter, the purchaser, the employer, the merchant, all these intermediaries have been removed, or rather have not been instituted.

"And so, as I say, the joy at Bartzan is not confined to the children, for whom Bartzan exists, but pervades the place like a salubrious air. I hope you may be able to come here, before many months, and behold for yourself this joy. You would find meat for many sermons."

Among those who had discovered a new kind of joy at Bartzan—and whom Lyle may have had particularly in mind in his letter to Coswold—was Paul Stepanovitch Markov. Paul had never thought of himself as an unhappy man; his Spartan-like nature was generally im-

pervious to sadness, and he had never fallen into the
temptations of seeking in sadness solace for his misfortunes. He found satisfaction in certain things—in doing
his duty, for one; in bringing order out of disorder, for
another—but his satisfaction seldom rose to the heights
of joy and never to that of exultation. But he was now
experiencing something akin to exultation.

Now that things were well-organized and running
smoothly, he found a growing pleasure in wandering
around the grounds and watching the children at play.
He found a refreshment in their spontaneous joy, and
he marveled at the fact that they seemed incapable of
holding a grudge against the world for its harsh treatment of them. They seemed long since to have forgiven
life for all the disasters with which they had been overwhelmed, and they began each new day as though it
were the first of creation.

Paul Stepanovitch, more and more, also, sought the
company of Sirani—on these walks and at other times. He
seemed to understand the children better when watching them with her. In some indefinable way, their joy
was translated through her into something he could
understand, and in which he could participate. She
seemed to give it a meaning for him which eluded him
at other times.

It was, no doubt, because Sirani was both child and
woman, and partook of the nature of each. She had the
qualities of childhood in her laughter, which was spontaneous and fresh, in her imagination, which was piquant
and fanciful, in her sympathies, which were quick and
clear; but she also had the qualities of womanhood in
her powers of affection and her perceptive understanding.

At the end of July there was held at Bartzan—at
Sirani's instigation—a big party for the children, to celebrate the close of the wheat harvest. It was not a great
harvest which they celebrated, but enough to be thankful over. Seed grain and plows and oxen to draw the
plows and men to scatter the grain had all been scarce,
but by a tremendous effort a hundred acres had been

planted. Though planted late, the grain sprouted, broke through the soil, and grew with such rapidity as to overtake the season. When the standing grain had become a golden coverlet billowing and shimmering on the plain, it was ready for the harvest. Paul Stepanovitch, remembering the harvests of his boyhood, threw himself to the task with the joy of refound youth. Everyone who could be spared was sent into the field.

The grain was cut, the fields were gleaned of the last wheat stem, the straw was threshed and winnowed on the open floor. And now the granary was filled with the grain; the straw was thatched; and the people of Bartzan were giving their thanks for the harvest and celebrating with games and dancing.

The scene was inconceivable in the time and circumstances. Here were the long gray military barracks, stern and severe; the immense parade grounds where in times past soldiers had maneuvered and pivoted to the command of officers and the sound of bugle; the plain which had reverberated with the rumble of artillery and rolling caissons and galloping cavalry; and in the distance, Ararat, brilliant in the clear sunlight, like a purple-and-gold backdrop. Now, instead of soldiers, in flashing array and resplendent uniforms, and prancing horses; instead of the shouting of officers and the martial music of drum and bugle, was a host of children, dancing and playing games, while their laughter, their cries, their occasional tears, rose into the air like the chatter of a host of birds.

At the granary the men who had gathered the grain were dancing a harvest dance to the singing and clapping of the women who formed a circle about them.

Paul Stepanovitch wandered over the grounds watching the games and play. He was in the mood of the harvest—contented with what he had accomplished since the spring, thankful for the security that had been erected against the winter—but restless, vaguely conscious of not being fully a part of the scene, imbued with a feeling that he did not really belong here, but somewhere else.

He observed Sirani among a group of the older children, teaching them to dance. She was in the center of a circle, and as the girls clapped time and sang, Sirani moved around the ring with a quick mincing step, her body swaying, her arms thrown out, her fingers snapping to simulate castanets. Her face was glowing, and her white teeth flashed as she laughed and sang.

Paul Stepanovitch watched from a little distance, unobserved, until she had finished, and then applauded vigorously.

Sirani looked up and saw him. The blush which she could not restrain when in his presence colored her cheeks, but she waved to him to come near.

"I am showing these young ladies how the *snopka* is done," Sirani said. "Come and I'll show you."

"Oh, yes, the *snopka*," he responded with gravity. "How well I remember the *snopka*, which we used to dance to the sound of *troika* bells on the Volga steppe."

"Now, Pavil," protested Sirani, drawing him along by the hand. "Don't tease us. You know very well you have never danced the *snopka*."

"No?" inquired Paul Stepanovitch, his eyes opening wide in assumed surprise.

"No, because it has never been danced before. I made it up, and Dina here named it."

"Dina, of course," said Paul Stepanovitch, delightedly, in recognition, but hesitant about drawing near her.

He was amazed to discover again the transformation which had taken place in the child. She was, it seemed to him, a good six inches taller than when he had picked her up by the railway tracks, and was now plump and ruddy of cheek. Her hair—he recalled how matted and unkempt it had been—glistened over her forehead and fell in shining braids upon her shoulders. Instead of coarse sacking, she was now clad in a fresh gingham dress, made from cloth received in a Relief shipment.

"It has been weeks since I have seen you. And how you are growing—almost to your sister Asta!"

Dina had come up and thrown her arms about Paul Stepanovitch's legs, hugging them happily. Paul let his hand rest upon her shoulder, and for a moment stroked her hair. Then, by a sudden impulse, he lifted her into his arms.

Dina looked at Paul Stepanovitch. Her little teeth showed as her lips parted in a smile. Then she put her arms around Paul's neck.

"Come," said Sirani, who had been talking to the other children. "You don't know all these children, and I want you to meet them."

"Yes, I want to know them all," replied Paul Stepanovitch, taking her arm, "and you must forgive me for spending so long with Dina, for, you see, we really are old friends."

In these past months Paul Stepanovitch had learned a great deal about child nature which he had never suspected before, and he was learning new things every day. He was beginning to see what children saw. It was a wonderland through which he had never traveled, or at best had traveled with closed eyes. Paul Stepanovitch, like so many others who spend their youth in growing up rather than in living, had hastened through his childhood in search of maturity, longing for the day when he would be a man.

He was beginning to discover for himself some of those things which Amos Lyle had written to Coswold—to discover how much "living" can occur during the years of childhood, and to wonder if possibly it were not in childhood that reality exists, that what the child sees is the truth, that what the man looks upon is the illusion.

Most of these ideas and discoveries came to him from, or through, Sirani. Sirani, who herself retained the freshness and ardor of a child in her young womanhood, understood how to reach the level of children and look through their eyes. Paul Stepanovitch always stood in a kind of awe when he watched her addressing a child. He observed now how she did not, for instance, patronize the children, but treated them with the dignity of equals, that as she pronounced the name of each she gave to her voice an inflection that showed an appreciation of the personality and individuality which each name represented. These were not just a dozen children gathered in from the storm: they were twelve distinct individuals, each with her own remarkable history, worthy of a story-teller's attention; each with her own gifts, many of which were rich and original; each with her own orbit, as majestic as that of a star.

Something of this he had perceived but not understood years before, when he first commanded troops. He had been taught in military school to look upon soldiers as so many units of offense or defense, like so many pieces on a chessboard. Problems of military strategy had been worked out in this logical, impersonal fashion. There was, of course, some mention of the fact that soldiers had temperaments and personality, and a good deal of talk of morale and *esprit*, and these had to be taken into account in getting the best results; but the whole idea of military discipline was to eliminate the variations of individuality as much as possible, to iron the men down to a dead level.

He had quickly learned from experience with troops that something was wrong with the military school theory of training men, though he had never attempted to analyze just what, and he had never been so rebellious as to question the theory. All he had learned was that while the theory may have had its merits, he had got the best results from his men when he had dealt with them as human beings, as persons like himself. And now he was learning that the three thousand or more children who formed the major population of Bartzan were not so many units to be fed and clothed and sheltered, but so many individuals.

Paul Stepanovitch spoke to each of the girls in turn, by name, as Sirani made the introductions, and asked a question or two.

"Navart Sedrakian? You have a brother here, too, do you not?" he inquired politely. "I know an Andranik Sedrakian who is learning from Mattios to be a carpenter. He is growing big and husky. Does he come to see you often enough?"

"He is very good and comes every day. It is Hasmik that I miss."

"That is too bad. Can we do something about it?"

"Hasmik is the baby of the family," explained Sirani, "and Hasmik is in the hospital with measles."

"In that case, you will have to be patient for some days but as soon as she is recovered I will see if she may not come and stay with you for a while, to make up for this absence."

"Oh, that will be wonderful," exclaimed Navart joyously. "Thank you. Thank you."

One of the children, Haikanush, a chum of Navart's, who had been standing with her arm about the other's waist, now spoke up:

"Navart has been embroidering a handkerchief for Hasmik."

"Oh, that is splendid," Paul Stepanovitch exclaimed. "Does she embroider well?"

"Oh, very well."

"Will you show it to me some time?" Paul Stepanovitch asked of Navart.

"I will embroider one for you if you like," she said, simply, neither flattered nor surprised at the request, but contented, as children are who have an interest.

"That would be very kind of you. I have a friend in Erivan to whom I would like to send one. Could you embroider me a very nice one?"

"I will try, but if it is to be extra nice—you, of course, understand that I don't embroider well—but your friend —he might not understand."

"Oh, I'm sure he will understand," smiled Paul Stepanovitch. "That is why I want to send him one—so that he will understand."

It turned out that each of the girls had some craft or art at which she was working. Haikanush, who had generously given tribute to Navart's embroidery work, was an excellent singer with the *tar*, a three-stringed musical instrument of the Caucasus. Arshalus was an accomplished story-teller and Vartuhi spent all her spare time in modeling clay. When he learned of this last, Paul Stepanovitch made a mental note to offer her an apprenticeship at the pottery kilns.

Evening came and with it the comfortable emptiness of hunger to remind the children of the supper board. Gradually the squares and areas became deserted, the air quiet. The sun was low in the west, a fiery ball above the plain, floating suspended in a golden mist. Above the mist the sky was violet, and a violet band encircled the horizon to the north and east; but in the south the violet became a mass of deep purple, streaked with ocher, which ascended and became embodied and took the form of the mountain, a purple and ocher mountain, capped by a dome of milky white.

Paul Stepanovitch took Sirani's arm in his. Together they strolled over the grounds, from which the sound of merriment had now subsided, toward the southern gate, where the plain swept without a break, save for the hidden gorge of the Araxes, to the base of Ararat.

They stood and watched the glory of the evening sun gather round the head of the mountain.

"I want to climb Ararat," Paul Stepanovitch remarked lightly, though there was earnestness in his voice.

Sirani asked why.

"Oh, because I am restless, I suppose, and mountain-climbing calms one," Paul Stepanovitch responded.

"That isn't the real reason, Pavil, and you know it," asserted Sirani.

Paul Stepanovitch tapped the palm of his hand with his fist, a characteristic nervous gesture when he was in thought. Presently he ceased his tapping, took Sirani's hand and kissed it.

"No, I can't keep anything from you," he said, turning and facing her. His expression was one of assumed playfulness. "I'll tell you. I feel at a complete loss. I find no answers."

Sirani waited, knowing that he would explain without being questioned.

"Maybe I could puzzle things out, if I could get away and look at myself."

"Yes, the saints used to go up into the mountains to pray."

"I want to understand this thing. I feel every now and

then that I have it in my grasp, and then it slips away."

"What is it you wish to know?" asked Sirani so softly that it was almost an inner voice prodding Paul Stepanovitch to speak.

"I want to know what I live for."

Then the words broke forth like an avalanche.

"I want to know what these children are living for," he hurried on. "I want to know whether any of them are growing up to be Belinskys and Baratoffs and Korsakoffs. How many of them are growing up to be offered as a sacrifice in the next war? What is the purpose of keeping these children alive? What is their destiny to be? Do they have any destiny, except one of suffering?

"I used to think I had a destiny, a destiny which I could carve out by my strong arm and will; I used to think my country had a great destiny to fulfill—mistress of land and waters, from the Baltic to the Pacific, from the White Sea to the Black Sea, a destiny to expand its arm and its majesty, to bring diverse peoples under its dominion.

"What is the Russian Empire now? Where are the great traditions, the mighty houses? Where is the memory of Peter and Catherine and Ivan?"

He paused, and then broke forth again:

"And what am I? For what do I live? And these children? Why Navart's embroidery, and why the songs of Haikanush, the clay-modeling of Vartuhi?"

"Pavil!" exclaimed Sirani, amazed at the violence of Paul Stepanovitch's words and voice.

"That's what I want to know," cried Paul Stepanovitch, his voice rising. "That's the way I feel. What is it all worth? What is it all for?"

"They're not growing up for anything, Pavil," Sirani responded quietly. "They are worthwhile now. They are at this moment fulfilling their destiny and God's plan for them. They are happy and their happiness is like a perfume that fills the air and floats to the far corners of the earth. What happens tomorrow is for God to say, but that will not mean that they have not already realized their destiny and expressed from life all the meaning that life has for them."

"It sounds very well for us, who have reached maturity to talk that way," said Paul Stepanovitch shortly. "It sounds all right for someone standing apart to say, 'Yes, they have fulfilled their destiny,' but what do they have to say? Perhaps they want to live, perhaps they feel that there is something yet to be done?"

"For those who have not found God, it is sad," Sirani acknowledged. "For them it can be said that they have not yet lived their life. But for those who have found God, life is already complete and perfect and fulfilled."

Paul Stepanovitch was not convinced, but he could not argue with Sirani. She was like her father, very positive on such matters, though unlike her father in that she had none of the insistence of the evangelist.

"Well, that's that," he said, shrugging his shoulders. "I am sorry I went on that way. I suppose old Noah must have felt the same way, as he watched his lands and barns and homes carried away in the flood, his friends gone, nothing left him but a boatload of assorted animals, and his dissimilar sons. And I can imagine his thoughts after the flood subsided, as he looked out and saw the earth only a sea of mud, with nothing on it that he could recognize. Everything gone—all the old landmarks washed away, his old home and fields hidden by silt, the towns which he had frequented, even his skeptical neighbors—all gone. No doubt he wondered what it was all about, and why he alone of men was chosen to survive, and what was the object and purpose of surviving. He may have felt as a lot of us have felt, that in selecting us to survive God is unkind. The Bible tells us only God's side of the story, the racial side, the side of posterity that would not have been if Noah had not survived. But maybe Noah had preferred to go down under the waters, to be drowned with his friends, rather than float alone upon the. . . ."

"Please, Pavil, don't say that," remonstrated Sirani.

"I'm sorry," apologized Paul Stepanovitch. "But it's when I am most happy and when everything seems to

be going well that these moods come upon me, that
these doubts arise."

"Have faith in God, Pavil."

"But how does one find faith? I would believe if I
could."

Sirani quivered ever so slightly.

"There are two things, I think, that are required. You
have attained one already."

"What is that?"

"One must first be emptied of self, before faith can
come in."

"I can understand that well. And what is the other?"

Sirani did not answer immediately. Then she said,
"That, Pavil, I cannot tell you. I do not know when
and how God chooses to enter the empty chamber."

"Pray to God, then, that He may."

5. *Haig Droghian*

PAUL STEPANOVITCH was overseeing the building of a
cote.

Amos Lyle had acquired, by gift from secluded villages in the north which had escaped the worst of the
denudation, some sheep and goats—a few here, a few
there, enough to make a small herd. Paul Stepanovitch
had carefully watched over them, and he hoped by next
year to have enough animals to provide milk for all the
children, with a crop of wool for spinning and weaving
into cloth.

The cote was necessary to fold the herd through the
winter, which was usually severe on this plateau. There
had been a small enclosure as an adjunct of the army
post, but it was near the abattoir and unsuitable. Markov
had chosen to reconstruct one of the remount stables
which stood on the range a verst away from the post.

The stable proved to be in sorry condition: though built originally of stone and apparently soundly erected, it was now well-nigh a ruin.

Markov had not expected to find it in such dilapidation. He had gone out one afternoon with Mattios—who had become his chief lieutenant in matters of handicraft and construction—expecting some repairs to be necessary, but he was shocked at the amount of work he would have to do.

He marveled at the ruin into which a product of human hands could fall in a few short years.

A mood came over him, the mood of restlessness and disquiet that had been recurring of late and seemingly growing in intensity in the degree that his happiness increased. He beheld the ruin of this stable, the effect of which was enhanced by the loneliness and desolation of the landscape, and it became a symbol of ruin everywhere. He was looking away from Bartzan now—the cries and laughter of the children did not reach him here—toward the north and away from Ararat, looking upon the same landscape that his father had looked upon so many years before, with the crumbling bastions of Ani pricking the horizon, and the ruins of Roman cities and fortresses scattered upon the plain, covered with dust and no longer visible. But Paul Stepanovitch was looking beyond the immediate landscape. He was looking beyond the horizon—beyond the Caucasus—looking at his native land, the once fertile fields of Russia, the busy cities, the traffic-laden roads. All this was a ruin, too, and everything associated with it had crumbled and decayed.

He wondered how long it would be before the same fate overtook the city of children at Bartzan. This was a house built of the ruins of other houses, destined itself to crumble into another ruin, for the building of yet another house. Was it not all endless and hopeless?

Paul Stepanovitch had had letters recently from Alexei Petrovitch. Alexei was enthusiastic about his work. He had at last been transferred from staff duty to the line, had been made colonel and was now training a regiment of recruits for the new Armenian army. Everything was hopeful. The Allies had recognized Armenia as a sovereign state and a delegation had visited Erivan, bringing promises of more loans and political support. When the organization of the League of Nations was completed, the Powers would move for the admission of Armenia—which would mean, under the Covenant, world support for Armenia should she be attacked. Added to all this was the treaty which was under negotiation with Georgia, the sister fledgling republic to the north, which would regularize trade and open up Armenia to trade with Europe through the port of Batum, making prospects bright indeed.

But Alexei's optimism did not move Markov. Despite his restlessness, he had no desire to return to the army life which he had forsaken. That now seemed to him to be a career without significance, a work even more hopeless and devoid of purpose than rearing orphans. If what he was doing here was but to raise children for their eventual destruction, certainly to train soldiers was to forge the instruments of that destruction.

Moreover, he understood, from reading between the lines of Alexei's letters, that despite the latter's hopes much was yet to be done before Armenia could be regarded as more than an experiment in statehood. These letters showed veiled impatience with the administration. Alexei had never been too efficient himself, and for him to complain or criticize suggested that glaring incompetence was prevalent. Without doubt, it was all due to inexperience; but there were bickerings and party strife. Apparently, the leaders considered that parties were a necessary habiliment of democratic government, and they cultivated party dissension as a mark of democratic unity.

There were other things more serious. Alexei had hinted of short harvests all over Armenia. Though the famine was no longer so severe as during the past winter, the sowing had been sparse—for all seed grain had gone to feed hungry stomachs, and the peasants, as before, were hoarding their grain. Alexei, Markov concluded, was talking academically, as people in the metropolis always do about agricultural prospects. Markov knew that there was more than "small harvest" and "short crop" and "hoarded grain." Even if they had a crop as good as was had here at Bartzan, hunger and starvation were again the outlook for the winter.

It was this academic view which the government apparently was taking, to judge from Alexei's letters, that made the situation for Armenia so dark. Were they doing nothing but talk? Food was now being shipped in by the Relief, but the Relief, great as it was, surely could not feed a whole nation. What was the government doing about it, except to drill soldiers!

The thought made Paul Stepanovitch gloomy.

Better at least to know the hopelessness of it all and go down with eyes open and fists clenched than to live in stupid, blind optimism, and finally to stagger into the abyss with a look of surprise on the face. . . .

"We will soon have this in shape," commented Mattios as he got out his tape and plumb line. Mattios was an old man, with a lame leg from a misplaced adz blow in his youth, and rheumy eyes produced by years of flying sawdust.

"I'm glad it doesn't dismay you," replied Markov.

"Oh, no. This is nothing. I've spent my life rebuilding things. Rebuilding houses, rebuilding furniture, rebuilding shoes. . . . What I haven't tried my hand at rebuilding you could put in your palm."

Mattios, despite his age—he was a contemporary of Amos Lyle, now approaching his seventieth year—and despite his lame leg, was as vigorous as any at Bartzan save Lyle and Markov. He was like a piece of well-seasoned oak, or a piece of well-tanned, well-beaten leather. He seemed to be shriveled and desiccated—but with the sort of dryness that is strength rather than decay.

Markov wished his other helpers had even a modicum of Mattios' vigor. The men at Bartzan, like this stable, were only wrecks of men. They were men from which all the strength, almost all the spirit, had gone. Of young men there were none. They had long ago been sacrificed to war—the war that had ended or, as recruits in the new Armenian army, the war that was now ahead. Only old men were here at Bartzan, men with aches and bruises, narrow chests and coughs, and frail arms and legs.

A summer on the sunlit plain, with regular if meager diet, had done much to revive strength and enthusiasm, and when the harvest was in, there had been enough spirit and gaiety for some of them to dance; but lifting stones and propping heavy timbers was a labor for which they were inadequate, and the work of rebuilding this single stable seemed almost to defeat Markov's will.

Day after day he worked with the men, spending almost his whole time at the stable, away from the post, away from the children, working until the sweat poured from his body, and his back ached and his muscles gave way....

While Markov was building his cote, Amos Lyle spent his time, as was his custom at this season of the year, touring throughout the province, searching out villages where he might preach the word of God and his faith in God's redemption, minister to the sick and broken-hearted, and gather the widowed and the orphaned to Bartzan. Through Lyle's preaching, word of this haven had spread far and wide, and every day there were new arrivals begging for shelter.

One day, while Markov was at work on his cote, there rode up to Bartzan from the south a party of armed men. They were, for the most part, dressed after the fashion of Kurdish mountaineers, and their mounts were shaggy hill ponies; they seemed to be tribal folk from some mountain region.

The company advanced toward the post, but when they came to the outer edge of the unfenced field that surrounded the barracks, they halted, while their leader rode on toward the gate.

Near the carpenter shed the leader came upon the boy Andranik Sedrakian who was on his way to work from a visit with his sisters Hasmik and Navart. At the sight of the armed tribesman—he looked very ferocious with his red beard, his many bandoliers of cartridges and the rifle across his back, and his heavily-bound turban—the boy stood terror-stricken.

The man addressed him, however, in Armenian.

"*Salem* [Peace], I come to see Pastor Lyle. Can you tell me where he is?"

The boy, still frightened, pointed dumbly toward the long building in which Lyle lived. The mountaineer curveted his pony and cantered off in the direction given.

Amos Lyle was in Bartzan, having returned but the night before from Gorem Chai, where he had been preaching. He saw the mountaineer from the window, where he was sitting writing, and hurried out.

The man leaped from his horse and ran toward the missionary.

"Pastor, pastor," he cried.

"Haig."

The two men embraced.

"God be praised that you have come again," exclaimed the missionary. "I knew it was you the moment I saw you ride up. What a blessed Providence that I was here!"

"So you know me, pastor?" laughed Haig, and his voice had a barrel-like boom. "With this beard?"—he drew at the heavy whiskers that covered his face—"and this girth?"—he stretched out his arms.

The insouciant urchin who had run away from Lyle twenty-three years before was now a man of massive proportions, with thick chest and mighty arms and legs, though he was still a good six inches shorter than the lanky Lyle.

"Were I blind, I would have known you. I knew you were coming."

"Knew I was coming?"

Lyle nodded.

"Have known it for years."

"Pastor," said Haig contritely, "I should have come long ago. I should never have gone away from you. I have prayed God day by day to forgive me for going away from you. I was not a good son."

"You are a good son if you have prayed day by day. No man who keeps his face turned toward God can live in darkness. It was His will for you to go away, His will for some great purpose."

"I know, I know," exclaimed Haig, proudly, his chest expanding. "I am no longer just Haig. I am Haig Droghian, Haig the son of Droh. And I am chief of the Kargaseurs."

"And those are your men? Come, while I see about quarters for them. You will stay awhile with us, of course?"

"We will spend the night, but in the morning we must return to camp. But I will be here again—many times."

"Where is the camp?"

"Yonder, across the Araxes—on Ararat."

"So near? We should have seen you before."

"I learned of Bartzan by chance. We winter in southern Persia. In summer, for some years, we have been tenting on the southern slopes of Ararat, near the Persian frontier. This spring the rains were scant and we came around to the north in search of grass, which, by God's bounty, we found, and found you to boot."

"The spring rains were abundant here, praise God, and for that reason we have had a good harvest, now gathered," said Lyle, as they walked out toward the tribesmen, who had dismounted and were leading their horses back and forth while waiting for their chief.

Amos Lyle welcomed the men and showed them where to stable their mounts and where they should quarter for the night.

"But where have you accumulated such a family, pastor?" inquired Haig, as they returned to Lyle's rooms. "There seem to be here a good many children for a bachelor like you."

He laughed in good humor and patted Lyle on the back.

Lyle told Haig about the work they were doing in

Bartzan, how they came to be there, about the children, and finally about Paul Stepanovitch.

"You will want to know Paul Markov," he said enthusiastically. "He has been God's hand in this city of children."

A frown passed over Haig's face.

"Markov? That's Russian. Is he a Russian?"

"Yes, Haig. Bread cast upon the waters."

"A Russian," Haig repeated.

Resentment began to show in his face.

"But you are a minister to the Armenians?" he asked, puzzled.

"Yes, to the Armenian people—thank God for the joy of serving them. And to all God's children, Haig. Paul Markov has made it possible to save these children."

"I am sorry, pastor. Forgive me, I see that you love him dearly. Let me meet this Paul Markov. I will love him, though he will be the first Russian whom I have not hated."

"You talk of hatred, Haig," Amos Lyle said a moment later. "And I observe that you and all your men are heavily armed. This is not the way of peace. This will lead to trouble."

"We are peaceful, pastor, but we carry arms for good reason. These are bad times. But I will tell you about that later."

"Let me understand about it now, Haig."

"Pastor, let us not differ now, at this moment of reunion. I know you are a man of peace. You have been a shepherd who has dared to cross the mountains into new valleys where grass is forever green and nights forever cool and delicious. But it is a stony path that we follow, a steep path, a path which your sheep cannot follow.

"I have remained on one side of the mountains, pastor, while you have crossed to the other. On my side the grass is scarce and brown, and whosoever pastures there must defend himself, lest someone stronger come and snatch the food while it is lifted to the mouth, yes, even pounce upon one to devour the carcass."

"But I have remained on your side of the mountain, Haig," replied Lyle, "and it is not I who am the shepherd, but He who is our divine Shepherd, who guards us so closely that should we pass through the valley of the shadow of death, we should fear no evil."

"I have not seen a good shepherd since I left you," responded Haig. "All I have seen are the hills and the pastures. The only refuge I know is the rocks—that rock yonder."

He extended his arm in a wide sweep toward the south.

"Ararat?"

"Yes, Ararat is impassable country, except to those who know it. It has its green fields and sylvan dells, but to him who does not know the mountain it is a place where the *jinn* and evil spirits play—a maze of valleys and abysses and insurmountable precipices, a land of nakedness and starvation.

"It was in the time of Droh that I first learned to know Ararat. Usually we followed the Persian ranges in our migrations, but in this year of which I speak the rains had been scant and we had crossed over into the Taurus. It was there that the Turkish *gizil bashies* pounced upon us, and harried us, until we fled to the Araxes, and there lost them. It was in that battle that Droh was killed. Later, by free election of the tribe, I became chief in his stead. Since then I have pursued the Turks. During the War I led foray after foray."

"With what army, Haig? With what army?"

"With no army, pastor. But because of Droh and because of all the persecutions of our race. We harried the Turkish armies, descending from the mountains, falling upon detachments of them when they entered the passes. When they pursued, we fled. Again, Ararat became our refuge. Once, in the spring, we were saved only by the Araxes, which flooded and cut off all pursuit."

"Whether you have sinned or not in taking arms against the Turks, I do not know," said Lyle. "That is a matter for God and you to judge. But the War is over, Haig, and your bearing of arms is not only without justification, but is a provocation to those who live in peace. Jesus said, 'Blessed are the peacemakers: for they shall be called the children of God.' And again He said, 'Ye have heard that it hath been said, An eye for an eye, and a tooth for a tooth: But I say unto you, That ye resist not evil.' "

"Pastor," interrupted Haig, "you err when you say that peace has come. Peace has not come. The Turks—I have seen it with my own eyes—are preparing for war, and they will attack Armenia."

"Preparing for war?" Amos Lyle was so surprised and alarmed at this news that his powerful, cracked voice became like the caw of a crow. "No, no. You must be mistaken there. They have signed an armistice. They will not go to war."

Haig took a boyish delight in being the bearer of bad news.

"You are too confident," he asserted, puffing out his cheeks. "The government that surrendered to the Allies is no longer known in the hills. Another army is forming. Everywhere I hear of their recruiting officers. Everywhere there is preaching, 'Redeem Turkey.' "

"It cannot be. Who are these men that are forming this new army?"

"Jemal Pasha, Mustapha Kemal, Ismet Bey, and others I have heard of. Among them is that one we know—Hashim Farouk."

"Hashim Farouk Bey!"

"No longer Bey, but Pasha. He is commander of the new Army of the East—the army on the Armenian frontier."

At the mention of Hashim Farouk, Amos Lyle's tanned, weather-beaten face grew pale, and his eyes became fixed in a stare across the plain. He saw rising again the waters of destruction that had so nearly overwhelmed his people in Dilijan and on the pass of Ghulam Dagh.

To face new dangers, new hazards, is something bearable; but to face old dangers, to recross old hazards, is something which will appall the bravest. A danger once met and eluded dies in the heart and fertilizes it for new virtue; but its second appearance is like the specter of death.

For twenty-four years Amos Lyle had met one reverse after another with courage, with confidence in his Lord, with increasing faith in Divine wisdom, love, mercy and justice. He had lost much in these years, but he had saved much. Never had he been left completely empty-handed. Always there had been left some crumb of hope to sustain him until another day should dawn and the world should be reborn.

But the mention of Hashim Farouk—the implacable enemy of the Armenian people, coupled with the armed and hostile aspect of this spiritual son of his—aroused such dismay in the breast of the missionary as to submerge for the moment his faith in God in a quaking fear.

Amos Lyle was no longer young. He could no longer contemplate with equanimity a long flight over the mountains, harassed by bloodthirsty horsemen. It was with him much as it might have been with Noah had the rains again come when he had established his new home and planted new vineyards and rested in his old age in the shadow of his own palm tree.

Yet it was only for a moment. Lyle's hope, lying on the ground like a fallen star, flickered, lighted, and became a devouring flame of renewed faith.

"God has preserved Hashim Farouk, as He preserved Lucifer, for His own greater glory," he exclaimed. "As the children of Israel were delivered from Pharaoh, and from Sennacherib, so shall these children be delivered. Wait, and you will see the Glory manifest; you will see the mighty power of the Lord for the redemption of His children. He will watch over them as the angel watched over the sleeping David. . . ."

He paused in his outburst, and it seemed for a moment that he was being carried away into a world of unreality.

Lyle recovered himself and continued:

"But of course Hashim Farouk is not a menace. The Turks are on the other side of the frontier, which is a long way from here, and they will abide by their treaty obligations."

"But if they do not, pastor, what then?"

"Not guns and swords, Haig! Not guns and swords! We will trust in God to abate their fury and to put love in their hearts."

"It will be many years before the Turks and the Armenians learn to live without hate of each other," said Haig shortly.

"Not so long as you may think. Time is as nothing to the Lord, and in a moment He can bring to pass that which men have not achieved in a thousand years. Within your time, Haig, you will eat from the same dish as a Turk, and drink from the same cup—if you but accept the gracious redemption of our savior Jesus Christ."

"Better ask Ararat to become as an ant heap than to ask me to love a Turk," replied Haig, with a bitter laugh.

"But come, pastor," he added, as they entered the barracks in which Lyle lived. "We have talked too much of this. Tell me about your blessings, about the years that have gathered around your head like a crown, about the Russian, Markov—whom I have a curiosity to see—and about our people, how they have fared."

The meeting of Markov and Haig Droghian was of that order which obtains between men of different stations in life. Markov, tired and disheartened by his labors in rebuilding the stable, looked upon this well-fed, ebullient mountaineer with a kind of resentment, or envy, that was not assuaged by the cordiality with which Droghian was treated by Lyle. Markov saw in Droghian, in his air of freedom and self-assurance, the man he might have been had circumstances been different, the man of war and action and impetuosity he still might be had he not accepted the yoke laid upon him by Lyle. Droghian had fled Lyle's influence and had remained a free man; Markov had stayed and allowed himself more and more to come under its subjection, until he was no longer free, no longer an independent spirit, but a bond slave to an authority which he did not understand.

While Haig Droghian talked—as he continued to do, regardless of where he was or who might be listening—Markov felt a qualm of fear—the same fear that had gripped Lyle's heart twenty-three years before, when Haig, as a lad, had forsaken him for the lure of the tribesmen—the fear that in devoting himself to the way of peace he was losing his manhood, becoming effeminate, craven. . . .

"You are building something?" Haig enquired, in the tone of one to whom details were of no consequence.

"I told Haig that you were working on some sort of building, but I did not know just what," Lyle explained.

Neither, then, thought Markov, knew what he was doing here at Bartzan. No one knew all the things he had been doing, details that were not visible to the eye, to make the children more comfortable, more secure, and happier.

"I am building a shelter for our herd," he explained.

"You are a military man—yes?—and you know how to care for herds and flocks and build shelters for them?" Haig asked.

His tone was not patronizing, but full of admiration. As Markov saw in Haig the Markov he might have been, so Haig saw in Markov the man he would have liked to be.

"I know little enough about tending herds," Paul Stepanovitch replied, "but of course I know something about construction."

"Will you teach me, and my men, how you do it? We have need of shelter for our herds, at times, and we are very ignorant of such things. When winter comes, we do not defy it, but flee from it, to a warmer land. But sometimes winter overtakes us, for the winds are swift and the legs are slow."

Markov's resentment dissolved.

"By all means," he exclaimed. "I shall be glad to show you."

A thought struck him. With the subtlety of which the Gospels speak, he added heartily,

"I can use a dozen of your brawniest men to finish this

cote, and while they are with me, I will teach them the art of building with stones."

"You are a shrewd man," roared Droghian, in high good humor. "It is a bargain. Let us learn of each other. And I shall add thereto a good number of goats from my own herd."

Amos Lyle smiled, with the benign smile of a father who sees his two sons reconciled from an incipient quarrel. He closed his eyes and murmured to himself a little benediction.

6. Ararat

WITHIN the vicinity of Bartzan nature had created two imposing works of contrasting character, symbolic, it might seem, of the polarity that is found in the relationships of the universe. These two works were Ararat and Araxes. Of the two, the mountain was the more impressive, the more majestic, aloof, inaccessible. It was, in the eyes of many, emblematic of deity—exalted, unchanged, eternal, serene, unmoved and immovable, an object which does not go out to men, but to which men must come by painful climbing and by slow degrees.

The river was of a different character. Less imposing than the mountain, it was of equal renown and antiquity, and in many ways a mightier work. Tradition places it as one of the four rivers of the Garden of Eden. Taking its source in the Taurus ranges to the west, it flows, turbulent and unpredictable, for a thousand miles to the Caspian Sea, and along its whole distance the hand of man has dared to throw but one bridge.

From Bartzan the river was not visible. Though it crossed the plain, circling about the mountain in a majestic arc, not a dozen miles from Bartzan, it was not apparent to the eye. One might live and die on Bartzan plain and never be aware of the Araxes River. While the mountain was lifted on high for all to behold, as the brazen serpent was lifted by Moses for the children of Israel to gaze upon, so the destiny of the river was cast upon the ground, as the serpent in the Garden of Eden was cast, by the decree of God, upon the ground, for the contempt of men, and condemned to crawl upon its belly among the crevices of the earth. The river, as if in submission to its destiny, had kept to the earth; yet, writhing with implacable energy and unappeasable will, it had cut for itself, with its swirling, turbulent waters, a deep, narrow, majestic and awe-inspiring gorge.

As the soul, according to Roman dogma, must descend into purgatory before it may ascend to heaven, so the traveler had to descend the gorge and cross the Araxes, before he could pass from the plain of Bartzan to the mountain of Ararat.

Paul Stepanovitch Markov had been many months at Bartzan and had looked daily upon the mountain—each time with an increasing desire to ascend its heights— but he had never beheld the Araxes.

Now, one day in September, he stood on the brink of the gorge, and looked down upon the river. Far below, almost lost among blue, hazy rocks, meandered what appeared to be a shallow, sluggish stream.

Markov looked upon the gorge and the stream for a moment, and his eyes returned to Ararat, upon which his thoughts were fixed. His manner, in averting his gaze, was not that of one to whom the river was undeserving of attention, but of one who was drawn ahead by something so compelling as to be stayed neither by river, nor gorge, nor flood nor fire.

"Be not contemptuous of its little size," warned Haig Droghian, who stood with Markov upon the ledge. "This is the season when Araxes sleeps. When Ararat thunders and shakes its forehead, then Araxes awakes and quivers and begins to writhe and hiss. It puffs and swells like an angry serpent. The water rushes in a torrent, filling the gorge as a cup is filled with wine. No man may cross it then. The water comes down like a clap of thunder, in a mighty wall, shutting Ararat from the plain as the sword of the archangel Michael shut Eden from the children of men. Then men may call to Ararat for help, but its help is not nigh, for Araxes flows between."

Haig lifted the reins of his mountain pony and entered the narrow trail that led down the gorge to the river level.

Paul Stepanovitch watched Haig for a moment, thoughtfully, observing the sun glistening upon the barrel of the rifle slung across his back, the swaying flanks of the pony, and the little clouds of dust kicked up by his heels.

In a moment Paul Stepanovitch would follow Haig. He would descend the gorge and cross the Araxes and ascend the other slope, and then he would stand among the foothills of Ararat. He looked again toward Ararat, now with eagerness mingled with anxiety. At last he was to challenge the mountain, at last he was to attempt the ascent.

He pressed his heels against the belly of his mount and started down the slope.

In an instant, the plain of Bartzan disappeared from sight; of a sudden, Paul Stepanovitch had left the world of reality, as he had known it, and had entered another world in which the only thing that existed was nature and the indomitable, challenging soul of man.

Nature was seductive at these portals to the world of Ararat. To descend the gorge of the Araxes was like entering a fairy kingdom. The imagination responded to the invitation; the rocks became castles and turrets; rising out of a lambent mist, they became of tender shape and tenuous outline, of the color of yellow and lavender and gold; they changed before the eye, dissolved and formed ahead into new and more fantastic shapes. . . .

Markov and Haig reached the water level; they crossed the Araxes, while the water, rising to the horses' bellies, swift and turbid and noisy, clutched at them with angry swirls as they pushed across the current. They attained the opposite shore, and mounted the heights. Again they stood on the level of the plain, but now they were separated from Bartzan by the Araxes, and ahead of them lay Ararat clothed in the iridescent mist of the morning, standing diaphanous and ethereal, as though separated from the earth, as though but newly sprung from the womb of creation, fresh and radiant.

"Here," exclaimed Haig in enthusiasm, pointing to the escarpments towering ahead of them, "here is peace and safety. No one knows this mountain so well as I, and our people. Ararat is our fortress, like that which David saw in his visions, and sang of in his psalms. Here, among the protecting walls of Ararat, we care neither for *ukase* of tsar, nor *irade* of sultan, for here we are free. No man pursues us here."

As they rode on toward the mountain, Markov understood the meaning of the chieftain's words. This side of Araxes was another sort of land, a sculpturesque land, a land naked and untidy, as though Ararat had surrounded itself with a vast moat of barrenness, a land whose natural beauties were fundamental—brilliance of sun, vast spaces of yellow gray earth, stern uplifted crags. For many miles they rode over a barren region of fine sand and hard yellowish clay, covered with dwarfish, almost leafless bushes, the monotony of which was relieved only by the butterflies which the horses, breaking through the trail, scattered before them like a hoard of golden bezants, and by the lizards of rainbow hue that scurried from beneath their feet. Each mile was like the last; there were no landmarks, and in the clear air Ararat seemed no nearer after three hours' travel than it had on first crossing the Araxes.

The ground gradually became rougher, and they came to a region where spring torrents had cut deep gullies into the volcanic soil. The elevation rose by a series of yellow hills, streaked here and there with a mold of green. In the sharp ravines they looked upon a world of pale golden color, a gargantuan cheese gnawed by gargantuan mice. And then suddenly, unexpectedly, they had traversed the moat of barrenness and were upon a vast plateau of verdant growth.

"We shall soon be at the encampment," shouted Haig exuberantly and began to curvet his mount, like a young warrior who has just received his plume of manhood.

Markov smiled at the chieftain's antics. He had been like that himself once. Now, though no older than Haig, he felt like a seasoned commander. His thoughts were upon his task ahead, the task he had set himself of scaling Ararat. Carefully, like a skilled officer, he was thinking out his strategy. Before he left Bartzan he had had fashioned alpenstocks and grappling irons and ice axes. These were packed and secure. It was men he would want now, men who knew the country, men who had the courage, with him, to scale the icy peaks and cross the glaciers and stand on dizzy heights.

"You think that some of your men will be willing to make the trial with me?" he asked as they rode along.

"Of that I am sure," Haig answered with conviction. "I need only ask and they will go. If not, I will go myself, though it is not a venture to my liking."

But Markov had not desired Haig's company on this venture. Not that Haig was not brave enough; but he was impetuous, hasty, lacking in prudence. In the short time that Markov had known the tribesman he had come to have a strong affection for him, but he had also shrewdly appraised his abilities. Leader though he might be to the crude tribesmen, to Markov he was a follower, subject to the Russian by the Russian's stronger will and more disciplined intelligence.

Shortly before sundown they reached the saddle that lies between Ararat and the turret on its southern flank, known as Lesser Ararat. They crossed an elevation and beheld the black tents of the Kargaseurs scattered over the grassy slopes of the valley. The Kargaseurs were a numerous tribe; their tents covered an extensive area, and there were many men, women and children about. Farther away, among the crags and grasslands of the higher slopes, horsemen were folding the herds in the lee of the escarpments, the sheep and the goats—so many black and white dots upon the green—collecting as though drawn together by a net.

The camp itself was astir with the labors of eventide; and an atmosphere of restlessness hung over it in the smoke haze of the lighted fires, like the purposeful rest-lessness of a flock of wild duck circling a pond before settling, or a hive of bees in swarm.

"My people are becoming anxious to move," said Haig, as they turned their mounts down the slope. "It is grow-ing late in the season, and they are afraid that the moun-tain passes will be blocked with snow unless we go soon.

"But they are too impatient," he added confidently. "The signs tell me that it will be another month yet before we need strike tent."

As they approached the camp the elders of the tribe rode out to meet their chief, led by Hairopet, the princi-pal lieutenant. This Hairopet was a tall, spare man, more handsome than the thickset Droghian, and more highly ornamented with scarves, cartridge belts and silver belt-tassels. The expression in his face, in contrast to that of the jovial Droghian, was sullen. Markov could not guess whether his expression represented his mood, or was the mask which nature lays upon the faces of those whose lot is hardship.

When the chieftain introduced his guest, Hairopet answered for the elders.

"You are welcome."

The words were curt, neither friendly nor hostile.

On the way into the camp, Haig and Hairopet talked about the affairs of the tribe, Haig in a hearty torrent of words, his lieutenant in monosyllables. Haig asked many questions concerning the condition of the pasturage, the health of the herds, the amount of cheese that had been made, the dyes gathered, the rugs woven, the number of deaths, and finally—the most important—the number of births, first of lambs and kids, and then of colts, and finally of babies.

"When do we strike tent and follow the storks south?" asked Hairopet, when he had given answers to the chief-tain's inquiries.

For answer, Haig Droghian reached down from his saddle as he rode along and plucked a handful of grass. He studied it for a moment. It was of the rich brown color which grass takes on in late summer, and was long and lustrous in the chieftain's hand.

"There is yet much food here for the herds. Are all the butter skins full?"

"All are full."

"We can still make cheese and weave carpets."

"It is growing late in the season."

"The signs tell me to wait. I know not why, but we must not leave for a while."

"What are these signs?" asked Hairopet stubbornly.

"Did you not observe the grass just now? How the stem was yet red above the joints? Have you looked at the condition of the horses' coats? And the scantiness of the wool upon the sheep? All the signs, Hairopet, point to a new spring, rather than the approach of winter. Never have I seen the like in my life. We must stay yet a while."

"It is true," observed Hairopet, without relaxing his stern countenance. "But the air is heavy, as though rain were nigh. The smoke clings to the tent tops. And the air itself is full of water—the tents are moist of mornings. What do these signs portend?"

"I know not, except that we must wait until the signs are clearer."

They entered the camp and were greeted by barking dogs, children *salaaming*, and women standing, dignified, in their traditional coronets, at the tent doors.

That evening, around the chieftain's fire, Droghian spoke of his guest's wish to scale Ararat. When this was announced there were shakings of heads and mutterings.

"Ararat has never been scaled."

"Russian audacity," muttered another, very low, so as not to reach the ears of the guest.

"It's making man equal to God, putting his will above God's."

"It is dangerous. The Russian will lose his life."

"Let him lose it!" whispered he who had condemned Russian impudence.

"The Russian has courage," spoke up Haig Droghian,

"but he needs companions. Are there those who will join him?"

There was no response.

"Why do you wish to scale the mountain?" asked Hairopet finally, in his short-breathed manner.

Markov looked at Hairopet long and hard, and in that scrutiny weighed the tribesman and knew his caliber.

"I have no reason except a desire to get up as high as I can for once," he answered firmly, as though what he willed was what the gods willed.

"I approve that reason," roared Haig Droghian. "I say that no man is a man who must give reasons for this and that. God created desires in man, and He does not call upon man to justify himself for them. The Russian has a desire to climb Ararat. I think it is dangerous and foolhardy, and not to be done. But I approve his desire, and will help him in every way except to climb the mountain with him. I belong on a horse, and my feet waddle when I put too many burdens upon them. Who will accompany the Russian to the mountain top?"

"I shall want two men to make the last climb with me, and six to keep the camps we shall make," Markov explained.

Again there was silence.

"I will go with you," said Hairopet, finally.

He who had condemned "the Russian"—Haratoun was his name, a small, slender, wiry man of about thirty— now spoke up.

"I will go also." Under his breath he growled, "To see him freeze or fall into the abyss."

Another offered—Petros, a solid, swarthy man—and another, and another, until the party was complete.

They were at an immense elevation. In the far distance the plain of Bartzan lay spread like a carpet; the Araxes had become a misty, dreamy valley that curved in a vast circle and lost itself, as it approached the southern boundary of the visible earth, in a tumultuous sea of rose-colored hills.

From the summit of a cliff, probably two hundred

feet in height, in the lee of which they had camped the night before, while the wind had whistled in fury about them in its headlong rush down the mountainside, the face of Ararat was visible in all its majestic proportions. In the midst of the mountain was an immense fissure, rising like an inverted V—a chasm left when the side of the mountain had been thrown out, disemboweled by some terrific explosion of nature. The chasm was visible from the plain—it is a principal feature of the great mountain—but from this elevation it acquired a new and supernal quality. In the morning sunlight it lay overcast with a violet pallor, a nebulous luminosity that seemed to be of infinite depth, as though one might walk into the solid rock, as if it were nonexistent, and penetrate into the very bowels of the earth.

The evening before, while the men were making camp for the night, Paul Stepanovitch had climbed the escarpment, following a narrow goat trail that led up its face, in order to survey the route for the morrow's ascent. They had come a great distance since leaving the tribal encampment—how far, it could not be said, for distance was not to be measured in versts but in changes in the landscape, and these had been such as to give the sensation of having left the inhabited world entirely and of having ventured into a spectral, lonely, half-world that was suspended between earth and sky, like neither earth nor sky but partaking of the qualities of both. In the same way, time had escaped reckoning. They were in a land where time, of the sort measured by the ticking of a clock, or the rising and setting of the sun, was nonexistent: it was all of one piece, a gossamer, misty veil that enwrapped all things in a swaddling of eternity. All that could be said was that they had gone far, had achieved much, had exerted seemingly impossible energies, had exhausted all ordinary strength, yet had acquired new reserves from the upper air, and that some were eager or willing to press on, while others were loathe to go farther, and complained of the cold and weariness, and of nausea from the sulphur fumes that issued from the volcanic ash.

Paul Stepanovitch was now completely under the spell of the mountain. Never in his life had he been so overwhelmed by the mightiness and majesty of nature, the insignificance of man. Yet though he was awed, he was not afraid. His sensations were rather those of one completely isolated, to whom the world and its affairs were nothing. The stupendous chasm in the face of the mountain, upon which his eyes had fixed, drew him on with an irresistible power. Bartzan and its children; the fate of his country, which had filled him with grief; his own fate; his despair—all were gone, all were of no consequence. . . .

Light had faded from the earth; the pallor that had filled the great chasm had spread, and had encompassed the whole mountain; the great boulders below had become roseate and tender and insubstantial; earth and sky had melted into one ethereal substance, unreal, impalpable, divine. Of this dissolution it seemed that all things partook. The thought occurred to Markov that, if by the effect of sunlight this hard rock could dissolve and become as nothing, might it not be that, by a diviner light, the hard woes of the world, the seemingly solid substance of misery, could reduce themselves to something nebulous, nay, disappear entirely? Indeed, might it not be possible, if one could catch that light, to dissolve all the barriers that shut mankind from the peace and joy to which it is rightful heir?

The men who accompanied Markov were growing weary. Though living in the mountains they were seldom moved to explore the heights, and spent their lives below the snow line. Moreover, they had not Markov's discipline and had wasted their energies early on the climb, nor did they have his driving urge to reach the top, which is, after all, a source of power as great as that of strength or training. Markov had finally told off two of the tribesmen to set a camp in the lee of the cliff, against the return of the others, with fires going and smoke constantly rising as a guide. The remainder had pushed on toward the great fissure, where they would reach the snow line.

All morning long they had fought their way up the slope. The firm rock and earth had been succeeded by lava gravel, strewn with black, igneous boulders that slipped beneath the feet and made the climbing doubly difficult. But now they were among the snowfields, and their eyes and nostrils were assailed by the pungent odor of sulphuric acid, the action of the water upon the sulphurous impregnation of the lava ash.

Toward noon they had come to a narrow valley, or defile, protected somewhat from the screeching winds and cold sulphurous blasts, where stood a grove of stunted, twisted trees. Here Markov had called a halt while the men rested.

A gazelle stepped from the glade and regarded them with timid, surprised eyes. Then it leaped nimbly away, springing on jeweled feet from crag to crag.

"See how he travels," panted Mesrob, one of the men who had been lagging for an hour past, and was obviously spent. "Why did not God create me with such legs, such nimble heels?"

"If you reproach God," growled Haratoun, "why not reproach him for not having given you wings? No legs will carry us where this conqueror would go."

"How much farther will you insist on going?" groaned Mesrob.

"Till my strength is gone," replied Markov. "I know not how long that may be."

"Oh, this man is like a devil who wearies not. I shall never see the camp again, or behold my wife or my children."

Mesrob began to wail.

It was true that Markov seemed tireless. The long arduous climb had seemed to touch him not at all. He had found, in the climbing, a vast exhilaration, a lightness of both body and spirit. He had experienced the afflatus which comes to mountain climbers from the breathing of rarefied atmosphere. The lungs must suck the air deeply in order to sustain vitality and in this intense respiration a physical and mental exaltation is achieved—a state somewhat like that which the *yogi* attain

their religious trances through the monotonous breathing of the chant "*Om mani padme om.*" Markov's body
was exhausted and purged by the struggle with natural
forces, but for that reason was the more ready to serve
his will, which now, more than ever, was bent on the
conquest of the mountain.

"His strength is not greater than ours," exclaimed
Haratoun. "He is a plainsman. I shall stay with him and
watch him drop in his tracks."

"I thought you would," said Markov, smiling. He had
guessed that Haratoun growled rather than bit. "You are
mountaineers and apt at this work. That is why I asked
for you. But as for Mesrob here, I think he had best
stay here and keep a second camp. I can see that his
heel is bruised by the gravel, and it is not good to trust
one's body to feet that are not sound. Will you keep a
fire going, Mesrob, with smoke rising, that we may mark
our return?"

Mesrob assented eagerly. Markov told off Petros to
remain with him, since it was safer that the men stay in
pairs; and the rest, consisting of Haratoun, Hairopet
and Markov, tightened and tested the stout thongs of
hides that bound them together, and started on.

Now they were well into the snows, and flurries struck
them in the face, while the wind screeched and howled
among the rocks, and great promontories stood forth—
massive rocks upon sharp abutments, like Crusaders'
castles—to forbid their approach. Following a ridge of
lava crags, which protruded from the snow like the verte-
brae of some extinct monster, they came to the brink of
the great fissure. Upon their right hand the earth disappeared into a seemingly bottomless chasm, vast enough,
it seemed, to swallow up all the towns and cities of the
universe.

They crept into the lee of a promontory, while the
storm roared and screamed in their ears. The heavens and
the earth were in tumult; it seemed at any moment they
would be seized by the snatching fingers of the wind
and hurled into the abyss. They were but three frail men

huddled together before the onslaught of all the force
of nature.

"We cannot go further," whined Haratoun, and hi
voice was now lost, now multiplied in the roar of th
tempest. "God forbids us. No man can reach the top."

Markov, who had braced himself against a rock, an
faced the full fury of the elements, grew suddenly furiou:

"God forbids us nothing," he roared against the win
"It is for us to say."

The wind took his breath, but only for a moment, an
then he hurled his words into the maw of the tempest

"I—am—going—to—the—top."

The wind howled down his words, but not before the
had fallen upon the ears of Haratoun.

"Blasphemy," he wailed, and his voice was like a mal
diction of the fates. "Blasphemy . . . blasphemy . . . W
must pray to God. . . ."

Toward dark, the wind subsided somewhat, and th
air grew warmer. They struggled out of the snow, whic
had drifted into their retreat and almost covered then
and clambered up the slope, where they found a roc
cairn that had been swept clean. Here they made cam
for the night, guarding themselves against the cold b
wrapping themselves up in their blankets, and beddin
down into the snow.

The wind had died now, except for a gentle soughin
as it slipped past the snowfields on its journey to th
lower regions. The skies cleared, and the stars sprinkle
the heavens with frosty scintillations, and in their ligh
the great rocks stood forth above the snow like watchfu
sentinels, dark and silent. And presently the moon ap
peared—suddenly, in mid-air it seemed, as though it ha
drawn aside its veil, though it must have just risen abov
the horizon—round and golden and benign.

Hairopet, who had remained silent during the violen
protest against going farther, now spoke:

"If the Russian wishes to climb farther, I shall not b
one to pull against the thongs."

"Good," exclaimed Markov. "Then we shall go on.

ink we shall reach the top tomorrow. We cannot be
r away."

The morning of the last day. As though bowing before
e conqueror's will, the mountain no longer defied the
imbers, and the aspect of nature was benevolent. The
ene, as they trod their way over the gently ascending
owfield, in the early morning, was one to etch itself
rever in Markov's memory.

They had started by the light of the moon, as it lay
w in the west, and were well upon the rounded dome
f the summit when dawn appeared. For the first time,
nce their encampment by the cliff, they were free of
e encompassing crags and could behold the expanse of
e lands surrounding Ararat. Morning had come on
viftly: first a coral mist that crept over the horizon,
dvancing upon a violet-colored emptiness that was the
ain. In a moment all was light: the plain became a
lver basin encrusted here and there with a patina of
reen, with the Araxes, like a crooked furrow, winding
a great horseshoe and disappearing in the mist of
e horizon. To the south and east lay a broken expanse
f hills, rounded like dust heaps, that caught the morning
nlight on their ridges and cast across the hollows a
acery of shadows.

The whole world was one of softened and tremulous
utlines, a silent and empty expanse, like the dawn of
eation, when the world had been laid and determined,
ut before it had been peopled with living beings.

They were not far from the summit. It lay not more
an a thousand feet above them. They had gained the
unded snow-packed dome of the mountain, and the
cent was no longer precipitous. In a little while they
ould be at the topmost point.

For this last stage of the ascent, Markov had as his
mpanion only Hairopet, the chief's lieutenant, and
aratoun, who had protested so violently. They were
w pushing forward earnestly, relieved that the end was
near, exultant at the prospect of victory.

But Markov had lost his interest in achieving the sum-

mit. For the moment at least, personal desire, the asser
tion of personal will, subsided and ceased to exist. Th
bitter words of Haratoun, "blasphemy, blasphemy," ran
in his ears. Markov had arrogantly challenged the moun
tain and now he was seemingly victorious. He had se
his foot upon the summit, but the great mountain ha
set its mark upon his soul. He felt humble. He had bee
willing to risk his life and the lives of his companions
for the sake of an egotistical assertion of will. In the sam
way, no doubt, men were willing to sacrifice peace, hono
and the lives of millions of their fellow men for the sak
of personal achievement with no other purpose than th
assertion of an egotistical will to power.

The three men were like flies that had alighted upo
the surface of a huge bowl of whitest porcelain. Below
the slopes of the mountain and the plain were becomin
obscured by the mist that collects about the head of th
peak toward mid-day, and the sensation it gave was tha
of being elevated over the surface of the deep. Marko
was suddenly aware of a loneliness, tremendous and ove
powering. Here, one did not belong to earth, whic
seemed a strange and distant place, connection or associa
tion with which had long since been lost; nor to the sk
which was tantalizingly blue and empty and distant.

Such a loneliness, the awful loneliness of abandonmen
Noah must have experienced as the Ark floated upon th
face of the waters, and he sent forth a dove, which foun
no rest for the sole of her foot and returned to him i
the Ark. . . .

Markov continued to climb. Some inner force, apa
from his conscious will, the same inner force that ha
led him to pick up Asta and Dina, that had led him
without knowing why, to return to Kars, and the sam
force that had kept him at Bartzan, was now directin
his steps toward the pinnacle. It was not his will. He ha
lost the will to conquer Ararat. It was to him as thoug
the same eternal will that had set Noah to building th
Ark, that had carried Noah over the deep, and had se
him upon this mountain, had taken charge of his will, an
had absorbed it within its own. And Markov, sensing th

will working within him, began to comprehend its quality, to understand that Amos Lyle, and Gregory Fedorevitch, and even Karim Agha, were moved by it, to grasp
the fact that millions of other men also were animated by
a will not their own, a will more powerful and irresistible
than the human will, which they knew not as will, but as
faith.

Gradually the path eased, and Markov felt the ground
leveling underneath; and at the same time the clouds
surrounding the summit began to dissipate. The three
had reached the topmost point of the mountain.

And now the mists that enshrouded the mountain top
were being broken by a stiff wind, revealing in patches,
as through a window, the country surrounding Ararat.
So tremendous were the distances, so great the altitude,
that the horizon appeared to rise to meet the sky, and
one seemed to be in the hollow of an enormous basin.
Far to the north, two hundred and eighty miles distant,
the summit of Mount Elbruz, in the Caucasus, was a
frosty point on the horizon. To the northeast lay the
Daghestan, a hundred and fifty miles distant, and caught
among them, like a silver comb in a woman's hair, the
sparkling surface of Lake Sevan. Nearer at hand, though
some seventy-five miles distant, rose Alagöz, an extinct
volcano, its three sharp peaks enclosing an ancient crater.
Toward the south, blue and lovely in the morning, lay
the mountains of Persia. Below, rising out of the mist,
was the peak of Lesser Ararat.

But these peaks seemed to rise from nothing at all. At
such a height as this the plain was but a diaphanous veil,
with no distinctness of color, as though nature were
shielding from sight the havoc that men had wrought
upon her bosom. Here, on Ararat, one was removed from
the earth, lifted into the formless void that lay over the
waters before God divided them and set the firmament
in their midst. The plain lay in a pale nebulosity like
that through which the archangel Michael must have
swum as he made his way from Heaven to Eden, a formless incandescence drawn between the beholder and a
fathomless void.

Gazing upon this sublime scene, this tremendous panorama that stretched before the vision, Markov felt his mind being emptied of every thought and emotion. There was an absence of exalted mood or conviction, and it was as though the whole purpose of nature was to deprive him of individuality and to render him insignificant. Loneliness was all he knew. He felt as though he were swallowed up in nothingness, overwhelmed by the waters and slipping irrevocably into oblivion. It was a sensation the like of which he had never experienced before, and he desperately thrust out tentacles of thought for something which he might grasp.

"There," said Hairopet, pointing, "is Bartzan."

Markov turned and looked. There it lay, a faintly discernible rag of white and green, waving to him through the mist. As he looked upon this patch of earth where he had labored to build a shelter for the homeless children gathered together by Lyle, there rose to his ears the laughter of their play and the sounds of contented activity in the shops and workrooms. Here was a spot of ineffable peace, an Eden where sorrow and pain and suffering had not yet mastered hope and faith.

The faces of the children at Bartzan seemed to appear out of the mist, beckoning him. But rising above all, like a guardian angel, was the face of Sirani, youthful, innocent yet wise, gay and yet grave, childlike yet full blown. . . .

Markov suddenly wanted nothing so much as to return to Bartzan.

7. Sirani

EVENING had fallen; the children of Bartzan were abed, and the barracks and playgrounds slept under a cloak of silence. Here and there, from some of the windows, lights still twinkled into the night, like stars upon the plain to counsel with the stars that shone in the sky.

One of the still lighted chambers was that of Lyle's sitting room. Amos Lyle sat at a table, under a lamp, writing a letter, his faculties absorbed and sublimated in his work.

Sirani, opposite, held a needle in her fingers, and in her lap lay some cloth upon which she had been sewing, but her expression was one of abstraction rather than absorption. She would sew busily for a while and then rest her hands in her lap while she gazed at the hearth with a concerned, somewhat worried, look. After a little she would shake her head shortly and quickly and work furiously again at her sewing.

Amos Lyle had already written ten pages of his letter, and it was not yet finished. It was to a certain pastor in St. Louis, David Walter. Lyle had never met Walter, but he had corresponded with him for a number of years, and he addressed him as a brother whom he had known always. A substantial gift of food had been forwarded to Armenia by the people of St. Louis, and Amos Lyle was expressing his thanks and the thanks of the children. As usual, these expressions ran to some length: he could not convey a sense of the gratitude felt without telling how the children had lived before aid came, and how they were living now. He had already told about their removal to Bartzan, and now he was telling how this city of children was organized, cared for, and managed by the young Russian, Markov, who had come to live with them.

When he came, however, to describe Markov to the Reverend David Walter, the swiftly moving pen paused. Lyle hesitated for words, and signs of agitation appeared on his massive face.

Who was this Paul Stepanovitch, and what were his purposes? Was he sent of God? Or was he sent of . . . ? The thought that Markov—or anyone else—could be sent of other than God was one utterly repugnant to Lyle, whose conviction it was that all things were of God and for His eventual glory. He had always looked upon Paul

Stepanovitch as one sent of God at a crucial hour, in a
time of great need, to finish the work which he had
begun, to fill out his inadequacies and make perfect this
work which God had given him to do.

But now, when he came to describe to the Reverend
David Walter, in terms of Christian service and disciple-
ship, what Paul Stepanovitch had done for the glory of
God, Amos Lyle hesitated. The young Russian did not
minister to these children in the name of Christ: freely
as Lyle had talked to him about his faith, he had never
got a response from Markov, and Lyle had never come
to the point—as he had with Markov's father—of the
direct question, "Are you saved?", of calling the young
man to redemption and salvation.

Could it be—the question obtruded itself despite the
missionary's resistance—that these children were being
saved and nurtured by one who did not believe in God,
who was unmoved by all the inspiration and injunction
of the Christian faith? And yet, if so, by what was he
moved, and by what hand was he guided?

The Apocalypse had been a portion of Scripture which
Lyle had never understood, and seldom read—his inspiration was drawn from the Gospels and the Epistles—but
the thought had crept into his mind, like a wolf in a
sheepfold, that Lucifer was arrayed like an angel, and
that Antichrist would come in the form of Christ. Could
it be possible that Paul Stepanovitch was . . . ? Again,
Amos Lyle, on the point of thinking the dread word,
rebelled with all the force of his spirit.

And yet, he could not go on with this letter until this
perplexing question was settled in his mind. Amos Lyle
had seldom struggled with doubt, but now doubt was
creeping in, like a noxious vapor through the crevices of
a wall.

Paul Stepanovitch seemed not only not to acknowledge
the will of God, but to be a living assertion of an independent will. He seemed to stand alone in his thoughts,
like Ararat, having connection with neither earth nor sky,
aloof, self-contained and self-sufficient, finding strength
not in prayer, not in submission to the will of God, but

from within, from a contentment in another will—his own.

Amos Lyle, in perplexity, laid his pen aside and turned to look at Sirani. Sirani was again gazing at the hearth, but at her father's movement she looked up at him.

"Father," she said, "you don't think anything has happened to Paul, do you?"

It was now ten days since Markov had left with Droghian.

"He is in the hands of God," Lyle said comfortingly, but the words did not comfort Sirani, upon whose face the look of worry increased. Lyle added hastily, "God will bring him safely home, I am sure."

"Do you think so, father? He is so good."

"Yes, he is good," said Lyle slowly. "He is good. . . . You are fond of Paul, are you not?"

"Oh, yes, aren't you?"

"Very."

Amos Lyle looked at his foster-daughter, lovely and serene, but now troubled, and he knew in his heart that she was no longer a child, but a woman. The thought gave him such mingled joy and sadness that his eyes dimmed.

"Yes, Paul is good, very good," he repeated. "Praise God for such."

He turned to his letter. Amos Lyle, who found comfort in resolution, decided quickly that if his Sirani found Markov good, then he was good; that if Sirani loved him, he was of God. He believed that goodness does not unite with evil, and that the love that awakens love is of God.

There was a noise at the outer door and the sound of quick, heavy footsteps in the hall; then the door to the sitting room was thrown open.

Paul Stepanovitch stood at the threshold, travel-stained, weary, but with eyes aflame.

At the sound of his feet in the corridor, Sirani had quickly laid aside her work and risen. Now, at the sight of Markov, her cheeks began to burn and her heart to quicken; but she did not speak, restrained by something she saw in his expression.

"Sirani," exclaimed Paul, and strode across the room.

"Pavil."

Markov had swept her into his arms, and was kissing her lips, her cheeks, her eyes, her forehead.

"Pavil."

"I love you, Sirani. I love you."

"Paul Stepanovitch," spoke up Amos Lyle, mildly disconcerted, "what is the meaning of this?"

"I love Sirani, Pastor Lyle. Have you not seen it in my eyes these months past, when I was too foolish to recognize it? You were my happiness, Sirani, my joy, my peace. Pastor Lyle, don't you see? I love her. Tell me we may marry."

Paul Stepanovitch continued to hold Sirani in his arms.

"Young man," said Amos Lyle, now quite embarrassed and perplexed by a situation of a sort he had not met before, and for which he could recall no remedy offered in Scripture, "it is our custom—I mean the American custom—to ask the young lady."

"Sirani, you love me, don't you? Tell me you do. I know you do. Tell me you love me."

"Pavil, I do. From the moment I saw you."

Paul Stepanovitch again took her in his arms and they clung together, oblivious of everything but each other.

Amos Lyle recovered from his momentary confusion and remembered the nuptial blessing.

"When do you wish to marry?" he asked.

"When Sirani is ready, pastor."

But Sirani was embarrassed now, and unable to speak.

"Then let it be after a fortnight," said Lyle, who intuitively recognized the urgency of love, and compromised between its necessities and respect for custom.

The wedding of Paul Stepanovitch Markov and Sirani Verian was a memorable event at Bartzan. Sirani had five hundred flower girls to attend her. There were dances without end. For the feasting a cask of hard candy— part of a donation to the Relief made by a Pennsylvania sweets manufacturer—was opened, and there were also cakes made of molasses and brown flour, and platters of pressed chicken—this last, by some happy mistake, had been mixed with a shipment of bully beef.

The wedding itself was celebrated in the open air—in order that the whole population of Bartzan might witness the ceremony—before an altar set in a bower of wild flowers and fragrant grasses to the making of which many loving hands had contributed. The children were seated on the grass, in groups according to their age and sex, divided by little pathways so that the "mothers" and patrol boys might move about to admonish the impatient ones and quiet those who were restless.

The children were, however, exceedingly well behaved, considering the occasion. They showed a genuine appreciation of the significance of the service. Its beauty they probably understood more than their elders, for they were not sophisticated and did not demand artificial adornment of that which is innately lovely. When Sirani came down the aisle between the banks of children, gasps of delight went up. She was dressed simply—a white dress, and a high coronet upon her head—but her face was radiant with a joy and beauty that needed nothing to enhance it.

"Isn't she beautiful!" "Just like the fairy princess!" "Isn't Sirani darling!" "Sirani's getting married. Oh, I'm so happy I could dance," were the appreciative and well-wishing exclamations that arose.

The ceremony was, of course, performed by Amos Lyle. His eyes began to moisten as he saw his lovely daughter approaching the altar, looking lovelier and more radiant than he had ever known her to look, and when he began to read the vows the tears dimmed his eyes so that he could hardly see the page. Impervious as he was to suffering, in the sense that he was never daunted by it, he was sentimental in the extreme at the sight of happiness, and this occasion was one of such joy as he had never known. He wrote of it later in a letter to James Lothrop of the Church of the Redemption, in Washington:

"You can imagine with what joy I beheld this new mark of Our Father's redeeming love. My Sirani, the circumstances of whose birth were so unpropitious—who while yet in the womb was encompassed with such storms of disaster as to make her appearance in the world a matter of doubt—who has been reared under conditions of stress and danger—a frail stem sprouting in a desert—who would have imagined, except those who know the Lord's goodness and infinite wisdom, such gorgeous flowering into womanhood, or such consummation of love? Of Paul, her husband, the same might also be said. What a regeneration I have witnessed in him these past weeks! He came to us cynical and disillusioned. He had not trust nor faith. But, miraculously, he has been touched by the grace of God. He has become a new man. He has become a Peter—no longer sand but rock—upon whom rests this great work we are carrying on. What joy it is to see his life fulfilled by his union with Sirani. For them both, my heart overflows with joy.

"When they stood before me, such was the radiance in the faces of both that it seemed as though the angels of the Lord were hovering in the air singing hosannas and covering us with their wings. After the service, as they returned down the aisle, man and wife, the whole gathering lifted its voice in song—four thousand children singing—

"Bartzan is a very happy place these days. I sometimes wonder if there are other places in the world as happy, as blessed of God."

To stand with him before the altar, Paul Stepanovitch had sent for Alexei Petrovitch Dosti to come from Erivan. Alexei was the only friend of the old days of whose whereabouts Markov had any knowledge. He had come by horse.

Alexei stood at the altar, erect, immobile, splendid in his colonel's uniform. This uniform was perhaps the only jarring note in the occasion, since the very sight of a uniform—even though that of their own country—raked the embers of fear in the hearts of many of the children. Though splendidly accoutered, Alexei's face was worn and tired, and worry was collected in pouches below his eyes.

He did not tarry after the festivities, hardly waiting until they were over.

"Why must you leave so soon, Aleisha?" Markov asked. "You have only just arrived. I want you to know Amos Lyle better, and I want Sirani to become better acquainted with you. Why do you leave at once?"

Alexei's gray eyes were sodden as he looked at him. Alexei was a man of intense moods, and at this moment he seemed to be carrying the load of Atlas.

"You have made a wise choice," he said sadly. "The fates have been kind to you."

"Fates?" smiled Paul, quietly. "Yes, the fates have been good to me. They have given me everything I couldn't get by my own efforts.

"But, come," he added gaily, slapping Alexei on the shoulder, "that's no answer. You're tired. I can see that. You have been drilling in the field too much. Why don't you stay awhile. You will find that the air here will do you good—it is fresher and more invigorating than at Erivan."

"Yes," sighed Alexei. "I know. Fresh and invigorating." He pulled himself together. "Pavil," he demanded, "have you forgotten all about the uniform and the army?"

"No, I have not forgotten about them. But I have no desire now. I am happy here with these children, and —my wife."

"Do you think you shall ever fight again?"

"By God," Paul Stepanovitch swore, "I hope not . . . I mean, I will not. I'm through with all that. I have a wife now. I will never leave my wife—as my father left his wife, and my grandfather his. And especially if there are children, I will not leave. It's a hellish life for a child to be brought up without a father."

"Do not be too sure that you will never fight," whispered Alexei. "Pavil, the wheel turns. But just between us, I should feel sorry. You have a wonderful prize in Sirani. I can see it in her looks."

"Thank you, Aleisha."

Alexei mounted his horse.

"But what do you mean about not being sure?" Paul Stepanovitch wanted to know.

"I mean that things are not going well in Erivan, or in Kars. No, nor anywhere—except here."

Paul Stepanovitch was concerned.

"What is wrong?"

"Maladministration. Ineptness. Communist propaganda." Alexei counted them off on his fingers.

"First," he continued, "there is the trouble with Georgia. Both governments are bumptious about their new-found sovereignty. Neither knows anything about diplomacy and negotiation; neither is willing to concede points. Diplomatic precedence, reciprocity of visas, and the like, are still unsettled. Then there are border incidents, and a boundary dispute. The fact is that Georgia is threatening to close the frontier. That would mean cutting Armenia's lines of communication with Europe by way of the Black Sea."

"That explains the delays in our last relief shipments," commented Paul Stepanovitch.

"Yes, if you've had trouble getting supplies, you now understand the cause of the delay.

"And now, second, the economic situation. Armenia is poor. How does this country ever expect to survive except as part of a greater whole? What does the country raise for export, in normal times—not to mention abnormal times like these? In normal times, some good cognac, some good rugs and fancy embroidery, generally a goodly supply of sheep casings and wool, as well as a few lambskins. Some dried fruits and nuts. What else? I can think of nothing. Yet the government goes ahead with magnificent plans for public buildings, parks, hydroelectric undertakings, industrial enterprises, as though it were a rich country like Germany."

"Well, the purse string is a good hobble," consoled Paul. "When taxes fail to come in, they will abandon such ideas."

"They might, if it weren't for the ineptness, which is my third point. I shouldn't be saying these things—it's disloyal. But you know me, Pavil, and you understand

I wouldn't say them to anyone else. But I've got to say them. It all goes against my grain. When things pile up and pile up, then I can't stand it. I'll explode. I don't understand these Armenians anyway—I mean the men," he apologized. "The women—well, a good woman is a jewel wherever you find her. But the men. They have marvelous ideas, I'll say that for them, but no practical experience in their execution. They discuss plans by the hour, and never come to agreement. I sit in at their conferences, until I grow wild. I want action or I must get drunk. One or the other. But they don't get drunk. They just argue, and finally they give orders, and the following day they countermand them.

"It's all theory with them—what is desirable—not what can be done with existing material. What is the result? Pavka, you would get drunk yourself. Supplies inadequate or late or misdirected. Orders countermanded, or never issued. Foundations for buildings laid, and no further work done. Alimentation failing. Sanitary services broken down, taxes levied but uncollected, public servants unpaid. And now there's popular unrest and discontent."

He paused rhetorically.

"Fourth—if you must have the list—where does this unrest lead to? To Communist propaganda and Communist success. Red agents are all through Armenia. They are now preaching openly. The government hasn't the nerve to stop them.

"And now, fifth. The Powers are gradually withdrawing their hand. But Armenia doesn't know it. They think they will receive aid should they be attacked. They know nothing of politics. They don't see that they are the dupes of the Powers, and that when Armenia no longer serves their purpose Armenia will be dropped like a hot chestnut. British and French prestige is all that supports the government now. When that is gone, the whole thing will collapse like a house of cards."

Paul Stepanovitch said nothing. He was thinking hard.

"Like a house of cards," Alexei repeated bitterly, slapping his boots reflectively with the tassel of his belt.

Paul Stepanovitch rubbed his hand along the flank of Alexei's mount.

"You are pessimistic," he said finally. "You are tired, and everything is brown to your eyes."

"As you will have it," responded Alexei, more easily now that he had unburdened himself. He was cheered at his friend's equanimity. "At least, I hope so."

"How will it crack?" asked Paul.

"Like an eggshell. Like a nut. Armenia is between the jaws. When the Turks and Reds get together, at that moment will the dam break. The Turks will pour in from the west, the Reds down from the north, by way of Baku and Azerbaijan. It's purely a question of which gets here first, how they divide the spoil, whether your children are to be spitted on Turkish bayonets or their souls burned out of them by the atheistic propaganda of the Reds.

"Well," he concluded, "maybe I have given you something to think about. Only I wish you were in Erivan with me. I would feel a lot better."

"I will see you in Erivan. I shall have to go there on business. And you have given me something to think about. But come to Bartzan when you can. It will do you good. You will find it like an elixir. I have."

When Alexei had gone, Paul Stepanovitch turned thoughtfully to his lodging—his and Sirani's now. Sirani met him not far from the gate.

"Come, would you like to walk, darling?" he asked.

Arm in arm they walked along, beyond the limits of the post, and out over the plain toward the Araxes. In the distance the lofty mountain of Ararat looked upon them, cool, serene, benign.

Paul Stepanovitch said nothing for a while, and then taking her in his arms, he said,

"Can you believe how much I love you?"

"Yes," she said gravely. "I know you love me. You have opened up a new world for me."

"I don't want to lose you now that I have you," continued Paul.

Sirani was thinking rapidly. Something that Alexei

had said had left her husband in a somber mood. It must be serious indeed to drive Paul's thoughts from her so soon after their wedding. She had no idea what it might be, but for herself she was certain that nothing could trouble her happiness, nothing could disturb her serenity. She wished that Paul might be equally impervious.

"What makes you think you may lose me?" Sirani asked.

"I want nothing to happen to you," said Paul earnestly, ignoring her question as well as her tone of assurance.

"Nothing will happen to me," said Sirani confidently. "Do you know what Alexei told me?"

"I am sure that it is nothing that can affect us."

"Why do you say that?"

"I don't know what Alexei said, but it doesn't matter. He may have talked about politics and troubles at Erivan. That is quite likely. He is in the capital, and that is where all the talk occurs. It is always that way. People in the cities are always excited about something. But what can happen to us?"

"A lot can happen if what Alexei tells me is true."

"I can speak only for myself, Pavil, but nothing, I am convinced, can happen to us."

8. The Menace

BARTZAN was prepared for the winter as well as any community of human beings can be prepared for what the future holds. During the autumn months, when the sun shone brilliantly and the air was alive with an early morning crispness, activity had been incessant.

The wheat had been sieved patiently by hand—with all the specks and grains of sand picked out one by one, the dust carried away by the wind—and now it was all carefully stored in sacks, in the granary, where it would keep dry and plump until needed. The cabbage crop had been gathered, the heads washed and chopped and then marinated for kraut in enormous vats which Mattios had fashioned. Root crops—turnips, potatoes, parsnips, carrots, and the like—were stored in long trenches dug below the frost line, where they would keep fresh throughout the winter. The carpenters had repaired all the occupied buildings, making tight the roofs and windows and door openings. Drains had been cleaned and flues inspected. In the work rooms, women had stitched many warm new garments for the children, and saddlers had made an immense quantity of shoes. In addition to all this, a goodly stock of supplies of the sort not to be provided locally—condensed milk, old clothes, medicines and hospital supplies, and other things of particular necessity—had been accumulated from the shipments that had now been coming regularly from America.

These gifts from America filled Lyle with wonder and gratitude at the goodness of God. As he phrased it, in a letter which he wrote about this time:

"The interest on the part of the American people, the outpouring of brotherly love, is to this troubled land like the moving of God's spirit over the waters, the parting of the waters and the appearance of the firmament.

"By these blessed gifts, the whole appearance of the country is being changed. A new day has dawned in Armenia. A whole nation is filled with gratitude to the Good Samaritan, America. . . ."

There were, indeed, many Bartzans now, scattered throughout the East. There were other Lyles and Markovs and Siranis devoting their energies to the relief of destitute children and harassed populations. From America and Europe had come these others, clad in gray whipcord, establishing their orphanages and refugee camps and feeding stations and hospitals and dispensaries in all parts of the East from Cairo to Samarkand, from the Black Sea to the Persian Gulf. In populous cities, in hamlets, in mountain valleys and desert plains, they worked and ministered; everywhere were the in-

ignia of the Relief—the White Star of hope to millions,
a star risen in the West to shine upon the darkness of
he East. . . .

Winter came to Bartzan, and with it Christmas and
days of festivities. One day was of course too short to
contain all the joy of the children; there were many
"little Christmases" celebrated before the "big Christmas," the actual Christmas. Every barracks building,
every chamber, was the scene of its own particular celebration; each group held its own watches, parties, exchange of gifts, and songs in preparation for the big
celebration on Christmas Eve in the long assembly hall.

Everyone was preparing gifts. A veritable deluge of
them appeared: gifts from the children to Amos Lyle
and Sirani and Paul Stepanovitch began to pile up in the
larger room which Lyle used for ceremonial occasions.
Navart, whose skill with the needle had become famous
at Bartzan, had made a long scarf for the table on which
Lyle kept his Bible, an exquisite piece of tatting and
drawn work on a strip of sheer muslin that had come in
one of the Relief shipments. Vartuhi, working at the
pottery, had fashioned and fired a pair of book ends,
representing a manger. Asta, who had shown an interest
in drawing, had designed a colored picture of the Three
Wise Men—most extraordinary Wise Men they were,
with miters on their heads and on their backs capacious
sacks filled with books and maps in addition to gold and
frankincense and myrrh. Haikanush's gift was nothing
tangible: it had no shape or color or smell; it was a song
which she had made up for the occasion and which she
sang for Sirani. It had to do with the birth of a baby,
in which the names of Mary and Sirani were inter-
woven. And from Andranik, who helped Mattios in the
carpenter shop, came a cradle for the expected arrival
in Paul Stepanovitch's household.

There were gifts, also, for the children, from far-distant
friends whom they had never seen. On Christmas morning every boy in Bartzan awoke to find in his bed a
brightly painted rubber ball; every girl, a rubber doll.

The donor of these was a New Jersey rubber manufacturer, a man whose business had been built by hard
work rather than by imagination. Nevertheless, he had
been touched by letters of Lyle's, read to him by a friend
with whom Lyle carried on correspondence, and he had
forthwith consigned a carload of his wares to the Caucasus as his contribution to the work of the Relief.

The climax of the celebration was, of course, the
Christmas Eve services held in the long assembly hall
for all the people of Bartzan. Amos Lyle's manner of
conducting a religious service well suited the temperaments of children; he was a minister who accepted the
Creed, acknowledged the Scriptures, honored the sacra-
ments, but believed not a whit in orders, vestments, rites,
litanies, liturgies and long sermons. All these latter he
adapted to the needs of the moment. As for orders which
involved his own authority as an ordained deacon and
priest, he was as much a Moslem as any Mohammedan:
he believed that nothing—neither priest nor man, nor
space nor substance—stood between man and God.

Christmas services were accordingly after the manner
of no Church nor rite, but were a mixture of old and
new, of Western and Oriental. The children had been
taught songs of the Western world—"Silent Night," "Tan-
nenbaum," "It Came Upon a Midnight Clear," "Hark
the Herald Angels Sing," "O Little Town of Bethlehem"
—but they also sang some of the melodic antiphonal
chants of the Oriental rites, chants that were ancient
when the Western world was young, that had in the
years lost none of their richness, their purity, and their
supreme devotional spirit.

Alexei Petrovitch had come from Erivan to celebrate
Christmas with the Markovs, and he stood and listened
to the singing of the children, the mass recitation of the
Psalm, and the reading of the Gospel story of the birth
of the Christ Child, as though he were gazing upon a
miracle.

Alexei was, on the whole, in better mood than he had
been on the occasion of the wedding, and as his stay

lengthened—he remained at Bartzan until after New Year's Day—he seemed to become almost gay again.

Seated around the fire one evening—Alexei and Paul and Sirani, while Amos Lyle sat in the corner, at his desk, writing letters—Alexei grew reminiscent. While the thistle roots blazed and crackled on the hearth he told amusing stories of army life, of the pleasant barracks days before the war, of adventures of his student years in Petersburg, before it became Petrograd, and then reaching further back into memory—for it seemed to be the effect of the fire and the quiet atmosphere to awaken dormant memories—he told incidents of his boyhood— of the time he slid down the mow into a nest of eggs which a setting hen had made in the hay, and how he had won a thousand walnuts in a guessing contest and become desperately sick from eating them.

The memories of boyhood aroused Alexei's dormant melancholy, and made him think again of the unkindness of his fate.

"I am like Lermontoff's Demon," he said. "Lonely, homeless, wandering in the empty, desolate spaces between heaven and earth. That is the curse of mankind— loneliness. Misfortunes, sorrows, sins and wickedness —they all congeal into loneliness. That is why Lermontoff has more aptly characterized the Evil One than Goethe or Milton. Goethe's Mephisto is cursed with cynicism; his sneering, superior contempt for all that is good and lovely is its own punishment. Milton's Satan is proud and defiant, and his arrogance is his fall. But our Russian Evil One, Lermontoff's Demon, has simply turned his face from fellowship, and for that he is lonely —the greatest curse of all."

He turned to Paul and asked, with affected humor,

"How does it happen, Pavil, that one like myself, who was so attractive to women as actually to be pursued by them, should at last be left in the lurch, while one like you wins such a prize?"

"It's because I have the need, Aleisha," protested Paul. "You talk of loneliness, but I die of it. You are self-sufficient—more than you think. I am not. I lack so many things, and Sirani supplies them. To each according to his need, you know."

"Oh, so you're coming to believe in Providence at last," laughed Alexei. "Because you are hungry, manna falls—in this case, Sirani. But I—I have no need, and so no white-winged angel comes my way?"

"Possibly," said Paul simply, stirring the fire.

The thistle roots crackled upon the hearth and showers of sparks flew up the chimney. In the glow of light that filled the room the faces of each revealed his mood and thought on this night: Amos Lyle, seated at his desk, his white hair falling over his bony forehead, one gaunt hand grasping a pen, the other resting on his knee, his face set in thought, but his eye alight with ardor and imagination, the whole giving an effect of engrossed majesty; Sirani, calm, seated beside the hearth, her eyes upon her knitting but raised now and then to look at her husband, as he spoke, with an expression of pride and happiness; Paul, contented, self-assured, pleased with himself and with life; Alexei, melancholy, with a kind of amused disdain of himself. Sitting directly in front of the hearth, the ruddy light of the burning thistle root illuminated every lineament of Alexei's handsome face —the lines of weariness, the pouches of dissipation under the eyes, the poetic, romantic sadness of his gray eyes, the prematureness of age showing in his thinning hair.

Sirani, lifting her eyes in pleasure over his appreciation of her, noted the signs of loneliness in his face and felt a compassion for him.

When Alexei returned to Erivan he wrote Paul Stepanovitch a letter, which Paul, because he did not wish to sadden his wife, did not show to her.

"When I go about this city," Alexei wrote, "I think of the retreat you have created at Bartzan—its peace, its quiet, the atmosphere of affection that envelops it, and above all its hope and promise for the future. Erivan is a city of old men; there is nothing here but senility and decay. Even the grandiose schemes of the administration seem like the visions and hallucinations of the dying.

"Though the Relief is doing much, conditions are indescribable. The wagon goes around each morning gathering up the dead: rottenness and filth fill the streets, mercifully covered over by a new snowfall. . . .

"People are hungry, but greater than the hunger of the belly is the hunger of the spirit. There are no children. In a way, thank God that you and Lyle have collected them out of the cities, for I do not know how they would survive. Yet how can age survive without children?

"I should leave, but Russian that I am, I have not the will. What can a soldier do but eat, and fill himself with food that the hungry need, clothe himself with cloth that the destitute want?

"You have created something at Bartzan. Yet when I think of it, I am filled with horror. At times it seems that you are arrogant and audacious—a Promethean pitting your will against the decree of the implacable Fates. You are to bring a new life into this world! You dare to offer a new mouth to be fed when there is already so little food. You dare to bring a new baby into this horror of horrors, and cast it upon the waters of trouble. May God have mercy upon you and forgive you for your presumption!"

The snow faded from the plain, and Bartzan shook off the coverlet of winter. Upon the brown earth appeared a patina of green, the reviving life of the earth. Where wheat had been planted the preceding fall, an emerald carpet appeared, which became thick and luxuriant under the influence of the spring rains. The winter had been hard at Bartzan, but not unendurable. Many of the children had succumbed to ailments contracted because of its rigor or because of bodies weakened by earlier privations, but still more survived, and the population of Bartzan had even been augmented by new waifs that had been gathered in by Amos Lyle.

With coming warmth, the plows which had been made at the forge and carpenter shop were broken out, and the moist earth was turned over to receive new seed for the summer crops. The big doors of the sheds were thrown open for the mellow sunlight to fall upon the looms and the benches, and the spinning women squatted with their spindles along the wall in the sunshine.

In May Haig Droghian's tribe returned from the plains of southern Persia, encamping again, as the year before, on the northern slopes of Ararat. When they had clipped their sheep and goats, Haig paid a state visit to Bartzan, bringing with him a long queue of pack donkeys laden with wool which he presented to Lyle.

During the succeeding months the tribesmen became a frequent sight at Bartzan. Their own labors over, now they could rest. During the migration northward the men had borne the toil and the strain of the journey—swimming the streams with the herds, carrying the exhausted lambs and kids up the steep slopes, packing their wearied children on their backs—and now it was the turn of the women. In camp, the routine labor fell upon them; they gathered the dye herbs, and churned the milk and spun and loomed the wool, while the men rode about on their horses watching the herds, or went hunting, or—in this case—visited Bartzan.

One of Droghian's young men fell in love with Badrani, a girl of sixteen whom Lyle had found homeless on the streets of Kars and had brought to Bartzan, and who was now "mothering" a brood of sixteen smaller children. Jared wanted to marry Badrani and take her to the tribal camp. He asked Haig's permission, and Haig asked Lyle, and Lyle consulted Badrani. Badrani admitted modestly that she reciprocated the tribesman's love. Accordingly, the marriage was performed; there was much ceremony and feasting, with food and presents from the black tents. But when Badrani came to take leave of Bartzan and bid her sixteen children good-by, she broke down in tears.

"Pastor, I would not have her unhappy," said Droghian. "Our tribe needs young blood; too many are lost on the long journeys. Let us have the children also."

And so Jared acquired a wife, and with a wife, an

extensive family. He proudly escorted his new possessions to the black tents and became the envy of the tribe. As property was communal, he received a tent suited to his requirements, and as the father of a large family he acquired importance in the tribe.

Haig Droghian came to Lyle.

"Pastor," he began, "we have many tents, herds and flocks, much cheese and butter stored in skins, and grazing land for all our needs. But of children, we are not so blessed. Some tents have no more than two or three, and many no more than four. Let us receive some of these fatherless and motherless ones. They are of our race, and our people shall receive them as their own."

Amos Lyle pondered.

"Our life is hard, but it is safe," urged the chieftain. "It is not like the life of the cities. We dwell in the tents, and the father sees his children from morning until night. We look upon children as a blessing, not as a curse, nor do we ask from whence this blessing comes. Let us have some of these children—as many as our tents will hold."

Amos Lyle was not unprepared for this request. Paul Stepanovitch had already, with excellent prescience, been giving thought to the ultimate disposition of their wards, and had discussed the possibilities with Lyle. It was admitted by both that Bartzan could, at best, be only a temporary home. The idea of a permanent orphanage was repugnant to Lyle; though such institutions were an accepted social method elsewhere, the thought of bringing children to maturity without the influence of a home was one which he could not contemplate. Paul Stepanovitch, who earlier had found a superficial satisfaction in the order and system he had introduced, had come to share this view. It was necessary to place the children in homes and under parental tutelage as rapidly as conditions would permit.

The coming of spring, with promise of harvests and more abundant food, and the continued quiescence of the country, despite the maladministration and the Com-

munist agitation, seemed to promise a rehabilitation of
the countryside—the return of the peasants from the
cities to the land, the reconstruction of villages, and the
restoration of peaceful routine. In such circumstances,
Paul and Lyle had believed it would be possible to find
homes for the children in the villages, with people who
themselves were bereft of children and who would take
them into their houses as their own.

The rehabilitation of villages, the repatriation of refugees on the soil, was, in fact, the next large program that
confronted the Relief, and to that end large quantities
of seed grain and farm tools were being assembled for
distribution. Paul Stepanovitch, whose work at Bartzan
was becoming widely known and respected, had been
called to Tiflis in February to attend a conference of
Relief administrators on the subject, and he had advanced
a number of well-founded suggestions.

Among the proposals that had appeared for the rearing of the orphans was that of removing some of them
to Persia, where various substantial colonies of Armenians lived and where the Armenian population had
enjoyed peace for many years. The proposal had been
tabled because of the objection of the Armenian government to losing any of its potential citizens, though it did
not appear how the government was prepared to care for
them. . . .

"This is not a matter for me, but for God, to decide,"
said Lyle, thoughtfully.

"Pastor, what do you mean 'for God to decide'?" Droghian asked impatiently. "Will He give me an answer out
of a thunderbolt? We want children. We will take care
of them, love them, make them as one of us. You have
them in charge. You can answer."

"No, I cannot. Though I am looking after them—after
a fashion, for it is really Paul and Sirani who do that—
they are not cattle, Haig, to be transferred by deed or
gift. You will have to ask them. Their childish hearts
are close to God. They will understand His will, and
answer to it."

"Oh," sighed Droghian in relief. "I think a good

spreading of *ghee* [goat's butter] on bread would tempt the Lord himself. They will come to the tents. . . ."

And so, whether in response to the will of God, or drawn by the prospect of plenty of *ghee*, within the month nearly two hundred children, male and female, found homes and parents among the Kargaseurs.

In June, Sirani was delivered of a son, ruddy and healthy and plump, who received the name Suren Palitch Markov.

In August, Alexei, on his way to Kars, where he had been transferred as colonel of a regiment of infantry, came to Bartzan for a short visit. When he saw the boy, laughing and playing with his toes in the warm sunshine, he pleaded forgiveness for all he had said.

"Ah, he is splendid," he exclaimed. "He draws your soul out."

He reached down and wiggled Suren's toes.

"Yes, something like that would be worth fighting for."

He sighed, and added:

"Worth dying for."

"Pray God there be no fighting nor dying over Suren," whispered Sirani.

"And so I pray," responded Alexei, "but pessimist that I am, I am afraid."

"Why do you say so?" Paul demanded quickly. While Alexei and Sirani were bending over the cradle, he had been sitting on his heels, tracing figures in the dust, in absent-minded preoccupation, raising his eyes every moment or so to take in—with the rapid, intent look of a sentinel—his wife and child, the grounds of Bartzan with all the varied activity, and beyond, to the great mountain rising serene and majestic in the distance.

"Why do you say so?"

The words were sharp, almost like a command.

"Well, for what other reason would they be sending me to Kars?" Alexei replied cynically, ominously. "If there's dying to be done, why, of course we mercenaries must do it."

"Nonsense," said Paul. "You talk as though a transfer read the same as a death warrant."

"No, it's more like slow poison, with agony at the end. The Turks are getting impatient, and it is likely that they won't wait for their partner at the kill. They don't trust the Reds; and if the Reds should break into the Caucasus, the Turks will be overflowing the borders next day. They are not going to let this rich prize go to the Soviets. And when they overflow, why, Kars is in their path, and Bartzan, and it will be just like another Flood—everything will go down before their fury."

Paul fidgeted.

"You talk too much, Aleisha," he said, glancing at his wife.

"Yes, of course," coughed Alexei, taking the hint, "and I'm pessimistic and gloomy—and a damn fool as well, or I'd have a nice wife like Sirani, and a son, and settle down. It's this barracks life that puts me down, and a change of barracks is just like going to a new prison, where you expect the worst."

"I understand, Aleisha," said Sirani. "There is danger —for us—for you. But please don't worry. Trust in God. Trust in God, please." Her voice choked and she could say no more. She turned to the baby and began to talk to it, while a tear coursed down her cheek and wet the pillow.

"I was delivered from the wrath when I was yet unborn, and even by a Turk," she said, talking more to herself or to the baby than to anyone else. "Surely God will be as gracious to my son."

9. Garabed Khansourian

GARABED KHANSOURIAN, whose services to the cause of Armenian independence had been long and indefatigable, had finally realized his ambition of a political appointment. When the new national state was organized, Khansourian had been rewarded by an advisory post and he had from time to time been the recipient of various honors, but he had never held a position of authority. He had been, for instance, a member of the Advisory Council on Public Education, a delegate to the Commission on Cultural Exchanges, chairman of the welcoming committee to distinguished foreign visitors, chief speaker at the Congress on Internal Developments. . . . But these honors, while they satisfied one's vanity, did not meet that urgent longing in Khansourian's heart to be in a position where he could do something for the welfare of his people besides talk and advise.

But political reward, if slow, is often ample, and when Khansourian's appointment came, it was, fittingly enough, as civil governor of Dilijan, the former Turkish *sanjak* in which he had spent his boyhood, and which now by grace of the treaties was included within the territory of the Armenian Republic.

Khansourian's first official act as civil governor was to decree the erection of a monument to the Armenians slain in the massacre of 1895. His second was to cause the Gapou, along the walls of which the shooting of the Armenians had occurred, to be razed. Since the Gapou had been the barracks and stockade of the former Turkish garrison, its destruction caused some inconvenience when it was later decided to post an Armenian garrison in Dilijan. Dilijan now lay but a few miles from the frontier between Turkey and Armenia, and there were increasing

rumors of Turkish forces massing in the neighborhood
in preparation for an attack.

Khansourian's third consideration on assumption of
his new duties was to select a uniform for himself be-
fitting the importance of his position. As civil governor,
he was under the authority of the military governor of
the province, and he had no military responsibilities that
would require a uniform; nevertheless, he was in charge
of the municipal police, and that, he thought, made a
uniform appropriate. Bari Pasha, he remembered, had
worn a certain amount of gold braid on his frock coat,
when he was governor of Dilijan. While Khansourian
would not think of aping a Turk, a plain frock coat was
of course too European. He finally selected, for his purpose, a coat of fine black broadcloth, that came to the
knees and buttoned tightly to the throat, like a military
tunic, with the coat of arms of Armenia worked into
the collar, and a cap of clipped lambskin. This uniform,
which gave him an impressive dignity, served as well to
conceal the portliness of his figure, which had been increasing with age.

These matters to which Khansourian gave his attention
were important apart from personal desire or whim. He
looked upon them as symbolic of the resurgence of the
Armenian nation and of its new dignity among the races
of men. Symbols were everything to Khansourian. He
lived in a land where symbols were the essence of life.
Had not the Roman emperors, noted for their tolerance
toward subject races and alien religions, insisted upon
the symbolic incense to Caesar? And had not the Christians been willing to suffer persecution and death rather
than render this same symbolic obeisance? Had not the
Christian world divided once on the relative appropriateness of images and portraits as symbols of the divine
character, and again, in the furious dispute over the
creed, as to whether Christ Himself were deity or the
symbol of deity? And who has not succumbed to this
same lure of the symbol? How many wars have not been
fought over flags and honors and precedence? And yet
is not the symbol itself something real? What are honor

and faith but symbols of the spirit? And morals, of the Universal Order? And perhaps God, the symbol of man's hopes and aspirations? Until we know ultimate reality, is not all existence but a symbol, an incense which is cast upon the altar of a Great Unknown? If all life should prove to be but a synthesis of symbols, must not the search for values be one of choice among the symbols, the selection of their relative quality and character and appropriateness?

Garabed Khansourian was walking in the outskirts of Dilijan one dewy morning in late summer, making an early inspection of some new precinct patrols that had been established. Of late, he had been giving considerable thought to the actual duties of the police. It was, indeed, a time and occasion for serious thought. In the old days the Armenians had been the predominant element in the population. Then, it had seemed an historical injustice that so populous an Armenian district should be governed by a Turkish minority. Now, the situation was reversed. In the decades just past, the district had been well-nigh depopulated of Armenians, and they were now a minority in a predominantly Turkish community. The Turks, though outwardly quiet under their new overlords, were growing restive. Every day new word came of the reviving strength of the Turkish government, and of threats of war to reconquer the *vilayets* that had been ceded to Armenia.

Garabed Khansourian was greatly disturbed by all this. He had discovered that it is one thing to be a member of a disenfranchised race agitating for power, and another thing to possess power and to be faced by a disenfranchised race demanding independence. He did not precisely know what measures he should take. It had seemed so pleasant, at first, to be returning to his native town as civil governor. He had looked forward to a resumption of the life and customs of those old days when Bari Pasha was governor—of renewing the soirées and receptions that Bari Pasha had been fond of holding and which Khansourian had attended as one of the leading Armenians of Dilijan—except that now it would be he instead of Bari Pasha who would be standing on the dais receiving the guests and beckoning the servants to serve the tea and sweetmeats. There had been a pleasant atmosphere to those gatherings: Khansourian recalled how he had talked gravely with Ibrahim Effendi the merchant, who had been everywhere and could quote the Persian poets without end, or with Assad Khodja, the ecclesiastic, with whom he would engage in polite argument over the respective attributes of the Christian God and the Moslem Allah. But they were all gone— Ibrahim Effendi and Assad Khodja; and so was Murad Bey, he who, Khansourian had heard, had befriended Miriam Verian in that awful day of massacre.

Those days were past. There was hunger now instead of abundance, ruins instead of the new public works Bari Pasha was so fond of starting, if never finishing, and strain and resentment and suspicion instead of contentment and insouciance and ease.

Garabed Khansourian had tried to revive the old spirit; he had tried to heal the wounds of war; he had tried to start new undertakings, to get crops planted and harvested, and to restore trade; but the task was beyond him. A new spirit was abroad; he could not quite fathom what it was, a spirit the old Turkish administrators had never permitted, or somehow had been skillful in holding in check. It was not only here, but everywhere; it came indeed, he suspected, from abroad—it was the thing he had sought in his youth, the gospel of individual freedom and self-determination nurtured by the democracies of the West. It was to have been the quickening leaven that would revitalize the ancient East, turn it from its somnolence and decay, and render it modern, progressive, alert. But this quickening leaven had become a malignant growth instead, a cancer of restlessness and insubordination.

It had begun long years before, with the first impact of Western democracy upon the peoples of Asia. Khansourian had found it, as a secretary of the Dashnak, wherever he had traveled; but he had not recognized its possibilities for destructiveness. He saw now how it had

uprooted settled ways and broken up the well-fitted ad-
justments by which diverse communities had existed side
by side for centuries in peace; how it had bred the ani-
mosities within the Turkish Empire that had led to the
massacres and spoliations; how it was not limited to Turkey, but was a devouring flame that had swept round
the world and was burning among every race and
people.

What was the answer to it all? Garabed Khansourian,
now that he sat on the governor's dais, was confronted
by this problem in a way that he had never been confronted before.

He wondered, as he walked along in the dewy morning, whether there was not something in the beliefs of
Assad Khodja, the *mujtahid*, that was eternally true, that
he had perhaps missed. Assad Khodja held that the
supreme duty of man on earth was *Islam*—submission to
Allah. Pastor Lyle, he remembered, seemed to hold the
same view, though Pastor Lyle's teaching had a lot of
other things mixed in with it, such as salvation of the
soul, seeking out the lost—and love. But Assad Khodja
had said simply *Islam*—submission to God.

Garabed Khansourian wondered if this generation did
not need more Assad Khodjas and Pastor Lyles. And
nervously he wondered how he should ever be able to
quiet the restive elements of Dilijan by calling them to
submission. He was not an ecclesiastic, but a political
administrator; his call must be that of submission to the
National Assembly of Armenia. How much contempt
did he already see manifest for the Republic among the
recalcitrant Turks of Dilijan—yes, even among the Armenians. Many of them were talking now of a Red
Revolution, a new government of the proletariat. The
soldiers themselves, who should be the most devoted to
the cause of the Republic, were showing disaffection.
He had had many talks with Major Dastian, in command
of the detachment at Dilijan, about this very situation.
Though as yet there were no desertions, the soldiers
were developing insolence toward their officers, and here
and there outright insubordination had appeared.

That was the chief reason why Garabed Khansourian had to give attention to the precinct patrols. They were manned by the municipal police, who were under his authority, and he took satisfaction in this, at least: the police were still loyal and devoted.

As Garabed Khansourian walked along, thinking of these things, he thought he heard the rumble of wagons in the distance. The air was filled with a heavy mist of morning, so that he could see no distance ahead, and he thought that some villagers were coming along the road with late produce. How pleasant, he thought, nostalgically, was the creak of the wheeled cart in the early morning mist. About him there was only the pearly grayness, like an aura, like a billowy carpet at the feet; only the muffled, distant sounds of awakening. Dilijan was a lovely city, thought Garabed Khansourian, its air so tender, its countryside so gentle.

Khansourian was now at some distance from the city, beyond his precinct patrols, and was in an open heath across which the road wandered. The mist, however, still clouded everything beyond the distance of a dozen yards; and he could only hear the rumbling, unable to make out what caused it.

The thought suddenly occurred to Khansourian that what he heard was not wagons, but caissons and artillery. He blanched. He had never heard the rumble of artillery, but he was certain now that this was what it was. It was artillery of the Turks! There was no mistaking it. He was on the road that led toward Trebizond, and if the Turks should be crossing the frontier it would be along this road that they would come.

Were there no advance patrols to give the signal, he wondered. Where were they?

He turned and walked rapidly toward the city. Almost immediately he broke into a run, and he ran until he panted heavily and his tongue lolled.

A military sentry challenged him.

"Garabed Khansourian, civil governor," he gasped. "The Turks are coming. Fire the alarm."

"I am under strict orders to give no signals unless I am certain."

"O God! It's the Turks."

"You may tell the captain of the watch."

"Where is he?"

"Up the road, five hundred paces," the sentry answered flatly.

Garabed Khansourian stumbled on. He did not find the captain of the watch. Perhaps he had passed him in the mist. He must hasten directly to Major Dastian.

He had not gone far before he heard the rifle of the sentry. It was immediately followed by the roar of a cannon. Stumbling, running, walking, running again, Garabed Khansourian hurried toward the town.

The report of the field guns was answered presently by a roar from the town, and then the air was full of excruciating sounds, sounds such as Garabed Khansourian had never heard before. A rattle like hail, and then a great shriek followed by the roar of an explosion. It was coming nearer, and now he could hear the confused shouting of men, and ahead, suddenly, a wall crumbled and broke into flame.

Garabed Khansourian fell flat on his face into a gutter. He felt he should move, but he could not, or did not dare—he knew not which. It seemed that nature itself had let loose fire and destruction. He thought, for a moment, that he was in the mountains, and he screamed to an imaginary companion that a rock slide was coming.

When Garabed Khansourian came to, men were running down the street with drawn revolvers, shooting all those whom they saw. He lifted his head and saw a man raise a rifle to his shoulder, fire, then shout and race on. Garabed buried his head in the angle of the gutter, and tried not to hear the scream that followed. . . .

Presently the artillery fire ceased. Garabed Khansourian wondered if the city were actually in the hands of the Turks. It was now day, but a wan, colorless day. He must have lain in the gutter a long time. The street was quiet now. He moved, found that he could rise, and got to his feet. His ankle was turned or broken, and

he could hardly bear the pain, but he must see wha
had happened. He was civil governor, and he could no
lie in a gutter.

He felt very miserable, very frightened. He was civi
governor, and he had been lying in a gutter while hi
city was being attacked.

But if Garabed Khansourian had continued to lie i
the gutter while the battle passed over his head n
doubt he would not have lost his life. If his race ha
been content with its prostration of a thousand years
the nation no doubt would have escaped the annihilatio
that now threatened. But the nation rose and asserte
its dignity as a nation, and Garabed Khansourian aros
to assert his dignity as civil governor.

He had not gone a hundred steps when a Turkish
soldier turned the corner ahead. He saw Garabed Khan
sourian in his uniform, with the coat of arms on the col
lar. He raised his rifle.

"No, no, no," screamed Garabed Khansourian. "Do no
shoot! Do not shoot!"

He felt a sharp stab in his chest and heard a soun
like the roar of water closing over his head. He felt hi
heart stop beating, and was suddenly frightened at th
thought. His knees buckled and he slipped to the street
while his life ebbed away like a wind dying in th
mountains. . . .

10. The Flood

"I WILL not again curse the ground any more for man'
sake. . . .

"While the earth remaineth, seedtime and harvest, and
cold and heat, and summer and winter, and day and
night shall not cease."

Paul Stepanovitch was thinking of these majestic

words of promise to man, as he stood in the rows of tall corn, and watched the harvest in progress. Listening to Lyle, he had absorbed more biblical lore than he had known in all his previous life.

Several large fields of late maize had been planted with seed supplied by the Relief, and though it was a product unfamiliar to the soil of Armenia, it had thriven, with rich long tassels and tall strong stalks, and finally with an abundance of plump ears. Since the harvest was heavy, and men were always scarce at Bartzan, several score of the Kargaseur tribesmen had, at Droghian's instigation, volunteered their services. The canny chieftain had quickly realized the possibilities of this new grain, and he had begged, as compensation for his men, a portion of the harvest.

All but the last field had been harvested, and the tribesmen, stripped to the waist, their rifles and other arms stored at the granary under the watchful eye of a sentinel, were in the field, going along the rows plucking and husking the ears and filling the panniers. As rapidly as the panniers were loaded, the willing donkeys carted them to the granary where the women were busy shelling the corn and storing it in bags. It was work to which the mountaineers were unaccustomed, but they took to it cheerfully. They were singing now, as Paul Stepanovitch watched them, and the odd, quavering notes of their song rose above the waving corn spears.

The corn crop was the last of a series of abundant harvests that had been gathered that summer at Bartzan. The seasons had come, according to the Promise, bringing their gifts; days and nights had passed in perfect procession, dewy mornings and golden evenings, and each had been fuller of peace and contentment than the last. Joy filled the hearts of those at Bartzan, like wine in a chalice, bubbling in the songs of the men in the field, in the humming of the women at their work, in the laughter of the children on the playgrounds.

Until three mornings before, Paul Stepanovitch's heart had been filled with the same joy as the others. It had seemed to him that never was there such happiness as

he found in the companionship of his wife, in playing
with his son Suren, in the fruitful work in which he was
engaged.

But three days ago word had come to him—privately
thank God; no one else had yet heard it—that was like
a cold finger upon his heart, chilling his life blood. The
Turks, in violation of the treaty into which they had
entered with the Republic of Armenia, in violation of the
peace settlement at Sèvres, which they had signed with
the Allied Powers not three months ago, had suddenly,
and without warning, begun hostilities. An army of fifty
thousand men, so the word was, had crossed the frontier
on a wide front, and was advancing, apparently unop-
posed, toward Kars.

The Turkish commander under whose orders this warfare had begun was Hashim Farouk Pasha. Hashim
Farouk had risen high in the Turkish service during the
War: Markov had heard his name many times, before
coming to Armenia, as one of the most resourceful and
redoubtable of the Turkish generals opposing the Russians. Hashim Farouk had been one of the master minds
in the massacres and deportations of the minorities during the War. Since coming to Armenia, Markov had
learned of Farouk's part in the massacre of Dilijan.

As yet, however, the word that had come to Markov
of the Turkish invasion was unconfirmed. It was possible
that the Turkish movements had been exaggerated, that
what had occurred was no more than a border incident.
Bad news enlarges as it travels. It was impossible that
Turkey, weakened as it was by the War—the general
reports were that the country was in almost as great a
state of anarchy and disintegration as Russia after the
Revolution—would dare risk the conflict with the powers
of Europe which would certainly follow an attack upon
their protégé Armenia.

Moreover, the Armenian army at Kars was substantial,
well-equipped and well-trained. It was certainly vigorous
enough to withstand any force which the Turks could
muster and send against it.

Markov took what cold comfort he could from these

thoughts, while he continued his work in the field, but the pessimistic warnings and prophecies of Alexei Petrovitch kept recurring to him. Could it be possible that he was being too hopeful, too sanguine? Could it be possible that he had been lulled by the peaceful atmosphere of Bartzan into a false sense of security?

While he walked up and down the rows of standing corn, the boy Andranik hastened to him from the barracks, a letter in his hand.

Paul Stepanovitch tore open the envelope. It was a letter from Alexei.

"I beg of you," it read, "if you cherish the independence of this little country, if you cherish the safety of your wards, of your wife and son, come and join us in the defense of Kars. . . .

"I cannot overstate the gravity of the situation, or the need of your services. Propaganda has undermined the spirit of the men. They have lost the will to fight. You could inspirit them. Everyone knows of Markov of Bartzan. Truthfully, for you to come to Kars would be to the men like the appearance of St. Michael with his flaming sword.

"The Turks are now some thirty miles away and no considerable force opposes their march on Kars. They are making a clean sweep of everything, burning villages, killing the inhabitants down to the last child.

"The fortress is impregnable, if properly manned, and the defense intelligently directed. The equipment is excellent and the magazines are full. The question is one of *esprit* and morale—the quality of will shown by the defense. . . .

"General Bazian hopes you will come. He knows of this letter."

Paul Stepanovitch stood a long time staring at Alexei's letter, reading and rereading its contents, as though he could not grasp its import. Finally, he looked up, and saw the tribesmen plucking the ears from the standing corn.

Haig Droghian alone, with a contempt for the accustomed ways, carried a long knife in his hand, and with it slashed the ears from their stalks, vigorously, violently, as though he were striking the heads from his enemies.

"Haig Droghian has kept to his path," Paul Stepanovitch thought, "while I have strayed."

His eyes fell upon the mountain beyond, across the plain, serene and unperturbed, its massive shoulders draped in a cloak of new-fallen snow.

"You're a mocker," he said to himself, "a mocker and deceiver of men. There's no such thing as peace; the idea that God is going to protect us is a chimera, a lie, a delusion."

He shook his shoulders with a violent movement and called to Droghian.

"You have always trusted in arms and might," he said, when the chieftain came up. "There is need for them now."

Markov's face was pale with resolution.

"No," protested Droghian, "it is just when I am on this side of the Araxes that I trust in arms. On the other side, I don't need to."

"Well, never mind," Paul Stepanovitch replied, clipping his words in his old-time military manner. "You're on this side now. Would you like to go to Kars with me?"

"For what purpose?"

"To fight the Turks!"

The words came out like the bark of a rifle.

"The Turks?"

Haig Droghian's face was full of consternation.

"Yes. They have invaded Armenia and are now outside Kars."

Haig Droghian took a deep breath, and then his teeth showed in a broad smile.

"There's nothing I would like better," he exclaimed, thrusting the long knife into his belt for emphasis. "When do we start?"

"Now."

Droghian called his men from the field, and they left the corn standing ripe for the harvest.

Paul Stepanovitch went to Sirani. He told her the contents of Alexei's letter.

"I shall go to Kars," he concluded. "There is nothing one can do here."

"Nothing?" questioned Sirani. Her face was pale, and she twisted her fingers nervously.

"Nothing. We might throw up earthworks around the post, but with neither men nor arms, they would do no good. Kars is where the stand must be made. The thing will be settled at Kars, and every available man should be there."

"Is that the only way?" Sirani questioned again. It was not so much a question as an attempt to realize the fact for herself.

"Yes. It must be decided by force of arms. If the Turks are not held back, there will be none of us left alive."

Sirani said nothing, but gazed into blankness, while she bit her lips and tried to repress her tears.

"I am going now," said Paul Stepanovitch.

Instead of reply, Sirani slipped down on a little ottoman. Paul saw that her lips were moving, but he could not hear what she said. He bent over her, putting his arms about her. He heard her whispering,

"'Lord, my heart is not haughty, nor mine eyes lofty. . . . Surely I have behaved and quieted myself, as a child. . . .'"

The words became inaudible. Sirani's face grew pale. Paul thought she might faint.

"Darling," he exclaimed, "if you do not wish me to go, I will stay."

Sirani was crying.

"Pavil dear," she said, forcing the words through her tears. "If you see it as your duty, then God wills it so. You wish to see Suren?"

"Yes."

Suren was asleep in his cradle when Paul and Sirani came in.

"Shall I wake him?" Sirani asked.

Paul looked at his son. The child's face was peaceful, the arms thrown back in characteristic infant pose, the tiny hands lying alongside the head, the little fingers half unclasped, half covered by wisps of golden brown hair.

Paul watched the baby's soft, rhythmic breathing.

"No," he said, "let him sleep on. If I don't—"

He did not finish the sentence, but drew Sirani outside.

"You go now?" she asked, her voice barely audible.

For reply, Paul took her in his arms and crushed her in his embrace, kissing her passionately, while tears blinded his eyes and wet her cheeks.

"Darling, I must go. Forgive me if it is the wrong thing."

A whistle sounded outside.

"Kiss me again, darling," Sirani said.

"I love you. I love you," he answered.

"Then nothing can matter."

Paul Stepanovitch and the tribesmen reached a village by the name of Goven, some ten miles from Kars, about dusk. Certain that their appearance at Kars after dark would alarm the sentinels, they decided to bivouac for the night and ride into the fort early the following morning.

While they were rubbing down their mounts—it had been hot and dry and the flanks of the horses were caked with brine and dust—Haig Droghian remarked,

"The air is thick. Rain is coming."

"It may as well rain. The crops are harvested."

"I care not about the crops, but rain in this season would be extraordinary. See how hot the horses are."

Markov was much more concerned about reaching Kars.

"So much the better," he said. "A good rain might stall the Turkish advance."

"Yes, and cut off retreat."

"Let us not talk of retreat," said Paul, pressing his lips together.

They set forth the following morning, while it was yet dark, under an overcast and lowering sky.

"It will rain," said Haig again, somewhat uneasily.

Paul Stepanovitch heard a sound which he was quick to recognize. It was a sound not unlike distant thunder. Haig heard it, too.

"It is raining in the mountains. Should it continue, Araxes will run full."

"That is not rain," said Paul, lifting his reins and allowing his horse to canter. "That is artillery. Surely the Turks can't be . . . ?"

He did not finish the words, for his horse broke into a gallop. They were on rising ground, and in a moment were at the top of the ridge.

In the distance lay the city of Kars, revealed by the dawn, as though a coverlet were being removed, shimmering in rose and ocher as the morning sun fell across the housetops. It lay in an atmosphere of profoundest peace. No movement was visible save for the wisps of smoke that rose in little puffs along the walls of the fortifications. From a fringe of field and orchard across the meadows answering puffs of smoke arose. The breeze was now against the city, and no sound came to those on the ridge; but presently the wind shifted, and the muffled roar of cannonading mingled with the rattle of machine guns and the crack of rifle fire became audible.

"The battle has begun," shouted Haig Droghian, and spurred his horse. "Come, let us have a part in driving back the Turks. We can reach the city from the other side."

"We're too late," said Paul Stepanovitch, without moving. "We would only run into the mouth of the pit. Look."

Droghian reined up his mount. Before their eyes was being enacted the prelude to the tragedy of Kars. The smoke from the fortress's batteries ceased, and at the same time men began to appear above the banks of the irrigation ditches. They advanced upon the city, slowly, mechanically, at even intervals, as though they were beads strung on wire. Long thin lines of them were now strung out over the basin before the city. They advanced without hindrance or opposition to the suburbs of the city, and disappeared among the walls and gardens like so many ants. On they came, endlessly it seemed, swallowed up by the walls and gardens of the city.

And now the party on the ridge could see the inhabitants of the city in flight along the Kutai road—the road they were upon. The roar of the cannon subsided, but as the wind died a horrible noise was borne to their ears. It was no precisely describable sound; on other occasions it might have been taken as the noise of revelry or the orgy of carnival, in which the sharp crack of rifle fire—which was the only recognizable sound—would seem to be that of exploding fireworks. But this sound was the mingling of women's cries and soldiers' oaths, the screams of the assaulted and the groans of the dying, the shouts of exultant victors and the pleading of the vanquished, all blended and confused and borne upon the air, to the utter stars, as the echoes of Walpurgis night might reach the tormented ears of this world.

"We must turn back," said Paul urgently. "They will press on toward Erivan, and Bartzan lies across their path. Unless we take measures. . . ."

He could not finish the sentence. What measures could they take? What defense could a hundred mountaineers offer? He could see what would happen as though he beheld it now before his eyes. Raiding parties of Turkish cavalry, or Kurdish irregulars, or even detachments from the main force, would descend upon Bartzan, would demand food and provisions, would find a pretext for insult, and an opportunity to vent their hatred of the Armenian and then the orgy would begin, a release of hatred and blood lust and sadism.

They turned back, riding silently, dejectedly, dispiritedly. The weight of their mood was increased by the heaviness of the atmosphere and the thunderheads that formed and re-formed in black tumbled heaps along the southern horizon. By and by clouds began to pass overhead, like crawling, bloated spiders, and the sun became obscured and the sky gray. The day grew sultry and close, the horses gathered lather about their harness and smelled of salty sweat. A rain would have been a welcome relief, as tears to assuage sorrow. But it did not rain.

They halted toward noon near a Roman ruin, where once had been a garrison post of the early Empire. Shade was afforded by a grove of trees and water bubbled from a well—bubbled as it had bubbled, no doubt, since the days of Pompey.

Ruins. Paul thought of all the ruins he had seen—and made—and wondered if that were not the ultimate purpose of life—to create and to bring ruin. What hope was there, ever, of erecting anything enduring, of building a house or a character that would survive? Was this —to die—the hopeless destiny of man? . . .

They stopped again at sundown for a brief rest and then, remounting, pushed on, arriving at Bartzan toward midnight. While the men stabled their horses, and spread their pallets in the loft, Paul went in to his wife.

"Paul, is that you?" Sirani asked. "God be praised."

They clung to each other for a time, while Paul's cheeks were wet with his wife's tears.

"I knew you would come back safely. I knew it."

She was stroking his cheeks and hair.

"Let me light a lamp so that I may see you."

Paul found a match and touched it to the wick. In the pale yellow light he thought he had never seen her look so lovely—her hair upon the pillows, like a net in which the lamplight was caught; her eyes as soft and gentle as the dawn; her skin like snow at eventide.

How could he tell her of their desperate situation?

"Sirani," he began, looking at her from above, "Kars has been taken."

Sirani did not seem to comprehend, for her only reply was to hold out her arms to him.

Paul, with sudden anguish, fell to his knees beside the bed and buried his face in Sirani's bosom, like a frightened child.

Presently, Sirani arose and, clasping Paul to her, said, "Let us go to father and talk with him."

Amos Lyle, who had heard the sound of the returning

horsemen, was awake and dressed when they knocked at his door.

"Let us read the Bible," he said quietly. "It is always a good prelude to mighty action or decision."

He took the book, which was always within his reach, and opening it haphazardly and settling himself, he began to read.

At another time Paul would have regarded this as the mark of an old man's dotage, as a superstitious rite of propitiation to which he was superior. Now, he listened with intent ears and expectant heart, like some ancient devotee before an oracle. The sense of defeat and personal insufficiency had burned down to a coal; no longer was he beaten to submission; there were within him a peace and confidence, like that induced by early dawn, by morning on the slopes of Ararat.

Amos Lyle had found a passage, and began to read:

" 'I will lift up mine eyes unto the hills, from whence cometh my help.

" 'My help cometh from the Lord. . . .' "

Paul's thoughts were not flowing rapidly; they lingered on each word that Lyle read, for they were for the most part unfamiliar words to him, and they awakened images that were new, yet somehow, in some fashion, old and familiar. His conscious mind lingered on the images, while his subconscious mind flowed ahead with the reading. Vaguely, he heard the rest of the passage:

" 'The Lord shall preserve thee from all evil: he shall preserve thy soul.

" 'The Lord shall preserve thy going out and thy coming in from this time forth, and even for evermore.' "

Amos Lyle closed the book.

"Shall we pray?" he asked, as he kneeled down by his chair. Sirani followed his example, naturally, easily; her husband, with a certain unaccustomedness.

"Our Father in Heaven," Lyle prayed, "we are Thy children, willingly Thine and obedient unto Thee as our strength and will confirms and permits. We love and worship Thee who art our strength and salvation, and the sweetness of our lives, our joy and our peace. . . ."

Paul heard all this in a dreamy reverie, in a mistiness of the mind in which all things blended, though not completely, and were harmonious, though not entirely so. Some faint voice within aqueous, pellucid depths, like a cry in a cavern, muffled by its own echoes, asked, "Can this be possible, that a man who has been buffeted so much by circumstance, can find such joy in the contemplation of the author of all his misfortunes?"

But all the time the more conscious parts of Paul's mind still clung to those first words upon which his attention had been fixed:

"I will lift up mine eyes unto the hills, from whence cometh my help."

The image of a hill had formed in Paul's mind, an image which at first was vague, and then became more clearly defined, and assumed the shape of various hills that Paul had known. . . .

Amos Lyle prayed on. It was a long prayer, for he had, as always, much to say to his God—praise of His name, sins to confess, confidence in His justice, trust in His care, joy in His love. . . .

"And now, our Father, give us wisdom to understand Thy will for those whom Thou hast committed to our care, and submission to accept Thy will, and strength to do Thy will in this matter. . . ."

Paul's head had not been bowed during this long prayer, though his attitude had been respectful, and now his eyes were directed toward the window and the scudding clouds of the sky. The moon was full and its light shone brilliantly upon the clouds, turning them into purple boats with silver sails. The clouds were scattering now and in the distance—

"Ararat!" exclaimed Paul, rising.

Amos Lyle halted in his prayer and looked at Paul mildly.

"Yes, Paul?"

"Ararat! God answers our prayer! We will take the children over into Ararat. Ararat is our refuge! The Turks will not follow us there. Ararat!"

"What do you mean, Paul? We cannot take four thou-

sand children across the Araxes on to Ararat," protested
Lyle.

"Of course we can. It is the only thing to do, and we
can do it. We can take them to hell, and back, if
necessary."

He paused, his jaws clamped together, his lips compressed, and then he added:

"By the grace of God."

"By the grace of God," echoed Lyle.

"Then, Ararat."

"Ararat."

Lyle's great cracked voice broke into a hymn.

> *"'God is my strong foundation;*
> *What foe have I to fear? . . .'"*

Paul Stepanovitch arose and quietly drew his wife
outside, while Amos Lyle continued to sing, swaying back
and forth, contentedly, confident that all troubles were
past:

> *"'What terror can confound me,*
> *With God at my right hand?'"*

11. The Deliverance

PAUL STEPANOVITCH did not go to sleep again that night.
Work had to be done, much work, if the extraordinary
plan he had conceived was to be carried out. From the
summit of Ararat he had viewed the land of Persia, which
came up to the base of the mountain on the south. He
had seen the prospect and the path. Twice yearly Haig
Droghian and his tribe followed the trail over the
shoulder of the mountain in the passage between summer
pasturage on Ararat and winter pasturage on the plains

of southern Persia. Soon, the tribe would again be taking that route.

What Paul Stepanovitch proposed to do was to transport the children over to Ararat, and thence south into Persia, safe alike from Turk and Bolshevik. There were Armenian communities in the Persian cities—Tabriz, Mervend, Urmiah—and there it would be possible to place the children among settled communities where they might be brought up in families and according to their own traditions.

Yet between Bartzan and the haven to the south lay obstacles the most forbidding—the passage of the gorge of the Araxes, the barren, uncharted foothills beyond, and Ararat itself. It was an exhausting journey for men on horses, as he had discovered on his journey to the encampment of the Kargaseurs, and would be one of multiplied hardship for so many children. If, however, they could reach the second band of Ararat—the grassy plateau where the nomads pastured their flocks—he had confidence that the rest of the journey south could be made in safety.

But to reach Ararat with the children, to bring them that far safely, was a task that called for every skill he possessed, all the foresight, all the capacities for organization and administration which he could command. His first concern was that of transport, both for the small children and for the food and water they would need on the journey. His second was the need for haste. What he must do must be done now, regardless of his weariness and fatigue.

It was three o'clock, and Bartzan lay under a sheen of moonlight. Paul awakened Mattios, and asked him to assemble all the workmen in the post.

"Yes, Paul Stepanovitch," said the old man, throwing off his coverlet, "I will see that they are roused."

Presently workmen began to appear, sleepy-eyed, squinting in the dazzling moonlight, drawing on their clothes as they came. While they stood before him, Paul told them about the disaster at Kars, of the threat to Bartzan, of his plan for flight.

"Yes," he continued rapidly, as the men sought to

interrupt him with exclamations and questions, "it will be hard, but on Ararat lies safety. You are willing to go?"

"Yes, *baroon*. Yes, *baroon*," a hundred voices answered.

"Then to work. Provisions and grain to be sacked. Many more pack saddles and panniers to be made, for we can't use the carts. Packs for strong backs—every man, every boy, every robust woman and girl must carry a pack. These must be made. Our goats and sheep we will take along also."

The men went to work. When early morning came they were joined by the women. The sun appeared on the eastern horizon and rolled a golden mist across the plain; the children awakened and the smoke from the breakfast fires began to curl up in little wisps. The work went on. The children, to whom the urgency of the situation was communicated, lent their energies to the task.

There was need for all this help. A well-equipped army may be able to move at an hour's notice, but four thousand children are not an army and they had not been equipped for travel. Among the children at Bartzan were babies hardly out of their swaddling clothes, little ones just learning to walk, pubescent ones with gangling legs, and robust, almost mature, adolescents.

All of them were doing their part—the youngest gathering up their treasured belongings, older girls watching the babies while the "mothers" hurried anxiously about, packing blankets and clothing, older boys helping the men wherever they could, others just doing their best to keep out of the way and restrain their curiosity, their excitement, their fears.

All morning the work went on.

Toward noon, Petros, one of Haig's men who had been riding scout duty, galloped in off the plain.

Haig hurried to Paul Stepanovitch.

"A party of Kurds is on the Kars-Erivan road. Shall we go out and give them a fight, Paul Stepanovitch? There are about two hundred of them. We can beat them. We can at least keep them from coming on to Bartzan."

"No," said Paul decisively. "We need every man here. If the Turks come in this direction, there will be time then for fighting. But we must trust that they will go on by. Post Petros again to watch, and keep me advised of their movements."

The word that the Kurds had been seen ran over Bartzan like fire in dry grass, and imparted a new quality to the activity—an urgency impelled by terror. Mattios hobbled here and there as he supervised half a dozen different pieces of work going forward at once. Haig's men, skillful from many migrations in the art of packing, worked deftly and were a mighty aid—save that now they refused to lay aside their arms and were greatly encumbered by them.

By nightfall much had been done, but much remained to be done. The work continued by lamplight until toward midnight, when at last everything seemed ready for flight, and Paul, who had seen no sleep for forty hours, lay down for a moment's rest.

The sun arose to behold the last breakfast at Bartzan. The children were assembled by their groups, with their guardians, and Amos Lyle spoke to them briefly.

"We are going," he said, "on a long journey. It will be tiring, but we shall go easily, so that you will not get overly fatigued. Do you know what we shall be like? We shall be like the children of Israel as they marched out of Egypt. The Araxes will be the Red Sea, and beyond the Araxes lies the Promised Land.

"We shall go forth by tribes, for the tribes of the Children, you remember, all had their appointed duties on the journey, and they encamped by tribes. And God will go before us, and we will trust in Him to guide our footsteps. As the Psalmist David says, 'The Lord is my shepherd; I shall not want . . . he leadeth me in the paths of righteousness for his name's sake.' And as he says in another place, 'He shall give his angels charge over thee. . . . They shall bear thee up in their hands, lest thou dash thy foot against a stone. . . .'"

At the close of his talk Amos Lyle led a prayer, and then the assemblage sang the Armenian words of "A Mighty Fortress is Our God."

Then, in the golden sunlight of the early morning, the children, with their mentors and protectors, set off for the Araxes and Ararat. In parties they went along, not according to age, but according as they might help each other. Little children were accompanied by the larger boys, to help them when they grew tired, to give them a drink from the water jugs they carried, to share the food in their knapsacks when the time for the mid-morning repast arrived.

The rear was brought up by the pack animals, and the goatherds and their flocks. The pack animals carried a variety of freight—babies in panniers that hung on the sides of the saddle, sacks of flour, tinned lard and milk, as much as could be transported.

A long procession it made, stretching across the plain in the direction of Ararat, like an enormous caterpillar, with the great mountain, resplendent and familiar in the clear morning air, seeming to beckon them on.

It was not high adventure and there was no gaiety, but songs and chatter rose into the air. Amos Lyle and Sirani were busy up and down the line of the procession, talking to the children, encouraging those who grew tired, telling them stories as they went along, starting new songs.

As for Paul Stepanovitch, he was, as usual, watching with eager eyes all the arrangements of the flight, seeing that the herders let no goat stray, that the pack saddles did not gall the backs of the donkeys, that the children who showed signs of exhaustion were lifted on to the backs of the men. He called for frequent rests, and since the more robust of the children had additional energy for play and wandering, he was careful to have a thorough count made after each halt.

The morning advanced; the day grew warm; the clear skies of dawn became opaque and gray; the air lay close and warm and stagnant upon the plain. It was not many miles to the Araxes, but the long train was creeping at a sluggard's pace, almost motionless it seemed to Paul Stepanovitch, whose anxiety was increasing momentarily.

Haig Droghian, who was in the van, leading the way,

fell out and waited for Paul to come up. His lips were thrust out in a pout and his bushy eyebrows half concealed his eyes contracted in a frown.

"Paul Stepanovitch, can we not go faster?" he wanted to know. "Those clouds mean rain."

He pointed to a ridge of purple black that had formed upon the western horizon.

"It will not rain, Haig," Paul replied reassuringly. "A shower, a local thunderstorm perhaps—no more. You know yourself that this is not the season for rain."

"The ways of the rains are not predictable, any more than the way of a goat returning to the fold. Every night they return, following the same path along the hillsides. Then, on a day, one goes astray. Why? Every year the rain comes in the spring, but this is a year of years. Since when, before last year, did we camp on the northern slopes of Ararat?"

"You are rightly concerned, Haig Droghian, but it will not rain—not before we have crossed the Araxes."

"So said the children of men in the time of Noah— 'It will not rain'—but God said 'Let there be rain' and there was rain. It will rain now, Paul Stepanovitch."

"We can only push on as fast as we can, as fast as the strength of the children permits."

The ridge of thunderheads along the horizon began to stir, like a sea rippled by a breeze; gradually the clouds became tempestuous, rolling up into portentous shapes, subsiding and mounting again, ever in new and more threatening forms. Toward midafternoon a gentle breeze sprang up, cool and refreshing. At the same time the thunderheads broke their bounds and, like an onrushing sea, swept over the sky and curtained the world in purple.

Haig Droghian came again to Paul Stepanovitch, running.

"Paul Stepanovitch," he shouted. "The wind. It is raining yonder. We must hasten, or Ararat is closed to us."

"Yes, Haig. I understand. I will pass the word along."

Paul hurried along the line, speaking a few words to each group leader. He did not wish to alarm the children, but it was vital to hasten them along the road at a swifter pace. He came to his wife, who was walking beside the donkey that was bearing Suren in one of its panniers.

"Darling, is the baby all right?"

Leaning over the pannier, he spoke to his son, who was asleep, and then turned to his wife:

"Sirani, we must go faster. Can you start the children singing again? There must be no panic."

Sirani started the song, "Onward, Christian Soldiers."

They were not many miles from the gorge now, and as the procession took up the song, the movement of the line perceptibly quickened. They swung along at a rapid pace. When the younger ones began to falter, the men picked them up, sometimes carrying one in each arm; and all the while the marching hymn continued to roll from a thousand throats.

At last they reached the Araxes, but they were still above the ford, which lay some miles downstream. From the edge of the gorge the water below appeared a muddy red, marked with little eddies.

"We can never reach the ford, Paul Stepanovitch," Haig exclaimed. "It is hopeless."

"Then let us try to cross here."

"As you will. But should we be in the gorge when the waters descend in a wall, as I have seen them descend, all will perish."

At this Paul paused. Should he make the attempt? Or should he return the children to Bartzan? He looked back across the plain. He could not see the post, which was hidden by the contours of the plain, but where Bartzan should be he thought that he could see a faint trail of smoke ascending.

Even as he looked, he saw Petros, the scout, riding in from the trail. When the tribesman came up, he leaned from his lathered mount to whisper,

"The Turks. They are at Bartzan."

"Many of them?"

"Not many, but enough."

"Then we must go on, Haig, and we can only pray that God will be merciful to us. Can we find a way down?"

"It is possible. Some of my men will go ahead and mark the way."

"Mattios," Paul called. "The ropes."

Mattios and two of his helpers unloaded the coils of thong that Paul had provided against such an emergency.

A dozen tribesmen started down the wall of the gorge, stretching the ropes along as they went, wrapping them about tree stems and jutting rocks for a guide to the children.

The way was steep and treacherous. Gravel showered down and rocks went bounding under the feet of the men. One of the tribesmen slipped and went sprawling down the slope, until the rope about his waist caught him up and held him fast.

As rapidly as the men marked a path and strung the cords, Paul Stepanovitch sent the children down. The larger boys—the "guardians"—he stationed at intervals along the path, clinging to the ropes, to take the hands of the smaller children and help them down. At wider intervals, and on the steeper declivities, he placed the men.

Slowly, but safely, the descent was made. The last child reached the valley floor, and Droghian, from below, called the number to Paul, above. All were down.

After them came the donkeys loaded with babies and gear, and finally the sheep and goats. They needed no urging. Last of all, Paul Stepanovitch and a number of the tribesmen descended, gathering the rope in as they went, for it would be needed for the river crossing.

And now the passage of Araxes. The water was rising, slowly but perceptibly, swirling in red whirlpools, lapping upon the dusty banks of the stream.

The men waded into the stream to form a human chain, two rows of them, while the rope ran between their hands from bank to bank.

"Come," shouted Paul, standing knee deep in the water.

But the children, brave as they had been on the perilous climb down the canyon, patient and willing as they had shown themselves to be on the long march from Bartzan, hesitated. They crowded upon the shelving shore of the river, staring at the swirling waters with the

look which can be found only in the eyes of children—
the look that comes when beholding something which
they do not understand.

A woman, Marta Hovasian, screamed:

"The waters! We'll drown."

Other women took up the cry and began to scramble
up the bank.

"The flood! The flood!" Marta screamed.

"The day of doom. We're lost," rose the frantic cry
from a dozen throats.

The children now began to wail and scream. Some
began to follow their elders up the bank. Others stood
transfixed, or clung to their playmates, while still others
were sobbing with such fright that they were well-nigh
in convulsions.

Among a band of girls, standing just above him, Paul
Stepanovitch saw Dina. She was clutching a little bundle
of rags, while she stood watching the water. In her face,
Paul Stepanovitch saw, was the same look with which
she had regarded him when he had called her and Asta
out from under the car wheels.

Paul Stepanovitch waded ashore.

"You're not afraid, Dina, are you?"

For answer, the child put her arms about Paul's neck.

"No," she replied, "not with you."

Paul picked her up and waded into the water.

"But don't get my dolly wet."

"We'll keep her dry."

"And you'll go back for Asta?"

"God willing, we'll save them all."

At the same moment, Paul heard, above the swirling
waters, above the screams of the women and the cries
of the children, the great, booming voice of Amos Lyle.
He was singing, in Armenian, the famous song:

> " 'He leadeth me! O blessed thought!
> O words with heavenly comfort fraught!
> Whate'er I do, where'er I be,
> Still 'tis God's hand that leadeth me.' "

As Lyle continued to sing, other voices joined in—the deep voices of the men, the quavering, frantic voices of the women, the tremulous, vibrant, high-pitched voices of the children,

> " '*He leadeth me, He leadeth me,*
> *By His own hand He leadeth me:*
> *His faithful follower I would be,*
> *For by His hand He leadeth me.*' "

Paul waded steadily and firmly across the river, reached the other shore, and deposited Dina on a rocky ledge.

Still singing, Lyle had followed Paul Stepanovitch into the river, leading a line of children, holding to each other's hands. Aided by the strong arms of the tribesmen, the children kept their footing and clambered, dripping, upon the dry rocks beyond.

The panic subsided. Fear gave way to courage. Others followed, going hand in hand, the tribesmen helping, the stronger boys lifting the smaller children to their shoulders, while the water rose steadily, clutching ever more insistently at the human chain stretching from bank to bank, and the song continued to rise upon the air,

> " '*He leadeth me, He leadeth me,*
> *By His own hand He leadeth me . . .*' "

The last child had scrambled, dripping, up the far bank, among the ledges of rock. The babies had been carried across, in the arms of the men, and deposited with the waiting women until the donkeys could be brought over. Sirani, who had waited until all the children were across, until she had seen Suren safely in the arms of Amos Lyle, was now across.

There remained only the herds and the provisions to be ferried over, for which purpose Paul Stepanovitch and a dozen of the tribesmen continued to struggle against the ever-rising waters. The goats were made to swim; the first casualty occurred when two or three kids were carried away by the stream past the reach of the waiting

men. The pack horses came last, their loads lightened
in order that they might swim the deeper parts of the river.

While this was in progress, the children, under the
guidance of others of the tribesmen, were being escorted
along the trail that led up into the foothills of Ararat.
This trail followed a broad ravine that curved and ascended sharply after leaving the main gorge.

Paul turned his attention now to the provisions and
baggage which had been left behind when the loads of
the pack horses were lightened, and which lay scattered
on the shore of the Bartzan side of the river. There was
still some light left in the sky; through the heavy curtain
of black clouds an evanescent pallor of evening illuminated the gorge—the red, swirling waters, the gray cliffs
dotted with scrub pine and brambles, and above, the
line of the canyon crest, barely distinguishable against
the darkness of the sky.

The children were no longer visible, hidden by the
bend in the ravine they were following, but their singing,
and the great, cracked voice of Amos Lyle came to Paul
faintly above the increasing rumble of the waters.

Paul had taken the lead horse of a train and had
waded into the water to recross to the Bartzan shore.

"Stop, Paul Stepanovitch, stop!" cried Haig Droghian.
"Look!"

Above, barely visible against the sky, stood a horseman.
As Paul looked, another appeared, and still others.

"The Turks! The Turks!"

As Haig shouted, the water in front of Paul Stepanovitch spurted. The crack of a rifle followed.

Paul Stepanovitch scrambled back to the bank, and
instinctively sought cover.

Petros, the scout, had taken shelter behind a rock and
was answering fire with fire. With him were Hombart
and Sassoun and others of the tribesmen—possibly two
dozen in all. Haig Droghian had unlimbered his rifle
and was taking aim.

The Turks were finding their way down the canyon
walls, firing as they came. More of them appeared on
the rim of the gorge. Paul Stepanovitch saw that there

was at least a full squadron of troopers. They came on with determination, as though by command, certain of their objective, sure of their quarry. Could it be possible, Paul wondered, that their hatred would extend to helpless children? He remembered all he had heard, in these last years, of the atrocities committed against the Armenians.

The vanguard of the Turks was now almost at the opposite bank of the river, firing upon the Armenians from their own level. Haig and his men were defending themselves valiantly, working with their rifles grimly, aiming slowly and making every bullet count. The crack of the rifles echoed in the walls of the canyon, and the bullets spat upon the rocks like the crackle of flame.

But the handful of rifles that were on the Ararat side were as nothing against the hundreds that were answering from the Bartzan side of the river. But above the barking of the rifles and the reverberating echoes, a rumble began to be heard from the gorge above, like distant thunder or cannonading.

Suddenly Haig ceased firing and slung his rifle across his shoulder.

"Back!" he shouted in a prolonged roar. "The waters! The waters!"

The men understood. Long experience with spring freshets encountered on the migrations had taught them the meaning of the fearful cry, the warning of a menace greater than flying bullets. With one accord they ceased firing, slung their rifles and began to scramble for higher ground.

For a moment longer they continued to be assailed by the fire of the Turks, and then it ceased. Paul Stepanovitch, who had followed the men, turned and looked. Across the canyon he could see the Turks. They too had seen their danger and were fleeing from the rising waters.

The river had assumed an awe-inspiring aspect. On the surface of the water there had appeared a huge foaming crest, and behind the crest was a dark and turbulent mass. Like a tidal wave, this mass, the head of the flood, came on, sweeping rocks and boulders before it. Paul beheld, in a flashing moment, the sacks of provisions and the baggage, which had been left on the far bank, being swept down the river in a rush of waters.

The Turks, interested only in regaining the heights, had abandoned all pursuit, and were driving their mounts up the slope. In their frenzy they were crowding upon each other; horses pawed the heels of other horses, whinnying and rearing; men shouted imprecations. One of the animals lost footing, began to slide back, belly scraping the earth; the horse behind reared, pawed the air, felled the rider of the first. In a moment both horses, both riders, were hurtling down the embankment, rolling and flying, crashing through bushes, until finally, with a splash, they struck the torrent and were carried away.

As for the mounts of the Armenians, they had, at the moment of the fighting, broken their tether and fled up the ravine in the direction taken by the main body of the company. The patient donkeys, however, had no more than gained a lower ledge of the trail, and there they stood, mutely awaiting their fate. Paul, from above, saw their peril. He leaped down the rocks into their midst and began to herd them along.

Haig Droghian, who had caught his horse and mounted, turned and saw what Paul Stepanovitch was doing.

"Leave them, Paul Stepanovitch!" he shouted in dismay. "Leave them. The waters will be upon you."

His words were lost in the roar of the flood.

Haig listened for a moment to the waters which were rising in a mighty crescendo and filling the gorge with the roar of a vast tumult.

"By God, what a man!" the tribesman bellowed both in exasperation and amazement. He turned his horse, and galloped down to Paul. Together they belabored the donkeys with cudgels and stones, and succeeded in getting them up the trail.

Behind them the writhing, tortured waters of the flood advanced, swallowed the ledge, surged up the ravine, lapped at their heels. But they were safe. . . .

The roar gradually subsided: the head of the flood passed, though the waters continued to rise. The agitation diminished, the water became a glassy sheet of turbid yellow. A ray of the evening sun, breaking through the clouds, fell upon the surface of the water, and turned it into a ruddy flame. The flame mounted, and filled the gorge, and was reflected against the darkening sky. It was as though the river was not a river of water, but a river of flame rushing between pursuers and pursued, the flaming sword of the Archangel drawn between danger and security, between death and life, casting a circle of magic fire about Ararat.

12. Haven

PAUL STEPANOVITCH was awakened by a thrush singing an aubade in the nearby brambles. Haig Droghian's tribe, with whom the children of Bartzan were encamped, was high on the green belt of Ararat, and the slopes now lay in a crepuscular light that softened the rocky escarpments into a delicate substance of violet and coral. At a little distance from the shelter in which Paul and Sirani had passed the night a fire of cedar wood was crackling and sending up spirals of smoke. Several of the tribesmen were moving quietly about the fire. Farther down the slope some of the younger children were awake, talking to themselves or their comrades with notes more musical than those of any thrush. The rest of the camp was asleep.

Paul raised himself and looked at Sirani. She was still sleeping, exhausted by the long journey. Paul arose quietly, so as not to disturb her, and went out. Mounting the slope, away from the main body of the camp, he came to a promontory which overlooked the plain.

The morning was dawning fresh and clear. It was such a morning as Noah might have beheld as he gazed from the summit of Ararat upon the receding waters. The world below was emerging from the mists of morning as though new made, with the tenderness, the freshness, the nebulous delicacy of the first days of creation.

The morning spread, leaping from summit to summit, creeping down the slopes of the far distant mountains, slowly spreading across the plain. The world was becoming visible part by part, as though an unseen hand were moving over the earth and endowing the void with color and form and substance. In the distance lay Bartzan plain, bathed in a nacreous haze, and to the left, the purple slopes of the Taurus ranges. To the south stretched the coral ridges of the Persian mountains, while seemingly directly below, like a serpent guarding the gardens of the Hesperides, curled the river Araxes.

Of infinite vastness, the world seemed from the slopes of Ararat, of infinite sweetness and surpassing purity and innocence. A garden, spacious and ordered, beautiful in design and marvelously arranged, for man to tend and make fruitful. Could this be the world, Paul Stepanovitch wondered, which the bitterness of hate, the bloodshed of war, had strewn with wreckage, had scarred with ruins, had denuded of its lovely and abundant life?

Could such order be no more than the haphazard product of physical force, moving by blind and compassionless law? Was such beauty born of no other union than the chance concatenation of molecules and atoms, aimlessly drifting in astral space?

No, there must be a guiding intelligence, a supreme will, working in the world, evolving its own plan for all the creatures of the world. Of that Paul was now sure. At last he had discovered in the universe about him the response to his own will, the greater Will toward which his own had been groping.

Paul Stepanovitch, gazing upon the world from Ararat, was filled with an aching tenderness for its creatures. His pity went out toward all men, toward all those children of God who still struggled against life, against each other, in hatred and arrogance, destroying themselves, and destroying the beauty and harmony which God so much desired for them.

Paul thought of the children encamped below, in the

tents of the tribesmen. Not one of them had perished in the flight, not one had been lost. Miraculous deliverance!

"I have saved them," Paul thought. "I have brought them out of the furnace."

This thought was succeeded immediately by a tremor of shame and humility.

"O God!" he prayed, "check my arrogance! Help me to look to Thee."

But even so, the thought returned, the consciousness that had it not been for his efforts the children would not have been saved. And then the realization dawned upon him that he should not be contrite, but proud. He grasped the mysterious, the incomprehensible truth, that salvation is a mutual product, the union of the Will of God and the will of man in joint enterprise. God holds forth His sanctuary, but of their own will must men enter into its peace; God's kingdom is nigh, but men of good will must rear its towers and lay out its pleasant gardens. Ararat offers its refuge to men, but capricious Araxes makes that refuge secure.

Still a perplexity remained. Though Paul Stepanovitch at last had come to recognize another Will, stronger than his own, which fulfilled rather than annihilated his own, the question arose—how may these wills be joined? What is the bridge that unites the will of man with the Will of God?

The light was now pouring over the rim of the horizon, down the sides of the valleys, dissolving the shadows as it advanced, and spreading over the plain like a sheet of limpid water. Its level rose, and the cupped world, like a silver basin, filled with a dazzling radiance. The sky clarified and expanded, receding as though to make room for the monarch of the morning. The sun arose, in crimson majesty, and assumed dominion of his realm.

While this levée of the heavens was taking place, the earth below began to stir and waken. A murmur arose from the camp, and movement became visible.

Sirani appeared from the tent which they had occupied. Paul saw his wife, and his heart quickened. Fairer, she seemed to him, than the golden splendor of the morning.

At the thought of her, perplexity dissolved in joy, uncertainty in peace. He beheld again the clouds of the sky as they were reflected on the surface of the Dasta, and heard the peaceful murmur of his boyhood fields. In a moment he had become a child again, encompassed by the simplicity and beauty of life that he had known in childhood years. All between then and now had been erased, and was as nothing. A bridge had been thrown across the years, and in the same moment a bridge was thrown across the gulfs of human mystery.

Here, he thought, was the secret of the mystery and the ineffable mystery itself. In love were the Will of God and the will of man united, in love was the understanding from which all harmony proceeds, and in love was the sanctuary and salvation which all men desire.

As he hastened down the rocks toward Sirani, Paul Stepanovitch heard, from below, a jubilant voice lifted in a hymn to the morning, that of Amos Lyle, in the midst of a group of children among the tents:

> "*Praise God from whom all blessings flow;*
> *Praise him, all creatures here below. . . .*'"